EXTINCTION
RETRIBUTION

SPECIAL EDITION

"If we look at the path, we do not see the sky.
We are Earth people on a spiritual journey to the stars.
Our quest, our Earth walk, is to look within, to know
who we are, to see that we are connected to all things,
that there is no separation, only in the mind."

Native American, source unknown

Praise for Joseph Massucci's Thrillers

"Amazing stuff, really trippy and very imaginative writing. And suspenseful!"
—*Ann Collette, Rees Literary Agency*

"Loved the characters, the action and the adventure!"
—*Dan Barbier, author of JUST 4 CHILLS*

"A very exciting and suspenseful read!"
—*Chris Beakey, author of DOUBLE ABDUCTION*

"This fiction can become reality. Our reality."
—*USA Today*

"Totally believable!"
—*Kirkus Reviews*

"A real page-turner."
—*World Entertainment*

"A perfect adventure."
—*Tulsa World*

"Truly frightening material."
—*Huntsville Times*

"Scary and mind-expanding."
—*Fredrickson & Friends*

"Joseph Massucci does an excellent job in combining New-Age literature with an action thriller."
—*Ron Callari, Editor, y-two-k.com*

"A good read, with plenty of bang for your Millennium buck."
—*Kevin Rittner, The Herald Tribune*

ALSO BY JOSEPH MASSUCCI

AMAN
GORGON
THE MILLENNIUM PROJECT
THE RESURRECTION OF ANDREW FINSBURY

EXTINCTION

RETRIBUTION

SPECIAL EDITION

JOSEPH MASSUCCI

Safari Multimedia, LLC

This Special Edition of EXTINCTION: RETRIBUTION delves deeper into the story's metaphysical foundation with enhanced scenes, richer dialogue, an extended climax, and more.

To Jennifer

"We all dance to a mysterious tune,
intoned in the distance by an invisible player."

Albert Einstein

DAY ONE

AWAKENED

Zbol, Iran

YOUNG JALAL FOUND herding sheep through the steep gorge far more difficult than anything his father had made him do. There were no wells along this route, and the unforgiving sun directly above stole his breath as it baked him. He could think only of water.

His father coaxed the animals along the rocky path with a constant stream of curses while whipping their legs with his staff. Jalal struggled to keep up. He had grown weary and parched from chasing strays back to the flock since sunrise.

Despite the steep terrain, they had no choice but to follow this twisting trail between the towering hillsides. Much was at stake. The sheep were worth twelve pounds each at the Bedouin market, maybe more if the region's drought continued. Jalal turned ten last week, and he had already betrayed his father's trust for the flock's safekeeping. Eight wandered off into the gorge during the night under his watch—another failed test of his manhood.

Jalal's father thrust a finger up the hillside, his leathered features stretched into a rare smile. "You are a very lucky boy."

Jalal shielded his eyes with both hands and saw his lost sheep grazing on the hillside high above.

His father gave no instructions, and Jalal needed none. His elder settled in the shade under one of the path's few trees with their water bottle. Jalal knew his father would share its contents only after he returned with the strays. Water would be his reward.

Jalal secured his leather pouch over his shoulder and began his struggle up the hillside.

"Faster," his father called to him. He laughed and took a long swallow of water, a sight that made Jalal's throat ache. The sooner I am back, the sooner I drink, Jalal thought.

The way up the hill was steep and rock-strewn, and Jalal was panting like a dog by the time he reached the strays. He felt his father's eyes boring into him, judging him. He vowed not to show his fatigue and fail yet another test.

Jalal chased after a young lamb that had strayed from the others and gathered it into his arms.

He froze.

Something was wrong. The earth groaned with a strange deep sound he had never heard before. The steep hill began to shake, sending rocks tumbling from above. A rumbling like distant explosions boomed down the gorge.

The devil was coming.

Frightened, Jalal stumbled down the hillside with the lamb. "Papa!"

Far below, his father was on his feet while the main flock scattered in a panic. The mounting tremors made it difficult to stand. Jalal never felt anything so violent, and it terrified him beyond reason. The lamb in his arms squirmed and thrashed. He pressed the animal tight against his chest.

Jalal heard his father shriek and saw him running down the gorge away from this hillside, leaving his flock behind. The youth's hammering heart choked off the air to his lungs. *Don't leave me!* He was too frightened to cry out.

The floor of the gorge disappeared in a massive fireball, followed by a great roar of thunder. Jalal eyes widened. He watched his father and every trace of their flock vanish into the inferno.

"*Papa!*"

Thick black smoke erupted and turned the bright sky into night. In seconds, fire consumed the bottom of the gorge. He felt the devil's callous breath wash over him, burning him.

Jalal could no longer distinguish the ground from the sky. He believed he would die on this hillside. He carried his lamb behind a boulder and hid, horrified, as larger rocks crashed past him in an avalanche and disappeared into the flaming abyss below. He could draw only short gasps of air into his lungs. Behind the thick shrieking storm of dust, he caught glimpses of trees, uprooted and thrown aside like sticks. Tendrils of fire reached up the hillside, hunting him. He hugged the lamb as he once hugged a toy animal, burying his face into its singed wool. What did it feel like to burn while alive, he wondered?

But Jalal did not die.

He did not know how long he huddled there. When he finally stood, ash fell from his clothing in a fine mist, the same ash that cloaked the hillside in a dull gray sheet of death. An acrid fog lingered. The floor of the gorge was gone. In its place lay a deep, charred canyon with no bottom.

The devil had awakened. And he was angry.

• • •

Global Consciousness Project
Princeton University, New Jersey

Dr. Irving Weissmann loved numbers more than he loved any human being. He explored them with his mind, calculating, manipulating, arranging, collating, studying, and showcasing them. And when he looked at those numbers closely, they revealed secrets to him—the universe's secrets.

The morning sun blazed through his lone office window, and with it came voices of the campus coming to life. He settled back into his abundant leather chair and frowned. A chronic insomniac since turning sixty a decade ago, he preferred the place to himself, free of noise.

"Go away and leave me alone," he ordered the window.

Weissmann returned to his computer screen's bar graphs, which represented the output from the project's global network of sixty-six random number generators placed strategically around the world. These sixty-six generators fed their data to the University's monitoring center, where workstations isolated non-random patterns. He was searching for proof of an emerging collective intelligence called the noosphere, humankind's next evolutionary step after the geosphere and the biosphere. The implications of a single mind for humanity were staggering, the results of his work always intriguing.

The monitoring software produced an audible heartbeat every second as it processed new chunks of data from the network. An occasional bell signaled deviations from average random values. The rhythmic pulse often put Weissmann into a meditative state. He closed his eyes and listened to those deviations, subtle signs of humankind collectively reacting to global events. The early morning transcendental experience helped make up for his lack of sleep.

A series of bells began going off like a pinball machine winning streak, jarring him from his trance. The bells gave way to abrasive gongs, signaling the most extreme deviations.

Weissmann scowled, annoyed. A damn software malfunction. He slipped on his reading glasses and squinted at the display's bar graphs. No system fault—the graphs showed a steady influx of new data. Yet the alarms, irritating and insistent, heralded that all sixty-six stations reported extreme non-random number variations.

Weissmann stood from his desk and stared at the screen, unbelieving. His breathing came in quick, short huffs, and he felt his blood pressure rising. Must be through the roof, he thought. Why was this happening? Had something profoundly awakened humankind's collective consciousness? He needed to verify the data's integrity.

And if he found no malfunction, a cataclysmic event had just occurred, the likes of which the world had never seen.

. . .

South Dakota foothills

The old man did not recall waking. He found himself standing in the first light of a new day, barely upright. His ancient eyes struggled to focus on a patch of violet windflowers at his feet, assuring him that life could still bloom from this depleted soil. He listened to the music of the flowers singing to each other and grinned.

He felt no pain. There was, however, an unusual sensation like a low-grade current running through his skeletal fingertips. As the sun cleared the mountaintops, his shriveled lungs inflated with the foothill's morning air. It smelled so sweet, so full of life. He indulged himself like a famished man, filling his lungs again and again.

Only six days.

He squinted against the dust spiraling off the plains and saw no trace of the community that once flourished here with its tall dome-shaped dwellings, stone streets, and roasting pits. Gone were the children that would ignore their elders to play with their puppets among the graves. What had become of the land's people so rich with life and love and hope? And what of his wife and two children he had left behind so long ago?

The *Paha Sapa* mountains, rising behind him like eternal sentinels, had seen everything yet told him nothing. His people had moved on and vanished, their dances still. He shook his head. The world had long forgotten his people. He listened for the slightest whisper of his wife's voice. *Speak to me, my love.* But even her lingering essence had faded. The wind and the elements, but mostly time, had taken everything.

He looked away, his throat swollen with grief. But his withered eyes could summon no tears. All that remained to mark the place where he had slept was a deep hole in the rough shape of a man, surrounded by a handful of pebbles.

His eyes turned skyward. The rising sun promised a sweltering day.

He must begin his journey.

Before him stretched a boundless prairie—the way to a new world he knew nothing about. Staring at the gravel path ahead, he wondered if his old legs would support him. Or would they collapse with the first step, his brittle bones shattering into a thousand pieces? There he would lie forever, his journey ended before it even began.

The old man took a tentative step. To his astonishment, his legs did not buckle. As he placed his full weight upon the desiccated bones, he felt neither feeble nor aged. His legs were firm. The barest smile stretched his thin parched lips, and he began walking across the scorched terrain with a slow but deliberate pace.

He had much to do in only six days.

HIGHWAY

SAMANTHA COYOTE ALMOST ran over the old man.

She had been cruising fifteen miles above the posted speed limit, drugged by the sameness of the rolling highway between the South Dakota mountains. Her 16-year-old Ford reliably ate the miles to Rapid City despite its cracked windshield and pockmarked blue paint, not to mention its 2-year-old engine oil. She patted the sun-weathered dashboard, a habit she knew the car appreciated.

Something made her eyes dart back to the road in time to spot a human lump sitting on the asphalt in the middle of the baked highway.

"What the—?"

Samantha jerked her tiny car onto the shoulder with a vicious spray of gravel against the undercarriage. She jammed her car into park, opened the door, and lost one of her summer sandals the instant her feet hit the ground. "*Damnit.*"

She grabbed her broken sandal and limped out onto the road, giving a small cry when the asphalt's afternoon heat scorched her bare sole. She thought about her boots in the hatchback – *screw it.* Samantha slipped on the sandal and continued at an uneven jog.

Her rush slowed to a tentative walk as she neared a slight man resting his forehead on his knees in the middle of the road. At that moment, the wind picked up, forcing her to cram her frayed straw cowboy hat onto her head while her shoulder-length black hair swirled around her face like a restless scarf. Through the haze of whirling dust, Samantha could see that the stranded man was old—exceptionally so. His tattered clothes were so badly worn, the material surely would fall apart if he stood. From the look of his bony extremities and leathery skin, she half expected to find a mummified corpse hunched here in the sun, well on its way to disintegrating into the dusty road.

If the next passing car didn't kill him, the heat would. Samantha glanced up and down the highway and saw no sign of another car coming. Why was he out here alone in the middle of the road twenty miles from town?

OK, you just turned forty, girl, she thought. You're too old for wild adventures but smart enough to figure this out. Wasn't 911 invented for this?

She reached for her belt before realizing that she left her phone between the bucket seats. Maybe this man was already beyond 911's help. She took a cautious step back.

To her astonishment, his head turned, and two sunken eyes looked at her from beneath a network of deep creases and wrinkles from temple to temple. As she approached, his eyes remained fixed on her face as though studying her. She was proud of her pretty features—although some told her they had hardened with age. Still, she grew self-conscious of his scrutiny. Perhaps he was trying to determine her Native American heritage.

His head bobbed slightly in greeting. *"Telan ay jun naq winaq yul b'e."*

"I'm sorry. I don't understand you."

She stiffened at the sight of his bare feet—split and bloodied and covered with gashes. A bloody trail of footprints across the road ended beneath him. Where did he walk from? How did he get this far? *What son'bitch dumped him here?*

"You can't sit in the middle of the road." She immediately regretted her dumb remark. "What I mean is, it's too dangerous to sit here. I'll help you up." She doubted he could hear, let alone understand her.

Those sunken eyes closed, and once again, he rested his forehead against his knees. "You are a kind woman to help an old stranger." His voice sounded strained and hoarse, barely more than a whisper, and with an accent she didn't recognize.

"If you would help me to my feet," he said, "I will continue my journey."

TRIAGE

Rapid City Regional Hospital

"I NEED HELP, please!" Samantha rushed into the ER's registration area, carrying her broken sandal. Several heads in the waiting area turned to watch.

A physician talking with the nurse behind the registration counter glanced up when he heard her plea for assistance.

Samantha drew a quick gulp of air when she recognized Dr. David Marshall. He had treated her here last year after she startled a prairie rattlesnake in the pile of logs behind her trailer. Dr. Marshall saved her life. He was in his mid-forties, with becoming features and thick dark hair that spilled over his forehead. Best of all, he wasn't married.

Marshall's expression brightened in recognition. "Sam, nice to see you again. How's your hand?"

Beaming, she let out her breath, impressed that the good doctor remembered her name. She held up her palm to show him. "Hardly a mark, thanks to you, Dr. Marshall."

He scowled and said with a grin, "David. Please."

Her expression sank when she remembered the old man in the back of her car. "I found a man on the highway. He's dying."

"What happened?" Marshall rounded the desk and motioned for an orderly.

"We was sitting in the middle of the road." Samantha slid on her sandal and led him outside to the curb. "He's in serious trouble."

Samantha opened the driver's door of her Focus and pushed down the seat to allow access to the back.

"Sorry," she said. "The passenger door doesn't open."

Marshall squeezed into the car's shallow opening and hovered over the old man lying in a fetal position across the back seat. The doctor's taut expression told Samantha that her layperson's prognosis was in the ballpark: her passenger was indeed in bad shape.

"He was sitting on the hot highway," Samantha explained. "Right in the middle of the road."

"Struck by a car?" Marshall asked over his shoulder.

"I don't think so," she said. "I think someone dumped him there."

An orderly pushed a gurney alongside the car. Marshall wrapped his arms around the old man's chest and lifted him out of the car while the orderly helped set him onto the gurney. It looked like easy work. The man appeared to weigh nothing at all.

"Can you tell me your name?" Marshall asked.

The old man's eyes remained closed. He appeared dead except for his shallow breathing.

"Let's get him into triage," Marshall instructed the orderly.

All heads in the waiting area turned toward the gurney rolling through the double ER doors. A Hispanic boy, no more than seven, cradling a swollen wrist, chased after the stretcher. The boy was barely tall enough to see the man lying on top.

"Are you an Aztec mummy?" the boy asked.

Samantha didn't think the old man could see much more than the boy's enormous brown eyes peeking over the edge of the gurney. The patient's mouth stretched into as much of a grin as his thin, cracked lips would allow.

The boy lifted his swollen wrist high enough to reveal his injury. "Papa says I broke it. But it don't hurt much."

The old man reached for the boy but managed only a quick touch of his broken wrist as the gurney rolled past. "Strong bones," he whispered.

The boy's father placed a hand on the youth's head and led him back to the waiting area while his own eyes, full of curiosity, watched the old man disappear through the security doors.

Before Samantha could follow them into triage, a nurse with a severe demeanor whose photo ID read "Rita Benz, RN, BSN, CGRN" stopped her with a firm, upraised hand. "Are you kin?" she asked.

"Well, no, as I told David, I found him on the road. I'm a waitress at Andy's Diner. I was coming back from—"

"Wait out here." The nurse indicated the area with the TV.

Samantha, disappointed, had hoped to watch David work. "The man's feet," she said. "He's walked them down to nothing."

"We'll take care of him." Nurse Rita closed the security door behind her with a metallic click.

Samantha turned and found herself staring down at the Hispanic boy, his eyes welling with tears. He held his wrist. "It hurts."

"You poor little guy." She squatted in front of him to inspect his swollen and bruised wrist. "They'll put a cast on it, and you'll be fine."

The boy could no longer contain his tears, and he began to cry, fluid running unchecked down his cheeks and out his nose. Samantha bit her lip and placed a gentle hand on his injured wrist to comfort him. His skin felt notably hot to the touch.

Marshall pulled the curtains around the examining cubicle and snapped on a pair of latex gloves. He couldn't recall the last time he saw a patient in this bad shape. "Rita, start an IV, please."

Nurse Rita wheeled an IV stand beside the gurney and mounted a clear fluid bag containing a solution of Ringer's lactate. She took the patient's hand to find a vein and looked up into the patient's eyes, confused.

Marshall noted her look of surprise. "You see something, Rita?"

"That's odd. His hand."

"What about his hand?"

"It's vibrating."

Marshall motioned the nurse to step back so he could have full access to his patient. He felt the man's hand, waited a moment, and then shrugged.

"I don't feel anything unusual." Marshall hovered over his patient. "Do you know where you are? What's your name?"

The old man stared up at him with a vacant look. "I—I don't know."

"We have a John Doe," Marshall told the nurse. "How old are you, sir?"

He rolled his head from side to side.

The doctor noted the deep lines on the man's face and assumed he was in his nineties—at least. "Are you Native American?"

The patient said nothing.

"His feet," Rita said. "The woman who brought him in was concerned about his feet."

Marshall moved to the end of the gurney and examined the man's feet. "I see a lot of dried blood here, but no open wounds." He probed several superficial scratches with his gloved fingers and, finding no visible external injury, felt the man's feet with both his hands. The old man didn't react. "No broken bones. Not even swelling."

While Rita searched the man's hand for a vein for the IV, Marshall directed an ophthalmoscope into his eyes. "His pupils are equal and reactive," he said to the nurse and then reassured his patient, "Your eyes are reacting normally." He put his thumb on the patient's chin and opened his jaw. "You still have your teeth. You've got great genes." He put his stethoscope on the man's gaunt chest. "Your pulse is slow."

"Are you admitting him?" Rita asked.

"Of course. Get him cleaned up and X-rayed. I'll order a blood workup—CBC, lipid panel, the works. Meanwhile, let's get these clothes off him."

Marshall pulled on the man's tunic. The material came apart in his hands, leaving a musty trail of dust-like fibers. "What the—?"

"Now that's interesting." Rita's fingers hovered over the fabric as though afraid to damage it further. "Hand sewn. And quite old. If I didn't know better, I'd say his clothes are as old as he is."

"Older," Marshall said.

AMAN

DR. MARSHALL LIKED what he saw on the boy's wrist X-ray. "Good news, Miguel," he said, indicating the image on a monitor. "Nothing's broken."

He turned to the boy sitting on the edge of the exam table and took the tiny wrist into his large, firm hand. "No swelling." Marshall ran his thumb along the underside of the boy's wrist and noted only trace discoloration, hardly a bruise. "You're a very lucky young man."

Miguel squirmed to get down off the table. "Nothing hurts me."

The boy's father shook his head, confused. "But his wrist looked very bad this morning after he fell. Twisted. Not a clean snap. He was in much pain."

Dr. Marshall shrugged. "Miguel's wrist isn't even sprained." He placed a hand on the boy's shoulder and showed him his most disarming grin. "You can run, jump, and play now. Just be careful climbing trees."

"John Doe's X-rays are ready," Nurse Rita said from the doorway.

"Excuse me," Marshall told Miguel's father. "I need to look after another patient."

The boy's father touched the doctor's arm before he could leave. "The old man," he said, "will he be well?"

Marshall looked at him without his obligatory frown of concern. "I'm doing everything I can for him."

Marshall entered the hospital room the old man shared with another elderly patient with congestive heart failure who most likely wouldn't survive the week. His new patient's withered face brightened when the doctor approached his bed. His gnarly features held a quiet resignation, suggesting a man who lived a long, hard life and now lay tattered and brittle in his final years. Yet the doctor noted a keen restlessness radiating from those aged eyes that spoke of a mind that had not yet surrendered to the many decades that had worn down and consumed his body.

"Mostly good news," Marshall informed his patient. "All your tests are normal. Except one. You have an unusual heart rhythm. I don't know what it means yet. But you're very fortunate you didn't die out on that road. You should thank Samantha. She saved your life."

"A lovely woman," the old man said in a low voice. "A good soul."

"Yes, she is."

"May I see her?"

"She had to go to work."

"May I leave?"

"Where do you live?" Marshall asked. When his patient didn't respond, he added, "Do you have a place to stay?"

"I am alone."

Marshall put a pensive finger to his lips. "I can't let you leave until I understand your arrhythmia. I want you to spend the night so we can observe you. In the morning, a social worker will find you a place to stay."

The old man nodded his thanks.

The doctor turned to leave.

"Aman," the old man blurted.

Marshall turned and looked at him. "I beg your pardon?"

"I remember my name," the old man said. "It is Aman."

DAY TWO

CELEBRATION

Rapid City Regional Hospital

NURSE RITA HEARD animated voices from the two men's double room. Had the social worker come early, she wondered? She rounded the doorway and was surprised to find her two critical care patients sitting up in their beds, alert and talking. Mr. Archibald Kravitz, whom she had never seen lucid—let alone sitting upright—greeted her with an expression of delight. He looked like a new man.

"It's a wonderful day, isn't it?" Kravitz beamed. He exhibited far too much vigor for a bedridden, near-comatose 78-year-old. He used the palms of his hands to brush back his long strands of gray hair, oily after two weeks in bed, until he looked downright presentable.

"Yes, Mr. Kravitz," Rita said. "Yes, it is."

She turned her attention to her newest patient, the man who almost died on the highway yesterday. She had wondered if he, too, would survive the night given his age and his condition when he arrived. But this morning, he was sitting upright in his bed, his arms folded in his lap while his deep-set eyes tracked her.

"And what about you, sir?" she asked. "How are you feeling?"

He offered a grin of affirmation and said, "My name is Aman."

"Aman? How interesting. Is that your first or last name?"

"Just Aman."

"What day is this?" Mr. Kravitz asked.

"It's Sunday, Mr. Kravitz." Nurse Rita took his right wrist to check his pulse.

Kravitz's grin expanded. "A day of worship. There's a chapel on the first floor. I very much wish to go there. It's been a long time."

"You'll do no such thing," Nurse Rita insisted. "You'll wait for your doctor. He'll want to know what's going on inside that chest of yours."

Kravitz waved away any notion of spoiling the morning with another examination. "No more tests." He shrugged off her hand. "I feel like celebrating. And I would very much wish to begin with a service."

"What's happened to you?" she said, astonished by his new-found strength.

"Gathering with others will be good for him," Aman said. His voice sounded stronger.

"I don't know about that," Nurse Rita said.

Kravitz thrust a finger at Aman. "The chapel will be good for you too, my friend. We will go together."

"The social worker will be here within the hour to talk to Aman," Rita said. "Besides, this isn't a good morning if you're looking for some quiet time. Second-graders from St. Elizabeth Seton are singing this morning."

Kravitz's features brightened further. "Wonderful. I would love to hear children sing. What about you, Aman?"

Aman nodded. "I would welcome the company of children."

WORSHIP

SISTER MARY KAREN, a pale and petite nun with large glasses, strummed an Ovation acoustic guitar, amplified by a frayed box the size of a footstool. Her second-grade students had just started Peter, Paul, and Mary's "500 Miles" when she observed two men sitting in wheelchairs at the end of a single row of orange plastic contoured chairs set up for twenty people. Only a quarter of those chairs were taken this morning. Crowds were never an issue here. The non-denominational chapel on the hospital's first floor was simply a place where patients could sit in solitude or mingle for some therapeutic camaraderie.

Sister Mary Karen recognized one of the men in a wheelchair as Mr. Archibald Kravitz. Her polite smile faded when she recalled last seeing the poor man struggling to breathe, his eyes half-buried up inside his head while lying stricken on what she was sure would be his deathbed. She had given him a blessing, passing on whatever comfort her small hands could provide. She never expected to see him outside his hospital room alive.

Reverend Ruth Chase, a large-boned, middle-aged woman with permed red hair, well known for her gentle rapport with patients at her little service, gave both men a nod of welcome.

When the children finished their song, Reverend Chase rose from her molded chair and stood before the morning's tiny congregation. "Welcome," she said with a smile for the few. "And I am gratified to see you here this morning, Mr. Kravitz."

Kravitz blew her a kiss from his wheelchair, enjoying his morning outing.

"Please introduce your friend," she said.

"This is Aman," Kravitz said, waving a hand toward the man in the wheelchair next to him.

Aman gave the Reverend a nod of greeting.

"He's as old as a fossil," one student exclaimed. Whispers and giggling rippled through the group of second-graders. Sister Mary Karen, still wearing her guitar, worked to quiet her students that would not stop stirring.

Aman smiled kindly from his wheelchair while Kravitz let out a healthy belt of laughter at the child's brazen comment.

One of the students, a girl with curly brown hair adorned with a blue ribbon and wearing a white dress with blue flowers, broke from her fellow singers and approached Aman, her eyes curious. She didn't try to conceal her right hand with mere nubs instead of fingers.

"Melissa," Sister Mary Karen called after her, "some of the people here don't feel well."

Reverend Chase allowed the child to proceed with an affirming gesture that suggested that mingling would be appropriate for the service and good for the faithful. Kravitz watched it all with a bemused grin.

Melissa stood before Aman's wheelchair and looked up into his withered face. "How old are you?" she asked him.

"I am blessed to have enjoyed a long and full life," he said in a raspy, winded voice.

"Are you an Indian?" she probed.

Aman's features relaxed, and he said to her in a thin voice, "I have no people now. They vanished long ago."

"But you were an Indian once, weren't you?"

"I'll bet he was a chief," one of her classmates called out from the front.

Melissa asked Aman, "Were you a chief?"

He shook his head. "No, my child."

"Where is your mama now?" Melissa asked.

A look of sadness crossed Aman's features. "Gone."

Melissa's bright expression crumbled. "Oh. You're all alone."

"No, child," Aman said. "My family's spirit flows through me. They are part of me."

"He's referring to God in heaven," Reverend Chase offered, nodding.

Melissa's blue eyes shifted from the Reverend back to Aman. "Is that what you mean? That God is inside us?"

Sister Mary Karen took off her guitar and leaned it against a rack of melted candles in colored glass votives. "Melissa, honey, you've asked the gentleman enough questions."

Aman raised a bony hand. "Please. I wish to speak to the child."

All eyes were on Aman and the girl.

"Very soon, your world will change," Aman rasped. "We will change. The wicked—those that do not cherish and protect life—will go away, while those whose hearts are forgiving and full of love like yours will grow stronger. There will be no more temples of worship, no more places of healing, no more coinage, no more imprisonment. None will be needed."

"And schools?" she asked, her eyes growing.

He smiled. "There will be nothing to learn. You will know everything. And the earth will be beautiful—a world of light, peace, and love. You will see colors and animals and flowers you never thought possible."

Melissa's teacher stepped forward and placed a hand on the girl's shoulder, protecting her. "You are referring to the afterlife in heaven, are you not?" Sister Mary Karen asked Aman. "You do believe in God?"

Reverend Chase spread her arms in an embracing gesture, but her cordial expression was visibly strained. "Of course he believes," she said. "And what a wonderful reward he describes for the faithful."

"I am describing our lives here and now," Aman said to the girl. "You should not be afraid."

Melissa held up her arm. "Will God give me a whole hand?"

Aman beckoned her with a wiggle of his thin fingers. "Come, child."

Melissa broke free from her teacher's grip, scrambled up Aman's wheelchair, and climbed into his lap. If her weight upset him, Aman showed no sign of it. The students gasped at her bold act and began whispering among themselves.

Sister Mary Karen put out a hand to the girl but stopped in midair, unable to intervene. "Melissa—"

Aman took the girl's hand with its finger stumps into his own and looked into her wide blue eyes. Tears spilled down her cheeks.

Kravitz's blithe expression turned somber.

Sister Mary Karen lifted Melissa from Aman's lap and led her back to her classmates. Once on her feet again, Melissa looked back at Aman while cradling her right hand. She was trembling. Tears began flowing unchecked down her soft tiny cheeks.

Sister Mary Karen placed a hand on Melissa's shoulder and glanced at Kravitz. He stirring uncomfortably in his wheelchair as though ready to stand and bolt from the room. Her students likewise looked on, unsure what had just happened.

Aman's tired eyes dropped to his lap. He appeared exhausted. Something was very odd about the old man, the Sister thought, something she couldn't attribute to old age or senility. An unsettling spark transcended the sound of his feeble voice, made all the more ominous by the strange message he had uttered to the child. She felt that the others sensed it too.

Reverend Chase turned away from the few who had come to her service today. She looked first at the children gathered upfront, then at Melissa, and then locked eyes with their teacher.

"I'll dismiss the children," Sister Mary Karen said.

Reverend Chase nodded. "Yes. Please. I have nothing more to offer anyone this morning."

CUSTODY

SAMANTHA GRIMACED WHEN she spotted the sheriff's SUV parked in front of the hospital's double doors. Police vehicles gave her the creeps—too many bad memories. But hospitals and cops went hand-in-hand, didn't they? *Just ignore them.* She didn't intend to spend the afternoon here. She planned to stay just long enough to check on the old man—and, frankly, assure herself that he was still alive. She'd brought him a leftover wedge of peach cobbler on a paper plate from the diner where she worked. Something about the man troubled her deeply. More peculiar, she felt an odd need to help him.

But as she entered the hospital lobby double doors, she never expected to see him with his hands cuffed behind his back, struggling to stay upright between Sheriff Bowman and his solid deputy. *Bowman!* The sheriff was the last person in the world she wanted to cross paths with today or any other day. Built like a horse with a long face and flaring nostrils, Sheriff Bowman marched his prisoner across the lobby wearing his signature brown Stratton triple brim felt hat with gold acorn cords that pushed down the top of his ears.

Several people, mostly hospital staff, stood watching. A very old man taken into custody was news, and any news in this town drew crowds. At least he looked better today, she noted. And he was walking, although with a pronounced limp. Dressed in blue hospital scrubs and slippers, he appeared ten years younger than when she'd found him yesterday. That was good news. She tried to read the look on his face to determine what he felt as they took him into custody. His eyes met hers as he passed, and he seemed to accept his situation with no quarrel or protest.

Dr. Marshall, trailing them, looked exhausted, as though he had just fought a hard administrative battle and lost. Samantha felt self-conscious seeing him again. She closed the diner very early this morning and looked like hell dressed hurriedly in a faded yellow T-shirt stuffed into a pair of tight torn jeans. Her dusty black cowboy boots needed a major scrubbing. And she hadn't showered yet.

Screw my appearance.

Samantha shifted her bag over her shoulder and weaved her way among the onlookers to the doctor. An older man she didn't recognize, carrying an overnight bag, walked with him. "David, what's going on?"

"Isn't it obvious, Sam?" Marshall said, letting her hear his frustration. "The Sheriff is taking him into custody."

"I don't understand," she said. "What's he done? Is he wanted for something?"

Marshall led her toward the lobby's wall for some privacy. The older man with the overnight bag followed. "It seems he was quite a hit at this morning's chapel service," the doctor said. "Reverend Chase said he told her congregation that the world is coming to an end."

Samantha shrugged. "So what? They're putting him in jail for that?"

Marshall scowled. "It gets better. A group of second graders who attended the service were pretty shaken by what he said to them—upset some of them bad. One of the students, a little girl, hasn't spoken since. She's traumatized after Aman touched her. Her teacher and her parents filed a complaint with the sheriff."

"Touched her?" She lowered her voice until it was hardly a whisper. "Did he assault her?"

The doctor spread his hands. "I can't get a straight answer from anyone. Something happened. But I'll be goddamned if I know what."

"He only held her hand," the elderly man interjected.

Samantha looked at him, curious. "Who are you?"

"Archibald Kravitz," the man said. "I was sitting next to him in the chapel this morning and saw everything. Aman did nothing inappropriate."

"Aman?" she asked.

"That's his name," Kravitz explained. "We shared a room last night. He said his father traveled the world and named him Aman in Timor where he was born. He's a good man. And smart. Very smart."

Marshall let out a sigh of frustration. "Nevertheless, he'll face formal charges when he appears before a judge tomorrow morning. Meanwhile, he gets to spend the night in jail. The sheriff is calling him a vagrant."

"What about his family?" she asked.

Marshall shook his head. "The only thing he owns in the world is a pair of my old scrubs. Aman's homeless. The judge will likely have him committed for a psychological evaluation. Maybe that's best."

"No, it's not." Samantha handed the pie plate to Kravitz before storming through the double doors after the sheriff. She caught up with the two law officers at the curb as they loaded Aman into the back seat of their police Excursion. A second police patrol car sat parked behind the sheriff's vehicle, its red and blue lights adding to the circus. She grabbed the sheriff's arm. "What the hell are you doing, Bowman?"

Sheriff Bowman grinned as though they were indeed old friends. "Well, well, if it isn't Samantha Coyote. Nice to see you again. Thanks for bringin' me more work."

"Cut the crap, Bowman." She pulled her sunglasses from her hair down over her eyes to cut the glare. "This man doesn't belong in jail. He can stay with me tonight."

"You're in no position to take boarders into your trashy little trailer—old man, or a young'un," he said.

She glared at him, her nose wrinkled in disgust as though a package of spoiled fish had been opened. "Go to hell, Bowman. This man's not capable of hurting anyone."

"Is that so?" the Sheriff said. "I've got a scared little girl, and her parents are all over me about it. The girl's teacher is also fretting that something serious happened to the girl under her watch." He gave her a callous scowl. "He ain't your business anymore. Now back off before I haul your pretty ass in, too, for obstruction."

Samantha felt a hand on her shoulder—Marshall's. Others gathered to watch. Archibald Kravitz stood next to the doctor, holding the pie plate.

"That's enough," Marshall said to them both. "This isn't helping him."

Bowman's tight expression broadened into a smile that flashed a set of large worn teeth that had gnawed through their share of T-bones. He ended the conversation with a tip of his large white hat, showing off a bandaged hand stained with dried blood from a recent injury. "Good day, doctor. Sam."

Still grinning, he slid his large frame behind the wheel of his SUV.

Chief Deputy Kirby Dawson, an ex-jock who could win a bear-wrestling match, touched his white cowboy hat in farewell. He seemed genuinely pleased to see Samantha, a gesture most likely reflecting a single date they had two years ago. She hadn't seen him since due to her lack of interest.

"Bye, Sam." The deputy joined the sheriff upfront.

Aman gave Samantha a nod through the rear passenger window. As the two patrol vehicles rolled away, she heard his voice as though he were whispering into her right ear, *"You have a strong will. I need you."*

. . .

"All the comforts of home," Sheriff Bowman said to his prisoner.

Deputy Kirby Dawson put Aman into one of the three six-foot holding cells. The back of the county jailhouse was a dark and airless vault. Those who spent any time in one of these cages likened the experience to slow suffocation. Kirby removed the cuffs from Aman's thin wrists and exited the cell in his usual quick manner. The sheriff chuckled. He knew his deputy hated spending even a moment inside one. Bad luck, he said. Kirby closed the heavy door on the cage behind him with a solid bang.

"He ain't goin' nowhere, boss," the deputy said.

Aman stood motionless in the center of the cell, his hands at the sides of his slim frame, his blank eyes fixed on the cinderblocks that made up the back wall.

The large prisoner in the cell next to him stirred on his bench. "I hate company," he growled.

Sheriff Bowman removed a toothpick from between his molars and jabbed it toward the second holding cell. "I don't want to hear nothing from that fat mouth of yours, Ronnie."

Aman's cell neighbor, a massive man with a reddish beard in desperate need of trimming, and sporting more tattoos than a sideshow freak, topped the scales at well over 300 pounds. Ronnie folded his tree-trunk arms across his chest and sat grinning at the Sheriff.

"Don't let that animal near my new prisoner," Bowman said to his deputy. "He killed one child molester that I know about. Can't prove it, though. Can't prove a thing. Isn't that right, Ronnie?"

"Shove it up your tight hole," the prisoner mocked.

"You're running late, boss," Kirby said. "The Coveys expected you an hour ago."

"I know, I know." Bowman turned and strode down the corridor, the clacks of his boot heels echoing off the cinderblock walls. "Can't keep the little girl waiting."

INTERVIEW

MATT HENDRIX, *Rapid City Journal's* youngest reporter, followed the deputy down the cinderblock hallway in front of the jail's holding cells. Matt was no stranger to the county's jailhouse. He often came back here to conduct interviews with a camera around his neck and a notebook in hand. Some of his best police beat stories came from men sitting in these cages.

Deputy Kirby Dawson extended a hand toward one of the cells. "He's all yours—the oldest prisoner ever incarcerated in this county. Calls himself Aman. Your readers are gonna love this guy."

Matt wore a loose-fitting long-sleeved shirt shoved into a pair of worn jeans. It was Sunday, and he could care less about presenting a professional appearance while conducting an interview in the jailhouse. The sheriff gave him the lead about the old man in custody, and he decided it sounded too good to pass up. Besides, he had nothing better to do with his afternoon.

Matt stepped to the bars and scrutinized the man dressed in blue hospital scrubs much too large for his small frame. Aman sat on the fold-down bench that doubled as his bed, his eyes fixed ahead as though in a trance. The reporter considered himself a pretty good judge of age, and he pegged this man to be at the top end of his eighties. How lucid would he be for an interview, he wondered?

"Sir, my name is Matt Hendrix," he began. "I'm from the *Journal*. I write news stories from police reports." When he got no reaction from Aman, he added, "I do longer pieces if the topic warrants. This may be one of those times. Would you like to tell me your side of the story about why you're here?"

"Don't tell him a thing," Ronnie blurted from the adjacent cell. "Everything you say is guaranfuckinteed to be used in court to nail your ass."

"I will talk to you," Aman informed the reporter. "Humanity must understand what is happening."

Matt thought he detected an accent, but Aman's voice was too soft for him to determine what it might be. "I'd also like to take your picture when we're through talking." He touched the Sony digital camera hanging around his neck and then opened his notebook. "How old are you?"

"I cannot answer that," Aman said.

"You can't, or you won't?"

"I do not know the answer to that question," Aman said.

"I'd forget my friggin' birthday too if my hide was that ancient." Ronnie chuckled and then muttered, "Senile asshole."

Senile my butt, Matt thought. "Who are your people, sir? Are you Native American?"

Aman moved his head from side to side, and when he spoke, his voice was coarse but even. "My people are the original ones—long forgotten. I will deliver their message."

Matt glanced up. "What message?"

"Everything is changing," Aman said. "You are changing. I am changing. Everything."

"Change? In what way?"

"Humanity is evolving rapidly beyond its present realm. As our collective harmonic frequencies rise, our bodies will undergo rapid changes so that we may survive the planet's shift. Our bodies will barely have time to adjust."

Matt stopped scribbling in his notebook. "I'm not following. How will you change?"

"I will become whole again," Aman said.

"Yeah? So, how will I change?"

"I am not your conscience and cannot see your fate," Aman said. "But you will know soon. It has started. You will begin seeing changes after sunset tonight."

"What's going to happen?" Matt asked.

"The wicked and the enlightened are woven together into a single fabric that must be unraveled before the loom can weave a pure cloth. Fear, greed, and a lust for power lead to warfare and violence between nations, ideologies, and even our relationships. This mentality lowers a body's frequency. Men with low vibration levels create disharmony and a dark imbalance that is not compatible with the New Earth. By morning, they will be purged."

The deputy let out a hoot. "You're a real piece of work, pop."

Matt scribbled in his notebook. Aman didn't talk like a nutcase—he sounded learned and rational. *Keep him talking.* "What do you mean by *purged*? Are you saying that bad people will die?"

"That is how it will begin."

Ronnie let out an explosive laugh from the neighboring cell that sounded like a spooked wild boar. "Shit—I better start packin'." Then his face darkened, and he glared through the bars at Aman. "You're full of shit, old man."

"I am here to tell you that what is happening to our world need not be the end of us. If we act immediately, humanity can be saved and experience a new beginning."

Matt stopping writing. "The beginning of what?"

"Our destiny," Aman said. "The reason why all of us are on this earth."

MELISSA

SHERIFF BOWMAN PARKED his Excursion at the end of a row of cars in front of the Coveys' small ranch house, where several people had gathered in the front yard. As he approached the front door, he observed more people on the porch holding glasses of lemonade, laughing and talking loudly. The last thing he expected to find here was a party.

Bowman didn't wait for an invitation to enter the Coveys' home. He never waited to be invited anywhere. His visit wasn't a social call, and Bowman affirmed that fact by keeping his official brown Stratton felt hat stuck firmly on his head.

Mrs. Covey, a heavy woman at the tail end of her thirties, greeted him at the door wearing an apron, her eyes wet with tears. She let the sheriff into the living room, where more people mingled while their children ran between rooms. A heavy aroma of smoked barbecue brisket wafted from the kitchen while festive music blared from distorted speakers. Bowman considered removing his hat as a sign of respect but thought better of it. He liked his hat perched just where it was. He wasn't comfortable with all these people around, and he wanted to finish his business here fast.

"All I need is a short statement, ma'am," he said, his voice raised above the party. "That is if she's talking now."

"Yes. Yes, she is," Mrs. Covey said. She led the sheriff to Melissa's bedroom door.

"Has the doc seen her yet?"

"He left an hour ago," she said. "She's been waiting for you. Sheriff, something's happened. A miracle. She wants to show you."

Sheriff Bowman tipped his hat. "Thank you, ma'am."

Bowman, his jaw clenched in restrained purpose, pushed open the door to the child's room and entered. He welcomed the relative quiet inside. The girl's room displayed an excessive mix of bright colors and lots of stuffed animals. He saw little Melissa sitting on her bed, smiling, wearing her Sunday white dress with blue flowers. She looked cheerful enough, he thought. Next to her sat a plump bald man with thick glasses he assumed was her father, Marvin Covey.

Bowman stood before the two. Instead of a look of grief the sheriff assumed would define the father's mood, Bowman saw—*joy?* Without a word of greeting to the sheriff, the girl's father stood and claimed an unobtrusive spot against the wall next to his wife. *Can't he talk?* The couple joined hands and watched.

The sheriff slid a tiny white chair from beneath the girl's little desk, spun it around, and sat astride to face Melissa. No sense delaying the ugly, he thought. Let's get right down to business. "I'm going to ask you some questions, sweet pea," Bowman began. "They'll be personal. Just tell me what happened so we can keep the bad man who hurt you in jail."

"Oh, he didn't hurt me." Her ponytail swung back and forth when she shook her head. "I felt something funny, but just for a minute. Then it went away."

Bowman nodded. "I understand." He glanced over his broad shoulder at the parents and said, "I need to ask her this." He turned back to the girl with a look of disgust. "Show me where he touched you."

"Here." Melissa wiggled her fingers. "He touched me here."

Bowman took her tiny hand into his bandaged palm. "So, he held your hand?"

"God forgot to give me fingers when I was born," she said. "The man touched me where my fingers were supposed to go."

She wrapped her fingers around the top of her hand to show him. "Here."

Bowman shifted his bulk around on the tiny chair to seek an explanation from the girl's parents. Mrs. Covey placed a palm over her mouth to stifle a sob. The father, his eyes glistening, nodded his affirmation.

Bowman had heard enough. Irritated, he stood and towered over the girl. "Are you expecting me to believe that you grew new fingers today because an old man touched your hand?"

"He did." Melissa's eyes were beaming. "The man touched me here and asked God for my fingers He forgot to give me. And God listens to him."

LEAVENWORTH

United States Disciplinary Barracks
Fort Leavenworth, Kansas

THE CREAK OF a cell door roused Captain Nick Judge from a shallow sleep. Nick sat up on his hard cot, disoriented, and stared across his four-by-ten steel box. What time was it? His cell's ever-present low light, insufficient for reading, gave no clue to the hour.

The jangle of chains and the shuffle of feet in the corridor told Nick that guards were removing an inmate from his cell. He bet himself that the reason was medical. But there were no stakes in this wager. As a member of the military's death row prisoners, Nick forfeited any claim to property, personal or otherwise. Even his socks—stamped "Leavenworth" on the soles—had covered the feet of at least one other prisoner before he inherited them.

Nick heard a groan from outside his cell. He grinned, enjoying one of his life's last satisfactions. Definitely medical. He rarely lost a bet with himself. Ah—but was the prisoner's medical problem real, or was something up? To answer that question, he needed to observe.

Nick moved to his cell door and peered through the eye slot. The corridor provided just enough light to see two guards half-supporting, half-dragging a doubled-over prisoner he knew only as "Samson," a brawny ape who kept his head shaven. A third guard walked behind the prisoner, slapping a wooden club against his palm.

A former member of the elite special forces, Samson had been on death row longer than any other Leavenworth inmate, and he might remain here long after Nick had been hauled away in a hearse. A rare military appeal after the intervention of some congressman dude had delayed Samson's execution by eight months. A retrial could buy him a whole extra year in this paradise. Some people have all the luck, Nick thought.

Samson was a classic psychotic the Army had turned into a monster killing machine. Nick figured the world would be a better place without him, and that day couldn't come soon enough. Regrettably, Nick wouldn't see it. In eighteen days, his life would end with a needle in his arm.

Nick decided to enjoy the show as long as he had the chance. Besides, Samson had pulled out all the stops for tonight's entertainment. The prisoner raised his head and coughed blood that spilled over his chin. Nick's grin vanished. Samson didn't get sick—his cell neighbor was faking. The blood most likely came from a chewed cheek or a bitten tongue. His two guard escorts wouldn't see this coming. He felt a pang of regret for them.

Nick didn't have long to wait for the show. As the two guards escorted their prisoner past Nick's cell, Samson jerked upright and ripped his wrist chains free from his leather belt. Samson wrapped the chain around the neck of the soldier to his right. Still handcuffed, he slammed the guard against Nick's door and jerked the chain back with a single swift pull. Nick heard the dry snap of bone.

Samson delivered a sharp blow with his elbow to the neck of the second guard. The guard dropped with a choking sound from a crushed windpipe.

A wooden nightstick came down hard on the back of Samson's head. The prisoner hardly wavered. Samson's club-like fist struck the face of the third guard, crushing his nose. Samson had little trouble wrapping the chain around the guard's neck, a green soldier Nick knew only as "Johnny."

The four remaining East Block inmates were on their feet, cheering and shouting their support—although most didn't have a view.

Samson flattened the guard against the cell and jammed an elbow into his spine. Johnny, his disjointed nose bloody, made eye contact with Nick through his door's eye slot. "Nick, he's gonna kill me ... help ..."

Nick was in no position to help anybody. "He needs you alive, Johnny. Just do what he says."

The overhead lights throughout the corridor flared on while sirens wailed through East Block.

Samson put his lips next to the guard's ear and hissed, "If I die tonight," he sneered, "you're going down with me."

The expression on Johnny's face was a blend of terror and submission, and Nick could smell the guard's soiled pants, front and rear. Tears streamed down Johnny's cheeks.

Two soldiers in fatigues raced across the overhead catwalk above the two. They saw Samson about to strangle one of their own while two guards lay at his feet, one with his neck twisted at a grotesque angle.

Samson whipped his prisoner around as a shield. "I want these cuffs off me in thirty seconds," he yelled up at the two soldiers.

More jeers erupted from the inmates, adding to the cacophony.

"He's killing me," Johnny croaked. Both his hands pulled down on his neck chain with no effect.

"No, he's not, Johnny," one of the soldiers called down to him, "no, he's not."

"Then I'll try harder." Samson tightened the chain until Johnny began choking, his eyeballs about to pop out of his contorted face.

"Take it easy," the other soldier yelled, his hands raised to show he wasn't armed. "We'll work something out—"

"*Bullshit!*" Samson roared. "If I'm going to hell tonight, I'm taking this little prick with me."

The second soldier, an officer holding a transceiver radio, ordered the other, "Give the asshole a key before he rips Johnny's head off."

The soldier glanced at his superior. "Are you kidding—?"

"You heard me, soldier," the officer said.

Nick knew that no one was getting off this block tonight, with or without chains. What did they have to lose by trying to save Johnny's life?

The first soldier produced a pair of cuff keys. "Here's what you want, asshole."

He dropped the keys down to Samson, who caught them in his left palm. The prisoner unshackled his wrist cuffs in seconds. Samson forced Johnny to his knees with the chain still around his neck and put the keys in the guard's hand.

"Get those cuffs off my ankles, prick," he ordered.

Johnny hurried to comply and tossed aside the shackles.

"Now open the rest of these cells," Samson ordered the soldiers watching from above.

The officer waved his arms. "Whoa! Can't do that."

Samson dragged Johnny to his feet by the chain. "This ain't no fuckin' negotiation!"

Nick's eyes narrowed. He could see activity in the guard station at the end of the block through the partly opened security door. Soldiers were rushing to get ready for something. This isn't going to end well, he thought.

"OK," the officer said, "OK. Don't hurt anyone. We'll do this your way."

The officer gave the other soldier a quick nod, a signal of some sort, and then barked an order into his radio. Finished, both soldiers raced down the catwalk toward the guard station.

A hard buzzer sounded, followed by the click of cell doors unbolting. The other four death-row inmates burst from their cells, screaming and yelling and slapping Samson's back. They couldn't believe their good fortune to be out of their cells on their terms. Nick made no move to join them.

Samson led Johnny around the corridor like a dog on a leash while the others whooped their approval. An inmate they called "Frankenstein," a tall, muscular commando with a face carved with deep scars, stormed toward the thick metal security door at the end of the corridor, the only way in and out of the cellblock. The door stood slightly ajar. "I'm pounding me some hamburger."

Nick pushed open his cell door. "*Wait!*"

There was an outburst of derision from the others. "You were always a pussy, Nickels," Frankenstein sneered. "What are you afraid of? No guns are allowed on this block. Whatever happens, I ain't giving those brass pricks the satisfaction of watching me hang."

"This is insane," Nick yelled after him. "No one's leaving this block."

"Screw him," another inmate said. "He's not one of us. Never was. If I'm going down, it'll be on my terms."

There was unanimous agreement among the other prisoners.

Samson flung Johnny aside, seized the front of Nick's overalls, and pushed him back into his cell. "You can stay here and enjoy your journey to hell. Have fun." Samson hurled Nick across his cell, where he landed with a thud on the floor in front of his bunk. Samson closed the cell door behind him with a metallic bang, locking Nick inside. "Have a nice short life, pussy."

Nick stood up and peered through his cell's eye slot just as Frankenstein yanked open the security door. The prisoner's vengeful smirk evaporated while he stared into the muzzles of a half dozen M16 rifles. Frankenstein was right—almost. Guns were forbidden inside the block. Unless there was a riot. The compound's SWAT team had arrived. Two soldiers lay dead, another in jeopardy, and there was blood to repay.

"Oh shit—"

A burst from the M16s tore a dozen holes through Frankenstein's chest. The volley forced him back across the concrete floor, where he landed heavily at Samson's feet. Frankenstein gazed up at him with the resigned, glassy look of a man on his way to hell. A gaping hole in his neck pulsed out a river of blood that slowed to a trickle.

At least Frankenstein got his wish, Nick thought—no one would have the satisfaction of watching his execution.

Another inmate hurled himself against the security door and slammed it shut as a second volley of fire erupted. Indentations appeared in the metal above his head, followed by the sound of bullets ricocheting inside the guard station. They could hear men shouting on the other side.

"What'll we do, Sammy?" the inmate shouted.

Samson sank into a sitting position against the wall while Johnny curled up fetal-like beside him. No one moved.

The corridor lights flared out, plunging East Block into darkness. The climate control fans whined to a halt.

Nick let out a long sigh of exasperation. He stretched across his cot, put his head on the flat pillow, and stared up into the blackness. He could hear Johnny's tortured sobbing, the only sound on the block.

This was going to be a long, hot night.

PROPHETIC

SHERIFF BOWMAN CLOSED the metal door to the jailhouse's holding area behind him with a *clack*. He moved to the first cell and stared at the ancient little man seated inside.

"Who are you?"

"I am Aman," his prisoner said.

Bowman pressed his face between the steel bars. "I want to hear for myself what you told my deputy and that reporter fella this afternoon."

Ronnie belted out a boar-like laugh from his cage that reverberated off the concrete walls and ceiling. "He's a frickin' prophet, Sheriff. Says the end of the world's coming tomorrow. Put him in here with me. In two minutes, I'll show him the end of the world."

Bowen ignored the brute. "Is that true, old-timer? I want to hear it from you."

"Sheriff Bowman, you should know that men whose dark nature promotes greed, control, and violence will be purged," Aman said.

"Purge my ass. What makes you so goddamn sure?"

Aman's eyes stayed riveted on the sheriff. "This is how it will be. No one can change it."

Bowman stepped back from the cell until his broad shoulders struck the cinderblock wall behind. He couldn't pull his eyes away from this man. He felt seriously rattled, and he was even more afraid to admit why.

Bowman's eyes dropped to his bandaged right hand, which hid a deep cut he received from replacing a section of his ranch's barbed-wire fence. His palm no longer throbbed. He unwrapped the thin strip of fabric slowly—reverently—as though it were a holy burial cloth, afraid of what he might find beneath. His jaw tightened as the last piece of cloth fell away to the floor.

The wound was gone, but the tattered black stitches remained embedded under the skin.

Bowman swallowed hard. He couldn't pluck out his stitches fast enough on what he concluded had been a very strange day.

"What makes you so goddamn sure, old man?" he muttered.

SUMMON

Brooklyn, New York

JACOB COHEN WOKE suddenly. He felt no lingering fatigue. In fact, he couldn't recall the last time he felt so awake. It was late, almost midnight by his table clock. He lay still on his bed, staring at vague shadows on the ceiling that, without his glasses, reminded him of gathering storm clouds. Instead of fading from memory, the strange dream that roused him only intensified.

He shifted his head on the pillow to look at his wife, but he could see only Martha's form, sleeping on her left side, facing away from him. It occurred to him that they had shared this same bedroom for the past forty-seven years.

Jacob grabbed his wireframe glasses from the bedside table and put them on. The worn room with its decades-old wooden furniture came into focus. He slipped from beneath his sheets as quietly as possible and stood motionless on the hardwood floor. He didn't wish to disturb his wife. An even stream of light traffic flowed from the street below the bedroom window, which he had opened wide to circulate the summer's night air. The old building's ancient wiring couldn't handle the demands of air conditioning.

The awkward squeaks of the floorboards made leaving the room in stealth impossible. But Martha never moved. Jacob closed his bedroom door gently behind him, creaked down the dark hallway to his study, and retrieved an archaic key from his bottom desk drawer.

Returning to the hallway, he stopped in front of the attic door and inserted the key into its lock. When he turned it, the sharp rap of the mechanism echoed down the hallway like a hammer dropping. He glanced toward the bedroom door but heard no stirring.

Jacob opened the door with a creak and stared up the vague attic steps that seemed to beckon him. He ascended at an even pace, mindful of the dimness. He felt for the light knob and rotated it with a snap, allowing a naked sixty-watt bulb to light the attic storage space. He passed familiar boxes, antique furniture, and scraps of dusty mementos—a long lifetime of accumulations. None of this would be of use to anyone again. The keepsakes included equipment that had served his family's jewelry business for generations. Every item was an antique. The collection would bring more at auction than his dwindling business was now capable of generating. But he refused to part with any of it.

Jacob used both hands to pull aside a scarred wooden table, revealing a fireproof safe purchased second-hand more than forty years ago. He eased himself onto his knees, placed his nimble fingers on the dial, and spun it back and forth, stopping at four different numbers. He turned the safe's handle and opened the thick door, releasing a musty waft of disintegrating papers laced with petroleum lubricant. His fingers slid under a stack of documents and withdrew a hand-made wooden container slightly smaller than a cigar box. The withered wood lid and base were held together by twin metal straps, as thin as paper, soldered together long before he was born.

Jacob sat back onto the floor with the old box in his lap while contemplating what he would do next. He ran his fingers over the wood's grain, a worn surface polished by the fingers of his father and his father's father, and so on, that all touched the box the same reverent way over many, many years.

A woman's voice shattered his thoughts. *"Jake?"*

Jacob jerked around to see his wife standing at the top of the attic steps wearing her nightgown and slippers. "Marti?"

"Jake," she said, crossing the attic, "what in heaven's name are you doing up here at this hour?"

"I couldn't sleep."

"Something woke me too," she said. "I dreamt you were meeting an unusual man in a very large room. The ceiling was high, and the rain that came down in torrents looked like blood. The man desperately needed what you brought for him. He couldn't go on without it."

"You weren't dreaming, Marty. I saw him too."

She spotted the box in his lap and put a hand to her forehead. "Jesus, Jake. When?"

"Tonight," he said without hesitation. "Now."

Her drawn look revealed deep apprehension. "Wait until morning."

"No," he snapped, refusing to look at her. He couldn't allow himself to be distracted. Not now. Certainly not now. "Morning will be too late. I must leave at once."

"Where are you taking that?" she asked. "Who is this man you need to meet?"

Jacob rose unsteadily to his feet and winced, his arthritic knees snapping. He looked at her somberly. "I don't yet know."

PHOTO

Rapid City Journal

MATT HENDRIX BROUGHT up the county prisoner's digital photos on one of the *Journal's* computer screens. There were six images in total. He had turned in his story minutes past deadline, and the paper's front-page editor was anxious for a photo to accompany the article. If the headline touted the county's oldest prisoner, the editor wanted a picture of the old man in his cell.

Matt paged through the images on his camera's SD card, looking for the two best photos from the series—one vertical and one horizontal. He wouldn't show any of the others. He didn't like anyone else deciding how best to illustrate his story with his own photos. He'd been burned too many times by lousy editorial calls.

Matt's grin faded, and his heart began to race. *Shit!* He moved closer to the screen for a better look. Strange, semi-translucent spheres of varying sizes and hues were visible in each photo, like floating balloons.

His fingers keyed through the images a second time and then a third. The orbs were arranged randomly in each photo.

Then something else caught Matt's attention. The prisoner staring into the camera from his jail bench was not the old man he had interviewed earlier. The photos depicted a younger man, middle-aged, with skin healthy and virile. Yet his features were undeniably those of the prisoner he interviewed.

"What the…?"

The longer Matt stared at the screen, the more disconnected he felt from his body. He knew he couldn't show these images to anyone—not now, not until he understood what had happened. *Christ!* He had already filed his glib story, and his boss needed these photos to finish the layout. His editor would question his competency as a reporter when he saw these. Worse, this would delay publication of the morning edition while his editor killed the story and scrambled to insert a new one. *Shit, SHIT!*

Matt fought to control his breathing. *Goddamnit—think!* He drew in a deep breath and held it, unclipped a cellphone from his belt, and punched the speed-dial to the editorial office while he still had the nerve. His hands were shaking. When his editor answered, Matt exhaled and blurted, "Jack, forget the photos for my article. I spilled hot coffee on the camera's SD card when I was rushing to make my deadline. The card's ruined. The photos are gone. Sorry." Could his boss hear the nervous quiver in his voice?

When the reprimands started, Matt ended the call and hooked the phone back onto his belt. He felt nauseous and needed fresh air—fast.

Matt popped the SD card from the computer's reader and pocketed it before leaving, not knowing if he'd still have a job in the morning.

• • •

LaGuardia Airport, New York City

Jacob Cohen stared up at the overhead departure display and scanned the list of international flights scheduled to leave over the next several hours. He was traveling light, wearing a black suit, and holding a single carry-on bag in his right hand. Tucked securely inside—sandwiched between an extra pair of trousers and a clean shirt—was the wooden box from his attic's safe.

Jacob's body stiffened when he spotted the US Airways flight direct to Frankfurt. He focused on the name of the city. There was no reason to look further. The flight was scheduled to leave at 1:30 a.m. He would be on it.

Jacob turned away from the monitor and noted the short line at the US Airways' international counter. He stepped behind a young couple who looked tired. Despite losing a night's sleep himself, he felt alert and focused. Odd. He always felt tired, even after a good night. He knew he wouldn't be sleeping much until he turned over the box tucked inside his travel case, something that had been in his family for more generations than he could fathom.

Only then would he rest.

DAY THREE

VISITOR

SAMANTHA WOKE TO a cold hand brushing her scalp. She jerked up and stared wide-eyed across the dark, unfamiliar bedroom.

"Kirby?"

No response. She lit the face of her wristwatch—two minutes past 5 a.m. She'd slept for more than seven hours without recalling any dreams.

The chill disappeared as quickly as it came, and she touched her hair, uncertain. Yet, she sensed a presence. As she sat there staring, the bedroom door opened, revealing a white vapor in the hallway.

The vapor drifted into the room and stopped at the foot of the bed. Samantha couldn't move. The walls seemed to move in around her, trapping her. *This isn't happening.*

She recalled a scary story her grandfather told her long ago about how fear attracts ghosts. 'Don't be afraid of them,' he warned her. 'Ghosts are lonely and miss the earth. If you fear them, they will come to your room in the night to crop your hair in spite to make you undesirable.' When she began crying, her grandfather laughed and told her he had made up the story. But she refused to believe that. Although she had never seen a ghost, she believed they were real, some of them angry, maybe even violent. She dreaded the day she would join them—

A cry caught in Samantha's throat when a woman's voice whispered, "Samantha, you must not leave him—"

Samantha threw off the sheets and charged into the hallway, her heart pumping pure adrenaline.

"David!"

The cloud followed her into the hallway, coalescing into a pure white profile of a woman. The sun hadn't risen, but Samantha could discern long hair and a flowing robe that tapered off into a mist. The featureless face appeared to be made of cotton. She sensed it staring at her, even without eyes.

Samantha's breaths came quickly, and she feared she might hyperventilate. She tried to think clearly. *Maybe I should speak to it—*

The mist dispersed when Hunter Rowe charged into the hallway holding his shotgun ready. Samantha watched what remained of the ethereal form regress into a shadow that moved across the living room. The whimpering dog hid behind Samantha.

Rowe appeared dressed in boxers and a sleeveless T-shirt. "What's going on here?" He rubbed his eyes, struggling to clear his vision. "Who's in there with you?"

Samantha lifted a finger toward the living room. "Out there."

"Samantha?" Marshall scrambled down the staircase from the second level, buttoning his shirt.

"A woman." Samantha pushed past Rowe and pointed toward a silhouette moving along the living-room wall. "That shadow. It's not human." The shadow faded.

Rowe swung his shotgun over his shoulder with a scowl. "So, we're chasing shadows now?"

"She spoke to me."

Marshall turned on the table lamp and joined Samantha in the center of the living room, his eyes bouncing from corner to corner.

Rowe turned on her, furious. "What the hell is wrong with you? You're fricken useless." He glared at Marshall. "I'll bet she can't even cook."

"Screw you, Rowe," Samantha shouted. "No one invited you to come along."

"You should not feel alarmed." Aman descended the stairway in slow, measured steps. He had found a pair of tan

Dockers, a long-sleeved plaid shirt, and dress loafers, all of which more or less fit him. "The woman you saw is important to me."

"What the hell are you talking about?" Rowe demanded.

"Sheema," he said at the foot of the steps. "My wife when she last walked the earth. She came a great distance to help me."

Rowe lunged at Aman and yanked the front of his plaid shirt into his fist. He pulled until their eyes were only inches apart. "You've brought us all this way out here to chase *ghosts?*"

Aman stared into the trooper's eyes without saying a word. Samantha watched, frozen, as the two men's eyes remained locked, boring into each other. God—!

"Don't you dare touch him," Samantha shouted. "Hit me, humiliate me, criticize me, but you don't dare touch Aman."

Marshall grabbed the trooper's arm. "Back off, Rowe."

Rowe let go of Aman in disgust. Samantha sighed in relief.

Marshall raised his hands in a surrendering gesture. "Let's all take it easy, cool down, and figure this out."

Rowe thrust a finger at Aman. "I want some answers from you."

"Everything will become clear in time," Aman said.

Rowe shook his head and stomped toward the back of the house, muttering something about finding coffee.

The old Victorian house felt even more claustrophobic to Samantha. A terrible ringing filled her ears. *What the hell am I doing here?* She retreated into her room, slamming the door behind her.

AB AMBAR

SAMANTHA ROLLED INTO a fetal position on her bed, knees tucked under her chin. She smelled flowers—lilacs. She observed movement, outlines, and shapes positioning themselves around the room. Three of them. *Oh my God ... oh my God ... oh my God—!*

Every muscle in her body tensed. She buried her head in the sheets, her eyes closed tight, and whispered, "Leave me alone ... please."

A gentle hand brushed her hair, forcing a scream from her throat.

"Do not fear them."

Her head shot up. "Aman—?"

Aman stood beside the bed, looking down at her with keen, warm eyes.

Samantha rolled to the edge of the bed and switched on the nightstand's lamp. The light's soft glow revealed that Aman had undergone yet another change she hadn't noticed in the dark hallway. He appeared ten years younger than the night before, his complexion softer and with more color. No frail elderly man here—this was a thoughtful fifty-something with graying hair, intense brown eyes, and smoother features. For a moment, she wondered if this was even the same man.

"They wish to help me," Aman said. "They will protect you."

Samantha could see them. She recognized "Sheema" with her long, graceful robe. The other two remained formless. She sensed a deep longing, as though these entities wished to speak to her, but to their regret, could not.

"Protect me from what?" she asked.

Aman sat on the edge of the bed across from her, easing her apprehension somewhat. She felt safe sitting near him.

"What began as a delirious old man's trek down a long, hot road has become a very dangerous path," Aman said. "Now I need your help to finish this."

His intense eyes peered into hers as though searching for something. Her trust? How could he think of her as an asset when she didn't believe it herself?

She lowered her eyes and shook her head. "I'll slow you down. Rowe's right. I can't even cook. I should go back to Rapid City."

Aman smiled. "Rowe knows nothing about you."

She glared at him. "I don't trust him. I think he's dangerous."

"He is a danger," Aman said. "To himself."

"Everything's coming to an end, isn't it, Aman?" Samantha asked. "We're all going to die, aren't we?"

"That is a real possibility," Aman said. "I cannot lie to you."

There came a gentle knock. The door opened, and Marshall peered around the edge. He raised a cup of coffee. "May I?"

Samantha felt a rush of relief seeing him. "David."

"Please join us, Dr. Marshall," Aman said, beckoning him into the room.

Callie trotted into the room behind him and jumped up onto the bed next to Samantha. The dog touched her leg with a cold nose.

Marshall presented the coffee mug to Samantha. "For you."

She accepted it, grateful. The brew was fresh and steamy, the mug hot. As she sipped, she noticed that the doctor seemed oblivious to the presence of the room's apparitions. No one other than she and Aman could see them. Well, maybe one other—Callie's head jerked, and her eyes scanned the walls, her ears high.

"We must proceed with caution," Aman said to them. "Your safety is of great concern to me."

Marshall sat on the bed next to Samantha. She saw him staring at Aman, seemingly fascinated by his continual age regression. But the doctor said nothing about it.

"Aren't we safer traveling now that these sudden deaths have eliminated the violent element?" Marshall asked.

"Not entirely eliminated, doctor," Aman said. "Those who harm and take another's life—directly or indirectly—have been purged first."

"So, what's the problem?" Samantha pressed, sipping from her mug.

"Individuals who would knowingly take or control another life, yet have not acted on that appetite because of circumstances, still walk among us," Aman said. "The possibility of violence remains."

"Terrific," Marshall said.

"So, where are you going?" Samantha asked, changing the subject.

"I must reach Ab Ambar within three days before the breach does irreparable harm to this planet," Aman said.

"What breach?" Marshall said.

"An interdimensional breach is responsible for all that is transpiring," he said. "At the same time, we are witnessing a shift that was meant to occur gradually over many years as Earth evolved and us with it. An accident forced this sudden shift on an unprepared world, a course that is now greatly accelerated. We cannot stop it. If my journey succeeds, humankind will realize its destiny long ahead of the Plan and allow us to live safe and in peace on a new Earth. If I reach Ab Ambar."

"I never heard of Ab Ambar," Samantha said. "Where is it?"

"The location is 31° 25' 24" North by 53° 42' 1" East," Aman said.

Marshall withdrew an opened envelope and a pen from his pants pocket to jot down the coordinates. "That's quite a way overseas," he noted as he wrote.

"Overseas?" Samantha's eyes darted to Aman. "You need to go overseas?"

"I must reach the source of this devastation," Aman said.

"The way is dangerous, but access is still possible."

"What will you do when you get to this—place?" Marshall asked. The doctor wasn't buying this, Samantha noted.

Aman spread his hands. "I am only aware of the breach and its location. What I must do when I reach Ab Ambar is not yet clear. However, I will become aware as I need to know."

"How will you get overseas?" Samantha asked.

"I do not yet know."

Marshall stood with a frown. "That's not good enough. You're not making much sense—not to me, nor will anyone else believe you. And now you're asking us to follow you halfway around the world without a plan." He shook his head. "I'm afraid this expedition of yours is getting too difficult."

Marshall had a point, Samantha realized. And who else would agree to travel with him under these circumstances?

"I am sorry, doctor," Aman said. "I must continue my journey with or without help. And I am in great need of your skills."

"If you really need me, I'll go," Samantha said. She tried her best to sound committed.

Marshall raised his hands to forgo further discussion for now. "OK, we'll think this through. In the meantime, let's keep the fact that you've got no plan between the three of us. We have enough problems."

Samantha sensed movement. She saw the ethereal shadows moving into a vague circle around the room, and she heard whispering, like anxious chatter. At the same moment, Aman's head snapped up, his expression drawn. He gripped the amulet around his neck.

"A man is approaching this house," Aman said. "He will interfere with what I need to do. We must prepare for his arrival."

An urgent rap on the door startled Samantha. Kirby burst in before any of them could move.

"Someone's coming," Kirby hollered.

They followed Kirby into the living room where Hunter Rowe stood peering out one of the front windows, shotgun in hand. Samantha stepped to the next window for a look. The sky to the east had brightened, and the day's first light revealed detail along the tree line. She saw headlights of an approaching vehicle coming down the long, gravel driveway. Marshall stepped next to her for a look.

Samantha appealed to him. "What do we do?"

Marshall said nothing and watched a late-model black Oldsmobile emerge from the tree line. The car pulled into the parking area next to their vehicles.

"Shit," Rowe said. "Shit. *Shit.*"

Samantha recognized the Olds from the checkpoint out of Rapid City—the car that belonged to the federal agent.

"*Sonofabitch* — it's Coffey," Rowe said.

"Who?" Kirby said.

"He's FBI Special Services," Rowe said. "Coffey has orders to bring Aman in for interrogation. At any cost."

AGENT COFFEY

"HOW DID HE find us?" Samantha said. "Does that mean the FBI knows Aman's here?"

"He must not enter this house," Aman said. "*He must not.*" Samantha heard the distress in his voice. She turned to him for some instructions, but he offered nothing.

"I'll talk to him," she said.

"The hell you will. Just stay out of my way." Rowe held up his 12-gauge. "This'll do my talking."

"*No,*" Aman said. "You will provoke an already dangerous situation."

Before anyone could stop her, Samantha punched open the screen door with a bang and stormed onto the porch. The federal agent stood outside his car, wearing sunglasses despite the dim light of dawn.

"What do you want here?" she called down to him. Even from across the yard, she could see that the agent looked tired and edgy, most likely from driving all night.

Agent Coffey removed his sunglasses and stroked back his hair to look presentable. He broke into a grin and stepped around the Oldsmobile while slipping on his black suit jacket. "I'm a federal officer. You're harboring a fugitive I'm taking into custody."

"You're here for the glory and fame," Samantha said. "You want to be a hero for capturing him."

Kirby stepped out on the porch next to Samantha, holding a revolver at his side. "Stop right there."

Samantha glanced at the deputy, uncertain of his intentions.

Coffey halted. "I'm the authority here."

"You don't have squat here," Kirby said. "How'd you find us?"

Coffey's smug grin returned. "You invited me. Your truck's GPS transponder led me right to you."

"*Shit,*" Kirby spat.

"The agency knows you took our fugitive and that you're hiding him out here," Coffey said. "You're way over your heads—all of you."

Kirby pushed Samantha away from him and pointed his revolver at the federal agent with both hands. "There's no way you're taking Aman."

Samantha raised a tentative hand toward him. "Kirby? What are you doing?"

"Put down your weapon, deputy," Coffey ordered. "You sideshow clowns are already facing federal charges of obstruction and interfering with a federal investigation. You're looking at years of prison time."

Samantha noticed Aman watching from the opposite side of the screen door.

"Mr. Dawson," Aman said. "Do not use your weapon. You will only destroy yourself. And I need you."

Kirby glanced over his shoulder. "What the hell does that mean—"

Coffey jerked a handgun from his back holster and squeezed off two rounds in quick succession. The first bullet streaked between Samantha and the deputy, and the second struck Kirby's arm below his right shoulder. He spun around with a surprised grunt and landed heavily on his back on the porch's worn timbers. "Son of a BITCH!"

"Kirby—oh my God!" Samantha dropped to Kirby's side and grimaced at the sight of the blood gushing from his wound. She didn't know how to stop it.

Kirby stared up at her, his face wide with surprise. "Sam," he managed, "how bad is it?"

"David, help," Samantha shouted. "He's bleeding badly."

Marshall opened the screen door and stepped out onto the

porch, his eyes on Coffey, his hands raised to show he wasn't armed. "Take it easy. I'm a doctor, and I'm going to help this man."

The federal agent mounted the porch steps, still pointing his gun. He intended to get his way.

"Don't point that gun unless you plan to shoot us all," Samantha said.

"That's not what I want," Coffey said. "Turn that man over to me, and no one else gets hurt."

"And if we don't cooperate?" she said.

"Your Constitutional rights don't apply here," Coffey said. "I advise you to do as I say. My orders are very specific about any interference."

Marshall crouched beside Kirby and examined his upper right arm. "The bullet passed through your muscle and exited." He looked up at Coffey. "We need to take him to a hospital."

"He's not going anywhere until I get what I want," the agent said. He pointed his handgun at Samantha.

A shotgun blast blew the screen door off its hinges and pounded Coffey's left shoulder with buckshot. The federal agent stumbled backward off the steps and landed hard on his back on the stone walkway. Samantha watched, stunned, as Coffey struggled to rise. The state trooper kept his shotgun barrel pointed at Coffey.

"Officer Rowe," Coffey managed. His forced grin showed off a bloody row of teeth. "I didn't recognize your patrol car."

Coffey reached for his lost gun. Rowe discharged a second round that shattered the federal agent's right arm up to his elbow. Coffey let out a wail and stared at his forearm stump in dumb astonishment.

Samantha reeled back, horrified.

Marshall rose and reached for the trooper's shotgun. "That's enough!"

Rowe pushed the doctor roughly away. "He would've killed us all to get to Aman. Now he can identify us. I'm finishing this bastard right here."

Rowe pressed the shotgun's stock into his shoulder and

peered down its barrel, his finger planted on the trigger. Samantha didn't recognize the man behind those soulless eyes.

"Stop it," she shouted. "He's not a threat to us now."

"I want him off this planet," Rowe sneered.

Blood spewed from Coffey's lips. "You're a pathetic traitor, Rowe. It's over, and you lost. You just don't know it yet—"

Rowe fired. The crown of Coffey's head vanished in a shower of blood, bone, and brain matter that splattered across the walk like a spilled plate of lasagna. Coffey's upper torso splashed down in the middle of the crimson swill.

Samantha stared at the agent's body in disbelief while a scarlet stream flowed down the walkway. She never saw a man killed before. Her eyes locked with Rowe's. He looked at her with an odd expression of amazement. The state trooper nodded, lowered his shotgun, and turned away. His skin paled.

Rowe leaned his gun against the wall beside the front door like a defeated soldier. He looked at Aman standing on the opposite side of the empty door frame, watching him.

"I understand now," Rowe said.

Aman said nothing.

"So tired." Rowe lowered his sturdy frame into a frayed rocking chair and let out a deep sigh of fatigue. "I understand now," he uttered to no one in particular.

He let out a long breath, and his chin dropped to his chest, his eyes partially open.

Hunter Rowe was dead.

THE ROAD

MARSHALL HELPED KIRBY into a sitting position on the porch's first step and pressed a towel against the gunshot wound. He needed his bag from the truck to treat the damage to Kirby's arm. "Keep pressure until I clean and dress your wound," he instructed.

Kirby nodded.

Aman descended the steps and placed the sofa's afghan over Coffey's remains. "More agents will be here shortly," he said. "We must leave at once."

Samantha headed for the front door. "I'll bring whatever food I can find in the kitchen." Callie followed on her heels, wagging her tail.

"There is no time," Aman said, his voice firm.

Samantha paused by the front door. "What about Callie?"

"She will be well cared for," he said.

Marshall stood, frowning. "Kirby needs emergency medical care."

"Wait a second, doc," Kirby said. He yanked on Marshall's arm with stubborn strength and pulled him down until they were face-to-face. Sweat poured over the deputy's features as he checked to make sure Aman was out of earshot. He looked terrified.

"I'm staying here," he whispered.

"You need surgery—"

"Traveling with Aman is a very bad idea," Kirby hissed. "He doesn't have the same DNA as us, like an alien or something. What if he used Rowe to kill that agent? Maybe he intends to use all of us. Maybe he brought me along to take a bullet for him. This whole mess is freaking me out, and I'm not going any farther. He doesn't need me."

"Yes, I do, Mr. Dawson," Aman called from the far end of the walkway. "And I will do everything in my power to keep you safe."

Marshall glanced at Aman in surprise, wondering how he could have overheard their whispered conversation.

"I'll slow you down," Kirby called to him. "Leave me here. I'll tell them you're heading back to Rapid City."

"They will not believe you," Aman said, approaching the steps.

"Jesus, Aman," Kirby shouted, "I'm dying!"

"You will heal quickly," Aman said. "We must all leave together. Dr. Marshall, please help Mr. Dawson to the vehicle."

Aman headed toward the cars.

"He's right," Marshall said. "Who knows what the Feds will do to you if you stay. If we leave now, I can treat you."

"Damn it," Kirby said, his eyes shut tight. "Damn it. Damn it."

Marshall didn't doubt that Kirby wished he could be anywhere but here. He helped Kirby to his feet. The deputy, grimacing, made it down the walk with the doctor's assistance.

"You drive the sheriff's truck, David," Samantha said, hurrying to catch up with Aman.

"We need to disable the GPS transponder," Kirby said. He winced, and Marshall knew he was in considerable pain.

"The authorities are looking for your truck, Mr. Dawson." Aman walked between the vehicles. "And they will find it, even without its locator."

Marshall watched Aman open the driver's door to Samantha's Focus and peer inside. Satisfied, he moved around the car to inspect it as though considering a purchase. Marshall wondered what, if anything, he knew about cars.

"No one is searching for this vehicle," Aman told Samantha. "The four of us will travel as one."

"The passenger door doesn't open," Samantha said.

"We will manage." Aman climbed into the back seat.

Marshall didn't like the idea of them crowded into such a small car, but there was no time to argue their situation. He settled the wounded deputy in the back beside Aman's slim frame. Marshall lifted the towel to inspect the wound.

"Bad, doc?" Kirby asked.

"Not exactly. The bleeding's stopped. Try not to move."

Kirby leaned his head back against the seat, closed his eyes, and let out a long sigh of frustration. Marshall retrieved his bag from the truck and slid into the front passenger seat as Samantha started the engine.

Callie sat down at the edge of the porch with a whimper and watched her new friends leave in their tiny blue car.

. . .

The Journal
Rapid City, N.D.

"These pictures are shit," muttered Jack Feehery, the *Rapid City Journal's* managing editor.

Feehery, a seasoned Irishman with a poorly trimmed red beard, shuffled through several 8x10-inch photos as though dealing a poker game, and always with the same results—a losing hand. He desperately needed an original photo for today's special edition about fallen world leaders and the rising global body count. His top story read: "National Manhunt Continues for Local Homeless Man."

An uninspired photo of the medical center represented the best of the bunch, while another showed a long shot of yesterday's crowd in front of the jail. The only halfway newsworthy image was an out-of-focus photo of a woman in front of the jailhouse helping a man into a small blue car. A local snapped the photograph with an old smartphone.

"This sucks," Feehery muttered. Motion blur was a big problem, the detail poor. He couldn't make out the car's plate number.

Feehery tossed the photos across the table harder than he intended and watched them fly onto the floor. Just as well.

He removed his reading glasses and ground a thumb into the bridge between his bloodshot eyes. How the hell did he let the scoop of the century slip through his fingers? *Jesus, I'd sell my own mother for one decent photo of this geezer.*

"Excuse me," said Matt Hendrix from the doorway. "Excuse me."

Feehery's long, leathery face turned toward the reporter. "Jesus, Hendrix, you've got a lot of balls showing up here." He let the reporter hear his disgust. "When you lost your pictures of this guy, you flushed away your chance at fame and made me look like a *goddamn* jackass."

Hendrix held up his camera's SD card. "Boss, if I had real balls, I'd sell these images to every news bureau from here to China for a lot more money than you'll earn in your career."

BIKER

THE MORNING SUN rose directly in Samantha's line of sight, triggering the first throbs of a nasty headache. At least her apprehensions eased a bit the more distance she put between them and that strange old house. None of her passengers said much, and that suited her just fine.

"Tell me about your parents," Marshall said to break the silence. A tattered U.S. highway map covered his lap.

Samantha threw him a sideways glance. "Why?"

He shrugged. "Just curious. Are they okay?"

She winced from the stab in her head. "They died together when I was nine. Grandma raised me, or rather let me live with her until she passed. I pretty much raised myself."

"How did your folks die?"

"A car crash in Nevada. Dad, drunk out of his mind, managed to find the only tree along a stretch of highway thirty miles outside Vegas. Tore his Mustang in two. The police discovered the accident at dawn. Never did find mom's lower body."

When Marshall didn't respond, Samantha added, "Aren't you glad you asked?"

Samantha hit the brakes harder than she intended when they neared a stop sign at the junction of Route 59. More than a dozen cars had backed up, waiting for a chance to pull out. That wouldn't be easy. A continuous stream of cars packed the two-lane road they needed to access.

"Where's everyone going?" she moaned, a hand against her

temple.

Marshall looked over his shoulder at Aman. "This trip of yours is going to take longer than you figured. I hope your schedule's flexible."

"It is not," Aman said.

Samantha shook her head. After a ten-minute wait, she finally pulled her car onto Highway 59 and fell in with a long line of cars snaking toward the I-80 onramp more than two miles ahead. Lots of people walked in the same direction along the road's shoulder. Two men passed, carrying between them a body wrapped in a bedsheet. The sight sickened her.

"Are we there yet?" Kirby muttered from the backseat, his eyes shut, and his head tilted back.

Samantha glanced at the dashboard. "I hate breaking the news, but we're down to a quarter tank of gas. We should have siphoned some before we left."

"We had no time," Aman reminded her and then touched her shoulder. "Take your vehicle off this road."

Samantha looked at him in her rearview mirror. "Where?"

"Here." Aman pointed to a grassy area beyond the road's shoulder. "Now."

Samantha shrugged, steered her Focus onto the grass, and stopped. "What's wrong?"

"Uncover the engine," Aman said. "Allow others to see our distress."

"Whatever you say." Samantha reached under the dashboard and popped the hood. She slipped out of the car to allow Marshall room to slide over her driver's seat to exit. Marshall lifted the hood, and she felt the engine's heat waft past her.

The rumble of a motorcycle brought her attention to the lighter traffic on the opposite side of the two-lane road. A Harley-Davidson decked in chrome with black lacquer slowed as it approached them. Samantha saw a lone rider wearing a black T-shirt and a black helmet with orange and red flames. The biker weaved a skillful path through the oncoming traffic and arched onto the grass beside them, the rear tire tossing up a trail of dirt like a cock's tail. Samantha noticed Aman watching from the back seat with a hint of a smile.

The biker cut the engine and rolled to a stop. "Car trouble?"

"You could say that," Samantha said. "We're trying to get to the East Coast on a quarter tank of gas by way of a jammed interstate."

The rider threw down the kickstand and slid off his bike. The lean young man pulled off his helmet and ran a hand through a short patch of dark hair. He moved with a confident, almost cocky stride. At least he didn't look dangerous, she thought. What did he want from them?

"No one's going anywhere on the interstate," he said. "It's backed up all the way to Des Moines. And there's no gas. When your tank's empty, you walk."

Samantha's heart sank for Aman. There was no way he could finish his trip now.

Aman thrust his head out the open window and said to the young man, "You are alone after such a long time away. I, too, am far from my home."

The biker's shoulders sagged, and he stood motionless as though his cowboy boots had taken root. He couldn't seem to find the words to respond and stared at Aman with a dumb expression.

Did he recognize Aman, Samantha wondered? How could he?

"Do you two know each other?" she asked.

The biker shook his head. "I had a strange dream."

"We all are having strange dreams," Aman said.

"Who are you?" Samantha asked.

The biker pulled himself up to his full height as though on a military inspection. "The name's Nick Judge. I have a suggestion."

Samantha settled against the side of her car, her arms folded. "We're wide open to suggestions."

"Fly to the East Coast," Nick said.

Samantha scowled. "Yeah, right."

"All flights are banned," Marshall said. "We need to admit that we're stuck here."

"Screw the ban," Nick said. He pointed back the way he came. "There's a municipal airport off 59, not five miles from here—all private aircraft. A skilled pilot could fly a single-engine plane low enough to stay off FAA and military radar."

Marshall wouldn't stop shaking his head. "That's crazy."

"Well, it sure beats walking," Nick grinned.

"But where will we find a pilot willing to ignore the ban?" Samantha asked. "And one who can fly that low?"

Nick bowed and presented her with a winning smile. "You're looking at him."

"You?"

"Yes, ma'am," Nick said. "I could use the work."

Samantha expelled a huff of incredulous laughter. Could this young man help Aman get to where he needed to go? "Are you serious?" she said. "We're in no position to hire anyone to help us."

Nick offered a playful smile. "Fine. You can owe me. Otherwise, I'm stuck here too."

"I want to see your pilot's license," Marshall said.

"I don't have anything like that with me. Not even a wallet."

"Why should we trust you?" Marshall asked.

"For the same reason I'm willing to trust you," Nick said. "I grew up inside the cockpit of a single-engine Cessna. I was trained to fly F-18 fighters over Afghanistan. I can fly anything that can get off the ground. It might not always be pretty, but I can get you anywhere."

AIRPORT

THE SMALL RURAL airport looked deserted. Despite common sense, Samantha allowed her hopes to rise while following Nick's Harley between the twin runways. They passed six single-engine prop airplanes arranged in a neat row alongside the airport's lone hangar. A sleek corporate jet sat inside the hanger's opened bay door. Could Nick fly one of those little planes? If it turned out he was full of shit, she figured they were no worse off than on the highway.

Samantha pulled next to Nick's bike in front of a one-story aviation office. A lone pickup truck sat in the first parking space. She didn't see a worker anywhere. Even on a typical day, she doubted this place saw much activity.

"I will stay with Mr. Dawson," Aman said. He appeared to have no interest in exploring the tiny airport.

Samantha stepped out of her car, followed by Marshall climbing across the front on all fours. She followed Nick and Marshall into the pilots' center. The air inside felt baking hot, despite a noisy window-mounted air conditioner. A lone older man she assumed took care of the place sat at a table behind a counter. His creased leather face boasted an impressive tan, and his shaggy white hair and a matching drooping mustache looked very non-corporate. The name "Mel" was embroidered onto his denim jumpsuit.

Marshall detoured into a small break area where he found a worn atlas on an end table. He retrieved the envelope from his pants' pocket on which he had written Aman's global coordinates.

"I'm closed," Mel said without looking up. "But you're welcome to what's left in the coffee pot. Otherwise, I'm tossin' it."

He stared through a pair of reading glasses at a newspaper spread over the table. A stack of today's newspaper sat on the counter. Samantha picked up one and noted coverage devoted solely to the cataclysmic events that began yesterday and had now captured the world's undivided attention.

Nick set his helmet on the counter and said, "We need to charter an airplane, sir. The Cessna 335 next to the hangar would be ideal."

Samantha thought about the thirty-odd dollars in her wallet. Even if the airport manager agreed, did they have enough cash between them to rent one of these things?

Mel tossed his reading glasses onto the newspaper with a frown and gestured to the muted TV in the break area. The scene showed a churchyard filled with uneven rows of dead bodies covered with makeshift materials from bedsheets to floral shower curtains.

"In case you've been smokin' your bloomers and just woke up," he said, "all flights are grounded. The new president is expected to order martial law at noon to control the panic. No one's goin' anywhere. I suggest you call it a day and go back home." He returned his reading glasses to the bridge of his nose. "I do have a '92 Mustang I can rent you. But you'll need to find your own gas."

Samantha stiffened when she saw Aman's face on the TV's news story. His picture was taken in the sheriff's holding cell, but he looked a good deal younger.

"What the—?" She couldn't hear the program, but a lot of talking heads seemed to have much to say about Aman. The screen caption read, "Nationwide Manhunt Intensifies." This is bad, she thought. *Really bad.*

Nick glanced over his shoulder at the broadcast.

Marshall stared at the TV screen until another segment began about a national week of mourning. He returned to the world atlas, thumbing through the pages.

"Everyone's looking for that fellow," Mel said with a nod toward the TV. "Seems he may know something 'bout all this. The paper says he might even be in the state. Wish I knew his whereabouts. There's a generous government reward for anyone that finds him—more than enough for me to retire and die comfortably. Meanwhile, a military task force is on the way to set up camp here. They need our long runways. I'm turning the airport over to them, and then I'm going home." He peered over his glasses at the chrome clock above the door. "They should be here in 'bout a half-hour or so."

Samantha placed both hands on the counter while she considered their next move. Dare they take a chance and confide in this man? They were out of options. "What if I told you that the man everyone is looking for must leave the country? Otherwise, we all might die."

Nick looked at her in surprise.

Marshall glanced up from his book. "Sam, are you sure you want to say anything?"

Samantha nodded.

Mel's shoulders jiggled as he chuckled. "Miss, I know when someone's blowing smoke up my backside. I may not know what's goin' on, but I do know that the world's not gonna end any time soon. No ma'am, nothing of the sort. When the Big Shout happens, I expect we'll see lots of angels—not just one little feller." He leaned back in his squeaky chair and gestured toward the TV. "Won't be nothin' like this."

"Don't take my word," Samantha said. "Ask him yourself."

Mel's grin vanished, and he squeaked forward in his chair. "Come again?"

"The manhunt is for a man who's sitting outside in my car," Samantha said. "We need an airplane to get him out of here."

"A plane that carries lots of fuel," Marshall added.

"You figured out where he wants to go?" she asked.

Marshall held up the world atlas. "Southern Iran. In the center of the most barren stretch of desert in the Middle East."

Mel expelled a blast of laughter. "Now I've heard it all." He wouldn't stop laughing. "No way you can get there from here."

"Follow me," Samantha said. "I want you to meet someone."

Mel kept shaking his head and chuckling while Samantha led him outside to her car. The airport manager stooped and peered inside at Kirby sitting with his head back and a bloodstained towel pressed against his upper arm.

Mel's grin faded, and his eyes narrowed when he spotted Aman. "I'll be a sorry son of a bitch. It *is* you!" He shook his full head of white hair. "Jesus in heaven. What have you folks gotten yourselves into?"

Aman reached out his window and offered his hand. "I am pleased to make your acquaintance."

Mel took Aman's hand into his calloused palm. Samantha saw his shaggy eyebrows lift and his facial lines stretch. His eyes took on an odd quality—fear?—not unlike the anxious look she had observed when Nick first saw Aman. Perhaps at some level, he understood the importance of Aman's journey—the same urgent energy that compelled the rest of them to help, even if they didn't understand why. She threw a glance back at Marshall. His nod said he noticed it too.

The old-timer wouldn't stop shaking Aman's hand. "Pleasure's mine, sir. Call me Mel—Mel Arterberry. Now let's see what we can do to get you on your way with all due Godspeed."

HANGAR

NICK GRABBED THE YOKE of the Cessna 355 and relished the possibilities beneath his fingers. He loved sitting in a cockpit—any cockpit. Flying meant freedom. An aircraft could take him to the top of the world away from the discerning eyes of humanity. His head bobbed approval. *Yes!* This baby would get them to the coast without much notice.

"I found the one," he called down to the tarmac. When no one responded, he strained his neck for a look outside. "Hello?"

No response. Nick climbed down from the Cessna and stood on the deserted tarmac. "Samantha? Dr. Marshall?" The others were gone.

Nick heard voices inside the hangar and went to investigate. He found the others gathered by a Gulfstream G550 corporate jet with no logo or company colors along its sleek one-hundred-foot surface.

"What's going on?" Nick asked, joining them.

"We're considering another option," Marshall informed him.

"This? You want to take *this*? We can't fly at treetop level in *this*. Every radar in the country will see us."

"Aman thinks this plane will work better for us," Samantha said. "Talk to him."

Nick marched to the nose of the aircraft.

"This beauty will cruise at Mach 0.86 into eighty-knot headwinds," Mel told Aman. He sounded like the consummate aircraft salesman, Nick thought. But this wasn't hype. Mel was risking everything—his job, pension, and maybe even his life—

to help Aman. And he saluted him for that.

"And its range?" Aman asked.

"Five-thousand miles," Mel said. "There's 30,000 pounds of fuel in the wings. She's primed and ready for a jaunt to Europe."

"Aman?" Nick said. "What are you doing?"

"Mr. Judge," Aman said. "This aircraft's range and speed will provide us with many benefits. Most importantly—time."

"But every radar will spot us," Nick said.

"The military chain of command has broken," Aman said. "That gives us the advantage. This aircraft will travel faster than most, well ahead of the military's ability to mobilize and intercept us. By morning, I will be halfway to my destination."

"You're serious, aren't you?" Nick said.

"Our time is dangerously short," Aman said. "Please follow me."

Aman led Nick up the stairs into the Gulfstream's cabin, a luxurious sitting room as sleek as its exterior. Nick stiffened when he spotted a man slumped in the rear of the cabin. He took several cautious steps toward a corpse of a suited middle-aged man spread over a fold-down oak table. His bone-white face had begun to wither. Nick felt his lips go numb. The man's unseeing, open eyes remained fixed on the table's surface, and his fists clutched a spread of papers as if he wished to finish one more report before his death. A laptop computer lay face down on the floor next to his polished Berluti shoes.

"He was purged like the others," Aman said.

"Why?" Nick asked.

"He stopped a crucial safety upgrade at one of his chemical plants to save money," Aman said. "Because of his decision, a preventable explosion killed fourteen workers and injured scores more."

"How do you know that?" Nick asked.

"That is what I am told. Do not concern yourself with him. Come this way."

Mel stepped behind the corpse. "I'll get him out of here."

Aman led Nick to the front of the aircraft and directed him into the cockpit. Nick forgot all about the corpse when he eased into the pilot's seat.

"Hey now!" He felt a surge of adrenaline while surveying the instrument panel's four Honeywell flat-panel displays. The flight deck had more in common with a computer control center than an aircraft. Sitting in the pilot's seat convinced him that this was a fabulous option. He liked Aman's thinking.

"Can you fly this aircraft without a copilot, Mr. Judge?" Aman asked from the doorway.

"Call me Nick," he said. "And the answer to your question is yes. This jet can fly itself. The hardest part is getting off the ground."

The whump of pumps starting and a muted forward bell indicated that Mel had switched on the auxiliary power unit. The cockpit instrumentation came to life as the aircraft automatically readied itself for takeoff.

Mel appeared beside Aman at the cockpit door. "She's programmed for a flight to Frankfurt. But you can change the flight plan once you're airborne. Shoot, take her anywhere you want."

"Thank you, Mr. Arterberry," Aman said. "You have been of immeasurable assistance. I am grateful."

Mel's bright expression turned cold. "The military transport will touch down on my runway in about ten minutes. They're coming for you."

Nick whipped around in his seat. "Ten minutes? I need time to review the manuals."

"If you can fly this aircraft," Mel said, "get her in the air pronto, son."

$$\bullet \ \bullet \ \bullet$$

Hotel Excelsior
Frankfurt, Germany

Jacob Cohen stepped out of the shower, grabbed a towel, and began wiping his slim body. He stared at his pure white beard trimmings lining the sink. The sight reminded him of his age, and he looked away. He should be home in Brooklyn, reclining in his study with a good book. Instead, he stood naked in a hotel bathroom a continent away. Waiting. For what?

He made his way into the bedroom, tracking a path of water across the white tiled floor. He thought of his Marti, who would wonder what had become of him. Since he landed, the phone circuit failure made calling her impossible. Was she safe? After all that had happened, he worried about her constantly to the point of obsession.

Jacob put on his thick glasses and focused his eyes on the bed. He froze, seized by a fear he had never known. The box he guarded so carefully for most of his life was gone. He could still see the slight indentation where it had sat on the top comforter. His eyes darted around the room and stopped at the door. It stood ajar. He felt lightheaded and thought he might pass out. He cursed his carelessness.

His fear yielded to a panic that he couldn't control. Jacob wrestled his way into a thick white robe from the hotel's closet and charged into the hallway without bothering to find his shoes. The corridor was empty.

Jacob hadn't the patience to wait for the elevator. He raced into a stairwell and half ran, half stumbled down the three flights. When he reached the lobby, he felt dizzy from hyperventilating. He had been panting like a dog and could feel his heart pounding against his chest. *I am too old to run down stairwells.*

Shouting erupted in the lobby by the double glass exit doors. Jacob hurried toward the disturbance and found several people gathered around a young man with curly black hair sitting on the lobby's cold marble tiles. The man wore a crisp oversized jacket to cover a worn T-shirt and torn jeans. Jacob's precious box sat between his legs.

Great waves of relief washed over him, and his breathing relaxed. The man's eyes were downcast and hidden, and he sat sobbing as if he were the one robbed. A bellboy spoke to him in German while a hotel guest pumped the man with questions about his health. The thief didn't appear to hear them.

Jacob knelt before the young man. The robber's head shot up, and he looked at Jacob with eyes glistening from weeping. Every muscle in his body seemed to tremble.

"You took what belongs to everyone," Jacob said to him, his tone curt.

The young man let out a gasp that hurled a rope of spittle down the front of his large jacket. Those watching grew quiet. Jacob put out a hand to the young man, palm up, non-threatening.

Without taking his eyes off Jacob, the man lifted the box from his lap and held it out for him with a shaking hand. The box's twin metal straps were still intact.

"I can't take it from the building." His accent was American. "It ... it won't let me."

Jacob accepted the box without a word. The other hotel guests watched Jacob rise awkwardly to his feet, his knees snapping, and make his way toward the lobby elevator. Several spoke to him, but he heard none of it. He felt weary in every extremity.

Once back in his room, he would sleep with the door bolted and the box secure in his arms.

• • •

Harlan Municipal Airport

Mel used twin red flags to direct the Gulfstream out of the hanger. Nick, smiling, gave Mel a thumbs-up from the cockpit and taxied the corporate jet out onto runway 15/33.

The screech of the hazard alarm brought Nick's eyes to the heads-up radar display. A large incoming aircraft—a military C-17 transport, according to its transponder data—was on final approach to his runway. The task force had arrived—two minutes to touchdown.

Screw it. Nick didn't think twice about violating a dozen FAA regulations. He touched the intercom button. "Make sure you're all buckled up back there for a quick, steep climb."

Nick disengaged the aircraft's auto-throttles and pushed the levers forward harder than he intended. The jet's twin Rolls-Royce engines roared. Within seconds the aircraft shot down the runway with 30,000 pounds of combined thrust. Through his headphones, Nick could hear the military pilot broadcasting a description of their plane.

He throttled to maximum power.

"Gulfstream G550, abort your takeoff. Repeat, abort your takeoff. You are violating national security—"

With one swift pull, Nick brought up the nose of the aircraft. The flat, endless Iowa landscape gave way to a thick, cloud-covered sky. *Sweet—nothing to it.*

He glanced at his radar and swallowed hard. The military transport had aborted its landing and flew a frightful 3,000 feet from their tail.

Close. Too close.

Nick engaged the auto-climb program that would take the jet to 37,000 feet in eighteen minutes.

The Gulfstream ascended and left the military transport far below them.

ASCENT

MEL ARTERBERRY STOOD at the bottom of the staircase he had pushed up to the C-17 military transport's cabin door. The day's insufferable heat and smothering humidity forced him to wipe his glistening forehead repeatedly with a stained rag that doubled as his handkerchief. *Couldn't pick a worse time of summer to stand on a tarmac.*

A tall young officer in an impeccably creased uniform and buzz haircut deplaned, followed by two military staffers, one of them a woman carrying a metal case. The team all wore somber expressions, as though they were returning from a covert mission that had gone bad. The officer and his team marched off the staircase and formed a rough circle around the airport manager. Mel looked into their solemn faces, all staring back at him through aviator sunglasses, out of place on this overcast day.

"I am Colonel Theodore Welch, head of a special military manhunt unit," the officer said. Mel saw his reflection on Welch's mirrored sunglasses and decided his rowdy mustache needed a trim. "I want to see the flight plan of that Gulfstream and a roster of everyone onboard."

"Whatever you say, Colonel," Mel said. Lean and all business, Welch smacked of West Point.

"And you are?" Welch asked.

"The name's Arterberry. Mel Arterberry."

Mel shielded his eyes to watch another figure make his way down the staircase clutching the rails with both hands. He was an older man, 70ish, and on the heavy side, with thinning white hair and bushy eyebrows. Instead of a uniform, he was dressed carelessly in a wrinkled tweed jacket and gray slacks with a blue dress shirt open at the collar. The word "professor" jumped to Mel's mind. The older gentleman joined the group and put on a pair of sunglasses with shaky hands. But these glasses were different. They had deep green lenses and thick black frames that resembled goggles.

The older man studied the cloud-covered sky through his green lenses. "Can we please hurry?"

"Hold Mr. Arterberry for interrogation," the Colonel said to his first lieutenant. Then he removed his dark glasses and directed a cold, penetrating glare at Mel. "Violating the flight ban is a federal offense. I'm taking you into custody."

• • •

Samantha sat mesmerized in a heavily padded seat, watching Marshall examine Kirby's arm wound. Thorough and precise. The deputy slept soundly on the executive leather sofa, thanks to the shot of morphine Marshall gave him before takeoff. The doctor finished and tossed the used towel into the receptacle under the cabin's wet bar.

"How is he?" Samantha asked.

"He's healing well," Marshall said. "Too well. It's remarkable."

"Mr. Dawson will mend rapidly," Aman said from the executive chair across from Samantha. "He will not notice the scar."

"Ladies and gentlemen," Nick announced over the cabin's intercom, his voice chipper, "we are approaching our cruising altitude of 37,000 feet with an airspeed of 640 miles per hour. Please sit back and enjoy the ride."

Something troubled Samantha, a point she had been reluctant to bring up before. "Tell me something, Aman," she said. "Why did Nick agree to help us?"

Aman swiveled his seat to look at her, and she saw the hesitation in his eyes as though he wished to avoid this topic. Why?

"Nick Judge is a gifted aviator," Aman said slowly. "We are

very fortunate to have his assistance."

Samantha frowned at Aman's reluctance to answer her question. "He's responsible for our lives right now. Why do you trust him?"

"Sam's right," Marshall said. "We don't know anything about him, just like we don't know much about each other, least of all you."

"What if I told you that yesterday Nick woke in a military prison seventeen days from his execution?" Aman said.

Samantha drew in a quick breath. *"What?"*

Marshall leaned against the wet bar with folded his arms. "That's just great."

"Nick is innocent of the offenses for which he was charged and convicted," Aman said.

"How do you know that?" Samantha asked.

"They told me," Aman said.

Marshall scowled. "So, you're talking to ghosts again."

Samantha scolded the doctor with a frown. "Tell us what happened."

"The incident occurred the night Nick arrived at a coalition training base in Pakistan," Aman said. "A soldier from another unit befriended Nick and took him to a local family's home to celebrate his last day in the country. The soldier put a drug in Nick's drink. While Nick lay unconscious, the soldier raped the 14-year-old daughter before taking her life and killing her parents. He planted evidence to make Nick look responsible. Nick was arrested and charged with the crime. He recalls nothing about that night, including the man who committed the atrocities. After a brief military trial, Nick was sentenced to die."

Samantha didn't dare ask for another detail. She regretted bringing up the topic, she regretted knowing. "How awful."

Aman's intense brown eyes softened. "Take comfort in knowing that as Earth's frequency rises, violence will become impossible."

Samantha wanted to believe Aman, she really did—but she couldn't put aside her doubts. "Are you saying there will be no more wars?"

"No more wars," Aman said. "No more killing. No more atrocities at the hands of another."

"You're describing paradise," she said, "a return to the Garden of Eden."

"Humanity has failed itself," Aman said. "We have struggled with our beliefs, our self-imposed morality, and the awareness of our eventual deaths. We are still under the delusion that the self is separate—and doomed. Humankind needed time to evolve past its naive and self-destructive nature and become aware of our peaceful place in this universe. However, because of the breach, radical shortcuts have accelerated this evolution."

"Tell me more about this breach," Marshall said.

"An inadvertent tear of spacetime is releasing a dark stream of radiation from an incompatible dimension we know nothing about," Aman said. "Its destructive force is tearing apart the Great Field."

"What's this great field?" Marshall asked.

"Our minds and bodies are not separate entities, but rather are part of a quantum field that transcends all matter. The original ones called this *Dzonot*. The discordant radiation from the breach is creating global chaos and death and must be closed before it does irreparable damage to the field and humanity's very existence."

"It sounds like you're going to need a lot of metaphysical alchemy to deal with something like that," Marshall said.

"I require metamaterial and energy density beyond humanity's engineering capacity," Aman said. "I will tap the gateway's energy flux to manifest what I need to close the breach."

"A lot of people would call that crap," Marshall said.

"This is all quite real, I assure you, doctor," Aman said. "The ancient knowledge that would allow us to manipulate the Great Field has been lost to us. Humanity must relearn what its ancestors understood and practiced."

"The Fold," Samantha said.

Marshall threw her a sideways glance. "The what?"

Samantha's eyes lost focus. "I can hear it. There is great intelligence. It wants to embrace and protect all of us in its fold."

Amen nodded. "It is as you say."

"When will we see this great new world of yours?" Marshall asked.

"We may never experience it," Aman said.

Samantha refocused her gaze on Aman. "Why not?"

Aman swiveled his seat toward the window and looked over the top of the clouds. "I must reach Ab Ambar before nightfall two days hence. And that probability is diminishing each moment as the laws of physics that run your machines continue to breakdown."

INTERROGATION

MEL ARTERBERRY SAT slumped in a wooden chair in the airport's aviation office. Through his brain's retreating fog, he watched the lone female member of the taskforce return several vials and a syringe with stainless steel thumb rings to her metal attaché case. Whatever she had done to him had produced a nice buzz. He didn't care what she did. Or had she already done it?

The last thing he remembered was someone introducing her as Specialist Sheila Moore. She didn't say much, yet Mel found the woman attractive despite the dark, soulless look in her eyes.

The other members of the military team were sifting through his office files. He wasn't sure what they were looking for or how long they had been searching his office, but he sensed that hours might have passed since their arrival.

Mel recalled the colonel grilling him with questions, but he couldn't remember what he had told the guy or if he'd answered him at all. Screw it. He couldn't tell them anything about Aman. As far as Mel knew, the interrogation might be over. Or had it even started?

The older man in tweeds, out of place among the younger team members, didn't like how the interrogation had been going or the methods used to facilitate it. The others addressed him as "Dr. Weissmann," and they deferred to him as if he were an essential adviser or perhaps a mentor to the team. He couldn't have looked less like a soldier with his broad, intellectual forehead and white, tousled hair. Mel enjoyed watching him. Weissmann appeared flustered, as though late for an appointment, pacing with sharp, agitated movements while absently handling his special green goggles.

Dr. Weissmann held up a traffic control printout. "Can we assume they will abandon the aircraft's original flight plan?"

Colonel Welch wiped his forehead with the back of his long-sleeved shirt. The municipal airport office felt obnoxiously hot despite the window air conditioner running full blast. "Absolutely. There isn't a chance in hell they plan to go to Germany."

"The Gulfstream is in Canadian airspace," said the lieutenant staffer, the office phone to his ear. "They haven't deviated from the plane's original flight plan."

"I don't get it," Weissmann said. "Why would he be so arbitrary about a destination?"

"He wants to leave the country and doesn't care where to," the Colonel said.

"Iran," Mel blurted.

Weissmann looked at the airport manager. "What did you say?"

"They're going to Iran," Mel repeated.

That got the Colonel's attention too.

Weissmann thrust his goggles into his jacket's pocket and squatted in front of Mel's chair. "Iran? How do you know that? Why didn't you tell us this before?"

Mel grinned, and when he spoke, he felt drool spill over his chin. "Because they can't get there from here. Told 'em so." He could hear his speech slurring. "Besides, your fella didn't say it. The guy with him, a doctor, said that's where they needed to go."

The lieutenant held up a world atlas he'd found next to the coffee pot. "The page of the Middle East is torn out."

Colonel Welch wouldn't stop pacing. "A pilot unfamiliar with a Gulfstream would be smart to allow the aircraft's preprogrammed flight plan to take him to Europe. He could study the flight system en route and, once in Germany for refueling, he could develop a new flight plan for Iran."

"But he can't just fly into Iranian airspace without getting attacked," Weissmann said.

"There's no one left to stop him," Welch said. "Except me."

Mel watched the professor sit back on the floor in front of him and run a hand through his white wisps of hair. Weissmann's eyes grew vacant, and he said to no one in particular, "One of the world's oldest civilizations once sat on land that's now Iran. He's going back to the beginning."

"Bullshit, doc," the Colonel snapped. "He's a terrorist heading back home. He's leading us right to his base of operation, probably aiding Iran's nuclear weapons program."

"I disagree." Weissmann pushed himself off the floor and rose to his feet. "This isn't about global nuclear or biological weapons terror. Whatever is happening will continue to affect everyone in every corner of the planet. There's no sanctuary anywhere." Sweat beads rolled down his forehead. "We need to find this man fast. All of our lives depend on it."

• • •

Dr. Weissmann led the way across the tarmac toward their aircraft while Colonel Welch and his two staff members jogged to keep up. Weissmann, an avid bicyclist, was in a hurry and gave the younger team members a workout. The air had become thick with humidity, and the gathering storm clouds appeared ready for a downpour. And only one more hour of daylight.

Welch walked up to the C-17 transport's pilot waiting at the foot of the staircase. "How fast can this plane fly, Captain?" he asked.

"She tops at 300 miles an hour cruising altitude," the pilot said.

Welch rubbed a hand over his buzz cut. "That's not fast enough. The Gulfstream will be traveling two, maybe three times that speed. And we'll need to refuel along the way. He won't."

Dr. Weissmann felt his blood pressure rising. "Jesus, do

something, Colonel."

Welch turned to his lieutenant. "There's a NOAA Citation II at Cedar Rapids. That should be fast enough. I want it here in thirty minutes."

The young man punched a number on his cellphone and listened with a scowl. "Can't get a signal."

"Then use the damn office landline," Welch ordered. "And get me in touch with Canadian Defense Minister McKay. I want his Air Wing to intercept this sonofabitch."

Dr. Weissmann felt his muscles tense. They couldn't afford an air disaster. "You mustn't take risks, Colonel. We need to find him—alive."

INTERCEPT

NICK HAD TWO words to describe flying the Gulfstream: *Fuckin' A!* The aircraft could indeed fly itself, thanks to one of the most advanced avionics systems he had seen anywhere, commercial or military. The flight over Canada proceeded uneventfully—just the way he liked it. Compared to his training flights over Afghanistan, this run was downright dull.

The last scarlet thread of day vanished over the Nova Scotia coastline behind them. It had been a long day, and he slumped down in his seat to steal a few hours of sleep while crossing the ocean. He closed his eyes.

The alert bell sounded.

Nick sat up, his neck muscles tightening. The Gulfstream's radar return had picked up signatures of two aircraft climbing rapidly. The transponders identified a pair of McDonnell-Douglas CF-18 Hornet fighters from Dartmouth airfield. *Uh oh.* What were the chances they were coming after another aircraft? None, he figured.

The warning indicator confirmed two armed fighters at his altitude with radars locked on him, shadowing thirty miles behind. The two fighters proceeded on an intercept course, one to his port, the other starboard. Nick glanced at the moving terrain map on the multifunction display and noted the coastline retreating behind him. *What the f—?* They were over international waters.

Nick disengaged the auto and grasped the yoke with both hands. He worked the pedals to assure himself the aircraft would respond. It did. The cockpit door opened, and Aman put a hand on the back of the pilot's seat to watch.

"Two Canadian Hornets are shadowing us," Nick informed him.

Aman stooped to peer through the windscreen. But there was nothing to see but blackness. "I am aware." He slipped into the copilot's seat. "And your reaction?"

"If they engage us, we have three options," Nick said. "One, we follow them back to their airbase. Two, I try to lose them. Three, we do nothing and let them shoot us down."

The cockpit's Traffic Collision Avoidance warning triggered. Nick noted the twin fighters were accelerating.

"Speak to them," Aman said. He slid on the copilot headset to listen in.

Nick put the Gulfstream back on auto. He selected the standard frequency for air-to-air traffic and began transmitting with a gentle press of his thumb on the yoke button. "This is Gulfstream five juliet charlie social," Nick said into his mic. "Traffic. Traffic. You're on my heading and altitude. Please disengage and drop 10,000 feet."

Nick heard no response and wondered if he had set the communications console correctly. Before he could try a different frequency, a voice filled his headset.

"Gulfstream juliet charlie social," the pilot said, "descend to 15,000 feet and proceed on a heading of one niner zero. We will escort you to Dartmouth Air Force Base."

Nick muted his headset mic and said to Aman, "OK, option one—we follow them back."

"That will end my journey," Aman said. He adjusted the headset microphone over the edge of his lip. "Allow me to speak to both pilots."

Nick opened the channel to Aman's mic and signaled him that he was live.

"You are addressing the pilot and a passenger of this aircraft," Aman said. "You must allow us to continue on our present course. We have an emergency. A delay will be catastrophic."

"Negative," the CF-18 pilot responded. "You do *not* proceed. You must comply with my order, or we will open fire."

Both CF-18 fighters surrounded the Gulfstream, port and starboard. Nick knew that aircraft model very well from his military training.

"These guys are serious." Nick looked at the CF-18 on his port side and could see the Hornet's pilot inside his cockpit. "This isn't a MiG fighter, Aman. We can't engage them."

"We cannot deviate from our course," Aman said into his mic. "If you attack us, you will kill four American men and one woman who mean you no harm."

Nick heard the second Hornet pilot say, *"He's out of our airspace. I'm disengaging."*

The CF-18 outside Aman's window dipped its wings ninety degrees and dropped away, vanishing into the blackness.

"Hold your position, alpha one niner," the lead Hornet pilot instructed his wingman. *"That is my order."*

Nick heard no response from the fighter pilot who had abandoned his flight commander. He heard the lead pilot mutter, "Asshole."

"Yes!" Nick shouted. He glanced at the second CF-18 off this port quarter. "What about this guy? Why hasn't he disengaged too?"

"He is no longer following his directive," Aman said. "This encounter has become his personal contest for supremacy."

Marshall opened the cockpit door. "Gentlemen, may I ask what the hell is going on?"

Nick glanced back and saw Marshall staring at the CF-18 Hornet out the windscreen. The sight of the fighter so close drained all the color from the doctor's face.

Aman twisted in his seat. "Nick and I will work to mitigate this situation."

"You'll do whatever that fighter pilot tells you, right?" Marshall asked.

"Buckle in tight back there," Nick said, ignoring his question. "Secure everything."

Marshall closed the cockpit door and returned to the cabin where Kirby slept in one of the executive chairs. He made sure the deputy's seatbelt was fastened tight. *Let him sleep through this.*

Samantha, sitting across from the deputy, turned to Marshall. "So, what's happening, David."

She wanted his assurance that they would be all right, but he couldn't lie.

"It looks like a dangerous situation," Marshall said. He put his syringe kit and a loose bottle of morphine inside his black case and secured it at the bottom of the coat closet. "Make sure you're buckled in."

She checked her seatbelt. "But we'll be all right? Aman will make sure we're safe, won't he?"

Marshall didn't look at her. He sat in the chair behind her and fumbled with the seat buckle. His hands were trembling. "Aman is a smart man. But I think we're going to need more than that tonight."

• • •

The Hornet disappeared from Nick's port cockpit windshield. A glance at the heads-up radar told him that the aircraft had fallen back for a pursuit vector behind and above him.

"So, you don't want me to follow him back to his base?" Nick asked.

"No," Aman said. "You must stay calm and think rationally. Do not allow what transpires to lead to recklessness."

Aman's steady voice had a calming effect on Nick—but only momentary.

The CF-18 opened fire with its six-barrel Gatling gun. Nick saw the 20mm tracers streak just feet above his port wing's leading edge.

"Jesus! He means to kill us. He actually means to *kill us."*

Aman put a hand on Nick's arm. "His fire missed us."

"Yeah? What about next time?"

Nick took the Gulfstream off auto and planted his feet firmly on the pedals. Acting on trained instincts, he moved the throttles forward and pushed the yoke hard, sending the jet into a steep one-hundred-degree roll while his feet worked the rudders like a dancer. He saw Aman clutch the hand rest.

"I'm going down to sea level," Nick shouted.

As he expected, Nick's maneuver took the Hornet pilot by surprise. The military aircraft overshot their flight path by a wide margin before the fighter pilot began circling back. Meanwhile, Nick maintained a steep dive at an alarming speed, pushing him back into his seat at four times the force of gravity.

Aman clutched the amulet. "Your actions are not advised—"

"When he returns to my tail," Nick said, "his radar will be in Situation Awareness Mode to hone his attack. He'll have no other visual cues in the darkness. If he's green, he won't watch his altitude and will ignore all alarms."

"Nick, listen to me—"

"No, you listen." Nick couldn't get his words out fast enough. "I'm going to pull out at a thousand feet. It'll be close. He'll be flying too fast to lift in time. The bastard will hit the ocean at Mach 1.5. Common mistake. God, I hope he's green."

"The pilot has no flight combat experience," Aman said. "He will not recover from your maneuver and will be killed. He is a stubborn aviator. He means only to intimidate. He has not armed his air-to-air warheads."

"You don't know that, Aman," Nick said.

"If you kill him knowing what I have just told you, you will be purged, and all of us will die when we crash into the ocean."

"Intentional or not, this bastard's dangerous," Nick said. "He could make a mistake and rip this aircraft in half!"

The altitude radar and infrared vision showed the ocean rising fast toward them. A dozen cockpit alarms blared at once. Nick leveled his wings. At this speed and altitude, he had no margin for error. The CF-18 roared toward them at Mach 1.5 on an intercept path.

"Right out of the textbook," Nick said. "I've got him."

"You are the superior pilot," Aman said. "You can out-think and out-maneuver him." When Nick didn't respond, Aman added, "Do not do this. Your life and the lives of your passengers depend on you abandoning this petty act of power."

Nick gritted his teeth. *"Jesus Christ*—if you're wrong—"

With a stiff pull of the yoke, Nick took the Gulfstream out of its steep dive. Likewise, the Hornet aborted its attack dive, swooping to within a thousand feet of the ocean's surface and leaving an explosive trail of water turbulence in his exhaust wake.

Both aircraft leveled off and began a steady ascent into the black night.

• • •

The Canadian fighter pilot felt oddly detached from his cockpit. He had just experienced a revelation. He almost died in this brief, foolish skirmish. But not the way he wanted to die in combat. There was no courage and dignity here. Instead, he almost killed himself and innocent others with his irresponsible arrogance. The Gulfstream pilot was good—damn good—a trained combat attack flier who could have let him die just now. But he saved him.

The pilot now understood the enormity of his shortcomings. He saw an image of himself as a soldier, and that image no longer worked for him. There was no honor in killing, even for a noble cause. That path led to an abyss. He decided at that moment to end his military career.

The pilot broke into elated laughter. Euphoric, he couldn't contain his broad smile while he brought up the nose of his Hornet and carved a huge arc in the sky on a heading back to his family.

SAFE MODE

NICK SAID NOTHING more while the Gulfstream climbed back toward its cruising altitude, unimpeded by military attack fighters. He stared at the nothingness outside the cockpit window until his heart slowed.

Aman unbuckled his seat's restraining strap and stood. "I will inform the others."

"Aman," Nick said, "I gotta be honest with you."

"Yes?"

"You're scaring the hell out of me. Who are you, man? Tell me why I shouldn't get as far away from you as I can before things get any stranger?"

Aman said nothing, which Nick found even more rattling.

"Damn it," Nick shouted. "Where did you learn to fly?"

"From you."

"Don't screw with me."

"I read the Field," Aman said.

Nick cocked his head. "What does that mean?"

"The sum of what we are is imprinted on a quantum matrix that surrounds everything," Aman said. "Nature's blueprints are there. If you listen closely, you can hear it."

"That's nice, but that doesn't answer my question. How do you know your way around a cockpit?"

"Our proximity allows easy contact with your field of experience. I then know what you know." Aman touched Nick's arm. "Excuse me. I must reassure the others."

A thousand questions spiraled through Nick's mind, yet he managed only a stiff nod. Something else captured his attention, but he mentioned nothing to Aman as he left the cockpit. Nick's eyes returned to a flickering indicator on one of the flight instrumentation's heads-up displays. He moved the cursor control with his thumb to scroll through the display windows to check the integrity of each aircraft system. The auto-flight system wanted a password.

What the heck is going on?

Nick unbuckled his harness and made his way back into the passenger cabin, where he found Aman telling the others about the encounter with the Canadian fighters. Nick's appearance brought the conversation to a halt.

"Nick," Samantha said, her eyes red from crying, "who's flying this plane?"

"This aircraft is doing an excellent job flying itself." Nick tried his best to sound upbeat. "In fact, it doesn't want my help." He forced a smile and rubbed his short, sweat-glistening hair. *I must look like shit.*

"Is everything all right?" Marshall asked.

Kirby moved his chair upright. Although some color had returned to his face, he looked exhausted. "What they're saying, dude, is that we'd all feel a whole lot better with someone at the controls."

"There is an issue with this aircraft," Aman said. "Describe our situation, Mr. Judge."

"This aircraft has gone into *safe mode*, a subsystem that shuts down all but its essential systems until I tell it otherwise. One of the flight computers may have been affected by my dive. I'll go below and check the connections."

"Wonderful." Kirby shut his eyes and put his head back against the seat.

"Are we going to be alright?" Samantha asked, her voice strained.

She was frightened. Nick hated when his passengers were frightened.

"I'm locked out," he said. "I need a ten-digit password to get into the flight system and run diagnostics. Meanwhile, the aircraft has assumed all flight responsibilities for a trip to

Frankfurt."

"I thought you could fly anything," Marshall reminded him.

"Yes, sir, I can. It's getting these things back on the ground that can be tricky."

Aman bowed his head and closed his eyes as though meditating. "A hydraulic line in the left rudder is leaking," Aman said. "The pressure is down four percent."

He opened his eyes. "The problem is not critical. However, if we attempt to override the auto-safety systems and fail, the aircraft's inertial navigation systems will abort our flight plan. This aircraft will divert to the nearest airfield large enough to accommodate our landing, which will force us back to Canada."

"So, can you get me that password or what, Chief?" Nick asked.

"That won't be necessary." Aman sank back into the chair's overstuffed leather cushions. "This aircraft has enough fuel and system integrity to get us across the ocean. Let it take us to Germany."

DAY FOUR

VISITOR

SAMANTHA WOKE TO a cold hand brushing her scalp. She jerked up and stared wide-eyed across the dark, unfamiliar bedroom.

"Kirby?"

No response. She lit the face of her wristwatch—two minutes past 5 a.m. She'd slept for more than seven hours without recalling any dreams.

The chill disappeared as quickly as it came, and she touched her hair, uncertain. Yet, she sensed a presence. As she sat there staring, the bedroom door opened, revealing a white vapor in the hallway.

The vapor drifted into the room and stopped at the foot of the bed. Samantha couldn't move. The walls seemed to move in around her, trapping her. *This isn't happening.*

She recalled a scary story her grandfather told her long ago about how fear attracts ghosts. 'Don't be afraid of them,' he warned her. 'Ghosts are lonely and miss the earth. If you fear them, they will come to your room in the night to crop your hair in spite to make you undesirable.' When she began crying, her grandfather laughed and told her he had made up the story. But she refused to believe that. Although she had never seen a ghost, she believed they were real, some of them angry, maybe even violent. She dreaded the day she would join them—

A cry caught in Samantha's throat when a woman's voice whispered, "Samantha, you must not leave him—"

Samantha threw off the sheets and charged into the hallway, her heart pumping pure adrenaline.

"David!"

The cloud followed her into the hallway, coalescing into a pure white profile of a woman. The sun hadn't risen, but Samantha could discern long hair and a flowing robe that tapered off into a mist. The featureless face appeared to be made of cotton. She sensed it staring at her, even without eyes.

Samantha's breaths came quickly, and she feared she might hyperventilate. She tried to think clearly. *Maybe I should speak to it—*

The mist dispersed when Hunter Rowe charged into the hallway holding his shotgun ready. Samantha watched what remained of the ethereal form regress into a shadow that moved across the living room. The whimpering dog hid behind Samantha.

Rowe appeared dressed in boxers and a sleeveless T-shirt. "What's going on here?" He rubbed his eyes, struggling to clear his vision. "Who's in there with you?"

Samantha lifted a finger toward the living room. "Out there."

"Samantha?" Marshall scrambled down the staircase from the second level, buttoning his shirt.

"A woman." Samantha pushed past Rowe and pointed toward a silhouette moving along the living-room wall. "That shadow. It's not human." The shadow faded.

Rowe swung his shotgun over his shoulder with a scowl. "So, we're chasing shadows now?"

"She spoke to me."

Marshall turned on the table lamp and joined Samantha in the center of the living room, his eyes bouncing from corner to corner.

Rowe turned on her, furious. "What the hell is wrong with you? You're fricken useless." He glared at Marshall. "I'll bet she can't even cook."

"Screw you, Rowe," Samantha shouted. "No one invited you to come along."

"You should not feel alarmed." Aman descended the stairway in slow, measured steps. He had found a pair of tan

Dockers, a long-sleeved plaid shirt, and dress loafers, all of which more or less fit him. "The woman you saw is important to me."

"What the hell are you talking about?" Rowe demanded.

"Sheema," he said at the foot of the steps. "My wife when she last walked the earth. She came a great distance to help me."

Rowe lunged at Aman and yanked the front of his plaid shirt into his fist. He pulled until their eyes were only inches apart. "You've brought us all this way out here to chase *ghosts?*"

Aman stared into the trooper's eyes without saying a word. Samantha watched, frozen, as the two men's eyes remained locked, boring into each other. God—!

"Don't you dare touch him," Samantha shouted. "Hit me, humiliate me, criticize me, but you don't dare touch Aman."

Marshall grabbed the trooper's arm. "Back off, Rowe."

Rowe let go of Aman in disgust. Samantha sighed in relief.

Marshall raised his hands in a surrendering gesture. "Let's all take it easy, cool down, and figure this out."

Rowe thrust a finger at Aman. "I want some answers from you."

"Everything will become clear in time," Aman said.

Rowe shook his head and stomped toward the back of the house, muttering something about finding coffee.

The old Victorian house felt even more claustrophobic to Samantha. A terrible ringing filled her ears. *What the hell am I doing here?* She retreated into her room, slamming the door behind her.

AB AMBAR

SAMANTHA ROLLED INTO a fetal position on her bed, knees tucked under her chin. She smelled flowers—lilacs. She observed movement, outlines, and shapes positioning themselves around the room. Three of them. *Oh my God ... oh my God ... oh my God—!*

Every muscle in her body tensed. She buried her head in the sheets, her eyes closed tight, and whispered, "Leave me alone ... please."

A gentle hand brushed her hair, forcing a scream from her throat.

"Do not fear them."

Her head shot up. "Aman—?"

Aman stood beside the bed, looking down at her with keen, warm eyes.

Samantha rolled to the edge of the bed and switched on the nightstand's lamp. The light's soft glow revealed that Aman had undergone yet another change she hadn't noticed in the dark hallway. He appeared ten years younger than the night before, his complexion softer and with more color. No frail elderly man here—this was a thoughtful fifty-something with graying hair, intense brown eyes, and smoother features. For a moment, she wondered if this was even the same man.

"They wish to help me," Aman said. "They will protect you."

Samantha could see them. She recognized "Sheema" with her long, graceful robe. The other two remained formless. She sensed a deep longing, as though these entities wished to speak to her, but to their regret, could not.

"Protect me from what?" she asked.

Aman sat on the edge of the bed across from her, easing her apprehension somewhat. She felt safe sitting near him.

"What began as a delirious old man's trek down a long, hot road has become a very dangerous path," Aman said. "Now I need your help to finish this."

His intense eyes peered into hers as though searching for something. Her trust? How could he think of her as an asset when she didn't believe it herself?

She lowered her eyes and shook her head. "I'll slow you down. Rowe's right. I can't even cook. I should go back to Rapid City."

Aman smiled. "Rowe knows nothing about you."

She glared at him. "I don't trust him. I think he's dangerous."

"He is a danger," Aman said. "To himself."

"Everything's coming to an end, isn't it, Aman?" Samantha asked. "We're all going to die, aren't we?"

"That is a real possibility," Aman said. "I cannot lie to you."

There came a gentle knock. The door opened, and Marshall peered around the edge. He raised a cup of coffee. "May I?"

Samantha felt a rush of relief seeing him. "David."

"Please join us, Dr. Marshall," Aman said, beckoning him into the room.

Callie trotted into the room behind him and jumped up onto the bed next to Samantha. The dog touched her leg with a cold nose.

Marshall presented the coffee mug to Samantha. "For you."

She accepted it, grateful. The brew was fresh and steamy, the mug hot. As she sipped, she noticed that the doctor seemed oblivious to the presence of the room's apparitions. No one other than she and Aman could see them. Well, maybe one other—Callie's head jerked, and her eyes scanned the walls, her ears high.

"We must proceed with caution," Aman said to them. "Your safety is of great concern to me."

Marshall sat on the bed next to Samantha. She saw him staring at Aman, seemingly fascinated by his continual age regression. But the doctor said nothing about it.

"Aren't we safer traveling now that these sudden deaths have eliminated the violent element?" Marshall asked.

"Not entirely eliminated, doctor," Aman said. "Those who harm and take another's life—directly or indirectly—have been purged first."

"So, what's the problem?" Samantha pressed, sipping from her mug.

"Individuals who would knowingly take or control another life, yet have not acted on that appetite because of circumstances, still walk among us," Aman said. "The possibility of violence remains."

"Terrific," Marshall said.

"So, where are you going?" Samantha asked, changing the subject.

"I must reach Ab Ambar within three days before the breach does irreparable harm to this planet," Aman said.

"What breach?" Marshall said.

"An interdimensional breach is responsible for all that is transpiring," he said. "At the same time, we are witnessing a shift that was meant to occur gradually over many years as Earth evolved and us with it. An accident forced this sudden shift on an unprepared world, a course that is now greatly accelerated. We cannot stop it. If my journey succeeds, humankind will realize its destiny long ahead of the Plan and allow us to live safe and in peace on a new Earth. If I reach Ab Ambar."

"I never heard of Ab Ambar," Samantha said. "Where is it?"

"The location is 31° 25′ 24″ North by 53° 42′ 1″ East," Aman said.

Marshall withdrew an opened envelope and a pen from his pants pocket to jot down the coordinates. "That's quite a way overseas," he noted as he wrote.

"Overseas?" Samantha's eyes darted to Aman. "You need to go overseas?"

"I must reach the source of this devastation," Aman said.

"The way is dangerous, but access is still possible."

"What will you do when you get to this—place?" Marshall asked. The doctor wasn't buying this, Samantha noted.

Aman spread his hands. "I am only aware of the breach and its location. What I must do when I reach Ab Ambar is not yet clear. However, I will become aware as I need to know."

"How will you get overseas?" Samantha asked.

"I do not yet know."

Marshall stood with a frown. "That's not good enough. You're not making much sense—not to me, nor will anyone else believe you. And now you're asking us to follow you halfway around the world without a plan." He shook his head. "I'm afraid this expedition of yours is getting too difficult."

Marshall had a point, Samantha realized. And who else would agree to travel with him under these circumstances?

"I am sorry, doctor," Aman said. "I must continue my journey with or without help. And I am in great need of your skills."

"If you really need me, I'll go," Samantha said. She tried her best to sound committed.

Marshall raised his hands to forgo further discussion for now. "OK, we'll think this through. In the meantime, let's keep the fact that you've got no plan between the three of us. We have enough problems."

Samantha sensed movement. She saw the ethereal shadows moving into a vague circle around the room, and she heard whispering, like anxious chatter. At the same moment, Aman's head snapped up, his expression drawn. He gripped the amulet around his neck.

"A man is approaching this house," Aman said. "He will interfere with what I need to do. We must prepare for his arrival."

An urgent rap on the door startled Samantha. Kirby burst in before any of them could move.

"Someone's coming," Kirby hollered.

They followed Kirby into the living room where Hunter Rowe stood peering out one of the front windows, shotgun in hand. Samantha stepped to the next window for a look. The sky to the east had brightened, and the day's first light revealed detail along the tree line. She saw headlights of an approaching vehicle coming down the long, gravel driveway. Marshall stepped next to her for a look.

Samantha appealed to him. "What do we do?"

Marshall said nothing and watched a late-model black Oldsmobile emerge from the tree line. The car pulled into the parking area next to their vehicles.

"Shit," Rowe said. "Shit. *Shit.*"

Samantha recognized the Olds from the checkpoint out of Rapid City—the car that belonged to the federal agent.

"*Sonofabitch* — it's Coffey," Rowe said.

"Who?" Kirby said.

"He's FBI Special Services," Rowe said. "Coffey has orders to bring Aman in for interrogation. At any cost."

AGENT COFFEY

"HOW DID HE find us?" Samantha said. "Does that mean the FBI knows Aman's here?"

"He must not enter this house," Aman said. *"He must not."*

Samantha heard the distress in his voice. She turned to him for some instructions, but he offered nothing.

"I'll talk to him," she said.

"The hell you will. Just stay out of my way." Rowe held up his 12-gauge. "This'll do my talking."

"No," Aman said. "You will provoke an already dangerous situation."

Before anyone could stop her, Samantha punched open the screen door with a bang and stormed onto the porch. The federal agent stood outside his car, wearing sunglasses despite the dim light of dawn.

"What do you want here?" she called down to him. Even from across the yard, she could see that the agent looked tired and edgy, most likely from driving all night.

Agent Coffey removed his sunglasses and stroked back his hair to look presentable. He broke into a grin and stepped around the Oldsmobile while slipping on his black suit jacket. "I'm a federal officer. You're harboring a fugitive I'm taking into custody."

"You're here for the glory and fame," Samantha said. "You want to be a hero for capturing him."

Kirby stepped out on the porch next to Samantha, holding a revolver at his side. "Stop right there."

Samantha glanced at the deputy, uncertain of his intentions.

Coffey halted. "I'm the authority here."

"You don't have squat here," Kirby said. "How'd you find us?"

Coffey's smug grin returned. "You invited me. Your truck's GPS transponder led me right to you."

"*Shit,*" Kirby spat.

"The agency knows you took our fugitive and that you're hiding him out here," Coffey said. "You're way over your heads—all of you."

Kirby pushed Samantha away from him and pointed his revolver at the federal agent with both hands. "There's no way you're taking Aman."

Samantha raised a tentative hand toward him. "Kirby? What are you doing?"

"Put down your weapon, deputy," Coffey ordered. "You sideshow clowns are already facing federal charges of obstruction and interfering with a federal investigation. You're looking at years of prison time."

Samantha noticed Aman watching from the opposite side of the screen door.

"Mr. Dawson," Aman said. "Do not use your weapon. You will only destroy yourself. And I need you."

Kirby glanced over his shoulder. "What the hell does that mean—"

Coffey jerked a handgun from his back holster and squeezed off two rounds in quick succession. The first bullet streaked between Samantha and the deputy, and the second struck Kirby's arm below his right shoulder. He spun around with a surprised grunt and landed heavily on his back on the porch's worn timbers. "Son of a BITCH!"

"Kirby—oh my God!" Samantha dropped to Kirby's side and grimaced at the sight of the blood gushing from his wound. She didn't know how to stop it.

Kirby stared up at her, his face wide with surprise. "Sam," he managed, "how bad is it?"

"David, help," Samantha shouted. "He's bleeding badly."

Marshall opened the screen door and stepped out onto the

porch, his eyes on Coffey, his hands raised to show he wasn't armed. "Take it easy. I'm a doctor, and I'm going to help this man."

The federal agent mounted the porch steps, still pointing his gun. He intended to get his way.

"Don't point that gun unless you plan to shoot us all," Samantha said.

"That's not what I want," Coffey said. "Turn that man over to me, and no one else gets hurt."

"And if we don't cooperate?" she said.

"Your Constitutional rights don't apply here," Coffey said. "I advise you to do as I say. My orders are very specific about any interference."

Marshall crouched beside Kirby and examined his upper right arm. "The bullet passed through your muscle and exited." He looked up at Coffey. "We need to take him to a hospital."

"He's not going anywhere until I get what I want," the agent said. He pointed his handgun at Samantha.

A shotgun blast blew the screen door off its hinges and pounded Coffey's left shoulder with buckshot. The federal agent stumbled backward off the steps and landed hard on his back on the stone walkway. Samantha watched, stunned, as Coffey struggled to rise. The state trooper kept his shotgun barrel pointed at Coffey.

"Officer Rowe," Coffey managed. His forced grin showed off a bloody row of teeth. "I didn't recognize your patrol car."

Coffey reached for his lost gun. Rowe discharged a second round that shattered the federal agent's right arm up to his elbow. Coffey let out a wail and stared at his forearm stump in dumb astonishment.

Samantha reeled back, horrified.

Marshall rose and reached for the trooper's shotgun. "That's enough!"

Rowe pushed the doctor roughly away. "He would've killed us all to get to Aman. Now he can identify us. I'm finishing this bastard right here."

Rowe pressed the shotgun's stock into his shoulder and

peered down its barrel, his finger planted on the trigger. Samantha didn't recognize the man behind those soulless eyes.

"Stop it," she shouted. "He's not a threat to us now."

"I want him off this planet," Rowe sneered.

Blood spewed from Coffey's lips. "You're a pathetic traitor, Rowe. It's over, and you lost. You just don't know it yet—"

Rowe fired. The crown of Coffey's head vanished in a shower of blood, bone, and brain matter that splattered across the walk like a spilled plate of lasagna. Coffey's upper torso splashed down in the middle of the crimson swill.

Samantha stared at the agent's body in disbelief while a scarlet stream flowed down the walkway. She never saw a man killed before. Her eyes locked with Rowe's. He looked at her with an odd expression of amazement. The state trooper nodded, lowered his shotgun, and turned away. His skin paled.

Rowe leaned his gun against the wall beside the front door like a defeated soldier. He looked at Aman standing on the opposite side of the empty door frame, watching him.

"I understand now," Rowe said.

Aman said nothing.

"So tired." Rowe lowered his sturdy frame into a frayed rocking chair and let out a deep sigh of fatigue. "I understand now," he uttered to no one in particular.

He let out a long breath, and his chin dropped to his chest, his eyes partially open.

Hunter Rowe was dead.

THE ROAD

MARSHALL HELPED KIRBY into a sitting position on the porch's first step and pressed a towel against the gunshot wound. He needed his bag from the truck to treat the damage to Kirby's arm. "Keep pressure until I clean and dress your wound," he instructed.

Kirby nodded.

Aman descended the steps and placed the sofa's afghan over Coffey's remains. "More agents will be here shortly," he said. "We must leave at once."

Samantha headed for the front door. "I'll bring whatever food I can find in the kitchen." Callie followed on her heels, wagging her tail.

"There is no time," Aman said, his voice firm.

Samantha paused by the front door. "What about Callie?"

"She will be well cared for," he said.

Marshall stood, frowning. "Kirby needs emergency medical care."

"Wait a second, doc," Kirby said. He yanked on Marshall's arm with stubborn strength and pulled him down until they were face-to-face. Sweat poured over the deputy's features as he checked to make sure Aman was out of earshot. He looked terrified.

"I'm staying here," he whispered.

"You need surgery—"

"Traveling with Aman is a very bad idea," Kirby hissed. "He doesn't have the same DNA as us, like an alien or something. What if he used Rowe to kill that agent? Maybe he intends to use all of us. Maybe he brought me along to take a bullet for him. This whole mess is freaking me out, and I'm not going any farther. He doesn't need me."

"Yes, I do, Mr. Dawson," Aman called from the far end of the walkway. "And I will do everything in my power to keep you safe."

Marshall glanced at Aman in surprise, wondering how he could have overheard their whispered conversation.

"I'll slow you down," Kirby called to him. "Leave me here. I'll tell them you're heading back to Rapid City."

"They will not believe you," Aman said, approaching the steps.

"Jesus, Aman," Kirby shouted, "I'm dying!"

"You will heal quickly," Aman said. "We must all leave together. Dr. Marshall, please help Mr. Dawson to the vehicle."

Aman headed toward the cars.

"He's right," Marshall said. "Who knows what the Feds will do to you if you stay. If we leave now, I can treat you."

"Damn it," Kirby said, his eyes shut tight. "Damn it. Damn it."

Marshall didn't doubt that Kirby wished he could be anywhere but here. He helped Kirby to his feet. The deputy, grimacing, made it down the walk with the doctor's assistance.

"You drive the sheriff's truck, David," Samantha said, hurrying to catch up with Aman.

"We need to disable the GPS transponder," Kirby said. He winced, and Marshall knew he was in considerable pain.

"The authorities are looking for your truck, Mr. Dawson." Aman walked between the vehicles. "And they will find it, even without its locator."

Marshall watched Aman open the driver's door to Samantha's Focus and peer inside. Satisfied, he moved around the car to inspect it as though considering a purchase. Marshall wondered what, if anything, he knew about cars.

"No one is searching for this vehicle," Aman told Samantha. "The four of us will travel as one."

"The passenger door doesn't open," Samantha said.

"We will manage." Aman climbed into the back seat.

Marshall didn't like the idea of them crowded into such a small car, but there was no time to argue their situation. He settled the wounded deputy in the back beside Aman's slim frame. Marshall lifted the towel to inspect the wound.

"Bad, doc?" Kirby asked.

"Not exactly. The bleeding's stopped. Try not to move."

Kirby leaned his head back against the seat, closed his eyes, and let out a long sigh of frustration. Marshall retrieved his bag from the truck and slid into the front passenger seat as Samantha started the engine.

Callie sat down at the edge of the porch with a whimper and watched her new friends leave in their tiny blue car.

• • •

The Journal
Rapid City, N.D.

"These pictures are shit," muttered Jack Feehery, the *Rapid City Journal's* managing editor.

Feehery, a seasoned Irishman with a poorly trimmed red beard, shuffled through several 8x10-inch photos as though dealing a poker game, and always with the same results—a losing hand. He desperately needed an original photo for today's special edition about fallen world leaders and the rising global body count. His top story read: "National Manhunt Continues for Local Homeless Man."

An uninspired photo of the medical center represented the best of the bunch, while another showed a long shot of yesterday's crowd in front of the jail. The only halfway newsworthy image was an out-of-focus photo of a woman in front of the jailhouse helping a man into a small blue car. A local snapped the photograph with an old smartphone.

"This sucks," Feehery muttered. Motion blur was a big problem, the detail poor. He couldn't make out the car's plate number.

Feehery tossed the photos across the table harder than he intended and watched them fly onto the floor. Just as well.

He removed his reading glasses and ground a thumb into the bridge between his bloodshot eyes. How the hell did he let the scoop of the century slip through his fingers? *Jesus, I'd sell my own mother for one decent photo of this geezer.*

"Excuse me," said Matt Hendrix from the doorway. "Excuse me."

Feehery's long, leathery face turned toward the reporter. "Jesus, Hendrix, you've got a lot of balls showing up here." He let the reporter hear his disgust. "When you lost your pictures of this guy, you flushed away your chance at fame and made me look like a *goddamn* jackass."

Hendrix held up his camera's SD card. "Boss, if I had real balls, I'd sell these images to every news bureau from here to China for a lot more money than you'll earn in your career."

BIKER

Central Iowa

THE MORNING SUN rose directly in Samantha's line of sight, triggering the first throbs of a nasty headache. At least her apprehensions eased a bit the more distance she put between them and that strange old house. None of her passengers said much, and that suited her just fine.

"Tell me about your parents," Marshall said to break the silence. A tattered U.S. highway map covered his lap.

Samantha threw him a sideways glance. "Why?"

He shrugged. "Just curious. Are they okay?"

She winced from the stab in her head. "They died together when I was nine. Grandma raised me, or rather let me live with her until she passed. I pretty much raised myself."

"How did your folks die?"

"A car crash in Nevada. Dad, drunk out of his mind, managed to find the only tree along a stretch of highway thirty miles outside Vegas. Tore his Mustang in two. The police discovered the accident at dawn. Never did find mom's lower body."

When Marshall didn't respond, Samantha added, "Aren't you glad you asked?"

Samantha hit the brakes harder than she intended when they neared a stop sign at the junction of Route 59. More than a dozen cars had backed up, waiting for a chance to pull out. That wouldn't be easy. A continuous stream of cars packed the two-lane road they needed to access.

"Where's everyone going?" she moaned, a hand against her

temple.

Marshall looked over his shoulder at Aman. "This trip of yours is going to take longer than you figured. I hope your schedule's flexible."

"It is not," Aman said.

Samantha shook her head. After a ten-minute wait, she finally pulled her car onto Highway 59 and fell in with a long line of cars snaking toward the I-80 onramp more than two miles ahead. Lots of people walked in the same direction along the road's shoulder. Two men passed, carrying between them a body wrapped in a bedsheet. The sight sickened her.

"Are we there yet?" Kirby muttered from the backseat, his eyes shut, and his head tilted back.

Samantha glanced at the dashboard. "I hate breaking the news, but we're down to a quarter tank of gas. We should have siphoned some before we left."

"We had no time," Aman reminded her and then touched her shoulder. "Take your vehicle off this road."

Samantha looked at him in her rearview mirror. "Where?"

"Here." Aman pointed to a grassy area beyond the road's shoulder. "Now."

Samantha shrugged, steered her Focus onto the grass, and stopped. "What's wrong?"

"Uncover the engine," Aman said. "Allow others to see our distress."

"Whatever you say." Samantha reached under the dashboard and popped the hood. She slipped out of the car to allow Marshall room to slide over her driver's seat to exit. Marshall lifted the hood, and she felt the engine's heat waft past her.

The rumble of a motorcycle brought her attention to the lighter traffic on the opposite side of the two-lane road. A Harley-Davidson decked in chrome with black lacquer slowed as it approached them. Samantha saw a lone rider wearing a black T-shirt and a black helmet with orange and red flames. The biker weaved a skillful path through the oncoming traffic and arched onto the grass beside them, the rear tire tossing up a trail of dirt like a cock's tail. Samantha noticed Aman watching from the back seat with a hint of a smile.

The biker cut the engine and rolled to a stop. "Car trouble?"

"You could say that," Samantha said. "We're trying to get to the East Coast on a quarter tank of gas by way of a jammed interstate."

The rider threw down the kickstand and slid off his bike. The lean young man pulled off his helmet and ran a hand through a short patch of dark hair. He moved with a confident, almost cocky stride. At least he didn't look dangerous, she thought. What did he want from them?

"No one's going anywhere on the interstate," he said. "It's backed up all the way to Des Moines. And there's no gas. When your tank's empty, you walk."

Samantha's heart sank for Aman. There was no way he could finish his trip now.

Aman thrust his head out the open window and said to the young man, "You are alone after such a long time away. I, too, am far from my home."

The biker's shoulders sagged, and he stood motionless as though his cowboy boots had taken root. He couldn't seem to find the words to respond and stared at Aman with a dumb expression.

Did he recognize Aman, Samantha wondered? How could he?

"Do you two know each other?" she asked.

The biker shook his head. "I had a strange dream."

"We all are having strange dreams," Aman said.

"Who are you?" Samantha asked.

The biker pulled himself up to his full height as though on a military inspection. "The name's Nick Judge. I have a suggestion."

Samantha settled against the side of her car, her arms folded. "We're wide open to suggestions."

"Fly to the East Coast," Nick said.

Samantha scowled. "Yeah, right."

"All flights are banned," Marshall said. "We need to admit that we're stuck here."

"Screw the ban," Nick said. He pointed back the way he came. "There's a municipal airport off 59, not five miles from here—all private aircraft. A skilled pilot could fly a single-engine plane low enough to stay off FAA and military radar."

Marshall wouldn't stop shaking his head. "That's crazy."

"Well, it sure beats walking," Nick grinned.

"But where will we find a pilot willing to ignore the ban?" Samantha asked. "And one who can fly that low?"

Nick bowed and presented her with a winning smile. "You're looking at him."

"You?"

"Yes, ma'am," Nick said. "I could use the work."

Samantha expelled a huff of incredulous laughter. Could this young man help Aman get to where he needed to go? "Are you serious?" she said. "We're in no position to hire anyone to help us."

Nick offered a playful smile. "Fine. You can owe me. Otherwise, I'm stuck here too."

"I want to see your pilot's license," Marshall said.

"I don't have anything like that with me. Not even a wallet."

"Why should we trust you?" Marshall asked.

"For the same reason I'm willing to trust you," Nick said. "I grew up inside the cockpit of a single-engine Cessna. I was trained to fly F-18 fighters over Afghanistan. I can fly anything that can get off the ground. It might not always be pretty, but I can get you anywhere."

AIRPORT

THE SMALL RURAL airport looked deserted. Despite common sense, Samantha allowed her hopes to rise while following Nick's Harley between the twin runways. They passed six single-engine prop airplanes arranged in a neat row alongside the airport's lone hangar. A sleek corporate jet sat inside the hanger's opened bay door. Could Nick fly one of those little planes? If it turned out he was full of shit, she figured they were no worse off than on the highway.

Samantha pulled next to Nick's bike in front of a one-story aviation office. A lone pickup truck sat in the first parking space. She didn't see a worker anywhere. Even on a typical day, she doubted this place saw much activity.

"I will stay with Mr. Dawson," Aman said. He appeared to have no interest in exploring the tiny airport.

Samantha stepped out of her car, followed by Marshall climbing across the front on all fours. She followed Nick and Marshall into the pilots' center. The air inside felt baking hot, despite a noisy window-mounted air conditioner. A lone older man she assumed took care of the place sat at a table behind a counter. His creased leather face boasted an impressive tan, and his shaggy white hair and a matching drooping mustache looked very non-corporate. The name "Mel" was embroidered onto his denim jumpsuit.

Marshall detoured into a small break area where he found a worn atlas on an end table. He retrieved the envelope from his pants' pocket on which he had written Aman's global coordinates.

"I'm closed," Mel said without looking up. "But you're welcome to what's left in the coffee pot. Otherwise, I'm tossin' it."

He stared through a pair of reading glasses at a newspaper spread over the table. A stack of today's newspaper sat on the counter. Samantha picked up one and noted coverage devoted solely to the cataclysmic events that began yesterday and had now captured the world's undivided attention.

Nick set his helmet on the counter and said, "We need to charter an airplane, sir. The Cessna 335 next to the hangar would be ideal."

Samantha thought about the thirty-odd dollars in her wallet. Even if the airport manager agreed, did they have enough cash between them to rent one of these things?

Mel tossed his reading glasses onto the newspaper with a frown and gestured to the muted TV in the break area. The scene showed a churchyard filled with uneven rows of dead bodies covered with makeshift materials from bedsheets to floral shower curtains.

"In case you've been smokin' your bloomers and just woke up," he said, "all flights are grounded. The new president is expected to order martial law at noon to control the panic. No one's goin' anywhere. I suggest you call it a day and go back home." He returned his reading glasses to the bridge of his nose. "I do have a '92 Mustang I can rent you. But you'll need to find your own gas."

Samantha stiffened when she saw Aman's face on the TV's news story. His picture was taken in the sheriff's holding cell, but he looked a good deal younger.

"What the—?" She couldn't hear the program, but a lot of talking heads seemed to have much to say about Aman. The screen caption read, "Nationwide Manhunt Intensifies." This is bad, she thought. *Really bad.*

Nick glanced over his shoulder at the broadcast.

Marshall stared at the TV screen until another segment began about a national week of mourning. He returned to the world atlas, thumbing through the pages.

"Everyone's looking for that fellow," Mel said with a nod toward the TV. "Seems he may know something 'bout all this. The paper says he might even be in the state. Wish I knew his whereabouts. There's a generous government reward for anyone that finds him—more than enough for me to retire and die comfortably. Meanwhile, a military task force is on the way to set up camp here. They need our long runways. I'm turning the airport over to them, and then I'm going home." He peered over his glasses at the chrome clock above the door. "They should be here in 'bout a half-hour or so."

Samantha placed both hands on the counter while she considered their next move. Dare they take a chance and confide in this man? They were out of options. "What if I told you that the man everyone is looking for must leave the country? Otherwise, we all might die."

Nick looked at her in surprise.

Marshall glanced up from his book. "Sam, are you sure you want to say anything?"

Samantha nodded.

Mel's shoulders jiggled as he chuckled. "Miss, I know when someone's blowing smoke up my backside. I may not know what's goin' on, but I do know that the world's not gonna end any time soon. No ma'am, nothing of the sort. When the Big Shout happens, I expect we'll see lots of angels—not just one little feller." He leaned back in his squeaky chair and gestured toward the TV. "Won't be nothin' like this."

"Don't take my word," Samantha said. "Ask him yourself."

Mel's grin vanished, and he squeaked forward in his chair. "Come again?"

"The manhunt is for a man who's sitting outside in my car," Samantha said. "We need an airplane to get him out of here."

"A plane that carries lots of fuel," Marshall added.

"You figured out where he wants to go?" she asked.

Marshall held up the world atlas. "Southern Iran. In the center of the most barren stretch of desert in the Middle East."

Mel expelled a blast of laughter. "Now I've heard it all." He wouldn't stop laughing. "No way you can get there from here."

"Follow me," Samantha said. "I want you to meet someone."

Mel kept shaking his head and chuckling while Samantha led him outside to her car. The airport manager stooped and peered inside at Kirby sitting with his head back and a blood-stained towel pressed against his upper arm.

Mel's grin faded, and his eyes narrowed when he spotted Aman. "I'll be a sorry son of a bitch. It *is* you!" He shook his full head of white hair. "Jesus in heaven. What have you folks gotten yourselves into?"

Aman reached out his window and offered his hand. "I am pleased to make your acquaintance."

Mel took Aman's hand into his calloused palm. Samantha saw his shaggy eyebrows lift and his facial lines stretch. His eyes took on an odd quality—fear?—not unlike the anxious look she had observed when Nick first saw Aman. Perhaps at some level, he understood the importance of Aman's journey—the same urgent energy that compelled the rest of them to help, even if they didn't understand why. She threw a glance back at Marshall. His nod said he noticed it too.

The old-timer wouldn't stop shaking Aman's hand. "Pleasure's mine, sir. Call me Mel—Mel Arterberry. Now let's see what we can do to get you on your way with all due Godspeed."

HANGAR

NICK GRABBED THE YOKE of the Cessna 355 and relished the possibilities beneath his fingers. He loved sitting in a cockpit—any cockpit. Flying meant freedom. An aircraft could take him to the top of the world away from the discerning eyes of humanity. His head bobbed approval. *Yes!* This baby would get them to the coast without much notice.

"I found the one," he called down to the tarmac. When no one responded, he strained his neck for a look outside. "Hello?"

No response. Nick climbed down from the Cessna and stood on the deserted tarmac. "Samantha? Dr. Marshall?" The others were gone.

Nick heard voices inside the hangar and went to investigate. He found the others gathered by a Gulfstream G550 corporate jet with no logo or company colors along its sleek one-hundred-foot surface.

"What's going on?" Nick asked, joining them.

"We're considering another option," Marshall informed him.

"This? You want to take *this*? We can't fly at treetop level in *this*. Every radar in the country will see us."

"Aman thinks this plane will work better for us," Samantha said. "Talk to him."

Nick marched to the nose of the aircraft.

"This beauty will cruise at Mach 0.86 into eighty-knot headwinds," Mel told Aman. He sounded like the consummate aircraft salesman, Nick thought. But this wasn't hype. Mel was risking everything—his job, pension, and maybe even his life—

to help Aman. And he saluted him for that.

"And its range?" Aman asked.

"Five-thousand miles," Mel said. "There's 30,000 pounds of fuel in the wings. She's primed and ready for a jaunt to Europe."

"Aman?" Nick said. "What are you doing?"

"Mr. Judge," Aman said. "This aircraft's range and speed will provide us with many benefits. Most importantly—time."

"But every radar will spot us," Nick said.

"The military chain of command has broken," Aman said. "That gives us the advantage. This aircraft will travel faster than most, well ahead of the military's ability to mobilize and intercept us. By morning, I will be halfway to my destination."

"You're serious, aren't you?" Nick said.

"Our time is dangerously short," Aman said. "Please follow me."

Aman led Nick up the stairs into the Gulfstream's cabin, a luxurious sitting room as sleek as its exterior. Nick stiffened when he spotted a man slumped in the rear of the cabin. He took several cautious steps toward a corpse of a suited middle-aged man spread over a fold-down oak table. His bone-white face had begun to wither. Nick felt his lips go numb. The man's unseeing, open eyes remained fixed on the table's surface, and his fists clutched a spread of papers as if he wished to finish one more report before his death. A laptop computer lay face down on the floor next to his polished Berluti shoes.

"He was purged like the others," Aman said.

"Why?" Nick asked.

"He stopped a crucial safety upgrade at one of his chemical plants to save money," Aman said. "Because of his decision, a preventable explosion killed fourteen workers and injured scores more."

"How do you know that?" Nick asked.

"That is what I am told. Do not concern yourself with him. Come this way."

Mel stepped behind the corpse. "I'll get him out of here."

Aman led Nick to the front of the aircraft and directed him into the cockpit. Nick forgot all about the corpse when he eased into the pilot's seat.

"Hey now!" He felt a surge of adrenaline while surveying the instrument panel's four Honeywell flat-panel displays. The flight deck had more in common with a computer control center than an aircraft. Sitting in the pilot's seat convinced him that this was a fabulous option. He liked Aman's thinking.

"Can you fly this aircraft without a copilot, Mr. Judge?" Aman asked from the doorway.

"Call me Nick," he said. "And the answer to your question is yes. This jet can fly itself. The hardest part is getting off the ground."

The whump of pumps starting and a muted forward bell indicated that Mel had switched on the auxiliary power unit. The cockpit instrumentation came to life as the aircraft automatically readied itself for takeoff.

Mel appeared beside Aman at the cockpit door. "She's programmed for a flight to Frankfurt. But you can change the flight plan once you're airborne. Shoot, take her anywhere you want."

"Thank you, Mr. Arterberry," Aman said. "You have been of immeasurable assistance. I am grateful."

Mel's bright expression turned cold. "The military transport will touch down on my runway in about ten minutes. They're coming for you."

Nick whipped around in his seat. "Ten minutes? I need time to review the manuals."

"If you can fly this aircraft," Mel said, "get her in the air pronto, son."

• • •

Hotel Excelsior
Frankfurt, Germany

Jacob Cohen stepped out of the shower, grabbed a towel, and began wiping his slim body. He stared at his pure white beard trimmings lining the sink. The sight reminded him of his age, and he looked away. He should be home in Brooklyn, reclining in his study with a good book. Instead, he stood naked in a hotel bathroom a continent away. Waiting. For what?

He made his way into the bedroom, tracking a path of water across the white tiled floor. He thought of his Marti, who would wonder what had become of him. Since he landed, the phone circuit failure made calling her impossible. Was she safe? After all that had happened, he worried about her constantly to the point of obsession.

Jacob put on his thick glasses and focused his eyes on the bed. He froze, seized by a fear he had never known. The box he guarded so carefully for most of his life was gone. He could still see the slight indentation where it had sat on the top comforter. His eyes darted around the room and stopped at the door. It stood ajar. He felt lightheaded and thought he might pass out. He cursed his carelessness.

His fear yielded to a panic that he couldn't control. Jacob wrestled his way into a thick white robe from the hotel's closet and charged into the hallway without bothering to find his shoes. The corridor was empty.

Jacob hadn't the patience to wait for the elevator. He raced into a stairwell and half ran, half stumbled down the three flights. When he reached the lobby, he felt dizzy from hyperventilating. He had been panting like a dog and could feel his heart pounding against his chest. *I am too old to run down stairwells.*

Shouting erupted in the lobby by the double glass exit doors. Jacob hurried toward the disturbance and found several people gathered around a young man with curly black hair sitting on the lobby's cold marble tiles. The man wore a crisp oversized jacket to cover a worn T-shirt and torn jeans. Jacob's precious box sat between his legs.

Great waves of relief washed over him, and his breathing relaxed. The man's eyes were downcast and hidden, and he sat sobbing as if he were the one robbed. A bellboy spoke to him in German while a hotel guest pumped the man with questions about his health. The thief didn't appear to hear them.

Jacob knelt before the young man. The robber's head shot up, and he looked at Jacob with eyes glistening from weeping. Every muscle in his body seemed to tremble.

"You took what belongs to everyone," Jacob said to him, his tone curt.

The young man let out a gasp that hurled a rope of spittle down the front of his large jacket. Those watching grew quiet. Jacob put out a hand to the young man, palm up, non-threatening.

Without taking his eyes off Jacob, the man lifted the box from his lap and held it out for him with a shaking hand. The box's twin metal straps were still intact.

"I can't take it from the building." His accent was American. "It ... it won't let me."

Jacob accepted the box without a word. The other hotel guests watched Jacob rise awkwardly to his feet, his knees snapping, and make his way toward the lobby elevator. Several spoke to him, but he heard none of it. He felt weary in every extremity.

Once back in his room, he would sleep with the door bolted and the box secure in his arms.

• • •

Harlan Municipal Airport

Mel used twin red flags to direct the Gulfstream out of the hanger. Nick, smiling, gave Mel a thumbs-up from the cockpit and taxied the corporate jet out onto runway 15/33.

The screech of the hazard alarm brought Nick's eyes to the heads-up radar display. A large incoming aircraft—a military C-17 transport, according to its transponder data—was on final approach to his runway. The task force had arrived—two minutes to touchdown.

Screw it. Nick didn't think twice about violating a dozen FAA regulations. He touched the intercom button. "Make sure you're all buckled up back there for a quick, steep climb."

Nick disengaged the aircraft's auto-throttles and pushed the levers forward harder than he intended. The jet's twin Rolls-Royce engines roared. Within seconds the aircraft shot down the runway with 30,000 pounds of combined thrust. Through his headphones, Nick could hear the military pilot broadcasting a description of their plane.

He throttled to maximum power.

"Gulfstream G550, abort your takeoff. Repeat, abort your takeoff. You are violating national security—"

With one swift pull, Nick brought up the nose of the aircraft. The flat, endless Iowa landscape gave way to a thick, cloud-covered sky. *Sweet—nothing to it.*

He glanced at his radar and swallowed hard. The military transport had aborted its landing and flew a frightful 3,000 feet from their tail.

Close. Too close.

Nick engaged the auto-climb program that would take the jet to 37,000 feet in eighteen minutes.

The Gulfstream ascended and left the military transport far below them.

ASCENT

MEL ARTERBERRY STOOD at the bottom of the staircase he had pushed up to the C-17 military transport's cabin door. The day's insufferable heat and smothering humidity forced him to wipe his glistening forehead repeatedly with a stained rag that doubled as his handkerchief. *Couldn't pick a worse time of summer to stand on a tarmac.*

A tall young officer in an impeccably creased uniform and buzz haircut deplaned, followed by two military staffers, one of them a woman carrying a metal case. The team all wore somber expressions, as though they were returning from a covert mission that had gone bad. The officer and his team marched off the staircase and formed a rough circle around the airport manager. Mel looked into their solemn faces, all staring back at him through aviator sunglasses, out of place on this overcast day.

"I am Colonel Theodore Welch, head of a special military manhunt unit," the officer said. Mel saw his reflection on Welch's mirrored sunglasses and decided his rowdy mustache needed a trim. "I want to see the flight plan of that Gulfstream and a roster of everyone onboard."

"Whatever you say, Colonel," Mel said. Lean and all business, Welch smacked of West Point.

"And you are?" Welch asked.

"The name's Arterberry. Mel Arterberry."

Mel shielded his eyes to watch another figure make his way down the staircase clutching the rails with both hands. He was an older man, 70ish, and on the heavy side, with thinning white hair and bushy eyebrows. Instead of a uniform, he was dressed carelessly in a wrinkled tweed jacket and gray slacks with a blue dress shirt open at the collar. The word "professor" jumped to Mel's mind. The older gentleman joined the group and put on a pair of sunglasses with shaky hands. But these glasses were different. They had deep green lenses and thick black frames that resembled goggles.

The older man studied the cloud-covered sky through his green lenses. "Can we please hurry?"

"Hold Mr. Arterberry for interrogation," the Colonel said to his first lieutenant. Then he removed his dark glasses and directed a cold, penetrating glare at Mel. "Violating the flight ban is a federal offense. I'm taking you into custody."

. . .

Samantha sat mesmerized in a heavily padded seat, watching Marshall examine Kirby's arm wound. Thorough and precise. The deputy slept soundly on the executive leather sofa, thanks to the shot of morphine Marshall gave him before takeoff. The doctor finished and tossed the used towel into the receptacle under the cabin's wet bar.

"How is he?" Samantha asked.

"He's healing well," Marshall said. "Too well. It's remarkable."

"Mr. Dawson will mend rapidly," Aman said from the executive chair across from Samantha. "He will not notice the scar."

"Ladies and gentlemen," Nick announced over the cabin's intercom, his voice chipper, "we are approaching our cruising altitude of 37,000 feet with an airspeed of 640 miles per hour. Please sit back and enjoy the ride."

Something troubled Samantha, a point she had been reluctant to bring up before. "Tell me something, Aman," she said. "Why did Nick agree to help us?"

Aman swiveled his seat to look at her, and she saw the hesitation in his eyes as though he wished to avoid this topic. Why?

"Nick Judge is a gifted aviator," Aman said slowly. "We are

very fortunate to have his assistance."

Samantha frowned at Aman's reluctance to answer her question. "He's responsible for our lives right now. Why do you trust him?"

"Sam's right," Marshall said. "We don't know anything about him, just like we don't know much about each other, least of all you."

"What if I told you that yesterday Nick woke in a military prison seventeen days from his execution?" Aman said.

Samantha drew in a quick breath. *"What?"*

Marshall leaned against the wet bar with folded his arms. "That's just great."

"Nick is innocent of the offenses for which he was charged and convicted," Aman said.

"How do you know that?" Samantha asked.

"They told me," Aman said.

Marshall scowled. "So, you're talking to ghosts again."

Samantha scolded the doctor with a frown. "Tell us what happened."

"The incident occurred the night Nick arrived at a coalition training base in Pakistan," Aman said. "A soldier from another unit befriended Nick and took him to a local family's home to celebrate his last day in the country. The soldier put a drug in Nick's drink. While Nick lay unconscious, the soldier raped the 14-year-old daughter before taking her life and killing her parents. He planted evidence to make Nick look responsible. Nick was arrested and charged with the crime. He recalls nothing about that night, including the man who committed the atrocities. After a brief military trial, Nick was sentenced to die."

Samantha didn't dare ask for another detail. She regretted bringing up the topic, she regretted knowing. "How awful."

Aman's intense brown eyes softened. "Take comfort in knowing that as Earth's frequency rises, violence will become impossible."

Samantha wanted to believe Aman, she really did—but she couldn't put aside her doubts. "Are you saying there will be no more wars?"

"No more wars," Aman said. "No more killing. No more atrocities at the hands of another."

"You're describing paradise," she said, "a return to the Garden of Eden."

"Humanity has failed itself," Aman said. "We have struggled with our beliefs, our self-imposed morality, and the awareness of our eventual deaths. We are still under the delusion that the self is separate—and doomed. Humankind needed time to evolve past its naive and self-destructive nature and become aware of our peaceful place in this universe. However, because of the breach, radical shortcuts have accelerated this evolution."

"Tell me more about this breach," Marshall said.

"An inadvertent tear of spacetime is releasing a dark stream of radiation from an incompatible dimension we know nothing about," Aman said. "Its destructive force is tearing apart the Great Field."

"What's this great field?" Marshall asked.

"Our minds and bodies are not separate entities, but rather are part of a quantum field that transcends all matter. The original ones called this *Dzonot*. The discordant radiation from the breach is creating global chaos and death and must be closed before it does irreparable damage to the field and humanity's very existence."

"It sounds like you're going to need a lot of metaphysical alchemy to deal with something like that," Marshall said.

"I require metamaterial and energy density beyond humanity's engineering capacity," Aman said. "I will tap the gateway's energy flux to manifest what I need to close the breach."

"A lot of people would call that crap," Marshall said.

"This is all quite real, I assure you, doctor," Aman said. "The ancient knowledge that would allow us to manipulate the Great Field has been lost to us. Humanity must relearn what its ancestors understood and practiced."

"The Fold," Samantha said.

Marshall threw her a sideways glance. "The what?"

Samantha's eyes lost focus. "I can hear it. There is great intelligence. It wants to embrace and protect all of us in its fold."

Amen nodded. "It is as you say."

"When will we see this great new world of yours?" Marshall asked.

"We may never experience it," Aman said.

Samantha refocused her gaze on Aman. "Why not?"

Aman swiveled his seat toward the window and looked over the top of the clouds. "I must reach Ab Ambar before nightfall two days hence. And that probability is diminishing each moment as the laws of physics that run your machines continue to breakdown."

INTERROGATION

Harlan Municipal Airport

MEL ARTERBERRY SAT slumped in a wooden chair in the airport's aviation office. Through his brain's retreating fog, he watched the lone female member of the taskforce return several vials and a syringe with stainless steel thumb rings to her metal attaché case. Whatever she had done to him had produced a nice buzz. He didn't care what she did. Or had she already done it?

The last thing he remembered was someone introducing her as Specialist Sheila Moore. She didn't say much, yet Mel found the woman attractive despite the dark, soulless look in her eyes.

The other members of the military team were sifting through his office files. He wasn't sure what they were looking for or how long they had been searching his office, but he sensed that hours might have passed since their arrival.

Mel recalled the colonel grilling him with questions, but he couldn't remember what he had told the guy or if he'd answered him at all. Screw it. He couldn't tell them anything about Aman. As far as Mel knew, the interrogation might be over. Or had it even started?

The older man in tweeds, out of place among the younger team members, didn't like how the interrogation had been going or the methods used to facilitate it. The others addressed him as "Dr. Weissmann," and they deferred to him as if he were an essential adviser or perhaps a mentor to the team. He couldn't have looked less like a soldier with his broad, intellectual forehead and white, tousled hair. Mel enjoyed watching him. Weissmann appeared flustered, as though late for an appointment, pacing with sharp, agitated movements while absently handling his special green goggles.

Dr. Weissmann held up a traffic control printout. "Can we assume they will abandon the aircraft's original flight plan?"

Colonel Welch wiped his forehead with the back of his long-sleeved shirt. The municipal airport office felt obnoxiously hot despite the window air conditioner running full blast. "Absolutely. There isn't a chance in hell they plan to go to Germany."

"The Gulfstream is in Canadian airspace," said the lieutenant staffer, the office phone to his ear. "They haven't deviated from the plane's original flight plan."

"I don't get it," Weissmann said. "Why would he be so arbitrary about a destination?"

"He wants to leave the country and doesn't care where to," the Colonel said.

"Iran," Mel blurted.

Weissmann looked at the airport manager. "What did you say?"

"They're going to Iran," Mel repeated.

That got the Colonel's attention too.

Weissmann thrust his goggles into his jacket's pocket and squatted in front of Mel's chair. "Iran? How do you know that? Why didn't you tell us this before?"

Mel grinned, and when he spoke, he felt drool spill over his chin. "Because they can't get there from here. Told 'em so." He could hear his speech slurring. "Besides, your fella didn't say it. The guy with him, a doctor, said that's where they needed to go."

The lieutenant held up a world atlas he'd found next to the coffee pot. "The page of the Middle East is torn out."

Colonel Welch wouldn't stop pacing. "A pilot unfamiliar with a Gulfstream would be smart to allow the aircraft's preprogrammed flight plan to take him to Europe. He could study the flight system en route and, once in Germany for refueling, he could develop a new flight plan for Iran."

"But he can't just fly into Iranian airspace without getting attacked," Weissmann said.

"There's no one left to stop him," Welch said. "Except me."

Mel watched the professor sit back on the floor in front of him and run a hand through his white wisps of hair. Weissmann's eyes grew vacant, and he said to no one in particular, "One of the world's oldest civilizations once sat on land that's now Iran. He's going back to the beginning."

"Bullshit, doc," the Colonel snapped. "He's a terrorist heading back home. He's leading us right to his base of operation, probably aiding Iran's nuclear weapons program."

"I disagree." Weissmann pushed himself off the floor and rose to his feet. "This isn't about global nuclear or biological weapons terror. Whatever is happening will continue to affect everyone in every corner of the planet. There's no sanctuary anywhere." Sweat beads rolled down his forehead. "We need to find this man fast. All of our lives depend on it."

. . .

Dr. Weissmann led the way across the tarmac toward their aircraft while Colonel Welch and his two staff members jogged to keep up. Weissmann, an avid bicyclist, was in a hurry and gave the younger team members a workout. The air had become thick with humidity, and the gathering storm clouds appeared ready for a downpour. And only one more hour of daylight.

Welch walked up to the C-17 transport's pilot waiting at the foot of the staircase. "How fast can this plane fly, Captain?" he asked.

"She tops at 300 miles an hour cruising altitude," the pilot said.

Welch rubbed a hand over his buzz cut. "That's not fast enough. The Gulfstream will be traveling two, maybe three times that speed. And we'll need to refuel along the way. He won't."

Dr. Weissmann felt his blood pressure rising. "Jesus, do

something, Colonel."

Welch turned to his lieutenant. "There's a NOAA Citation II at Cedar Rapids. That should be fast enough. I want it here in thirty minutes."

The young man punched a number on his cellphone and listened with a scowl. "Can't get a signal."

"Then use the damn office landline," Welch ordered. "And get me in touch with Canadian Defense Minister McKay. I want his Air Wing to intercept this sonofabitch."

Dr. Weissmann felt his muscles tense. They couldn't afford an air disaster. "You mustn't take risks, Colonel. We need to find him—alive."

INTERCEPT

NICK HAD TWO words to describe flying the Gulfstream: *Fuckin' A!* The aircraft could indeed fly itself, thanks to one of the most advanced avionics systems he had seen anywhere, commercial or military. The flight over Canada proceeded uneventfully—just the way he liked it. Compared to his training flights over Afghanistan, this run was downright dull.

The last scarlet thread of day vanished over the Nova Scotia coastline behind them. It had been a long day, and he slumped down in his seat to steal a few hours of sleep while crossing the ocean. He closed his eyes.

The alert bell sounded.

Nick sat up, his neck muscles tightening. The Gulfstream's radar return had picked up signatures of two aircraft climbing rapidly. The transponders identified a pair of McDonnell-Douglas CF-18 Hornet fighters from Dartmouth airfield. *Uh oh.* What were the chances they were coming after another aircraft? None, he figured.

The warning indicator confirmed two armed fighters at his altitude with radars locked on him, shadowing thirty miles behind. The two fighters proceeded on an intercept course, one to his port, the other starboard. Nick glanced at the moving terrain map on the multifunction display and noted the coastline retreating behind him. *What the f—?* They were over international waters.

Nick disengaged the auto and grasped the yoke with both hands. He worked the pedals to assure himself the aircraft would respond. It did. The cockpit door opened, and Aman put a hand on the back of the pilot's seat to watch.

"Two Canadian Hornets are shadowing us," Nick informed him.

Aman stooped to peer through the windscreen. But there was nothing to see but blackness. "I am aware." He slipped into the copilot's seat. "And your reaction?"

"If they engage us, we have three options," Nick said. "One, we follow them back to their airbase. Two, I try to lose them. Three, we do nothing and let them shoot us down."

The cockpit's Traffic Collision Avoidance warning triggered. Nick noted the twin fighters were accelerating.

"Speak to them," Aman said. He slid on the copilot headset to listen in.

Nick put the Gulfstream back on auto. He selected the standard frequency for air-to-air traffic and began transmitting with a gentle press of his thumb on the yoke button. "This is Gulfstream five juliet charlie social," Nick said into his mic. "Traffic. Traffic. You're on my heading and altitude. Please disengage and drop 10,000 feet."

Nick heard no response and wondered if he had set the communications console correctly. Before he could try a different frequency, a voice filled his headset.

"*Gulfstream juliet charlie social,*" the pilot said, "*descend to 15,000 feet and proceed on a heading of one niner zero. We will escort you to Dartmouth Air Force Base.*"

Nick muted his headset mic and said to Aman, "OK, option one—we follow them back."

"That will end my journey," Aman said. He adjusted the headset microphone over the edge of his lip. "Allow me to speak to both pilots."

Nick opened the channel to Aman's mic and signaled him that he was live.

"You are addressing the pilot and a passenger of this air-craft," Aman said. "You must allow us to continue on our present course. We have an emergency. A delay will be cata-strophic."

"Negative," the CF-18 pilot responded. "You do *not* proceed. You must comply with my order, or we will open fire."

Both CF-18 fighters surrounded the Gulfstream, port and starboard. Nick knew that aircraft model very well from his military training.

"These guys are serious." Nick looked at the CF-18 on his port side and could see the Hornet's pilot inside his cockpit. "This isn't a MiG fighter, Aman. We can't engage them."

"We cannot deviate from our course," Aman said into his mic. "If you attack us, you will kill four American men and one woman who mean you no harm."

Nick heard the second Hornet pilot say, *"He's out of our airspace. I'm disengaging."*

The CF-18 outside Aman's window dipped its wings ninety degrees and dropped away, vanishing into the blackness.

"Hold your position, alpha one niner," the lead Hornet pilot instructed his wingman. *"That is my order."*

Nick heard no response from the fighter pilot who had abandoned his flight commander. He heard the lead pilot mutter, "Asshole."

"Yes!" Nick shouted. He glanced at the second CF-18 off this port quarter. "What about this guy? Why hasn't he disengaged too?"

"He is no longer following his directive," Aman said. "This encounter has become his personal contest for supremacy."

Marshall opened the cockpit door. "Gentlemen, may I ask what the hell is going on?"

Nick glanced back and saw Marshall staring at the CF-18 Hornet out the windscreen. The sight of the fighter so close drained all the color from the doctor's face.

Aman twisted in his seat. "Nick and I will work to mitigate this situation."

"You'll do whatever that fighter pilot tells you, right?" Marshall asked.

"Buckle in tight back there," Nick said, ignoring his question. "Secure everything."

Marshall closed the cockpit door and returned to the cabin where Kirby slept in one of the executive chairs. He made sure the deputy's seatbelt was fastened tight. *Let him sleep through this.*

Samantha, sitting across from the deputy, turned to Marshall. "So, what's happening, David."

She wanted his assurance that they would be all right, but he couldn't lie.

"It looks like a dangerous situation," Marshall said. He put his syringe kit and a loose bottle of morphine inside his black case and secured it at the bottom of the coat closet. "Make sure you're buckled in."

She checked her seatbelt. "But we'll be all right? Aman will make sure we're safe, won't he?"

Marshall didn't look at her. He sat in the chair behind her and fumbled with the seat buckle. His hands were trembling. "Aman is a smart man. But I think we're going to need more than that tonight."

. . .

The Hornet disappeared from Nick's port cockpit windshield. A glance at the heads-up radar told him that the aircraft had fallen back for a pursuit vector behind and above him.

"So, you don't want me to follow him back to his base?" Nick asked.

"No," Aman said. "You must stay calm and think rationally. Do not allow what transpires to lead to recklessness."

Aman's steady voice had a calming effect on Nick—but only momentary.

The CF-18 opened fire with its six-barrel Gatling gun. Nick saw the 20mm tracers streak just feet above his port wing's leading edge.

"Jesus! He means to kill us. He actually means to *kill us."*

Aman put a hand on Nick's arm. "His fire missed us."

"Yeah? What about next time?"

Nick took the Gulfstream off auto and planted his feet firmly on the pedals. Acting on trained instincts, he moved the throttles forward and pushed the yoke hard, sending the jet into a steep one-hundred-degree roll while his feet worked the rudders like a dancer. He saw Aman clutch the hand rest.

"I'm going down to sea level," Nick shouted.

As he expected, Nick's maneuver took the Hornet pilot by surprise. The military aircraft overshot their flight path by a wide margin before the fighter pilot began circling back. Meanwhile, Nick maintained a steep dive at an alarming speed, pushing him back into his seat at four times the force of gravity.

Aman clutched the amulet. "Your actions are not advised—"

"When he returns to my tail," Nick said, "his radar will be in Situation Awareness Mode to hone his attack. He'll have no other visual cues in the darkness. If he's green, he won't watch his altitude and will ignore all alarms."

"Nick, listen to me—"

"No, you listen." Nick couldn't get his words out fast enough. "I'm going to pull out at a thousand feet. It'll be close. He'll be flying too fast to lift in time. The bastard will hit the ocean at Mach 1.5. Common mistake. God, I hope he's green."

"The pilot has no flight combat experience," Aman said. "He will not recover from your maneuver and will be killed. He is a stubborn aviator. He means only to intimidate. He has not armed his air-to-air warheads."

"You don't know that, Aman," Nick said.

"If you kill him knowing what I have just told you, you will be purged, and all of us will die when we crash into the ocean."

"Intentional or not, this bastard's dangerous," Nick said. "He could make a mistake and rip this aircraft in half!"

The altitude radar and infrared vision showed the ocean rising fast toward them. A dozen cockpit alarms blared at once. Nick leveled his wings. At this speed and altitude, he had no margin for error. The CF-18 roared toward them at Mach 1.5 on an intercept path.

"Right out of the textbook," Nick said. "I've got him."

"You are the superior pilot," Aman said. "You can out-think and out-maneuver him." When Nick didn't respond, Aman added, "Do not do this. Your life and the lives of your passengers depend on you abandoning this petty act of power."

Nick gritted his teeth. *"Jesus Christ*—if you're wrong—"

With a stiff pull of the yoke, Nick took the Gulfstream out of its steep dive. Likewise, the Hornet aborted its attack dive, swooping to within a thousand feet of the ocean's surface and leaving an explosive trail of water turbulence in his exhaust wake.

Both aircraft leveled off and began a steady ascent into the black night.

• • •

The Canadian fighter pilot felt oddly detached from his cockpit. He had just experienced a revelation. He almost died in this brief, foolish skirmish. But not the way he wanted to die in combat. There was no courage and dignity here. Instead, he almost killed himself and innocent others with his irresponsible arrogance. The Gulfstream pilot was good—damn good—a trained combat attack flier who could have let him die just now. But he saved him.

The pilot now understood the enormity of his shortcomings. He saw an image of himself as a soldier, and that image no longer worked for him. There was no honor in killing, even for a noble cause. That path led to an abyss. He decided at that moment to end his military career.

The pilot broke into elated laughter. Euphoric, he couldn't contain his broad smile while he brought up the nose of his Hornet and carved a huge arc in the sky on a heading back to his family.

SAFE MODE

NICK SAID NOTHING more while the Gulfstream climbed back toward its cruising altitude, unimpeded by military attack fighters. He stared at the nothingness outside the cockpit window until his heart slowed.

Aman unbuckled his seat's restraining strap and stood. "I will inform the others."

"Aman," Nick said, "I gotta be honest with you."

"Yes?"

"You're scaring the hell out of me. Who are you, man? Tell me why I shouldn't get as far away from you as I can before things get any stranger?"

Aman said nothing, which Nick found even more rattling.

"Damn it," Nick shouted. "Where did you learn to fly?"

"From you."

"Don't screw with me."

"I read the Field," Aman said.

Nick cocked his head. "What does that mean?"

"The sum of what we are is imprinted on a quantum matrix that surrounds everything," Aman said. "Nature's blueprints are there. If you listen closely, you can hear it."

"That's nice, but that doesn't answer my question. How do you know your way around a cockpit?"

"Our proximity allows easy contact with your field of experience. I then know what you know." Aman touched Nick's arm. "Excuse me. I must reassure the others."

A thousand questions spiraled through Nick's mind, yet he managed only a stiff nod. Something else captured his attention, but he mentioned nothing to Aman as he left the cockpit. Nick's eyes returned to a flickering indicator on one of the flight instrumentation's heads-up displays. He moved the cursor control with his thumb to scroll through the display windows to check the integrity of each aircraft system. The auto-flight system wanted a password.

What the heck is going on?

Nick unbuckled his harness and made his way back into the passenger cabin, where he found Aman telling the others about the encounter with the Canadian fighters. Nick's appearance brought the conversation to a halt.

"Nick," Samantha said, her eyes red from crying, "who's flying this plane?"

"This aircraft is doing an excellent job flying itself." Nick tried his best to sound upbeat. "In fact, it doesn't want my help." He forced a smile and rubbed his short, sweat-glistening hair. *I must look like shit.*

"Is everything all right?" Marshall asked.

Kirby moved his chair upright. Although some color had returned to his face, he looked exhausted. "What they're saying, dude, is that we'd all feel a whole lot better with someone at the controls."

"There is an issue with this aircraft," Aman said. "Describe our situation, Mr. Judge."

"This aircraft has gone into *safe mode*, a subsystem that shuts down all but its essential systems until I tell it otherwise. One of the flight computers may have been affected by my dive. I'll go below and check the connections."

"Wonderful." Kirby shut his eyes and put his head back against the seat.

"Are we going to be alright?" Samantha asked, her voice strained.

She was frightened. Nick hated when his passengers were frightened.

"I'm locked out," he said. "I need a ten-digit password to get into the flight system and run diagnostics. Meanwhile, the aircraft has assumed all flight responsibilities for a trip to

Frankfurt."

"I thought you could fly anything," Marshall reminded him.

"Yes, sir, I can. It's getting these things back on the ground that can be tricky."

Aman bowed his head and closed his eyes as though meditating. "A hydraulic line in the left rudder is leaking," Aman said. "The pressure is down four percent."

He opened his eyes. "The problem is not critical. However, if we attempt to override the auto-safety systems and fail, the aircraft's inertial navigation systems will abort our flight plan. This aircraft will divert to the nearest airfield large enough to accommodate our landing, which will force us back to Canada."

"So, can you get me that password or what, Chief?" Nick asked.

"That won't be necessary." Aman sank back into the chair's overstuffed leather cushions. "This aircraft has enough fuel and system integrity to get us across the ocean. Let it take us to Germany."

DAY FIVE

ALLENDORF EDER AIRFIELD

THE GULFSTREAM ENTERED German airspace a little after 8 a.m. local time. While the others slept, Nick monitored the cockpit's flight systems on the heads-up displays. There hadn't been much to do during the transatlantic crossing except read manuals, and he even managed to catch a couple of winks just south of Greenland.

However, as the flight computers positioned the aircraft on an approach vector to Frankfurt International Airport, Nick grew increasingly uneasy about the avionics readings. The weather had deteriorated with excessive rain and limited visibility, but that was the least of his concerns. He felt abnormal vibrations in the airframe, an aberration he had never experienced before as a pilot.

He scrolled through the display windows again and again, monitoring the integrity of each aircraft system. The readouts showed values fluctuating in and out of the normal range. Every one of his flight systems was compromised, and he hadn't a clue why.

The prospect of attempting an emergency landing in the unfamiliar aircraft in lousy weather terrified him.

• • •

Airframe tremors jarred Samantha awake. She sat up on the executive sofa and lowered her feet to the floor. The steady vibration against her toes felt like a washing machine out of balance. An airplane wasn't supposed to feel like this, she decided. The others began stirring too.

Samantha noticed Aman standing at the front of the cabin, watching them. He looked to be in his forties, sporting thick brown hair with only traces of gray brushing his temples. His dark features appeared solid and handsome, and his eyes glistened with new energy.

Samantha couldn't stop staring. "Aman?"

He put a finger to his lips. "Another time."

Marshall stretched his arms with a yawn. "What's going on?"

"Nick requires my assistance," Aman said. "While we work, I suggest you all prepare for an interesting landing."

• • •

The cockpit door opened. Nick glanced over his shoulder and saw Aman standing behind his seat. He thought he had a pretty good handle on what Aman looked like. Several moments of scrutiny failed to assure him that this was the same man who had sat next to him in this cockpit last night. *What the hell?*

Aman's eyes scanned the bank of flight displays. "How can I assist you?"

Nick returned his attention to the controls. "We've got problems, Aman. A shitload of problems."

The radar alert signaled another aircraft approaching their airspace. "Great," Nick said. "And we've got company again." He reached for his headset.

Aman leaned over Nick's shoulder to peer into the dull morning sky outside the windscreen. The rain hammered its surface like a fire hose. "Four NATO F-16s," he informed Nick. "They have been scrambled to escort us to the Stuttgart airbase in Echterdingen. A division of troops is assembling there to take us into custody."

"How the hell do you know—" Nick caught himself. Of course, Aman was right.

The radar showed the F-16s forming a box around them, one forward, two to port and starboard, and a fourth on their tail.

"I could've diverted," Nick said. "But I'm locked out."

Aman placed a hand on Nick's shoulder. "You have done exceptionally well. Do not concern yourself with our escort. They are unimportant. Tell me about the integrity of this aircraft."

Nick strained to keep his voice calm. "This aircraft isn't stable. The inertial navigation system failed. Other systems are at risk."

"All machines around the world are unstable," Aman said.

"*What?* Why?"

"The breach," Aman said. "The physical laws that govern our world are changing rapidly."

"What are you talking about?"

"These changes are still quite small," Aman explained, "mere particle fluctuations in the discrete quantum electrodynamics. But, in time, all machines will cease functioning."

"Screw that. Can I land this thing or not?"

Aman sat in the co-pilot's chair and buckled his restraining harness. "Activate your emergency transponder. Send a message that we are making an emergency landing."

Nick enabled a beacon that would notify air-to-air traffic and ground traffic that the Gulfstream was in trouble. He slid the headset over his ears.

Aman brought up the aircraft's inertial navigation systems on a heads-up display.

"Don't waste your time, Chief," Nick said. "We're locked out."

"This aircraft will not reach Stuttgart," Aman said. "I will override the flight plan. We must divert to Allendorf Eder Airfield sixty miles north of Frankfurt. The runway is long enough to accommodate us."

"Not without a password," Nick warned.

Aman keyed in a string of ten numbers and letters, a colon separating every two digits. Finished, he entered the string, which gave him full access to all flight systems.

"Holy—"

"Make your call to air traffic control," Aman reminded him.

Nick opened the traffic frequencies. "This is Gulfstream six juliet charlie social—I have an emergency." Nick heard no response—only static. "The radio's not working. Screw it."

Nick began working the rudder and fin like a barnstormer. The aircraft responded sluggishly when he maneuvered the elevators and horizontal stabilizer to compensate for the airframe vibration. The NATO fighter escort widened their box around them, allowing the Gulfstream to ease out a formation for a new heading to Allendorf Eder Airfield.

"Their aircraft are also at risk," Aman said. "I do not advise proximity."

Minutes later, as the Gulfstream made its final approach to Allendorf Eder Airfield at 5,000 feet, a more severe round of tremors rocked the aircraft. *What the hell just failed?* Nick, his jaw set, wrestled the controls as though he were gripping the handlebars of an off-road bike hurling down a steep, rocky trail. He doubted his ability to compensate for something this bad.

"She's fighting me," Nick said. "This is insane."

"Put the landing gear down before the controls fail," Aman said.

Nick pulled the lever to the down position and heard the reassuring *boom* of the gear dropping.

Aman began keying in more instructions with his left hand. His fingers worked the keypad swiftly and without thought, reminding Nick of a seasoned tax accountant tallying columns of numbers on an adding machine.

When he finished, all four of the cockpit's heads-up displays went black. Nick felt an immediate drop in vibration. The yoke and pedals responded more efficiently, and he had manual control of the aircraft.

"What did you just do?" he asked.

"I powered down the aircraft's computers. They are now disengaged from all flight operations."

Nick's expression sobered. "You realize that I'm now flying

this bird as though it were an old-fashioned 1950s prop plane."

Aman said nothing.

"I need gauges," Nick said. "I need to know how fast we're descending."

"You must do without them and use your trained instincts."

Nick felt his back muscles threatening to spasm. He ignored the fatigue and brought the crippled aircraft on its final approach to the rural German airfield. Thanks to the driving rain, he could barely make out a long runway at twelve o'clock.

"Two miles," Aman announced.

The jet descended rapidly with no way to deploy the wing-edge flaps to slow them. Nick glanced out the windshield and saw a patchwork of farm fields surrounded by wooded hills.

"I'll circle to lose speed," Nick said.

"No."

Aman placed his feet on the co-pilot's rudder controls and grabbed the yoke. He pulled back the throttles. "One thousand feet."

"This is gonna be tricky," Nick said.

Working together, they eased the aircraft down over the runway and deftly nosed the plane onto the tarmac. Nick reversed the engines and felt the main wheels touch the airfield's water-swept tarmac and begin to hydroplane. He brought the jet to a sliding stop with 500 feet of runway to spare.

"Thank you, Mr. Judge," Aman said.

Nick responded with a belt of laughter and taxied the aircraft off the runway. He noted the F-16s circling the airfield. "I don't see any of them getting into a landing pattern."

"The pilots are burning fuel with the probability of ejecting." Aman unbuckled himself from the copilot's seat and headed for the passenger cabin. "We must disembark quickly before the authorities arrive. I will inform the others."

Nick taxied the Gulfstream off the runway toward the airfield's hangars. He saw a few workers milling about with umbrellas, watching them. Nick figured these folks hadn't seen a plane take off or land here in days.

Nick spotted a line of trucks moving down the airport access road in single file. His expression dropped. These vehicles sported camouflage paint—military troop transports, enough to carry one-hundred soldiers. "Uh-oh."

He moved the aircraft to the edge of the runway, set the brakes, and powered down the engines. He unbuckled his harness and headed back to the cabin.

Nick found his passengers gathered around Aman, engaged in a lively conversation about their landing. "Military trucks heading our way," he called to them.

Their chatter ceased, and all solemn faces turned to him.

"Dozens of them," Nick added.

Marshall moved to a window for a look while Samantha swiped her few belongings into a large tote bag.

"A garrison stationed at Hallenberg arrived in less time than I estimated," Aman said. "This changes our options."

"I thought you had this all figured out," Kirby said. He was on his feet, wincing while stretching and twisting his stiff arm.

Nick unlatched the cabin door and, with Marshall's help, pulled it inward and lowered the passenger stairs to the tarmac. The airport workers refused to approach the plane. They would leave their unlawful arrival to the military convoy.

The others joined Nick and Marshall at the door to watch the parade of military trucks come to a quick stop on the runway in front of them. Soldiers stormed off the vehicles in the heavy rain and formed a tight skirmish line around them with guns held ready.

Nick placed a hand on Aman's shoulder. "I trust this is all part of your plan, Chief." When Aman didn't respond, he added, "Or should we be scared shitless?"

BUNKER

Leighton Barracks
Wuerzburg, Germany

WHAT HAVE WE gotten ourselves into? Samantha kept asking herself.

The interior of the military transport reminded her of a car-rental courtesy shuttle. But this was no vacation ride. For the past two hours, Samantha and her friends sat shoulder to shoulder on a bench seat, their wrists bound in front of them with plastic cuffs. She sat next to Marshall while facing a row of young soldiers—peacekeepers, Nick called them—dressed in light blue uniforms with matching berets. They kept the butts of their rifles planted on the floor between their feet.

"Are we in serious trouble, or what?" she asked.

Marshall didn't answer.

The rain hadn't let up since they left Allendorf Eder Airfield, and the air had become hot and humid—an unpleasant climate made even more uncomfortable with so many bodies crammed inside the small vehicle. The musty and rancid smell inside threatened to choke her. She wanted out.

Despite the heat, Samantha was trembling. Her feeling of dread grew worse each mile of the long road trip taking them to—well, she didn't know where they were going. The last hopes for Aman and his journey had evaporated, an unfortunate situation that left her exhausted, not to mention jet-lagged. They were in military custody after violating German airspace—during an international flight ban, no less—which didn't bode well for their freedom. What had they hoped to accomplish traveling halfway around the world, anyway? People everywhere were dead or dying. Who did they think they were? A league of superheroes trying to save the world? What possessed her to think—?

Stop it!

Samantha still believed in Aman. She promised to help him complete his journey any way she could—whatever it cost her. But now this?

"These cuffs," she said to Marshall, "they're just a precaution, aren't they?" She felt him shift restlessly beside her.

Before he could answer, Nick blurted, "No."

"Zip it, Sam," Kirby said. He looked tired and pissed off. "They shoot talkers."

Marshall scowled. "Don't be ridiculous."

After another long silence, Samantha asked Marshall, "Have you ever served in the military?"

Marshall shot her an anxious sideways glance. "No. But I have an older brother in the army."

"Really? What's he do?"

"He's a Special Forces major." Marshall looked away. "I haven't been able to reach him since this business started."

"Oh." Samantha regretted bringing up the subject. "Well, I haven't seen my brother since grandma passed. Last I heard, the jerk was hauling fuel tanks somewhere out west."

Marshall said nothing while staring at the young German peacekeepers sitting across from them. He didn't feel like chatting.

Their vehicle crossed an armed checkpoint and then proceeded into a military compound. Samantha saw Nick straining to see out a tiny meshed window above his left shoulder.

"Of course they would bring us here," Nick said.

Samantha felt a fresh wave of anxiety. "Here? Where's here?"

"Leighton Barracks," Nick said. "It's the U.S. military headquarters for the First Infantry Division. I was stationed here for two weeks before deployment. It's also the headquarters for military intelligence in Europe."

Samantha glanced through the meshed window for a look. They were passing row after row of long barrack-like buildings with stone facades and pointed orange roofs. Jeeps, troop trucks, and German soldiers on foot lined the road as though a military operation was underway.

"If this is an American headquarters," she said, "why don't I see any American soldiers?"

No one had an answer.

"They are taking us to the base's emergency command center," Aman said, speaking for the first time since they were taken into custody. All eyes shifted to him, even the peacekeepers. He sat at the front of the compartment, too far from a window to see. "Our confinement will be in a bunker 700 feet beneath the surface, surrounded by bedrock and fourteen feet of reinforced concrete."

"That's pretty damn secure," Kirby said.

"The center can withstand a blast from a twenty-kiloton nuclear detonation," Aman said.

"Good Lord," Samantha gasped.

Marshall let out a long, resigned sigh that summed up their collective frustration. "OK, so we're not going anywhere," he said. He glanced at Aman. "You do realize that your journey is now officially on hold?"

Aman didn't respond, his hollow eyes fixed forward as though in reflection. What was he thinking, Samantha wondered?

The transport stopped abruptly and threw everyone sideways on the bench. Then, with a grinding of gears, the vehicle began creeping back into a faceless structure through twin steel blast doors encased in concrete collars.

Samantha shielded her eyes from the entrance's annoying rotating amber lights. Another wave of dread rippled over her. This building sure looks like a prison, she thought. She glanced at Nick, who watched their arrival with a scowl, understandably troubled by being locked up again.

Their vehicle jerked to a stop. There came a clatter of metal against metal as a soldier opened the rear door.

"The circus is about to start," Kirby said. "Welcome to the show."

The soldiers sitting across from them deployed one by one with practiced precision. A soldier outside the rear hatch instructed them in curt English, "You will all exit at this time. No talking."

The Americans complied. When Samantha stepped off the back of the truck, the building's substantial blast doors began closing with a mighty pneumatic hiss that startled her. The doors connected with a hollow boom that resonated through the hangar-size area. No one could get past those doors—coming or going.

The bunker's top level was constructed with countless yards of poured concrete and tons of steel, all bathed in a canopy of harsh floodlights. The smell of machine oil permeated the air. Samantha spotted a row of vehicles against the far wall.

Two lines of soldiers in blue uniforms facing each other came to attention, reminding Samantha of a firing squad.

"Aman, please tell me we're going to be all right," she whispered. "I need to hear you say it."

Aman's intense eyes remained alert and roaming as though searching for something. "Always stay behind me," he said over his shoulder.

Samantha and the others followed Aman in single file between the two rows of troops, who watched them with curious looks. They were famous—not just Aman, but all of them. The international headlines must have preceded them, catapulting Aman to the status of a notorious world figure. Each of them most likely had photos plastered throughout the world's media next to Aman's.

A tall, lean officer, older than the others, stood rigid at the end of the line of soldiers, his hands clasped behind his back. Two soldiers with rifles stood at attention on opposite sides of him, ready to provide muscle if needed.

"Should I address you as God?" the officer called out to them.

Aman raised his cuffed hands to bring their little party to a halt. His eyes scanned each of the soldiers' faces. He senses something, Samantha noted.

One of the German soldiers wearing an MP armband suddenly broke from the ranks and took several large strides toward them. He drew a handgun from a side holster, his face twisted with maniacal determination.

"Aman!" Samantha grabbed Aman's shirt at the shoulder and tried to jerk him out of the way, but the narrow row of troops prevented her from moving him.

She felt Marshall's hand on her shoulder. "Sam!"

The desperate soldier charged to within an arm's length of Aman with his handgun pointed at the center of his chest.

With a speed that surprised her, Aman's arms sprang up like twin pistons and grabbed the soldier's weapon between his bound hands and shoved it upward. The gun fired. The bullet found the eye orbit of a soldiers in the line, and an explosion of red brain matter sprayed the concrete floor behind him.

Several soldiers wrestled the would-be assassin to the ground in front of Samantha, while others rushed in to protect Aman, forming a human shield around him. The handgun clattered to the floor.

The German officer stormed through the skirmish with his handgun drawn. *"Standplatz beiseite!"* he ordered the soldiers pinning the assassin to the floor. The officer thrust his pistol into the attacker's face, and those holding him scrambled clear.

The assailant sat up on the floor at Samantha's feet, disheveled and bleeding from a cut down his forehead from the scuffle. His wide, intense eyes glared up at the officer pointing the gun. Samantha could smell the uncontrolled perspiration wafting off both of them.

"Er wollte uns alle zu töten!" the assassin said. He spotted the handgun on the floor by his feet and lunged for it.

The officer discharged a single bullet into his forehead. A cry of astonishment caught in Samantha's throat. The soldier fell back onto the concrete floor with a grunt, and blood formed a puddle around his head.

No one dared move or say anything. Samantha looked up at the gun-wielding lieutenant, and their eyes locked for a moment. His breathing was rapid, and she was sure this was the first time he'd ever killed a man.

The officer raised his handgun as a warning to his troops and addressed them in English: "I will shoot any man who attempts to—"

The German officer fell silent. His complexion drained of color, and he began teetering as though about to swoon. His eyes rolled up into his head, and he collapsed next to the man he had just killed.

Marshall squeezed past Samantha to assist. The officer's chest grew still, and his wide, sightless eyes remained fixed on the doctor. Marshall looked at Samantha and shook his head.

The sound of approaching hard-soled shoes echoed across the concrete cavern. Samantha saw a neat, solid woman in her fifties marching toward them. Her light brown hair touched her neck, and she wore a dark, well-crafted suit. Samantha stiffened in recognition. The soldiers guarding Aman stepped aside and stood at attention.

The woman ignored Samantha and the others and addressed Aman. "I am Anne Osthoff, Germany's Chancellor," she said with only a trace of an accent. "With the world in chaos, I no longer am certain how I can help the people of my country. For now, I am in charge of this base, which the Federal Republic of Germany took possession of when the Americans evacuated yesterday."

She gestured toward the two bodies on the floor. "Please forgive this most unfortunate welcome. This is a difficult time for everyone. Most of us haven't slept for the last thirty hours. Under these circumstances, none of us can predict what a man will do."

Aman raised his hands to show the chancellor the plastic wrist cuffs. "If you cannot guarantee my safety," he said, "please remove my bindings so I am better able to protect myself."

QUARTERS

MARSHALL STOOD NEXT to Chancellor Osthoff while their lift car descended deep inside the underground command center. The Chancellor had ordered their cuffs removed before herding them into a secure cargo-size elevator that worked with a unique keycard only she and her senior staff carried. She had dismissed the soldiers from her entourage, much to Marshall's relief. After the fatal incident upon their arrival, they couldn't trust anyone.

Even without cuffs, Marshall hardly felt free. He didn't like any of this. He pondered the sanity of taking the lift key by force, an idea he quickly abandoned. Even if he succeeded, what would happen when they reached the top level crawling with soldiers? And how would they get past those blast doors?

"I hope you appreciate that my primary concern is your safety," Osthoff said. "Please don't think of this place as your prison. You are here for your protection. I want to help you."

Marshall detected a careful accent that sounded like the product of an English university like Oxford.

"With all due respect, Madam Chancellor," Nick said from the rear of the car, "I know something about prisons. And this place sure feels like one."

Osthoff offered him a forced smile. "If it's any comfort, I am also staying in this facility with my staff one level above you— for our safety as well. We have few options to accommodate a group of your notoriety. The world media is full of stories about each one of you. You're all a social media legend." She looked directly at Aman. "Now I'm responsible for protecting the man who many believe is the one person who knows what is happening to the world. Is it true that a little girl grew a new hand after you touched her?"

Aman, his eyes fixed forward as though in deep thought, said nothing.

The elevator halted at the ninth sublevel, and the floor-to-ceiling door opened. The door was titanium, Marshall noted. No wonder she dismissed the guards so readily. This place was more secure than any prison.

Marshall followed Aman off the car into a light-blue hallway lined with doors and overhead strips of fluorescent lights, some of them flickering and buzzing like trapped flies. The air felt warm and stuffy down here despite the even rumble of the air circulation system. Tight spaces never bothered Marshall. However, he felt a shiver when he considered the massive concrete and steel above their heads.

Aman stood aloof, his keen eyes taking in their accommodations. He glanced at an overhead security camera before looking away without comment.

The chancellor followed them out into the hallway. "I have ordered your level cleared of all other occupants. You will be safe down here, I promise you. I think you will find everything you need."

Aman faced her and said, "Thank you. Your hospitality is most appreciated, Madam Chancellor."

Osthoff's voice dropped to a whisper, her words meant only for him. "Aman, we need to talk. I must know what is happening."

"I will share what I know," Aman said.

Her face lit up. "Excellent. We will not be disturbed down here. Let's find a place to talk." She glanced at the others. "In private."

"My friends and I first need time to ourselves," Aman said. "A brief period, I promise you."

Osthoff's smile faded, and Marshall read her disappointment. She seemed overly anxious to find out what Aman knew, and that made him suspicious of her. Perhaps she wanted fame by revealing Aman's secrets to the world. Or was she frightened and desperate for answers like the rest of them?

"Very well," she said. "A 9.4 earthquake in the Adriatic devastated the coastline. Venice is gone. We cannot render aid until transportation systems are functioning again. After I meet with my staff, I will join you down here for lunch."

Aman consented with a courteous bow. She returned to the lift and slid her security keycard into the control panel. The car's door closed in front of her.

"Our party just had cold water dumped on it," Kirby said, rotating and stretching his wounded arm, which seemed to afford him full use.

"Didn't the Führer kill himself in a place like this?" Nick said.

"What about beds?" Samantha asked. "And a shower?"

"We will require few amenities," Aman said. "We must leave here before nightfall."

Nick whirled at the news. "How's that going to happen, Chief?"

"I do not have an answer yet to that question," Aman said. "But I must find a way."

"Leave or not, we could all use food and some rest," Marshall said.

"An excellent idea, Dr. Marshall," Aman said.

"I'm hungry enough to kill something with a fork," Kirby said.

Marshall led the way down the hallway. The group began opening doors and exploring rooms, calling out their finds—a workshop, a filing room, personal quarters.

Samantha peered inside a personal quarter and saw a bed and a bathroom. "Oooo—my own private shower." She swung her tote over her shoulder. "If I'm not out in a half-hour, don't wake me up." She disappeared inside the room.

Sam had the right idea, Marshall thought—after two days of traveling, he wanted a shower and a bed too.

"I'm not getting a signal down here," Kirby said, holding up his phone.

"Even the most robust communication networks will fail by morning," Aman said.

"That's just terrific," Kirby scoffed.

Marshall found a door labeled "Climate/*Klima*" and heard the even drone of compressors on the other side, probably the air circulation system and perhaps a generator or two. Access was only possible by entering a code on the door's numeric keypad.

The next door had a name card on it—*Erich Kästner*. Marshall opened it and stepped inside. A small lamp on a corner desk provided a soft glow to a private room. Clothing lay draped over a chair. He saw no phone or any device to contact the rest of the center. He wondered if anyone outside of this center knew they were here.

A Bible lay open on the single bed. He picked it up and began scanning the page. The first verse was Acts 16:

"Suddenly there was a great earthquake so that the foundations of the prison were shaken: and immediately all the doors were opened and everyone's bands were loosed."

Marshall grinned at the text's irony and set the book back onto the bed, leaving it open to the same page. He wondered what coincidence had driven the room's owner to refer to that particular passage at this time.

He withdrew and noticed Aman standing at the end of the hallway by the closed elevator door, watching them, making no move to find a room for himself. Does he ever sleep, Marshall wondered?

"I found food," Kirby called to the others.

Marshall's stomach groaned at the mention of food. He joined Kirby in a small dining area with two round tables and a restaurant-sized refrigerator. Kirby helped himself to a loaf of rye bread, a container of sliced ham, and a wrapped wedge of Swiss cheese.

"I can't work when I'm hungry," Kirby said.

Marshall surveyed the racks of beverages and pulled out an iced tea for himself. The other shelves offered an assortment of packaged meats, produce, and condiments. At least they wouldn't starve down here.

Nick followed them into the dining area. "A couple of brewskis would hit the spot right now."

"No one must consume alcohol," Aman said, making his way down the hallway. "And I do not advise heavy foods. Six-ounce portions every four hours will serve you best."

Kirby, wielding an overstuffed ham sandwich, took a seat at one of the tables. "Yeah, right."

The level suddenly plunged into absolute darkness, followed by the sound of the air system's compressor whining to a halt. No one moved or said anything. Marshall had no fear of the dark, but the total blackness and the deep silence down here raddled him. A hundred imaginary phantoms paraded in front of his sleep-deprived eyes.

The emergency lighting blinked on, giving the corridor minimal amber illumination. Marshall let out a long breath, grateful for the modest light.

"This isn't cool," Kirby said. "I'm claustrophobic."

Samantha emerged from her room wearing a white robe that belonged to the center. "What the hell happened? It's pitch black in the shower."

"We're screwed, folks," Nick said. He shoved his slim frame into a chair at Kirby's table. "Did anyone consider that they put us down here to kill us?"

"Screw that shit," Kirby said.

"That is not their intention," Aman said. "The equipment is failing."

"Intentional or not," Marshall said, "we need a way to notify the chancellor what's happening down here. And without a working elevator, we're trapped."

"You're scaring me to death, guys," Samantha said. She moved beside Marshall and took his hand. He loved the feel of her warm presence and her scent. He felt more at ease.

Aman stepped in front of the door to the climate control room.

"You're not getting in there without a code," Marshall said.

Aman entered four digits into the numeric keypad. He opened the door and disappeared into the dark room. A moment later, the hallway's fluorescent lights blinked back on, its light steady and flicker-free. Marshall heard the whine of a generator powering up, accompanied by the even rumble of the air system resuming. A reassuring flow of cooler air brushed his face, and he drew in several deep breaths to reassure himself.

Nick stood up from the table with a grin. "Ok—I'm impressed."

Aman emerged from the utility room and joined them in the kitchenette. "The equipment will operate for another seven hours."

"Then what?" Nick asked.

"That is not our concern," Aman said. "If we are not underway by then, nothing will matter."

Kirby took a large mouthful of his sandwich. "The sooner we leave here, the better," he said, his voice muffled by the food.

Marshall released Samantha's hand and peered into the climate equipment room. He saw nothing disturbed and no toolkit.

"Mr. Judge," Aman said, "I want you to get three REM sleep cycles before we leave tonight. Your mental acuity is critical. We have a long night ahead."

Nick shrugged. "Sure, Chief. But—"

"How can you be so sure they'll let us out of here?" Marshall asked. The idea of leaving, with or without the Germans' help, seemed absurd.

"I must travel an additional 2,300 miles no later than nineteen hours from now," Aman said. "The consequences of my failure to do so will be catastrophic."

• • •

Stuttgart Airfield,
Echterdingen, Germany

Dr. Weissmann was the first off the crippled Cessna Citation II remote sensing jet after its dangerous landing at Stuttgart Airfield. He stopped halfway down the plane's staircase in the pouring rain, coughing so hard into a handkerchief that he feared his lungs would collapse from acute bronchospasm. Black smoke billowed from one of the aircraft's twin engines, which had seized and caught fire over the Netherlands. They should have made an emergency landing at Düsseldorf, but Colonel Welch insisted the pilot get them to Stuttgart or die trying. They succeeded, although just barely.

Weissmann stepped off the bottom of the staircase and staggered across the tarmac. He didn't get far before he collapsed onto his hands and knees in a puddle of water, struggling to breathe. The rain transformed the soot on his shirt into black muck. He felt the pockets of his jacket for an inhaler.

While the airfield's fire squadron attended to what remained of the burning engine, a paramedic hurried to Weissmann's aide. A gurney appeared alongside them.

"Smoke got into the cabin," Weissmann groaned to the EMT between coughs. "I've got asthma … my allergies…"

The paramedic helped him to his feet. He placed a bronchodilator over Weissmann's nose and pumped two doses of spray into his lungs. He then put a medical mask over Weissmann's nose and mouth with a flow of Albuterol. Weissmann's coughing fit eased. Still, he felt awful, his eyes streaming with tears from the smoke.

"Relax, sir," the paramedic said, checking his pulse. "I'm putting you in that ambulance." A second EMT appeared with a blood pressure meter.

Weissmann waved them away. "I can't. There isn't time."

The paramedic gave him a stern look. "We're taking you for treatment."

Colonel Welch marched up to them with a huge black umbrella. "This man is coming with me."

The woman staffer with the metal attaché case stood behind him, watching the doctor with her dark eyes. Weissmann removed the facemask and passed it back to the paramedic with a nod of thanks. He knew better than anyone that his health, however compromised, would need to serve him "as is," at least for another day.

"What time is it?" Weissmann asked.

The lieutenant staffer checked his wristwatch and frowned. "It stopped."

Weissmann clutched the Colonel's arm for support. "Will they hand him over to us?"

"Negative," Welch said. He escorted Weissmann to a waiting car. "No one is allowed to meet with him. The chancellor is prepared to use force to keep him secure."

Weissmann slid into the back seat and ran a shaking hand through his rain-soaked hair. "So, what do we do? Negotiate a meeting?"

"The U.S. operation to retake the base is underway," Welch said.

MADAM CHANCELLOR

SAMANTHA HEARD A light knock on her door. Before she could move, Marshall slipped inside her quarters. She stared in surprise.

"David...?" She felt self-conscious sitting on the edge of the single bed with a thick book on her lap, wearing a sleeveless T-shirt and a pair of jogging sweats she found in a drawer. Her eyes were red and puffy from crying. *I must look awful!*

Marshall stood awkwardly by the door. "I was just passing by."

That was not what she wanted to hear.

When she didn't respond, he said, "This was a bad idea to barge in here. I'm sorry. I just thought..." Marshall reached for the door handle.

Samantha sprang from the bed and wrapped her arms around him. "Don't go."

Marshall looked into her eyes with concern. "Sam, why the tears?"

She brushed a hand over a wet cheek. "Because I don't belong here."

He shrugged. "What are any of us doing here?"

"No—me. I shouldn't be here. Trooper Rowe was right. I'm no use to Aman. He doesn't need me."

He smiled and used his thumb to wipe away a stray tear from her cheek. "You're the one who found him, Sam. You saved Aman's life. You earned the right to come."

She returned his smile with a small stretch of her lips. "Anyone coming along that highway would have done the same.

David, I'm the very definition of a loser."

"That's ridiculous—"

"I've latched onto Aman—like a father or something—hoping he'll give my life some direction and meaning. A purpose."

"Sam—"

"Forget it. I want to show you something." She turned to the bed and picked up an encyclopedia of geographic names she had found on the closet's top shelf. "According to this, the name Aman means *safe* and *secure* in Indonesia. And it's Serbo-Croatian for *compassion* and *forgiveness*. I think that's fitting, don't you?"

"Sure. His old friend at the hospital said something about a connection to Timor."

"Timor?" She searched for Timor, flipping pages until she found a photo of an island at the southern end of Maritime Southeast Asia. "Here it is. It says the official languages spoken in East Timor are Tetum and Portuguese. In Portuguese, Aman means *love*." She looked at him, beaming. "That's awesome."

"What about Tetum?"

She flipped more pages until she found Aman's name in Tetum. She closed the book, her eyes glistening. "It means *father*."

"Well, well." Marshall took the book from her, tossed it on the bed, and pulled her close. He looked deep into her eyes. "You're more than capable of taking care of yourself. You're strong and very special. I like what I see very much."

She gazed up into his blue eyes. A tangle of emotions stirred inside her, and she rested her head on his chest with a soft sigh. "Oh, David."

She loved the way he felt against her, so strong, so warm. She drew in the faint lingering fragrance of his cologne and smiled.

He lifted her chin. "Sam—"

She planted a quick kiss on his lips to silence him. He held her tightly and returned her kiss with a passion that surprised her. Her heart thumped with excitement. The dance of their tongues felt so amazing, so natural, and she savored every sweet sensation.

Samantha kissed him more urgently, and she felt his hands moving down her back. She arched her back slightly when he kissed her neck. She moaned. Their breathing intensified—

A sharp rap on the door made Samantha jump back, startled.

"Are you expecting someone?" Marshall whispered.

Samantha pressed a hand against her flushed cheek. "Do I look as warm as I feel?"

She cracked the door and saw Aman standing in the hallway.

"I need a word with Dr. Marshall," he said.

Samantha opened the door wide.

"What is it, Aman?" Marshall asked.

"I wish you to accompany me to meet with Madam Chancellor."

"Right now?"

"Yes. Our situation is changing."

"Changing? How?"

"You will know soon."

Marshall gave Samantha an apologetic look.

"I'm going with you." Samantha turned to find decent clothing.

"No," Aman said. "You will be safer here. The doctor will bear witness for all of you. Meanwhile, you must rest."

Samantha acquiesced with a disappointed nod. Marshall planted a quick kiss on her cheek before following Aman out of the room and down the hallway.

Marshall swore to himself and stifled a swell of resentment. He wanted to spend time with Samantha before they left. If they left. He also needed a shower—a cold one.

"Why do you need me along to see the chancellor?" he asked, letting Aman hear his frustration.

"Many would do me harm," Aman said. "An incident is less likely with you present. I will see what you see."

Great, now I'm a bodyguard.

Marshall's hopes of remaining on this level rose when he spotted the proximity reader next to the closed elevator door. "We're not going anywhere without a pass card."

Aman placed the fingers of his left hand on the card reader until the pin light switched from red to green.

The lift motor whined inside the shaft. Marshall looked at Aman, curious. "How did you do that?"

"Simple electromagnetic manipulation, an ability we all can master."

Marshall noticed Aman's complexion had paled, and his breathing quickened as though he had just finished a brisk jog. Had the electro-manipulation trick depleted his strength?

"Can I ask you something?" Marshall said.

Aman looked at him expectantly.

"Kirby thinks you have alien DNA, an idea that I dismissed at the time," he said. "But what I've seen lately, I'm not sure he's wrong."

"He is not wrong," Aman said. "My physiology is more evolved. You have two strands of DNA—I have twelve."

"*Twelve!?*"

"Yes. Our species' DNA is evolving as well. When the shift is complete, none of us will be human in the way we now understand it. Our new species will be far superior."

Before Marshall could follow up with another question, the lift's titanium door opened. They stepped inside. None of the panel buttons worked for Marshall. Summoning the car was one thing—they needed the chancellor's key to get it moving again.

"You got us into this car," Marshall said, "but can you make this thing move?"

"In a moment." Aman's fingers clutched Samantha's amulet.

Let's get this over with. Marshall grabbed the metal panel under the key slot and unsnapped it from the wall, exposing three wires. He pulled two of them from their soldered terminals and twisted the bare ends together. The door closed.

"OK, so in high school, I used to hot-wire cars," Marshall said, "a little trick my older brother taught me. I wasn't seriously bad."

Aman nodded his thanks. "Level five."

Marshall touched the number for the floor four levels above. The car began to rise. He didn't know what Aman would say to the chancellor if they could even find her. And he didn't ask.

"If something should happen to me," Aman said, "persuade the others to remain in this facility for their safety."

Marshall stared at him, unsure what he was saying. "You *are* expecting trouble."

"There is a possibility," he said. "The infirmary has abundant medical supplies. Find them. If your blood oxygen level reaches eight kilopascals, administer morphine to yourself and the others. There is no point in making your way outside. You would not survive."

Marshall couldn't believe what he was hearing. "Are you saying we should kill ourselves?"

"I'm suggesting a level of comfort in the final hours," Aman said. "This advice is a precaution and only necessary if I cannot elicit the help I need quickly."

"You're kidding me, aren't you?" Marshall thought of Samantha again and considered heading back down to her room.

The door opened to a large circular area with sputtering overhead lighting—the heart of the command center. An impressive array of large screens, displaying mostly static, hung suspended over workstations operated by a dozen people dressed in civilian clothing. To his relief, Marshall saw no soldiers or weapons.

When Aman and Marshall stepped out of the car, most of the staff stopped what they were doing to watch them. Marshall noted their gaunt faces and crumpled clothing as the two made their way across the command area. These people looked worse than a class of medical students at the exhausted end of finals. At least no one made a move to stop them.

A young Asian woman in sweats stood next to the double glass doors, watching Aman approach her. She let out a soft yelp of surprise when he grabbed the ID card dangling from her neck and touched it to the access reader. There came a soft click of the door unlocking.

Aman pushed through the double doors and continued down the corridor while Marshall walked quickly to keep up. Aman no longer appeared fatigued. In fact, he was the only person in the center who didn't look burnt out. Marshall thought about his unshaven appearance and the same slacks and white shirt he had worn for two days. He hoped the chancellor wouldn't notice.

Aman stopped in front of a door labeled "Conference Room." He turned down the handle and entered unannounced.

Chancellor Osthoff sat at the head of a large conference table while four people occupied the chairs closest to her.

Osthoff rose with surprise. "Aman—?"

"Forgive my interruption," he said, "but we must have a conversation immediately. It is imperative."

An older man in a dark suit with a harsh demeanor and pure white hair combed straight back drew a chrome-plated revolver from beneath his jacket. He laid the handgun on the polished mahogany table in front of him as an unmistakable warning. The three other staff members traded uneasy looks.

"Put it away, Krueger," the Chancellor ordered.

"The U.S. First Division will arrive in seven minutes to reclaim this base," Aman said.

Marshall looked at him in surprise.

"You can't possibly know that," Osthoff said. "There is minimal communication services in and out of this facility."

Marshall rolled back a chair and took a seat at the table, grateful to get off his feet. "You'll find that Aman is very well-informed."

Osthoff, looking far from convinced, said to Krueger, "I need some privacy."

Krueger never took his eyes off Aman while he put away his handgun and ordered the others to gather up their notes and leave. The staffers filed out of the conference room, and Kruger closed the door behind him with a bang that rattled the military artwork across the room's wall.

"Please sit down, Madam Chancellor," Aman said, taking a seat beside Marshall. "There is nothing you can do to keep the Americans out of this facility."

Osthoff settled into her conference chair with a sigh. "Do you know why Krueger fears you?" Before allowing him to answer, she said, "Like so many others, he believes you are the *devil*." She spat out the word like a stone. "And others revere you as the world's new savior. They say you heal the sick. You punish the wicked. You end wars. In one night, you turned hatred into fear. In less than a week, you have become the most famous man in the world—maybe of the century. You are already a legend, sir. But tell me. What are you really?"

"I assure you that I am of flesh and blood and not the cause of what is happening to the world," Aman said. "I have been summoned to perform a task—nothing more. I did not seek this notoriety. I would have preferred to travel without notice."

"Summoned?" she asked. "By whom?"

"That is complicated," he said.

"If you are claiming to be a Divine agent," she said, "you should know I stopped believing at a very young age. God would never forsake his creation by allowing so many to suffer while he watched. I grew up believing in nothing except what I was capable of achieving."

"What do you believe now?" Marshall asked.

Osthoff glanced at the doctor, an awkward expression that betrayed her doubts, and then lowered her eyes to the pages laid out in front of her. "I don't know what to believe." She glared at Aman. "So, what do you want from me?"

"I must first tell you that the power that created this world can also destroy it," Aman said. "That is not its design nor its intention, but circumstances have forced this dire possibility upon us. I will do everything in my power to prevent that. But for me to succeed, I need your help and the resources of this base. You must do as I request immediately, or we are all doomed. Time is critical."

The Chancellor sank back into her chair with a sigh. "I have very little power left, as you can see. I cannot help you."

Aman stood. "The Americans have arrived to reclaim their base."

"How do you know that?" Osthoff said.

"Madam Chancellor, please," Marshall said. "Just take his word for it."

She stood from the table. "What if you are wrong?" The Chancellor stormed out of the conference room and marched down the hallway. Marshall and Aman scrambled to follow her. Most staff members throughout the command area were staring up at video displays with snowy feeds, allowing them a glimpse outside. An officer sat at a desk with a phone receiver to his ear, asking questions in German.

Krueger confronted the Chancellor and shouted, "*Die amerikanischen Hundesöhne denken, dab sie können hinein Marsch lassen!*" Marshall's limited German understood something about American sons of bitches.

One monitor showed a line of trucks, a tank, and American foot soldiers moving down the compound's main road between the barracks. Smoke billowed from the guard station. Marshall could hear nothing from outside. However, occasional muzzle flashes from the advancing troops' rifles indicated gunfire erupting between the two forces.

A loud metal clatter made Marshall jump. He swung around to see a soldier opening a floor-to-ceiling metal cabinet that held a row of rifles and boxes of ammunition. The soldier began lifting the guns from the rack and distributing them to the others in the room, military staff and civilians alike. Marshall looked up at another static-laden monitor to see a woefully small cluster of young German soldiers gathering in front of the bunker's entrance, preparing to stop the approaching forces with rifles.

"The Americans cannot penetrate this building," Osthoff said.

Aman approached her. "The Americans are intimately familiar with this facility and its security. Allow them entry. Sacrificing lives to protect this structure will gain nothing."

The Chancellor glared at Aman. "Has it occurred to you that

they may want you dead? I am protecting you—"

"You must do as I say," Aman said.

"And what about my staff?" Her once commanding voice sounded thin and strained. "The Americans could shoot every one of us on sight."

"The Americans do not want a battle," Aman said. "They want me."

ASSAULT

Leighton Barracks

JACOB COHEN CLUTCHED his leather satchel against his chest as though protecting a newborn. He squinted against a pervasive acrid haze while a hard, steady rain splashed off his black suit. He had traveled most of the morning from Frankfurt in the rear of a packed bus, arriving in Wuerzburg to intense weather. The chaos he found here troubled him deeply. Black smoke wafted from a rubble heap that had once been the military base's guard station, and the remains of a massive iron gate lay contorted and twisted to one side. American military police shouted orders while civilians and soldiers raced in every direction. He was alarmed for Aman's safety.

An MP the size of a horse shoved him aside with a leather-gloved hand. "Get out of here *now!*"

Jacob looked at the soldier, astonished to be stopped so close to finishing a task entrusted to him after so many generations. "But I must go inside. I am here to see Aman." Jacob raised his voice to a shout. "I must see the man who was brought here today."

"You and everyone else, old man," said an American officer holding a large, black umbrella. He filed past Jacob with his entourage.

The arriving officer flashed the MP his military ID. "Colonel Theodore Welch." He pointed toward a wheezing older man behind him with white hair and a pallid complexion. "This is Dr. Weissmann. The other two are my staff."

The man identified as Dr. Weissmann glanced back at Jacob, curious, before he passed through the MP checkpoint and vanished into the haze inside the compound.

. . .

Colonel Welch parked his borrowed Suburban a safe distance from the command center bunker. He raised a pair of binoculars to his eyes and watched a single round from a U.S. MIA1 Abrams tank strike the steel gates. The blast ripped the rails from their mounts all the way to the four-foot collars, opening a path to the bunker.

The Abrams lurched forward and crushed what remained of the twisted rails. U.S. foot soldiers followed the tank into the compound, where a contingent of German troops formed a rough line in front of the bunker's sealed blast doors. Colonel Welch spotted one of the soldiers hoisting an anti-tank RPG onto his shoulder. He scowled. *Stupid kid.* Last week these guys probably were drinking buddies with the Americans.

The Abrams responded to the threat with a single anti-personnel canister cartridge. More than a thousand tungsten projectiles erupted from the tank's smoothbore muzzle in a shotgun pattern that swept through the line of young soldiers like a firestorm from hell. In an instant, every soldier brave enough to take on an Abrams tank lay dead in front of the blast door, their bodies rendered unrecognizable.

Welch heard the gasps from his staff seated behind him. "What'd they expect?" he said. "Gift cards?"

None of his young team members said a word. Weissmann looked down at his trembling hands.

Welch returned the binoculars to his eyes to watch the Abrams fire another round at the bunker's blast door, this one a 120mm armor-piercing long-rod penetrator. The blast door, made of composite reactive armor over uranium mesh, showed a single broad depression where the shell had struck.

"One round isn't going to do it," Welch said to no one in particular.

The tank moved into closer proximity to fire a second projectile at the door. But the round never discharged. The Abrams tank just sat there with its turbine engine idling, its gun silent.

"Why aren't they firing?" Welch said.

Weissmann fidgeted beside him as though he knew the answer. But he volunteered nothing.

• • •

Major Yates, the division's deputy commander, put down the phone and confirmed, "The gunnery crew is dead."

General Lawrence Thompson stood rigid in silence. He regretted his decision to use deadly force. At the age of forty-one, Thompson was the youngest man ever to assume the rank of field commander of the First Infantry Division, a role that also gave him authority over all U.S. troops in Europe. Only two days into his new position, he was in the middle of his first military operation—this assault on Leighton.

"I'm ordering a cease-fire," the General said.

His staff relayed the order to all U.S. units engaged in the offensive.

A sudden wave of dizziness swept over the General, and a cold sweat drenched his face. He put a hand to his head to staunch a mounting sensation of lightheadedness. "I made a mistake—" He forced out the words through his rapid breathing.

Major Yates hurried to assist his commander. "Sir, are you all right?"

The General couldn't catch his breath. In a sudden moment of clarity, he realized he was dying. "I want it known," he gasped, "the plan and the orders to mount this assault were mine alone. I take full responsibility."

Yates grabbed the general's arm. "Sir, sit down—"

Thompson brushed him away. He took one step before losing his balance and collapsing onto the war room's floor. The world faded into blackness.

He remained unconscious as he exhaled his last breath.

• • •

Marshall couldn't stomach watching the massacre and turned his back to the monitor. All eyes in the command center shifted to Chancellor Osthoff, awaiting her next order. Her expression was a smear of regret and shame. Aman lowered his head as if in mourning.

"What must I do to put an end to this insanity?" Osthoff asked.

Aman raised his eyes to her and said, "Allow the Americans inside this facility."

A sneering Krueger stormed forward and said to the Chancellor, this time in English, "You would surrender our base on the counsel of this abomination?" He thrust his chrome revolver at Aman and glared at him with an intensity that elicited a collective gasp around the room.

Marshall remained very still, taking in everything.

"Krueger!" Osthoff shouted. *"Ich verbiete Sie!"*

Krueger ignored her.

Marshall stepped in front of Aman, shielding him. "You'll need to shoot me first." He wanted to say more, but his tongue adhered to the roof of his bone-dry mouth.

Krueger's hand began trembling. Marshall watched as Krueger's mouth opened, and out came a lame squawk from deep in his throat. His complexion turned crimson. He looked like he's about to stroke out, Marshall thought.

The handgun slipped from Krueger's grip, hit the floor, and discharged. Marshall flinched as the round ricocheted off the far wall and struck a rack of electronics, darkening an entire bank of red pin lights. Krueger collapsed into a sitting position with his knees raised.

The Chancellor took a tentative step toward him. "What's happening to him?"

Marshall knelt beside Krueger and grabbed his wrist for a pulse. Drool spilled from Krueger's lips and formed a meandering yellow creek down a crease on his dark jacket.

"A cerebral hemorrhage," Aman said. "An arterial rupture in the frontal lobe."

"We'll need tests." Marshall raised Krueger's chin and examined his bright red eyes, the result of massive brain swelling. Aman's diagnosis was probably correct, he thought, which meant Krueger was dying. In minutes, his blood pH would be critically acidotic.

"High blood pressure most likely caused a rupture," Marshall said. "He needs immediate surgery."

"We have no surgical capabilities here." The Chancellor's tone was curt and dismissive, as though Krueger's imminent death mattered little to her.

Marshall considered the medical supplies in the center's infirmary, none of which would help him. Krueger's grim fate was sealed.

Osthoff whirled to face the officer in charge. "Raise the *goddamn* door."

. . .

Colonel Welch watched a team of combat engineers attached Semtex C-4 explosives to critical points around the blast door. They were placing enough explosives to separate the door from the surrounding reinforced concrete walls—and take down a good portion of the building's facade with it. Once finished, the troops withdrew to a safe distance.

The amber warning lights surrounding the door flared on and began spinning. With a loud pneumatic hiss, the mammoth door began opening with a screech on damaged rails. Welch removed his binoculars with a frown, disappointed to miss what promised to be a spectacular demolition.

The blast door hadn't reached its apex when the U.S. troops stormed inside the bunker. Welch followed them, driving his SUV around the bodies and into the concrete structure. His vehicle came to a quick stop in the loading area, and Welch and his staff quickly exited the vehicle. The American troops searched every corner of the cavernous top level. The Colonel saw no one to oppose them, only a single row of troop trucks parked along one wall. He spotted several closed-circuit security cameras mounted near the ceiling.

A woman's voice blasted from a static-laden loudspeaker: "This is Anne Osthoff, Chancellor of Germany," the voice said. "Aman is here with me. I will allow a meeting with your commander as allies. Proceed to the lift car, which will hold seven. That is all I can accommodate. I will not allow weapons."

The service elevator door opened to an empty car. Welch and his two staff members rushed across the floor and gathered in front of it. Weissmann followed. A group of U.S. Army Special Forces soldiers stood ready behind them.

"Make him come up here," insisted the colonel's young lieutenant.

Welch watched the surge of troops continue to storm into the loading area. "Too many guns up here. I can't protect him."

"What if it's a trap?" Weissmann asked. He shifted a soft leather briefcase uneasily from one hand to the other.

"Then a lot of people are going to get hurt down there," Welch said. The Colonel placed a hand on Specialist Moore's metal attaché case and said to her, "Have your needles ready."

He turned to the Special Forces squad. He wanted soldiers with him who could take down hostiles hand-to-hand if needed. "Four of you come with me. Rubber bullets only." The soldiers replaced their rifle magazines in a series of *clacks*. He turned to his lieutenant and said, "You're staying up here. I need as many guns with me down there as I can fit."

Welch stepped onto the elevator between Weissmann and Specialist Moore. The four Special Forces soldiers in combat camouflage squeezed in front of them, holding their weapons raised and ready.

The lift door closed.

• • •

Krueger lay face up on a black leather sofa in the command center's executive office. An inconceivable pain pounded his head while tears streamed from his right eye. All he could do was draw in air through gritted teeth. He wanted any kind of relief, even death, which he knew was only moments away.

Through blurred and distorted vision, he saw a lone figure hovering over him. The room seemed to tilt sideways, and as hard as he tried, he could not focus on the only person who had come to his deathwatch. He squeezed his bloody eyes shut, bitter at the thought of dying without seeing his wife and son one final time. He regretted so many things about his sad, selfish life.

Krueger felt a hand cover his eyelids. "Sleep now, and take note of your dreams." He recognized Aman's voice. "You will wake in the morning with a slight discomfort behind your left eye. But that will pass."

The terrible throbbing inside Krueger's skull faded. He saw countless tiny silver spots spinning like pinwheels. And then he slept.

THREE QUESTIONS

THE ELEVATOR DOOR opened to the bunker's command center. The four Special Forces soldiers rushed out of the car, leaving Weissmann, Welch, and Moore standing with their backs against the rear wall. The soldiers took up defensive positions in front of the open lift door with their assault rifles pointed at the terrified faces of a dozen members of the center's staff.

Chancellor Osthoff approached the car and said to the Colonel, "I said no weapons. Who are you?"

"Colonel Theodore Welch, U.S. Special Military Unit." He flipped the car's emergency stop button before stepping out.

Neither Weissmann nor Moore made a move to follow.

"I ordered my staff to put down their arms," Osthoff said. "You will do the same."

Weissmann knew the colonel would determine for himself if he needed weapons down here or not. Welch surveyed each face around the room as though on inspection duty. When he came to one particular man—crumpled and unshaven—he paused and stared.

"Dr. David Marshall," Welch said. "You look like you haven't slept at all this week."

Weissmann recognized Marshall from the media photos, and the good doctor didn't appear in the mood to discuss personal grooming.

"I'll sleep later," Marshall said.

"Please, Colonel," Osthoff said, "we will accomplish much more without your intimidations."

Welch's roaming eyes lingered on a small arsenal of rifles stacked against the far wall. He turned to his troops. "Stand down."

The four soldiers directed their rifle barrels upward, fingers on the trigger-guards.

Welch called to Weissmann, "Get out here, professor. I'm turning this inquiry over to you."

Weissmann stepped off the elevator, his soft leather briefcase pressed to his chest like a shield. Specialist Moore remained inside the car, her shoulders slouched, as though unwilling—or afraid—to come out.

Weissmann's elevated blood sugar level made the room appear foggy. He struggled to focus his eyes, searching the same dozen faces the colonel had just inspected.

Weissmann turned to Colonel Welch and said, "He's not here."

Osthoff stepped into the man's path, blocking him. "Who are you?"

"Forgive me, Chancellor Osthoff," he said. "I'm Dr. Irving Weissmann, professor emeritus of Applied Sciences at Princeton. I have lectured and published extensively about plasma dynamics, fluid mechanics, quantum mechanics, and engineering anomalies."

"Why are you here?" she demanded.

Weissmann glanced at Welch for a reply—an explanation of their taskforce's mandate—but the Colonel said nothing. Welch wasn't a PR man for the team.

"I represent a global scientific consortium," Weissmann said. "Five days ago, my research lab's random event generator experiment began returning statistically significant results that captured the attention of the world's scientific community."

"What experiment?" Osthoff asked.

"ElectroGaiaGram, or EGG for short," Weissmann said. "An international collaboration of scientists, engineers, and researchers has been collecting data from random event generator stations around the world since 1998. Each station records a 200-bit trial sum of random numbers every second. Our laboratory at Princeton collects and studies this data."

The Chancellor cocked her head, puzzled. "I don't understand. Why are you studying random numbers?"

"When you flip a coin," Weissmann explained, "the laws of chance say that over time you should see an equal number of heads and tails. When plotted on a graph, these results look like a flat line, and any deviation would display a curve on this graph."

The Chancellor's glare intensified. "So?"

"As extraordinary as it may sound," Weissmann said, "we've found patterns representing significant deviations hours before major world events. We saw these deviations just before the Sept. 11 attacks on the World Trade Center in New York, and the deep sea earthquake that triggered the 2004 tsunami in Asia, one of the deadliest natural disasters in recorded history."

She shook her head. "Dr. Weissmann—"

"Just before cataclysmic events, our numbers cease to be random," Weissmann summarized. "Patterns began emerging that chance alone cannot account for."

Weissmann noted puzzled looks around the room, and he realized his dissertation confused everyone.

Marshall approached the professor and said, "What does any of this have to do with Aman?"

Weissmann squinted at Marshall, attempting to bring the doctor into focus. "Five days ago," he said, "our global network recorded a sudden and massive shift in these random numbers—huge deviations from the norm the likes of which we've never observed. The odds of such patterns emerging are one in ten trillion—approximately."

Osthoff's expression displayed a blend of doubt and annoyance. "Are you saying that your machines can predict the future?"

"Madam Chancellor," came a voice from the far end of the room, "the laws of physics do not forbid seeing the future."

Weissmann whirled toward the double glass doors. A slight man stood just inside the room, his hands at his sides. Aman? Weissmann frowned. This was a younger man than the media presented, smaller in stature than he had expected, with striking features. Handsome. The man walked across the command center, his movements sharp and self-assured. The word *prince* came to mind. Weissmann's heart raced when he considered that he was about to meet the prize of their global military manhunt, the man he had traveled halfway around the world to find.

"Who the hell are you?" Welch said, his hard, narrow eyes following him.

"I am Aman."

"Bullshit," Welch said. "We're looking for a much older man."

Aman approached Weissmann, ignoring Welch, and said, "Think of your brain as a radio receiver. Your random number experiment demonstrates your hypothesis that all humanity shares a single mind. This mind, linked to the intelligence that defines our world, can make decisions and think as a single entity. The anomalies in your experiment are a small demonstration of that power, Dr. Weissmann."

Aman's eyes were so intense and penetrating that Weissmann swore he felt an electrical current. He tried to read the soul beneath those dark pupils, but they revealed nothing but darkness. "How do you know my name?"

"They told me about you," Aman said. "You have been brought here to establish whether or how I am connected to the events reshaping the world."

"Who are *they?*" Questions began rolling through Weissmann's mind. "Where do you come from? Why have so many died in a single night? *Tell me!*"

"I have very little time to explain," Aman said. "I need the resources of this base to finish my journey. To gain cooperation, I must persuade you and your commander of the urgency of my task in a very short time. You have prepared questions to determine what I know. Please proceed."

He was right—they were wasting precious time. "Yes, of course. I have just three questions." Weissmann moved to a chart table and set down his soft leather briefcase on its lighted surface. With his hands free, he removed his fat digital wrist-watch and handed it to Aman. "My first question is—why has my watch stopped working?"

He heard scoffing around the room, mocking the question. Weissmann anticipated their scorn. If Aman were a genie granting him three wishes, observers would assume he had just wasted his first.

"Quiet," Welch ordered.

Aman took the timepiece from the professor. "The battery's electrons no longer have sufficient velocity to pass current through the integrated circuit due to a rapid symmetrical disintegration of its quark mass," he said. "This phenomenon will continue to increase exponentially and affect larger power sources. The region's electrical grid is struggling to keep up with demand. By tomorrow morning, the network will lack sufficient current to power this base."

Restless whispers of concern rippled through the room.

"However, even if sufficient current were applied, this timepiece would not display the correct information." Aman returned the watch to Weissmann. "The resonance frequency of Caesium-133 that controls atomic clocks on which this timepiece is based no longer is nine billion cycles per second because of an expansion of the element's atomic radius."

"He might as well be speaking Aramaic," Osthoff said to Weissmann. "Do you know what he's talking about?"

"Yes, Madam Chancellor. You need not concern yourself with the details." Weissmann glanced at his watch's display and grinned. The timepiece functioned once again, showing what he believed to be the correct time. He held up his watch for Welch to see. "He did this."

While others strained to see, Welch said nothing, his expression unaltered, chiseled.

"What is your second question, professor?" Osthoff said. Weissmann knew the Chancellor wanted more substantial proof, something she could understand.

"Yes, of course." Weissmann snapped the watch back onto his wrist and removed several bundles of paper from his briefcase. He put on a pair of half-reading glasses and shuffled through the sheets until he found one in particular. Weissmann looked at Aman over his glasses. "Our global network of random event generators displays exactly seventeen deviations at seventeen-second intervals. The squared mean deviation across all recording stations every seventeen minutes is always one point seven. What message are we to infer from the number seventeen—the seventh prime number and the sum of the first four primes?"

He noted more puzzled glances around the room, but this time no one uttered a note of ridicule.

Aman extended his hand to Weissmann. "You also see examples in your own life, doctor. Please share that information."

"Yes. Yes." Weissmann selected another paper and ran a trembling finger across a row of numbers. "My phone number adds up to seventeen, and four of its components are divisible by seventeen. When I dial any number, it now takes seventeen seconds for someone to answer—not a second more or less. Seventeen days ago, I published my seventeenth paper on fluid mechanics. My name has seventeen characters."

Marshall held up his Seiko watch with its traditional hour and minute hands to show that it had stopped at seventeen minutes past twelve. Others also checked their watches.

"The sudden and inadvertent release of a powerful energy awakened a shared consciousness in a way we were not meant to experience until our brain's neocortex had evolved," Aman said. "This energy flux is attempting to fill the core of mathematics once riddled with holes of our uncertainty. A new algorithmic axiom is emerging based on a factor of seventeen, which we are not yet ready to understand. All of us can observe this phenomenon if we look for it. Humankind is destined to know what was once believed to be unknowable."

"Number games," Welch said. "Doesn't prove a thing."

Weissmann disagreed. He now understood the significance of these catastrophic world events. Dare he ask his final question?

"You don't look well, Dr. Weissmann," Osthoff said. She

placed a hand to her temple. "I must admit that all this has my head spinning."

Weissmann removed a handkerchief from an inside jacket pocket and wiped his glistening brow. "Yes, yes, I will continue. I must continue."

The subterranean temperature was rising, even this far underground. The climate units could no longer keep up with the bunker's rising heat and humidity.

"I have one final question." Weissmann removed his reading glasses and looked at Aman. "How long before Earth can no longer sustain life?"

Aman returned Weissmann's piercing stare. Despite his failing eyesight, Weissmann saw sorrow in Aman's vibrant, handsome face.

In a voice loud enough for everyone to hear, Aman said, "Eight days."

SHOCK WAVE

RESTLESS MURMURS OF DISBELIEF, alarm—even anger—spread across the control center. Weissmann knew Aman was right. All scientific evidence supported his statement.

Osthoff confronted Aman. "What do you mean? *Tell me.*"

Aman remained stoic, his eyes fixed on hers, and offered no elaboration. The room grew loud with concern.

"It's true, Madam Chancellor," Weissmann said over the growing clamor. "NASA's EOS satellite network is monitoring a catastrophic breakdown of the earth's atmosphere. By tomorrow, there will no longer be sufficient power to maintain communication with these orbiting observatories. We'll be blind to this catastrophe."

A woman sank to the floor and cried, "My girls...."

A man waved a book—a Bible. "For there shall arise a false prophet, and shall show great signs and wonders, and he shall deceive us."

Welch frowned. "I've heard enough. I'm taking this man back to the States."

Weissmann raised a hand. "*No!*"

"This is over," Welch said.

"I believe I'm still in charge of this inquiry," Weissmann said with a note of anger. "And there are still matters we need to know."

Welch's crimson face dripped with sweat. "I'm giving you five minutes to wrap up this nonsense."

Osthoff, her face flushed, appealed to Weissmann. "Why, professor? Why is this happening?"

"Earth's magnetic field is shrinking," Weissmann said. "The ozone layer above the poles is already ninety-seven percent depleted, and the lighter gases are escaping rapidly. An accelerated greenhouse effect is heating the surface. And we don't know why."

"A quantum slowdown of the planet's liquid outer iron core," Aman said. "Anyone can observe the shift in the atmosphere's electromagnetic radiation in the near-infrared spectrum, just as you have been observing with your thermal lenses."

Weissmann slipped a hand into the pocket of his tweed jacket and wrapped his fingers around the goggle-like glasses.

"As the earth's outer core continues to slow," Aman continued, "the decaying magnetosphere will no longer deflect the sun's radiation. Without intervention, eight days from now, at 6:42 a.m. local time, our world will no longer support life."

Weissmann scanned the room's blank faces. The shock of Aman's words was sinking in slowly.

The elevator door began closing. Specialist Moore stood at the controls, staring at Aman with wide, terrified eyes. She was closing the door, separating them.

"Stop her," Welch ordered. "None of this leaves this *goddamn* room."

The two closest Special Forces soldiers charged the door, but they weren't quick enough to block it. Specialist Moore was gone. Others, also wishing to leave, stormed the door.

"Call our security," the Colonel ordered.

"Can't get a signal out of here, sir," his lieutenant informed him.

"Forget it, Colonel," Marshall said. "She's not doing anything we all won't be doing soon enough."

Welch thrust a finger at the professor. "What about it, Weissmann? *Goddamnit*, is the man bullshitting us or what?"

"No, Colonel," Weissmann said. "His explanations are consistent with our understanding of these extraordinary events. He is correct in describing Earth's ghastly future and the end of humanity."

More questions erupted until the room roared. Weissmann

feared that unchecked panic could get people hurt. He felt powerless to calm them.

"Listen to me," Marshall shouted. He waved his hands to get everyone's attention. *"Listen to me."*

"Quiet," Welch shouted. "Everyone quiet."

A full minute passed before the room calmed, and all eyes settled on Marshall. Weissmann observed terrified looks on the faces around the room. Pure fear. Like his own.

"Aman's come a long way to try to prevent this catastrophe," Marshall said. "I don't know how he plans to intervene, but he must be allowed to finish what he set out to do." He extended a hand to Aman. "Tell them."

A wave of cautious whispering swept the room.

"Dr. Marshall is correct," Aman said. "I must complete my journey by nightfall tomorrow. If I am successful in closing the breach, the damage done to the world can regenerate. If I fail, the earth is doomed."

Shouting erupted, demanding immediate action.

Osthoff asked Aman, "Where do you need to go?"

The room quickly quieted to hear more.

"My journey will end at 30° 54' 0" North by 53° 19' 60" East," he said.

Osthoff turned to a female technician seated at a console. "Bring up those coordinates on this table."

Marshall handed the technician his wrinkled envelope with writing on it. The top of the chart table brightened when she began keying in the coordinates.

A topographical map of Iran appeared from an altitude of 200 miles. Weissmann saw no cities, villages, or other populated areas within five hundred square miles of those coordinates. What was Aman looking for?

Welch stepped up to the table. "Shiite territory. A dangerous militant training region."

Osthoff joined the Colonel. "Closer, please," she requested.

The map zoomed in on the coordinates from an altitude of 2,000 feet. There were no labels or landmarks, just contour lines. Weissmann watched the colonel closely. Welch's keen scrutiny of the map suggested he knew something about this region.

"Show me a satellite image," Welch said. The topographical map disappeared, replaced by a satellite image from the same altitude. A detailed photo showed a barren desert with very few features.

"Tilt this ninety degrees," Welch said.

The image tilted ninety degrees to reveal elevations in rough three dimensions.

"Rotate 360 degrees," Welch instructed.

The photo rotated around several hilltops. Weissmann saw nothing to distinguish this particular stretch of desert from the desolate land around it—except for a lone road that appeared to end abruptly in the sand.

"Aman, are you certain these are the right coordinates?" Osthoff asked. She turned to the technician operating the screen. "Recheck your coordinates."

Aman stepped to the table between Welch and the chancellor. "The coordinates are correct." He placed a finger on a shallow hill. "I must be at this point tomorrow."

"But there's nothing there," Osthoff said.

"A powerful energy portal appeared five days ago," Aman said.

"But are you certain of its exact location?" Weissmann asked.

"An intense wave of electromagnetic radiation is emanating from that point." Aman pressed a palm against the display. The satellite map zoomed out to an altitude that showed most of the Middle East. He placed a finger on a barren area in southern Iran. "A sudden release of massive kinetic energy at this point five days ago sent a shock wave along this fault line that destroyed scores of villages in its wake."

Weissmann looked up from the map in disbelief. "A nuclear detonation."

All eyes turned to the colonel for an answer. Welch's jaw tightened. "An earthquake."

The professor knew Welch was lying. Top secret. Of course,

there would be denial, even in the face of a great disaster. *Humanity did this to itself.*

"A high-energy particle accelerator," Aman said.

Osthoff whirled while the others looked on in surprise. *"What?"*

"Yes, I'm afraid it's true," Weissman said. "For three years, a U.S. security task force monitored the construction of a circular tunnel beneath one of Iran's most desolate areas. The scientific community learned of this ambitious project only four months ago. The accelerator has been kept a carefully guarded secret from the world for national security purposes."

"Why on Earth did Iran build such a thing?" Osthoff said.

"To recreate the Big Bang," Marshall said. "Isn't that what particle accelerators do?"

"They can do other things besides smashing particles to probe the limits of physics as we know it," Weissman said. "Iran paid enormous sums to some of the best minds in the world to conceive and construct an ultra-high-energy electron-beam accelerator as a quick way of enriching weapons-grade plutonium. Within months, they could create enough to build scores of nuclear warheads." Weissman shook his head. "The risks from what they're doing are unfathomable. Theoretically, this accelerator is capable of producing cataclysmic antimatter. And, if superstring theory is accurate, it has the potential to create black holes, the most destructive objects in the universe."

"A micro black hole created from this process produced an irrotational plasma vortex," Aman said. "An intense gravitational field absorbed the elementary particles into a void, and the rapid spin of the black hole produced a vortex. The accelerator burned a quantum tunnel through space-time."

"Impossible," Weissman said. "A vortex such as you describe would disappear in a microsecond."

"The enormous pressure from the black hole coupled with a highly destructive gravitational wave is too strong to allow the vortex to collapse," Aman said. "The interdimensional radiation pouring through that portal is incompatible with our planet, causing chaos and destruction. This will be the end of us all without immediate action."

More gasps and whispers spread through the room.

"And you say you can fix this?" Osthoff asked.

Aman removed his hands from the chart table and static erased the satellite image. Other screens around the center went blank. "Our world is in great danger, and it is imperiled further the more we delay swift action," he said. "Each minute spent here discussing this lessens my chances."

"You will need weeks to get to Iran by ground and sea," Osthoff said.

"I must fly," Aman said.

"That's out of the question," Weissmann said. "Metal compounds continue to break down. Even an aircraft's titanium components are rusting. No engine will hold up during that flight. Your aircraft would experience a catastrophic failure. That is if you could even get one off the ground."

"The equipment will need modification," Aman said. "All mechanical components must be treated continuously during flight."

"This is bullshit," Welch said. "This man is *not* going to Iran. I'm taking him back stateside for interrogation. Those are my orders from the Joint Chiefs."

"Colonel—" Osthoff began.

"Wake up, people," Welch said. "You don't seriously believe a word this man is telling you. There is no vortex. His story is pure fantasy. He is not going to change the world's climate and prevent a global catastrophe by tomorrow night." He thrust a finger at Aman. "He is a very clever con man on the run. He's conning us to help him escape to a remote corner of the world where he can hide from authorities."

"I disagree," Weissmann said. "These events are real. Even the most hardened skeptics must give Aman the benefit of the doubt. Our lives depend on immediate action."

"Colonel Welch," Osthoff said firmly, "as Germany's chancellor, I will tell you who and what you can and cannot remove from my country."

Welch ignored her. He turned to his Special Forces team

and ordered, "Escort this man out of here."

None of the soldiers made a move to carry out their commander's directive.

"*Now,*" the Colonel demanded.

The squad's team leader snapped to attention. "No, sir."

Welch's cold eyes narrowed. "I'll have you all court-martialed." He reached inside his jacket and withdrew a Glock pistol.

The Special Forces squad lead directed his assault rifle at the Colonel.

Welch froze, holding the handgun at his side. The standoff shocked the room into silence.

"Think about what you're doing," Welch told his soldiers. "You will be executed for treason."

"No one's going to be executed," Marshall said. He held up Krueger's chrome-plated revolver for all to see. "Everyone stop and take a deep breath. Enough talk. It's time we do something about all this."

"What do you think you're doing?" Welch demanded.

Marshall, his gun pointed, relieved the colonel of his sidearm. "If anyone tries to interfere with what Aman needs to do, they'll go through me first. And if I understand the process, I won't get purged when I defend myself—at least I hope that's how it works." He said to the soldier, "You can stop pointing that thing, son."

The soldier raised the muzzle of this assault rifle. Marshall handed over Welch's sidearm to the center's officer in charge.

"Thank you, Dr. Marshall," Osthoff said. She made a point of giving Welch a glare of repugnance before turning to Aman. "Tell me what you need to complete your journey. My staff is at your disposal."

"I must be underway no later than five hours from now," Aman said. He approached Welch, his hand extended. "I need your help, Colonel. Your military has the equipment and the technicians I require."

Welch made no move to accept any alliance. His face remained stolid and expressionless.

"For God's sake, Colonel," Weissmann implored. "Work with us. You can appropriate the resources he needs."

When Welch didn't move, Aman reached over and grasped the Colonel's hand. Welch gasped in utter astonishment, and his expression widened with a look of profound wonder. His legs buckled. He attempted to ease into a rolling technician's chair, missed it, and landed on the floor on his back, flailing like a drunk. The Colonel's wide, unblinking eyes stared up at the ceiling while the center's staff stepped around him.

Weissmann knelt and helped Welch into a sitting position. He placed a finger on the Colonel's neck for a pulse. Strong and rapid. "Tell me what you just experienced."

Welch's eyes darted about in bewilderment. His breathing quickened, and he appeared incapable of speech. Finally, he gasped, "So ... real...."

"What did you see?" Weissmann pressed.

Welch's far-off gaze was full of dread. "I experienced my death at the hands of a mob—as the world ended."

BLUEPRINTS

"SAMANTHA."

Samantha jerked up in her bed and stared unblinking into the darkness, disoriented. Had someone spoken to her? Her heart beat triple-time. *Where am I?* Memory fragments seeped back. Single bed. Germany. Nuclear-proof bunker.

"Who's in here?" she said.

No answer.

She snatched her phone off the bed's nightstand for its light, but it wouldn't turn on. *Damn battery.*

"Figures."

The voice came again. Pleading. "Don't leave him, Samantha."

She gasped. A woman sat at the edge of her bed, a woman that glowed. Her long white hair flowed down her back, and she wore a white robe. Samantha recognized the woman from the old farmhouse—Aman's wife.

"Sheema?" Samantha gasped.

"Don't leave him inside," Sheema said, her voice desperate. "My husband is a stubborn man, and he will keep you at a distance for your safety. But don't leave him. Please. If he remains inside, we will not see each other for a very long time."

Astonished, Samantha stared at the woman's natural beauty and kind eyes. She wanted to know more—much more. "I don't understand what you want me to do. What sort of place is he going to? If he stays in where?"

The room darkened, and Sheema was gone.

"Damnit, Sheema? Stop running away. Tell me what's going

on. Please."

A full minute of silence passed while she watched and listened. Nothing.

Samantha untangled herself from the sheets and stood up from the bed wearing only a sleeveless T-shirt soaked with sweat. *Goddamn, it's hot in here.* Blood rushed from her head when she stood, leaving her dizzy.

Samantha snapped on the room's harsh overhead light and grabbed her wristwatch from the nightstand. She couldn't activate its blank face—damn battery.

Samantha considered crawling back into bed to see if Sheema would return. But that probably wouldn't work, she decided. Besides, she was too wired to go back asleep. The visit left her with a terrible feeling. As her head cleared, she couldn't shake a sense of foreboding that Aman—maybe all of them—wouldn't survive the next twenty-four hours. She needed to find out what was going on. She needed to find Marshall.

Samantha slid on her jeans and a *Universität Würzburg* sweatshirt she found folded in a drawer and pulled on her boots. She stepped to the dresser's mirror and pushed back her unwieldy curtain of hair until she declared herself presentable.

Grabbing her tote bag, she slipped into the hallway with its stark fluorescent lighting. Absolute silence. Where was everybody? For a terrifying moment, she feared they had left her behind. They wouldn't do that, would they? Why wouldn't they?

To Samantha's surprise, the elevator's door at the end of the hallway stood open as though waiting for her. She jogged the length of the hallway and stepped inside. A couple of twisted wires dangled beneath the control panel.

Without her touching anything, the door closed, and the car began rising. Her mind stirred with doubts about leaving this level. What if leaving got her into serious trouble? When the door opened, would armed soldiers threaten her with weapons—or worse?

The car stopped, and Samantha drew in a deep breath and held it. The door slid open. Samantha looked out at a command center with people dressed in uniform and civilian clothing, some conferring, others scurrying about as though in the middle of a crisis. A war room. Overhead widescreen monitors were dark, as were most of the banks of electronics.

Samantha let out her breath in relief and stepped off the car. The temperature was higher up here. She walked among the staff, searching for a familiar face. No one greeted her, but no one seemed to object to her being up here either.

Two men in uniform brushed past her. "He's going to kill himself," one man said to the other. "He'll never get that thing off the ground. Even if he manages to get airborne, the flight won't last two minutes."

Samantha saw Chancellor Osthoff leading an entourage through a double glass doorway and down the corridor beyond. To her right, a white-haired man wearing a tweed jacket stood at one of two large lighted tables. He was locked in a heated exchange with several geeky types.

To Samantha's relief, she spotted Aman at another table, surrounded by military types. He looked anxious, his dark, thick hair tousled. Blueprints of a fat four-engine airplane were spread out before him. A U.S. officer with a buzz cut sat to his right, sipping from a coffee mug and nodding. He looked exhausted. Or was he ill? His name tag said "Welch."

Samantha moved to the table and stood next to a chunky man in overalls. He reeked of cigars. "What's going on?" she asked him. The stocky man said nothing as if she wasn't there.

Aman glanced up at her. "I want you to stay below. We are very short of time and cannot afford distractions."

"I saw Sheema again," she said.

Aman's eyes betrayed a curiosity.

"She's concerned about you," Samantha said.

"She worries too much about me."

"Why is she worried, Aman?" Samantha asked. "What are you planning to do with this airplane?"

Aman didn't answer her. Instead, he returned his attention to the blueprints and said to the men gathered around the table, "Your new C-130J will no longer fly. Its avionics are useless.

However, your C-130H, built in 1968, uses analog equipment fourteen generations removed from current electronics. That aircraft will prove more stable. However, I will require the extra thrust of the modern Allison turboprop engines. They must be remounted on this older frame. Their six-blade composite propellers will need less treatment during flight."

The chunky man in overalls bit down on an unlit cigar. His tanned and leathered face smacked of working outdoors for a living. "It's your show," he said. "I'll have those engines changed out by morning."

"That is unacceptable, Mr. Malone," Aman said. "You must finish mounting those engines no later than four hours from now."

"That's impossible—"

"Employ eight teams," Aman said, his tone firm.

"Manpower isn't the issue, for chrissake. I'll need half the night to figure out how to rewire the engines and route the fluid lines. Maybe longer. I'm not a wizard, sir."

Aman unrolled a schematic that showed a cross-section of an aircraft engine. He studied the diagram for a moment, his piercing eyes darting from point to point. "May I borrow a writing instrument?"

Officer Welch produced a pen from beneath his jacket. "Here."

Aman took the pen and began marking the schematic with its felt point—adding lines, labels, values, and legends. His pen movements were brisk and confident and faster than Samantha ever imagined a drafter could work. His penmanship was flawless, nearly typeset quality—no one would misunderstand his notes. He must have already worked out these plans in painstaking detail with a team of engineers, she concluded. Didn't he?

Finished, Aman presented the blueprint to the man in overalls. Malone, his brow furrowed, grabbed the large sheet of paper and studied it while chewing the end of his cigar. Aman returned the pen to the colonel.

"Very unconventional," Malone said, studying the blueprint. "But will it work?" When Aman didn't answer, he addressed him in a curt tone. "How in the hell do you know this will work?"

"The solution is written into the Records," Aman said, his voice edgy, as though he didn't like explaining.

The engineer scowled. "*Records?* What records?"

Samantha winced. This guy wasn't getting it and wasting time. Where was his faith in Aman?

"The Records detail what you and any number of other experts know," Aman said. "I can read it quite clearly. You can, too, if you open your mind to the possibility."

Malone pointed his unlit cigar at Aman. "You're scaring the shit out of me, mister. Maybe I don't know how to make this engine work on the old frame. Maybe my goddamn record is wrong." He tossed the blueprints onto the table with a scowl. "*Jesus*—we may not have the engineering ability to get you off the ground."

"We will work with what we have, Mr. Malone," Aman said.

"I'm assembling a crew," Colonel Welch said. "I know two pilots who have experience flying in severe weather. A navigator and a couple of flight engineers are standing by."

"They will not be necessary," Aman said. "Nick Judge is quite capable."

"One man?" Welch scoffed. "You'll need a couple of hands just to monitor the flight systems."

"I must keep the crew to an absolute minimum," Aman said. "I am taking only the four who came here with me." He looked at Samantha. "I have complete trust in them."

A woman in military fatigues, holding a clipboard, appeared behind Aman and said over his shoulder, "We've located every item on your list except for the Makita portable electro-mechanical breaker. But I can get you an industrial hydraulic pneumatic drill."

"I need the Makita for its size and portability," Aman said. "You will find one at a depot in Arnstein belonging to a company named Mainz. Please hurry."

The procurement sergeant jotted down his instructions and

vanished.

"Aman," Samantha said, "where are you going with all this?" When he didn't answer, she raised her voice. "I want to know what you're planning."

A gentle hand came down on her shoulder. Samantha turned to see Marshall holding a mug of coffee with cream. She felt relieved and excited to see him.

"You look like you could use some caffeine after your nap." Marshall led her away from the table, away from Aman.

"You're a godsend, David." She accepted the mug, grateful, and then admitted, "I'm a distraction up here, aren't I?"

Marshall gave her a disarming grin. He wouldn't stop staring at her, which made her self-conscious. Clean-shaven and groomed, he wore a pair of khaki slacks and a dark green polo shirt too large for him. He looked younger and more handsome. She wanted to put her arms around him right here.

"Sheema visited me again," she said. "Her voice out of nowhere gave me a helluva a scare."

Marshall looked at her, curious, and she wondered if he believed her.

"She's afraid of something, afraid for Aman's safety," Samantha said. "She expects trouble. I tried to tell him."

"What kind of trouble?"

"That's just it, David—I wish I knew. Where are the others?"

"Nick's still sleeping," Marshall said. "Aman doesn't want him disturbed for any reason. Kirby's topside trying out a backhoe that Aman plans to bring along. I didn't realize Kirby could operate heavy equipment."

She bobbed her head. "He was a construction foreman before becoming a deputy." She frowned. "Why does Aman need a backhoe?"

Marshall shrugged. "I haven't a clue. He's too busy to let anyone in on his plans."

Samantha put a hand on his arm. "David, would you please tell me what's going on."

"A lot happened while you were napping," Marshall said. "Where do I start?"

• • •

Weissmann stepped into Aman's path as he left the chart table.

"May I have a word?" Weissmann asked with what he hoped would pass for a blend of academic authority and collegiality.

"Walk with me, doctor," Aman said. "I must meet a friend."

"Of course." Weissmann followed Aman across the center in silence, his hands trembling with nerves. When they reached the elevator, Weissmann gathered the courage to say, "I must go with you."

Aman stepped into the lift car and pressed the button for the top level. "That is not possible, Dr. Weissmann."

The door began closing. Weissmann bolted into the car and grabbed Aman's arm harder than he intended. He realized his desperation was overtaking common sense and released him.

The car began rising.

"This is very important to me," Weissmann said. "I can help you."

"You will remain here," Aman said.

"But—"

"For your safety." Aman leveled his penetrating eyes at him. "I cannot protect you."

Weissmann hesitated. *Protect me from what?* "If you can see the future," he said, "tell me if you will succeed."

"There are many futures, Dr. Weissmann. None are certain. Each has its consequences."

The car glided to a halt at the top level, and the door opened to the bunker's hangar-like loading area. Aman stepped off the car and walked briskly across the concrete bay. Weissmann hurried after him. Workers in hardhats were stacking crates on pallets while a large man worked a backhoe on the opposite side. The air felt thick and damp. The blast doors stood open, offering a dismal view of the torrential rainfall outside.

A frail-looking man with a white beard stood in the center of the area with two soldiers on either side of him. Workers and military types hurried past them. The elderly man wore thick glasses, a plain black hat, and a rain-soaked black suit that appeared too large for his lean frame. A well-traveled leather satchel, dripping wet, hung from his left hand.

Aman greeted the man with an embrace as though they were kin. The man wept.

Weissmann's eyes narrowed. He recalled seeing this man at the base's demolished gates upon their arrival. The MP wouldn't let him inside the compound.

Aman released the man and said to Weissmann, "This is Jacob Cohen. He traveled a great distance to find me."

Jacob, his face dripping with rainwater, fumbled to open the buckle on his dull leather case. He slipped a boney hand inside the satchel and withdrew a wooden box held together with twin metal straps. The box looked medieval, possibly Celtic. Weissmann very much wished to examine it.

"This belongs to you," Jacob said.

Aman took the box and held it with both hands with special care, as though it were sacred. He closed his eyes. A moment later, he opened them with a smile. "Thank you, Jacob Cohen. The world owes you a great debt."

A debt that may never be repaid. Weissmann's gaze returned to the hard rain outside the open blast doors. A plane couldn't take off in this weather, and conditions were deteriorating each hour. *He's too late.* Despite everyone's best efforts—despite Jacob Cohen finding him with that box—Aman's plan would never get off the ground.

DOWNPOUR

A VOICE SNAPPED Nick out of a deep sleep: "Time to go."

Nick wasn't ready to go anywhere, and he let his dream about flying a recreational ultralight reclaim him.

But the voice came again, this time its tone sharp. "Get your ass up, Nick. We're leaving."

A cruel overhead light came on, striking Nick like a hard slap. A hand came down on his shoulder and shook him until his eyes stayed open.

Nick rolled onto his back and squinted at Marshall standing over him. "What time is it?"

"Seven p.m., give or take," Marshall said. "I can't find a working clock."

"*Shit.*" Nick threw off the sheets and ran a hand over his cropped hair. "I overslept."

Marshall opened the dresser drawers one by one and rummaged through clothing. "Aman wanted you to sleep for as long as possible. He's with Kirby at the hangar with your aircraft. He needs you there, pronto. By the way, the weather sucks."

That got Nick's attention. He stood and stretched his arms behind his back until the cartilage cracked. "What's with the weather?"

"Rain."

Nick shrugged. "I've flown through rain lots of times."

"Not like this," Marshall said. "We're in the middle of tornadic cells, each squall line worse than the next. We're getting a good four inches every hour."

"*Jesus.* Aman can't leave now. We'll need to wait it out."

Marshall stacked two pairs of thick athletic socks and a Beatles baseball cap on the dresser. "Sorry, Nick. The weather is going to get a lot worse."

. . .

Leighton Airfield

Marshall figured they were still about a quarter-mile from the base's airfield. He sat in the back of a Chevy Suburban with Samantha, their hands locked. Nick, in the front passenger seat, stared grim-faced at the rain hammering their windshield. The young lieutenant from Colonel Welch's staff drove them capably through a torrential downpour in a vehicle that had become increasingly prone to stalling. Sundown was a half-hour away, but the thick, murky green cloud cover forced an early dusk.

Lightning struck the road ahead, accompanied by a car-rattling explosion of thunder that made them all jump. Marshall reached over Samantha's shoulder and pulled her closer. His nerves were frayed. Her warmth and subtle flower fragrance helped calm him.

"Maybe this will blow over," Samantha said.

Marshall shook his head. "A much more intense system is heading our way."

"I've seen mission-critical military flights grounded in weather better than this," Nick said.

Marshall understood Nick's apprehension. This was the sort of evening you stayed home—and prayed you didn't get flooded out.

Marshall touched Samantha's chin and looked into her eyes. They looked as vibrant as they had back in her room. "I want you to stay behind."

She looked down. "No. He needs me."

"You don't have to—"

"I'm going with him." Her tone was firm, and he knew it was pointless to argue.

Marshall heard shouting and leaned against the passenger window for a look. He was surprised to see people, all civilians, making their way down the road in the same direction. Scores of them. Where are they going? The driving wind and rain didn't deter them. Some carried umbrellas, some wore full-body ponchos, and some had no rain protection at all.

Marshall spotted a few wielding chains and one taking home-run-size practice swings with a metal baseball bat. Several others carried rifles. He could hear yelling and screaming all around them. A liquor bottle hit their hood and shattered.

Samantha spun in her seat to take in the scene around her. "This is freaking me out."

Marshall didn't like this either. He disliked crowds, especially rowdy ones, and he felt anxious as the mob thickened and the shouting grew louder.

Nick turned to check the road behind them. "Is some sort of evacuation underway?"

"I don't think so," Marshall said. "The chancellor ordered a curfew."

Marshall spotted floodlights ahead. As their vehicle approached the airfield entrance, the forest of people became too thick to drive through. The crowd had knocked down a chain-link fence and crawled over the mesh to get into the field. The lieutenant kept hitting the horn between mutters of profanity while working the accelerator to keep the engine from stalling.

Samantha put a hand to her cheek. "I get it. They're coming here for *Aman.*"

Of course. Marshall shifted in his seat, trying to calm his growing unease. "*Damnit!* This flight was supposed to be secret."

"News travels fast when the world's ending," Nick said.

Marshall let out a nervous huff he tried to pass for laughter. It didn't.

Several MPs appeared in front of them and waved their SUV into a gauntlet created by two solid lines of soldiers, their hands locked to form a human passageway. The SUV passed between them. Marshall saw hundreds of people gathering on the airfield beyond.

When their truck reached the hangar, Marshall rolled down his window, amazed by what he saw inside. The Lockheed Hercules C-130H cargo hauler was much bigger than he imagined. A network of cables and hoses hung from it like umbilical cords. Dozens of men and women in overalls worked beneath each of its twin high wings, while others wearing ear protectors stood up top, inspecting the engines. A company of soldiers pushed the arriving pedestrians off the runway.

The lieutenant drove the Suburban inside the hangar and jerked it to a halt beside a fueling tank truck.

Marshall watched the mechanics and technicians scurrying with final preparations. *Impressive.*

"I've never seen anything like this," Samantha said. "It's scary."

Nick scrambled out of the vehicle. A U.S. soldier in combat fatigues opened the rear passenger door for Samantha. She slid out, her expression betraying her uncertainties. Her strained expression mirrored Marshall's own doubts.

The lieutenant driver reached over the back seat and offered his hand to Marshall. "I'm glad I'm not going with you guys," he said. "Take care of yourselves."

"We'll try not to do anything foolish." Marshall grasped the lieutenant's hand before joining Samantha and Nick outside. Each of them carried a single cloth bag containing grooming items and whatever extra clothing they could find back in the command center.

It was loud in here. The sky pulsed with lightning. The air felt oppressively hot and humid, and the hard rain pounding the hangar's high metal roof sounded like a field of snare drums. Marshall could hear little else. Sweat rolled down his back, and his palms were sweating.

Nick pointed to the rear of the aircraft. Marshall spotted Kirby driving a forklift with a load of pallets up the plane's rear loading ramp.

"You've flown this kind of aircraft before, haven't you, Nick?" Marshall asked.

Nick waved away Marshall's concern. "Piece of cake. The hard part is getting her off the ground—and back down."

Marshall scowled. "So you keep saying."

He spotted Aman hurrying across the hangar toward them, leading an entourage of officers and civilians. When Aman reached them, he extended his hands to Marshall and Samantha, who each gripped a hand like a prayer group. Marshall felt strong confidence and energy in his touch, which helped reassure him.

"Allow me to present my friend Jacob Cohen," Aman said with a nod toward a frail-looking elderly man with a white beard and dressed in a dark suit and hat.

Marshall cocked his head, curious. "Are you coming with us?"

"I cannot," Jacob said. "I need to start making my way home. Marti must be worried sick."

"What's the plan, Aman?" Samantha asked.

"There will be a break in the storm in fourteen minutes," Aman said to the group gathered around him. "That window will allow us eight minutes to depart before another intense storm cell reaches this area. We cannot fly above it. Our lives will depend on our ability to stay ahead of the new weather line."

Jesus help us. Marshall watched the mechanics, still racing around the aircraft. "The plane isn't ready."

"The engineers will continue to inspect this aircraft until we are underway," Aman said. "They do not trust my instructions."

Samantha gestured toward the growing crowd assembling in front of the hangar. "What are they doing here? What do they want?"

"Most are friends who wish us success," Aman said. "Others are frightened."

Marshall felt his back muscles tighten. *And pissed off and hostile.*

Chancellor Osthoff joined them. She brought with her an older man in an officer's uniform, bearing a clergy insignia. "Aman," the Chancellor said, "it would mean a great deal to these people if you spoke to them."

"Perhaps someone else, Madam Chancellor," Aman said.

"This crowd should be dispersed, not entertained," Marshall said. "Besides, no one would hear him."

"This airbase has an oversized siren system that will work for voice," the clergyman said.

"Please, Aman," Osthoff urged. "Everyone is frightened. These people are desperate to understand what is happening. In this important moment, please offer them hope."

Marshall watched for Aman's reaction. He expected him to turn her down—for everyone's *goddamned* safety.

He was astonished when Aman bowed and said, "I will speak to them as a favor for your invaluable assistance."

Osthoff, smiling broadly, hugged him. "Thank you, Aman."

"I would be happy to translate for you," the clergyman said.

"That will not be necessary," Aman said. "They will understand me when I address them in my original tongue."

The clergyman stared at him, puzzled. Marshall glanced at Samantha, who returned a skeptical look of her own. Osthoff, ignoring his statement, led the cleric away to prepare.

The storm intensified, the rain falling in thick sheets with gale-force winds that shook the hangar. Marble-size hail fell with it. The pounding on the roof was deafening.

"Are you sure about speaking to them?" Marshall shouted to Aman over the downpour.

"I will be brief." Aman faced Nick. "Please start preflight procedures. In seven minutes, throttle all engines for taxi. And tell the workers to withdraw."

Nick, wide-eyed and flushed, drew in a deep breath as though it were his last. He looked scared shitless. Marshall could read his deep reservations, which he knew the young pilot would never articulate. Nick was a doer, not a naysayer. Besides, there was no turning back. They had this one chance.

"You got it, Chief." Nick removed the Beatles baseball cap from his carry-on bag and jammed it onto his head for luck. "Let's get this band in the air."

Nick bounced up the mobile steps two at a time and disappeared inside the aircraft. The plane's rear hydraulic cargo door whined shut beneath the plane's high-mounted tail.

Marshall saw the clergyman setting a microphone with a stand on a small portable podium inside the hanger. Finished, he hurried off. Everything looked ready.

Marshall placed a hand on Aman's shoulder. "Looks like you're on."

BLASPHEMY

SAMANTHA GUESSED AT least 2,000 people had gathered outside the hangar, with a steady stream still flowing onto the airfield. Aman watched the crowd grow, his eyes continually moving. He seemed reluctant to proceed with his address, and she didn't blame him. The soldiers had done an exceptional job containing the unexpected multitude. Still, the situation frightened her. Men and women in military ponchos, their arms and hands locked, formed a barrier in the rain outside the hangar. In front of them, soldiers with rifles stood every ten feet, facing the crowd. The hangar's perimeter appeared secure.

"You don't have to do this," Samantha said.

Aman reached for her hand. "I will be quick. Come with me."

"I'll come with you," Marshall said.

Aman waved him back. "Just her."

Samantha gave Marshall an apologetic frown while Aman led her across the hangar. Facing so many people intimidated her. She hated public speaking. A terrifying thought occurred to her: *I hope he doesn't expect me to speak for him. I can't even make a toast!*

A small wooden platform, large enough for one person, sat inside the hangar. A lone microphone on a stand stood on top. Samantha expelled an incredulous huff. Aman's short address could very well become a historical event—if anyone survived to read about it.

"I hope you don't want me to say something," Samantha said.

"No," Aman said. "I need you to watch the assembly. And be alert for trouble."

"What will you say to them?"

"I will tell them what I know," he said, adding, "or as much as I can in four minutes."

When the two reached the platform, the crowd quieted under the driving rain. Countless eyes watched them with anxious expectation. Samantha heard only the rainfall, hard and steady, hammering the hanger's iron roof and the tarmac.

Osthoff, standing to the side of the hangar, waved her hand as a signal to begin.

Aman stepped onto the box and stood before the microphone stand, adjusted too low for him. He slid the mic from its sleeve and brought it to his lips. Samantha winced at a momentary squeal of feedback from the loudspeaker horns. When Aman spoke, his voice boomed across the base like thunder, masking the drumming rain.

"*Grüße an meine Freunde,*" Aman began. "If I can leave this airfield tonight, my journey will end in a desert region near Ab Ambar 2,300 miles from here where a dangerous machine lays buried. This machine opened a tunnel to a violent dimension whose unrestrained energy is destroying the Great Field—a Divine intelligence that protects and nurtures all life on this planet. It holds the blueprint of our existence—the total of our experience in this realm. It is a field beyond the physical that governs all things." Aman extended a hand toward Samantha. "She calls it The Fold. It is the fabric of life itself."

Samantha's throat swelled with emotion.

"When humanity lost the Wisdom of our ancestors eons ago, we became blind to our true nature," Aman continued. "The seeds sown here so many years ago would allow the human race to shed the ignorance that caused fear for countless centuries and allow us to blossom into humankind's next and most significant evolutionary order. In time, we would learn to manifest from the Source to provide for all, fulfilling our every need and desire—and more. When we awaken to higher states of consciousness and vastly increased intelligence, Earth's masterworks and of all the heavens and beyond would belong to us all. Our days would fill with wonder and our nights of joy and peace."

As Aman spoke, the rain lessened as the intense squall line passed, just as he predicted. Samantha glanced skyward and thought she glimpsed a dim star through the parting dark clouds.

"All that is in peril," Aman said. "To advance its arsenal, one rogue nation carelessly allowed this machine to create a dangerous vortex that is ripping apart the Great Field with catastrophic consequences. Safeguards to repair and stop this sudden and uncontrolled release of conflicting radiation have thus far failed. Our world is in a desperate state, and we are all in grave danger. Our bodies are changing much more rapidly than planned. What should have been a purposeful transition to universal love and enlightenment is deteriorating into chaos. The continuum of this planet is in serious jeopardy."

Samantha scanned the crowd's solemn faces. The multitude listened to his every word, and, despite language differences, they all appeared to understand him. She spotted Jacob Cohen standing near the hangar's entrance. Their eyes met, and he offered her a thoughtful nod.

"I have been given the task of repairing this breach and restoring balance." Aman extended a hand toward the C130 cargo transport behind him. "It is my hope that this retired aircraft with all its fallibilities will allow me to complete my journey." He held out his hand to Samantha. "I have chosen this woman and three others to accompany me. They are humanity's last hope. Together we must close the breach by tomorrow at this time. Or everything we have achieved as a species will mean nothing. All will be lost forever."

Restless movement and murmurs swept through the assembly.

A man shouted, *"Blasphemy!"* Others began hooting and jeering.

Before Aman could respond, the aircraft's four engines powered up with a roar that shook the hangar. Nick had begun his taxiing sequence. The rain slowed to a drizzle. Samantha observed many in the crowd shifting anxiously.

Aman dropped the microphone to the podium floor, producing a gunshot-like bang that reverberated across the airfield. He stepped from the tiny platform and grasped Samantha's hand.

"You're done?" she asked. When he didn't answer, she added, "Of course you are."

They hurried back toward the aircraft while Aman continued to scan their surroundings. They hadn't gone far when frantic shouting erupted from the crowd behind them—unintelligible questions. Others began applauding, a sound that grew thunderous. The growing clamor frightened Samantha. She could feel the panic. The hysteria. She glanced over her shoulder and saw soldiers struggling to hold back a surge of movement. *Dear God—*

"*Aman,*" Chancellor Osthoff shouted, racing after him. "*Wait.*"

Colonel Welch led a group of officers behind her.

"We're leaving," Samantha hollered back. The two reached Marshall standing at the bottom of the aircraft's staircase.

"Aman," Osthoff said, catching up to them. "I must know something—"

Marshall stepped in front of her, a hand raised. "He can't answer any questions now. Our timing is critical."

Osthoff's intense expression betrayed her desperate desire for answers. "Aman, please. I must know what will happen to us if—"

"If I am successful, we will have much time to talk," Aman said. "If I am not, none of this will matter."

Hundreds broke through the barrier of soldiers like water from a burst levee and rushed toward the aircraft. Others fought to restrain them. The encounter escalated into a skirmish of wildly exchanged blows.

Aman faced Colonel Welch and said firmly, "This runway must be cleared immediately."

Welch roared at his team, "Get these people off the base.

Clear this runway *now!*"

His lieutenant began blowing a whistle and shouting orders in the face of the onrushing multitude. A company of soldiers ran to assist with crowd control.

A rifle shot rang out over the din. Samantha watched in horror as Colonel Welch collapsed onto his knees, blood bubbling from his lips. Welch looked up at Aman, his eyes wide with shock before he collapsed facedown onto the concrete.

Aman turned and began climbing the staircase.

More gunfire rang out, more screaming. Sirens blared across the airfield.

Marshall followed Samantha as she raced up the steps after Aman. Two soldiers with rifles stood at the bottom, blocking further access.

Samantha passed a man climbing up the side of the staircase. *"Take me with you!"* he screamed. A woman sat on the concrete below him, sobbing uncontrollably.

A bullet struck the wing above Samantha's head, just missing an external fuel tank. She stared, dumbstruck. *A bullet hole in the wing!* Aman continued without pause and entered the plane.

"Keep moving!" Marshall shouted behind her.

Samantha reached the doorway and dashed inside. Marshall followed.

Kirby watched the chaos below. "Holy Mary. What did he say to get them so riled up?"

Samantha glanced down the staircase. People had crushed past the guards at the bottom and were scrambling up the steps toward them. She heard more gunshots.

"How do we move the staircase away?" Samantha asked, her voice bordering on panic.

"They pull it away from the bottom," Marshall said. "Doesn't look like that's going to happen."

"Close the door," Aman said. The urgency in his voice sent a shiver through Samantha.

Marshall helped Kirby secure the fuselage door.

"Let's see them get through this," Kirby said.

They heard the crash of the staircase falling onto its side.

Samantha breathed easier, relieved.

She moved among pallets of cargo containers tied down to the floor's roller tracks. A yellow John Deere backhoe earthmover, attached to an armored Humvee with massive tires, sat in the center of the cargo bay. Bulky spare fuel tanks were mounted on both sides of the fuselage. *Please, God, don't let a bullet hit one of these tanks.*

Aman's voice shot across the bay. "Strap in."

Samantha found three fold-down seats along the far wall, the exact number they needed, assuming that Aman stayed in the cockpit with Nick. Substantial metal struts had been welded to the airframe around them for extra support.

Marshall and Kirby each scrambled into a seat on either side of her.

"Forgive me my trespasses," Kirby said, fumbling with his strap.

Samantha restrained herself with a reinforced shoulder and waist harness. Finished, she exchanged glances with Marshall, who looked unbecomingly pale.

"You don't look so hot," she said.

Marshall stretched his lips into a forced grin. "Is it too late to back out?"

Samantha touched his hand and tried to sound encouraging. "David, we're about to see what few will ever witness."

He threw her a sideways glance. "If we get there."

Nick scanned the cockpit's '60s-era control banks one final time to assure himself that he had set all switches correctly. He wasn't sure.

His gut twisted when the enormity of this audacious flight hit him, draining his confidence like a sinkhole. *What the hell have you gotten yourself into, dude?* A state-of-the-art cargo plane couldn't fly in a gale-force storm, let alone a hastily modified relic like this one. He was about to get everyone aboard killed. *Screw this!*

Aman entered the flight deck. "Proceed."

Nick whirled in his seat. "I'm not so sure about—"

"You must get us airborne with haste. Time is critical." Aman buckled himself into the copilot seat.

"Maybe we should—"

"*Proceed!*"

Nick, his jaw clenched, placed a hand on the throttles. The vibration beneath his fingers told him the machine was ready. Aman was right about one thing—they couldn't stay here.

"*Yes, sir!*"

Nick throttled up the aircraft's four massive turbofan engines with a roar. *Plenty of power.* Outside the large cockpit window, he observed soldiers fighting to move the crowd away from the hangar—and failing.

"Here goes."

Nick taxied onto the airbase's long runway, forcing people to scatter. The rain had started again. He saw no obstructions, just rows of halogen runway lights encircled with clouds of steam. The cockpit's retrofitted weather radar showed a violent new squall line bearing down on them. *Now or never, dude.*

Nick throttled the engines. The aircraft began rolling down the runway, its 80,000 pounds of combined thrust pushing him back into his seat. He caught a glimpse out the side windscreen of the crowd pushing through the last of the military barricades and charging across the field.

The Hercules swayed and bounced, gathering velocity while he watched the lights at the end of the runway race toward him. Nick pulled back the yoke. With a final bump, the modified cargo transport lifted into the air, gaining speed and altitude.

"We have wheels up," he said.

Nick banked the aircraft to the west, taking the C130 into the black, lightning-streaked sky.

DAY SIX

DAWN

NICK GLANCED AT the flight compass again. Each time he checked it, the dial showed the aircraft heading in a different direction from the last reading. Useless. *And totally nuts.*

For the past nine hours, Nick saw nothing but relentless rain, hard as spikes, hammering the aircraft's windscreen. These weren't separate storm cells—a single, violent weather system was sweeping the globe. Aman directed him around the most active weather, and Nick took modest comfort in knowing they were staying ahead of the most violent disturbances.

"We are leaving Turkey airspace," Aman said from the copilot's seat. "We are on course and only twenty-two minutes behind schedule. The additional thrust from the modified engines is helping to compensate for the headwind."

Nick threw him a sideways look. "Quit peeking inside my goddamn brain—"

Nick fell silent. Aman had changed yet again. Here sat a man in his thirties, with sharp features, a slim but muscular physique, and thick black hair without a trace of gray. *Definitely nuts.*

Nick spotted a sliver of light on the eastern horizon. He filled his lungs with a long, deep breath, grateful for whatever small weather break nature cared to give him. "It's morning."

"You are observing a new equatorial weather system," Aman said. "In forty-three minutes, we will enter a large low-pressure mesocyclonic system caused by the earth's slowing rotation. It holds no moisture. But you will encounter severe surface winds."

What the hell did he just say? Nick was too exhausted to pepper Aman with questions about meteorology. Later. "We've got a heavy payload back there," he said. "How long's our runway?"

Aman touched a throttle lever to increase one of the engine's RPMs. "There is no runway. You will put down this aircraft in a sand trench."

"Are you friggin' kidding me?" Nick said. "When were you gonna tell me that? How do you expect me to get us off the ground again?"

"Our fuel capacity will only get us there."

"You're insane," Nick shouted. "How the hell are we getting back?"

Aman didn't respond. His eyes narrowed with a look of concern that rattled Nick.

"Boss? Is everything's okay with this baby?"

Aman unbuckled his shoulder harness and stood with a hand on the back of the copilot chair for support. "There is a matter I must attend to."

"Don't you dare leave me," Nick shouted. *"Don't you dare!"*

"The others are not yet secure," Aman said. "I must prepare them for our landing."

● ● ●

Samantha woke to the sound of sporadic banging in the cargo hold. At first, she dismissed the noise as part of the compartment's constant shaking. The uneven shuffling, coupled with occasional gasping sounds, convinced her that someone was moving about the hold.

She sat up in her sleeping bag and peered into the dimness, letting her eyes adjust. Marshall, lying next to her, appeared oblivious. The air inside the hold was warm and humid, the smell a thick blend of sweat and motor oil.

She pushed wet hair off her face. "Aman?" she whispered. "Nick?"

Samantha stared, astonished, as a silhouette climbed down from the all-terrain vehicle, clutching the door frame for support. She gasped in surprise when a man with white hair and a tweed jacket staggered into the compartment's half-light in front of her. His complexion was pale, and he kept dabbing a handkerchief on his pasty forehead. He looked like he might puke.

"I know you," Samantha said. "You were in the command center's war room."

"I don't feel well," the man said. "I get motion sickness." He wavered and grabbed a pallet for support.

He's going to hurl right in front of me!

Marshall stirred. "What's going on?" He twisted around inside the same sleeping bag and stared into the dim light.

"You are not welcome here, Dr. Weissmann," Aman said, stepping around the Humvee to join them.

Samantha noted Aman's youthful appearance. *He's younger than I am.*

Marshall sat up and scowled when he saw Weissmann. *"Jesus*—what are you doing here, professor?"

Aman's tone turned bitter. "You are a distraction and a danger to us all. I blame myself. My preoccupation with preparing this aircraft blinded me to your boarding."

Kirby stirred in his sleeping bag and muttered, "What the hell's going on?"

Weissmann lowered himself into a sitting position with his back propped against a cargo pallet. He lifted an unsteady hand to his forehead. "I had to come. My life depends on it."

Samantha scrambled out of the sleeping bag and stood over him. "How did you get in here?"

"In the back of that truck." Weissmann lifted a trembling finger toward the Humvee behind him. "You were all too distracted to notice me. I hid inside the truck's troop compartment before they brought the vehicle aboard."

"You are in grave danger." Aman's piercing eyes bored into Weissmann like a high-speed drill. "I cannot protect you."

Weissmann waved away Aman's concern. "I accept the risks. I'll take my chances like the rest of you."

"You are different," Aman said. "My meeting these people

was no accident. I chose them. Not you."

Samantha looked at Aman, confused. "Come again?"

"I found you on that road," he said to her.

"Found *me?*"

Aman's eyes shifted from Marshall to Kirby. "Each of you is essential." His eyes settled on Weissmann. "You, however, are a gross liability. Your presence jeopardizes everything."

Weissmann, staring, said nothing.

Kirby sat up in his sleeping bag. "Want me to cuff him?"

Aman, frowning, headed for the cockpit. Samantha could sense his disappointment in himself for letting this happen.

"I must ask you something, sir," Weissmann called after him. "Your answer is worth risking my life to come with you."

Aman faced the professor.

"Each of our bodies is undergoing a physiological change, correct?" Weissmann said.

Marshall rose to his feet and tossed their sleeping bag into the corner. "Are you talking about rapid tissue regeneration?"

"I'm referring to radical aging acceleration," Weissmann said.

Samantha looked at him, curious. "You mean we're getting older?"

"Not everyone," Aman said.

Samantha's confusion mounted. "Are you going to fill me in, or what?"

"He means," Weissmann said, "the Field can retard aging and perhaps even stop it. It can also speed the aging process to cleanse defective specimens from the genus."

Samantha looked at Aman. "Is this true?"

"It is not quite so drastic as eliminating the lowest overnight," Aman said, "nonetheless effective over time. If I am successful today, those who are ready will transition to a new world. Our DNA is evolving rapidly, and the physiology of those with higher frequency levels will regress or stop at the physical age of twenty-seven with bodies that will be healed and rebuilt. Aging and diseases will not exist. The brain's circuitry will also undergo an expansion, and we will have more senses and much higher intelligence. We will become perfect entities."

Samantha cocked her head. *Perfect entities?*

"Are you saying that we're undergoing an accelerated process of natural selection?" Marshall asked.

"The process is out of control and unpredictable," Aman said. "To save humanity, the matrix is attempting to complete in one week what should have occurred over several generations. My physical state is regressing to facilitate my journey, as you all have observed. If the breach's toxic radiation continues to flood our world, I will cease to exist in three days. Meanwhile, those unenlightened who are a burden to the species will experience swift aging and death."

"Sounds more like Hitler's Final Solution," Kirby said. "Kill the ones that don't fit in."

Samantha inspected her palms, then turned her hands over and back again. Her skin and nails were undeniably softer, younger. *Is it possible?* She ran her fingers through her silky hair while scrutinizing Marshall. His facial lines were smoother, his hair darker and wavier. The stubble over his chin and along his jaw was thick and black.

She looked at Weissmann. "But you're getting older?"

Weissmann managed a feeble nod. "Yes. At this rate, I will be a very old man by week's end."

"Why is this happening to you?" she asked.

Weissmann fidgeted as though unwilling to answer. Finally, he blurted, "Because I am being eliminated as an undesirable."

She looked at Aman for an explanation, but he kept his intense eyes fixed on the professor.

"When I was a young man working on my Ph.D.," Weissmann said to no one in particular, "I stole my mentor's theory of dark energy's role in universe inflation. Markin described a compelling picture consistent with what we now understand from COBE data. It was his life's work. I convinced him not to make his findings public without more quantifiable proof. I put doubt in his mind. Markin suffered from bipolar depression and came to see himself as a failure. He took his life. After his death, I used his notes for my fourth paper on cosmic inflation, which secured me the Nobel Prize in physics."

"You don't care about the rest of the world," Samantha said. "You came all this way to get Aman to save your sorry ass."

Weissmann ignored her and implored Aman. "You must remove this curse before it kills me."

"I can do nothing for you," Aman said. "Your insatiable avarice has lowered your frequency to a level incompatible with the New Earth."

Weissmann was unable to control his rapid breathing, and his anxious eyes darted from side to side as though calculating another ploy. "Then tell me what will become of me. When I die, will my memories disappear as if I never existed? What will happen to my personality, my individuality, my identity? Will I lose all awareness of who I was? Will I exist in any form?"

"The universe will transmute your physical state," Aman said. "Your essence will be cleansed while experiencing neither emotion nor desire. In time, you will realize what you have done and must repay, and you will see the truth and the opportunities you missed in this life, which will teach you a great deal. Your essence will join others of your kind, and you will begin again as an individual in this or another universe and continue your work to grow and evolve as one to the Source."

Weissmann sat very still, his shoulders slumped, eyes downcast. "I wish to keep my memories."

For a moment, there was only the deep rumble of the engines. Then Aman said, "We will be down shortly." He looked at Weissmann, his features cold. "You will do as I and the others tell you. For our safety, not yours.

SENTINEL

"TURBULENCE IS GETTING worse, Chief," Nick said.

Aman slid back into his copilot seat, his eyes scanning the aircraft's instrumentation.

The plane dropped through 7,000 feet into the heart of a violent sandstorm. Debris battered the cockpit windshield while Nick struggled to keep the C-130's wings horizontal against brutal crosswinds. A powerful force he had never experienced before threatened to rip the aircraft from the sky. How much longer could he keep them airborne?

Sweat trickling down Nick's temples from under the brim of his cap felt like a line of marching ants. "The radar's gone, and the instruments are useless. I'm flying blind."

"Reduce your airspeed to 200 knots and descend to 3,000 feet," Aman instructed.

"This isn't going to work," Nick said. "The engines will starve in this sandstorm."

"The modified air inlet barriers will give the engines another eight minutes of power," Aman said. "We will be down before they fail."

• • •

"Dr. Weissmann!"

Samantha found the professor face-down on the floor beside a cargo pallet. All color had drained from his face, and a yellow puddle of vomit rolled around the floor by his left ear.

He looked terminal.

The aircraft jerked and shuddered, and Samantha grabbed the all-terrain vehicle to keep from falling. The loud drone of engines numbed her ears. She hadn't flown enough to know much about airsickness, but she expected to get a firsthand lesson any moment. She glanced at Kirby strapped into his seat next to her. He also appeared ill, his complexion sallow.

"Make sure you've secured yourselves back there," Nick said over the aircraft's intercom, his voice unbecomingly strained. *"Prepare for a hard landing."*

"That's just great," Marshall mocked. He stepped around her, grasping an overhead strap for support.

"What about the professor?" Samantha said.

The doctor crouched beside Weissmann, keeping one hand on a pallet to steady himself. "I don't carry anything in my bag that will help you."

"Then leave me," Weissmann groaned. "If I'm doomed, let it end now and save me the drama."

Marshall helped raise Weissmann into a sitting position and then onto his feet. Some color returned to his features.

"Thank you," Weissmann said. "I can manage from here."

Marshall put a cargo strap in Weissmann's hand and pointed to the cargo netting hanging from the aft bulkhead. "Tie yourself into that mesh. The taut netting will keep you from striking a surface. Can you do that? It's all we've got."

"Interesting idea," Samantha said.

"I think I can do that." Weissmann staggered toward the mesh, leaning on pallets along the way to keep from falling.

"Our landing will be a controlled crash," Aman said over the intercom. *"Dr. Marshall, there are medical supplies in a locker bolted to the bulkhead wall."*

Marshall spotted the container. "I see it."

"Help the ones that can be saved," Aman said. *"Don't jeopardize a life while attending to someone who has no chance."*

Samantha put a hand on her forehead. *"Jesus,* you're scaring the living crap out of me. Are we going to be okay?" She felt Marshall lay a comforting hand on her shoulder.

"Secure yourselves immediately," Aman said. *"Under no circumstances will you unfasten your restraints until we are down."*

Samantha returned to her seat. She met Marshall's gaze, but he said nothing—not a word of reassurance. She looked away. They couldn't do anything about their situation now.

"This is *horseshit*," Kirby said. "I didn't sign up for no crash landing."

"Would you like to get off here and walk home?" Samantha teased, trying to ease his apprehension.

Another violent tremor shook the aircraft, turning Kirby a shade paler. He looked like he might hurl.

"Fasten up," Marshall said.

Samantha locked her waist and double shoulder harness and cinched the belts as tight as the thick fabric would allow. Weissmann hoisted himself up onto the cargo netting as Marshall had instructed and stood suspended on the mesh between the bay's rumbling floor and ceiling. He appeared unsure about how to secure himself with the strap. Samantha grimaced. *A child could figure it out.*

Weissmann's head snapped around suddenly, his eyes and mouth opened wide. His weird expression alarmed Samantha. He climbed down from the netting and made his way toward them.

"What are you doing?" Samantha shouted. "Tie yourself—"

Samantha felt—dizzy? The cargo bay walls began moving in irregular patterns, splitting into shifting pieces, one overlaid atop another. She glanced at Marshall, who was watching her.

"Are you okay?" he asked.

"Something's wrong. I'm … disoriented … woozy."

"Close your eyes," he advised.

"This isn't airsickness."

Weissmann stumbled toward them while dragging his cargo strap. He placed his hands on both sides of the porthole beside Samantha to steady his view and stared out at the violent sand storm that obliterated everything.

"I can feel the gateway's energy," he said, "and I can hear it as well. It's speaking to me."

The aircraft banked sharply. Weissmann spilled sideways and tumbled at Samantha's feet.

"*Damnit*, Weissman!" Marshall shouted.

"It feels like we're turning," Kirby said.

Weissmann sat up on the floor. "We're very close."

Samantha grabbed her harness buckle to assist the professor, but the strange disorientation prevented her fingers from working the clasp.

Marshall loosened his shoulder harness and reached as far as his waist restraint would allow. He hurried to wrap one end of the cargo strap around Weissmann's forearm and put the end with a clasp in the professor's hand. "Lock this onto something solid."

Weissmann slid backward and pressed his body against the Humvee. He reached up and hooked the strap's clasp onto one of the vehicle's restraining catches.

"That won't be enough," Marshall said. "Wrap the strap around your chest and hold it tight under your arms."

Weissman made no effort to follow the doctor's instructions. His eyes remained fixed and glazed. "The Field is telling me its secrets."

A strange flow of geometric shapes twirled in Samantha's head. Through the myriad of interconnecting patterns, a single image percolated to the front of her mind—a vision of an ancient city built of stone. And people. Thousands of people. She closed her eyes to experience the fantastic image fully. *Incredible!*

"A great metropolis once flourished on the land below us," Weissmann said. "The ancients knew about the energy vortex that gave life to this region. They built structures to channel the stars' energy into healing chambers to cleanse and purify and reach higher levels of consciousness. They worshipped its power."

Samantha opened her eyes and looked at the professor. "*Wow*," she said. "We see the same thing."

"I don't see anything but the inside of this damn plane," Marshall said.

"David," Samantha gasped, "it's unbelievable."

She glanced at Kirby. He looked ill, his eyes closed and his head back. Oblivious.

Samantha closed her eyes and saw two duplicate Earths splitting from each other like dividing cells, one dark, the other light. The image of the two worlds faded, and a great cosmic tunnel appeared in front of her. She soared toward its black center and sucked in her breath in wonder. *So real—so frightening!*

Weissmann exploded in a shriek of laughter. "For thousands of years, humanity believed God created the heavens and the Earth and even humanity out of nothing. We were sadly mistaken."

Samantha plunged into the tunnel's dark nucleus. She closed her eyes to make it go away. But the experience intensified. "Professor—" she gasped.

"A door to another universe," Weissmann said. "A very strange universe."

She opened her eyes. "Yes, a door."

"What door?" Marshall said. "What are you talking about?"

Weissmann gazed past Marshall, ignoring him.

Samantha saw a row of men dressed in dark robes, carrying strange tools and implements into a grand white temple. The scene was so vivid she thought she could walk with them. Who were these men?

"Entire armies and civilizations once watched over the earth in the event of a catastrophe like the one we're now experiencing," Weissmann said. "But that was cons ago. Now that task is the responsibility of one man—a *sentinel*—a mortal with sacred knowledge of the Universe. There are two sentinels left. If for any reason, one sentinel is unable to avert a calamity under his watch, the other must perform the duty in his stead."

The aircraft plunged with an appalling bang, dropping them hundreds of feet.

"*Damnit*, Weissmann," Marshall shouted, "you're going to get yourself killed."

Weissmann ignored him. "A sentinel will use whomever

and whatever he needs to save Earth," he continued, "even if it requires great sacrifice. Even death."

Samantha saw a vision of Aman as a very young man. He stood alone in a massive room—inconceivable in its technical complexity. He wore a robe similar to the men she had just seen. Aman's hands were severely burned, his charred fingers glowing a fluorescent blue. *What the—?* The Aman in her mind looked up and beckoned her to help him.

"I ... can't," Samantha gasped.

He let her see his disappointment before turning away and vanishing. The vision and her strange disorientation faded. She saw only the inside of the shaking cargo hold.

Marshall kept his eyes focused on her. "You look like you just saw the devil."

"There was another breach," she said. "A long time ago. I know where it happened."

Marshall shrugged. "Where?"

"Under the Black Hills near the town where I grew up," she said, "not far from where I found Aman."

<u>DOWN</u>

EVERY COCKPIT WARNING alarm blared at once. Nick ignored them all. He dropped the C-130 to 1,500 feet while the plane pitched and rolled like a rowboat in a typhoon. He couldn't see the ground through the storm.

Aman tightened his seat harness. "Descend twenty-five feet per second. Impact in seventy-four seconds."

Nick fought to keep the massive wings level without a working attitude indicator. He was acutely aware that another wind shear could send the aircraft into a nosedive with no room to recover. His hands ached from gripping the yoke, and his arm muscles threatened to spasm.

"There's no way I can land in this shit," Nick said. "I'm aborting. I need to climb—"

"*No,*" Aman shouted. He reached for the console and activated several switches.

"What the hell are you doing?" Nick shouted.

"Purging the remaining fuel," Aman said. "The impact will rupture the auxiliary tanks and fill the hold with fuel. Ignition is possible."

"But—"

"You do not need all engines to land."

They descended below the dust clouds, and Nick got his first glimpse of high dunes broken by peaks of reddish rock, a sight that terrified him. Hitting just one of those peaks would rip them in half. Thanks to Aman, he had one shot to put her down. *Goddamn it!*

Aman activated another switch.

"Now what?" Nick shouted.

"I am opening the rear cargo ramp," Aman said.

"You're doing *what!?*"

"The impact will jam the ramp closed," Aman said. "I must be able to remove the cargo."

• • •

Samantha heard the pneumatic whine of hydraulics and felt the floor shake. The compartment's rear loading ramp began to open. *What the f—?* She stiffened and watched the barren landscape rolling below the opened cargo door at a fatal speed. The wind roared in her ears as the desert rose up to meet them. *We're crashing!*

She shouted at Marshall over the rising clamor, "David, we're going to crash!"

Before he could respond, howling wind swept the hold, hammering them with sand and debris.

"*Jesus Christ,*" Kirby yelled, protecting his face with his arms.

Samantha covered her eyes, terrified. "*David!*" Big mistake— she spat out a mouthful of sand. She thought she heard Marshall say something, but the blast of air masked his voice.

• • •

One of the windscreen panels cracked, forming a spider-web pattern in front of Nick's eyes. *Uh, Oh.* The panel imploded. A sliver of glass struck Nick's forehead and knocked the cap off his head. Blood cascaded down his face, blinding his left eye. He pressed a hand against his forehead and felt a deep gash just below his scalp. Blood flowed between his fingers, spilling onto his black T-shirt. A storm of grit poured through the damaged windscreen like a firehose. A single thought filled his head—*put this aircraft on the ground without killing my passengers.*

Nick grabbed the yoke in his bloody hands and worked the controls on feel and instinct to keep the aircraft's wings stable.

"Aman, I can't see."

He felt Aman push the copilot's yoke forward and the throttle back. Nick struggled to see the readouts, but the hazard lights were a blur.

"Focus on your training rather than your pounding heart," Aman said.

The C-130 continued to drop. Nick clenched his jaw, determined, and worked to hold the controls steady with Aman's help. He kept wiping blood from his eyes with the back of his hand. He was too wired to feel any pain.

Nick heard a single, sharp bang like a pistol crack. "We've lost an engine."

"Yes," Aman said.

"Throttle closed, autothrottle disengage."

"Closed. Disengaged."

"Glide path seven degrees," Nick said. "Flaps down." Every light in the cockpit went dark. "Generator's gone. No power."

"Understood."

Another bang.

Nick could no longer control the rudders, elevators, or wing flaps. "Hydraulics are gone. I have no way to slow us down."

Aman pulled back on the yoke, pulling the C-130's nose up slightly. The aircraft's undercarriage sheared off the top of a rocky peak like a chisel blade before sinking into a channel between twin dunes. "*Sonofabitch—*"

The jagged hills rose around them as the plane hurtled downward. The aircraft glided just above the ground, refusing to touch down.

Aman cut the remaining two engines. The airframe's underbelly dropped onto the valley floor with a terrifying roar. Nick released the yoke—he was no longer in control. The aircraft began a long, grinding skid at 100 knots like a derailed freight train.

• • •

The fuselage bucked violently, as though the aircraft were

dragging across one mound after another. Samantha took Marshall's hand and squeezed it tight. Their eyes met, and she braced for the impact she believed would kill them. *His face is the last thing I'll ever see.*

She heard him say, "I want you to know something, Sam—"

Powerful tremors rocked the cargo hold as the plane hit the ground and began skidding across the desert's surface. The aircraft rolled hard to the right, yanking their hands apart. Samantha glanced out the porthole and saw a wing shear off and vanish inside a massive cloud of sand.

God—

Without the wing, the airframe leaned hard to starboard, throwing them back against the fuselage. Samantha stared transfixed at the armored Humvee and backhoe hanging perilously over them like slabs of loose concrete.

Weissmann dropped straight down from the swaying vehicle, tethered to the strap. He hung tangled by one arm just above Samantha, spinning out of control like an acrobat in trouble. His mouth opened in a cry, but she couldn't hear him over the roar.

The C-130 rolled hard to port. The remaining wing tore away with an unsettling screech. Wall sections ripped free of their seams like shredded paper. A rivet, traveling at the speed of a bullet, shattered the porthole beside Samantha's head, peppering her cheek with fragments.

The aircraft continued to roll until Samantha was staring down at the heavy equipment. Weissmann fell over the top of the Humvee and vanished beneath it, his restraining strap torn from the catch. The strap's severed metal clasp shot across the compartment, striking Kirby's knee. He let out a howl that faded into the appalling din.

The aircraft righted itself and came to a sudden, vicious stop. Samanta flew sideways against her shoulder restraints, hard enough to knock the wind out of her. All lights inside the cargo area went dark.

Samantha, her heart racing, wiped her eyes. *How are we still alive?* The compartment filled with smoke and dust. Marshall's face was filthy, and he, likewise, struggled to clear his eyes. On her opposite side, Kirby made the sign of the Lord's cross while tears streaked his soot-covered face.

No one spoke. Samantha heard only the brutal wind howling outside the shattered fuselage.

WRECKAGE

DAZED, MARSHALL MADE his way to the cockpit with a medical bag while cyclones of sand and debris hammered the aircraft's metal surfaces. He heard something else too—a peculiar rumble of thunder.

The doctor expected to find two corpses when he peered through the flight deck's doorway. He saw Nick crushed between the pilot's seat and the flight controls. Aman stood beside him, his forearm bloody. The crash destroyed the cockpit, and the plane's nose and half its fuselage lay buried under a hill of sand. What few shards of glass remained in the windscreen dangled from their frames like snowflake ornaments.

Marshall slipped inside and watched while Aman placed one hand on Nick's seat, his other on the control surface, and pushed the tangled pieces apart with what appeared to be brute strength. *Unbelievable.* Nick's body fell loose. Aman grabbed the young pilot under his arms and dragged him back to the only clear area in the rear of the flight deck.

"*Jesus!*" Marshall knelt beside Nick. He was alive, but the good news ended there. A mask of blood covered Nick's face from a slice on his forehead. He had other visible lacerations and contusions, a left leg bent impossibly sideways, and probably internal injuries. Except for an occasional spasmodic tremor, Nick appeared dead.

"He has a fractured skull, a crushed pelvis, a broken forearm, and his left femur is shattered into nine pieces," Aman said. "There is also damage to his left lung, his spleen, and his liver."

He's a human MRI machine, Marshall thought. Both seats were mangled beyond recognition. *How can Aman be standing here?* "You're hurt. Let me see your arm."

Aman waved away the doctor's request. "I do not require medical assistance."

Nick's eyes opened and rolled up toward Marshall, but they couldn't focus. Blood bubbled from his lips when he tried to speak.

"*Damnit,* he needs a trauma room." Marshall appealed to Aman. "What can we count on from this field of yours?"

"He could die from his injuries before there is sufficient tissue regeneration," Aman said. "You must keep him stable. I suggest you start with morphine for the pain."

Marshall removed an intravenous drip from his bag. He shook his head in frustration while his soot-covered hands rigged the IV. "This isn't going to help him much."

Aman placed a hand on Nick's forehead and then curled his fingers around the back of his neck.

Nick let out a cough that hurled a stream of blood at Aman. He couldn't catch his breath due to a collapsed lung. Aman placed a hand on Nick's chest until his breathing eased.

"Looks like I need to find another line of work," Marshall said.

"If our species survives to see the New Earth, you will become a great healer," Aman said.

"A healer? You mean like a medicine man?"

"Much more. You will learn to use your hands more efficiently and effectively."

"If you can do this healing yourself, why did you drag me along?" Marshall said.

"I brought you to look after Samantha," Aman said. "And you have been very accommodating in that regard."

"What are you—?"

"*Ooooh.*" Nick struggled to sit up.

"Don't you move a muscle," Marshall insisted. He inserted a catheter into Nick's forearm.

Nick lay back with a groan. "Should've aborted."

"You put us down better than any pilot could," Aman said. "My equipment has not been damaged. If we succeed, the world will owe you a great debt."

Marshall injected morphine into the catheter hub. "This should ease the pain so you can rest."

Marshall checked for other open wounds. Thankfully, his bleeding had stopped.

"Where ... are we?" Nick managed.

"Three kilometers from the breach," Aman said. "We have arrived."

Nick clenched Aman's sleeve into his bloody fist. "Leave me. Finish what you came here to do."

"Soon." Aman placed a hand on Nick's cheek. The pilot's eyes closed, and his breathing slowed as he nodded off.

Samantha appeared in the doorway. "Oh, my God!"

A bruise the size of a half-dollar circled her right eye, and a streak of blood smeared one nostril. She wouldn't stop coughing from the thick haze permeating the hold.

"How bad is he?" she said.

Marshall shot her a severe look over his shoulder. "Bad."

Aman touched Marshall's arm. "Mr. Dawson's knee is shattered. See that he can operate the backhoe."

Marshall finished with Nick and returned to the wrecked cargo hold. He opened the crushproof container of emergency medical supplies and sifted through its contents—every item from the command center's infirmary, including pharmaceuticals. He let out another sigh of frustration. Nick needed much more than this, starting with a state-of-the-art operating theater and a team of surgeons.

Marshall secured a bottle of Novocain and grabbed a knee brace, then made his way to Kirby. Samantha followed, still coughing, her eyes red and weepy.

Marshall knelt before Kirby and tore away the fabric around his left knee. The joint was red and swollen. He felt for separations and fragments. Kirby gritted his teeth in agony and rubbed a muddy mix of dirt and sweat from around his eyes.

"Damn clasp got me good," Kirby huffed.

"Your kneecap is in three pieces," Marshall said. He helped Kirby into the knee brace. "I'll give you a local for pain."

Aman arrived and crouched beside Marshall. He placed a hand behind Kirby's knee. "Mr. Dawson, your injury is unfortunate. Regardless, you must operate this equipment."

"I know. I know." Kirby winced from the pressure of Aman's fingers. "I made it this far. I sure as hell ain't sitting on the bench now."

Samantha's coughing concerned Marshall. Their lungs were vulnerable to acute respiratory inflammation.

Aman unhooked the latches of a military-style case and threw open its lid. The container held a row of half-face respirators and a bundle of fabric caps. He removed three respirators and gave one to each of them. "You will not survive outside without these."

"You've thought of everything." Marshall injected the last of the anesthetic into Kirby's knee. He helped Samantha place the respirator's mask over her face, then put on his mask and pulled the straps snugly around his head. "Anyone see Weissmann?"

"He disappeared over the top of the truck during the crash," Samantha said, her voice muffled beneath the mask.

Marshall grabbed his bag and led the way around the equipment. On the opposite side, he found Weissmann's body jammed between two torn sections of the fuselage.

Samantha's hand sprang to her face mask. *"Whoa!"*

A steel bar the size of a ski pole had pierced Weissmann's lower back and jutted from his pelvis. Marshall was surprised to find him still conscious.

"It's about time you paid me a house call, doctor," Weissmann wheezed.

The professor's breathing was rapid and shallow, his eyes swollen. Marshall didn't doubt his body screamed with inexpressible pain. He set a respirator on the floor beside the professor.

"Is there any way you can help him?" Samantha asked.

Marshall knelt before Weissmann and touched the steel bar.

Nothing he saw gave him hope. There wasn't anything he could do without killing him.

"Doctor," Weissmann said, "whatever you need to do, please hurry."

"The shaft punctured your inferior mesenteric artery," Aman said.

"So, tell me the bad news," Weissmann said.

"The shaft is keeping you alive," Marshall said. "If I move you, the artery will rupture. You'll bleed out in thirty seconds."

"You expect me to spend the rest of my life pinned to this wall like a moth?" Weissmann spat.

When Marshall didn't answer him, Weissmann placed his shaking hands on the fuselage panels behind him and pushed. He was trying to free himself, even if it meant hastening his inevitable death. He coughed and spat out a crimson stream of drool.

Samantha turned away.

"Stay still," Marshall ordered, pushing him back.

Weissmann slumped back against the fuselage, his arms spread helplessly at his sides, his beet-red face distorted in agony.

Marshall began preparing another syringe of morphine.

Weissmann glared up at Aman. "What about your medicine? Can you mend me?"

"Neither Dr. Marshall nor I can help you," Aman said.

Weissmann's swollen eyes remained fixed on Aman. "A sentinel will use whomever and whatever he needs to complete his task. Even if it requires sacrifice and death."

"This was your choice," Aman said. "You were warned. I am sorry."

Samantha groaned and leaned against a pallet. She grabbed a restraining cable to keep from falling.

Marshall sprang to her. "What is it?"

"That strange feeling I had when we were landing," she said, "it's back, or something like it."

Her face above the mask appeared pale, and she looked like she might faint. Marshall put her arm over his shoulder and helped her to the opposite side of the hold, where he eased her into the seat beside Kirby.

Samantha drew in several deep breaths through her mask. It didn't help. "I'm dizzy. Much worse than before. I can't take this."

Marshall checked her facemask's filtering elements but found no blockage.

"I feel something too," Kirby said, fumbling to put on his mask. "It's shitty. Like a bad shroom trip." He tilted his head back against the fuselage. "This is worse than whirly beds after a couple of six-packs with the boys."

Marshall's ears began to ring, and his vision blurred. The strong winds battering the airframe sounded like kettle drums. He grabbed an overhead strap to steady himself. "Something's wrong here."

"The breach's radiation is disrupting your brain's neurotransmitters," Aman said. "Continued exposure to the emission at this amplitude and frequency will shut down your autonomic nervous system."

"That's frickin' great," Kirby said, his face a stream of sweat.

"This isn't going to work," Samantha moaned. "I can't move. And I think I'm going to pass out."

"This will kill us all, for chrissake," Marshall said. How ironic, he thought, that they'd come so far to fix this thing, only to die an excruciating neurological death not three miles from their destination. "So, what are we supposed to do now?"

Aman retrieved a handful of gray fabric headcovers that resembled ski caps from the respirator case. He gave one to each of them.

Kirby turned over the fabric in his hands. "What the hell, Aman?"

"They are woven from unique composite ceramic fiber," Aman said. "The material will shield the brain from the emission's stronger wavelengths."

Marshall ran his hand over the foreign material, which felt coarse under his fingertips, like steel wool. He recalled wearing aluminum foil hats with his brother and friends as kids to protect their brains from alien signals. He didn't find that memory amusing now.

Samantha pulled the cap over the top of her head and closed her eyes. She could breathe easier and let out a sigh of relief.

Kirby pulled on the cap. "Great. We're sitting in a hot zone with no way out. That pretty much fries our asses."

Marshall worked the stiff fabric over his head. He noted that Aman didn't keep one for himself. "You're not affected?"

"No," he said.

Marshall's disorientation vanished. "How much time will these give us?"

"Approximately 157 minutes." Aman handed him two additional caps. "For Mr. Judge and Dr. Weissmann."

There came another low rumble of distant thunder.

"Aman, whatever you need to do to fix this thing," Marshall said, "you better get started."

"Indeed." Aman faced Kirby. "Mr. Dawson, I want you to release the vehicles in all due haste."

Marshall knelt in front of Samantha's seat. "Sam."

She opened her eyes. "I can still feel something—some sort of current—crawling over my skin like dancing needles."

"I want you to stay here."

"Dr. Marshall," Aman said, "she must come with me. You will remain here and attend to Nick." His tone was emphatic. Final.

"You can't make her risk her life," Marshall said, standing. "You've withheld information about a hazardous situation to get us here—"

"I'm going with him, David," she said. The intensity of her eyes behind the face shield told him she had made up her mind.

"Sam," Marshall said, "I'm not letting you out of my sight."

She stood up from her seat and slipped her arms around his neck. Her eyes softened. "I'm going to help Aman. That's why I came. That is where I belong."

"Please, Sam—"

She put a quick finger to his lips to silence him. "Not another word."

He knew he couldn't change her mind. And he no longer wanted to. Her life had been harsh and full of regrets. To deny her this would devastate her in these last days. "Aren't you afraid?"

She smiled. "I'm frigging terrified."

He pulled her close and pressed his mask against hers.

• • •

Marshall helped Samantha into the back of the armored Humvee. She squeezed beside Aman in a compartment crowded with three military cases. There was no room left for Marshall, even if Aman wanted him along. The thought of staying behind filled him with frustration. Nick and Weissmann desperately needed advanced medical attention, which undoubtedly was the real reason Aman brought him along. But their first-aid supplies wouldn't help them—not by a large margin.

The bitter storm outside raged with gale-force winds. Kirby started the engine and revved it in neutral. The machine fired rough, banging and jerking and tearing itself apart, spewing a gray exhaust plume into the hold. Marshall knew a little about engines, and this one was in trouble. How in hell would this vehicle carry them through a sandstorm while pulling a backhoe?

Kirby twisted around in the driver's compartment, his nose and mouth buried beneath the respirator, its straps stretched over his ceramic headcover. The knee brace and local injections would keep him functioning for the moment. How he faired later was another matter, Marshall thought.

"The fluids in this thing suck," Kirby said.

"It must take us three kilometers, Mr. Dawson," Aman said from the back.

"Please stay out of trouble, all of you," Marshall said.

She set down her sand goggles, grabbed his hand, and

squeezed it—hard. He could see the passionate look in her eyes behind her respirator mask. "I love you, Dr. Marshall."

He felt an adrenaline surge that forced tears into his eyes. He knew nothing would persuade her to trade places with him. He squeezed her hand.

"I will do everything in my power to protect her," Aman said.

"You damn well better." Marshall forced a smile under his face mask. "Or you'll answer to me."

Marshall closed the carrier's rear cargo door and stepped back. He glanced at the exit ramp's twisted frame, no longer wide enough for the vehicle. Would the truck's compromised engine have sufficient power to tear through and let them out? A part of him wished they were stuck here. Then at least he and Samantha would be together at the end. But what about the rest of the world? *Damnit, Aman better be a helluva miracle worker.*

The transmission engaged, and the Humvee jerked forward, pulling the backhoe. The carrier's deep treads tore up the floor's cargo rails.

Kirby jammed the throttle to the floor. The diesel engine howled in protest, and Marshall expected to see the clattering rods and pistons shoot through the hood like rockets. He stepped back against the fuselage next to Weissmann. Miraculously, the engine held together. The carrier rammed through the twisted sheet metal, then charged down the ramp. The vehicle hit the sand with a bounce and drove out into the storm, its diesel engine sputtering like a tired lawnmower.

Marshall exhaled slowly inside his respirator. He stepped to the edge of the cargo compartment and watched the Humvee and backhoe disappear into the storm's black clouds. "Take care, Sam."

Once again, he heard a rumble of thunder and glanced to the sky. All he could see were looming ridges of dark, spinning debris.

Marshall stiffened when he realized the sound he heard wasn't thunder.

JAMAL

JAMAL AND HIS five sons sat on horseback atop a dune overlooking a wrecked aircraft. These men were the last survivors of a strange plague that wiped out most of their Shi'a clan three days ago. Jamal had led his terrified boys across the remote, barren province, determined to reach a refugee camp near Mittica. The ride had become a death march. Their minds and spirits had weakened, and they were in desperate need of shelter and food.

Jamal watched the armored vehicle with its trailer race off the aircraft and disappeared into the ravenous storm. He grimaced in disgust. Visitors were not welcome in his province, especially non-believers arriving in a U.S. military aircraft. Too many of his people died at the hands of these filthy dogs and their war machines.

But finding this wreckage was Allah's blessing. A gift of life. The strange storm grew progressively worse, and their chances of reaching a refuge diminished with each passing hour. Perhaps the Americans had brought food and water.

Jamal adjusted the layers of fabric over his face and urged his terrified horse forward. His five sons followed, and together they made their way through a blizzard of sand down the steep dune.

When the six horsemen reached the base, Jamal raised a hand to signal the others. They split into two groups and broke into a gallop. Jamal and his two youngest rode toward the wrecked aircraft. The second group of his three eldest charged across the desert in pursuit of the armored vehicle.

• • •

"Goddamn you," Weissmann shouted from the hold. "Help me."

Marshall ignored Weissmann while he attended to Nick, who was awake and in considerable pain. After Marshall finished dressing Nick's open wounds, he would give Weissmann another shot of morphine. That was the best he could do. Without trauma surgery, both men would die. That much was obvious. They needed a miracle. Would Aman's field provide that miracle in time?

"I can't touch your femur without an X-ray," Marshall said.

"Screw the X-ray," Nick said. "I trust you."

"I could puncture an artery."

Nick closed his eyes with a scowl. "Too much information."

Marshall reached into his medical bag. "I'll give you another injection—"

Men began shouting inside the cargo area. The doctor stood, his heart beating fast and hard. *Who the—?*

Marshall peered out into the hold and saw three men in rags enter the rear cargo door. One carried a rifle. They unwrapped layers of fabric from around their faces while staggering like drunkards. The effects of the breach's lethal emission?

Adrenaline coursed through him. Marshall glanced at Weissmann, trapped on the opposite side of the stacked pallets. The intruders hadn't spotted him yet. Weissmann grabbed a long sliver of glass from the floor beside him and held it like a knife. And waited.

The crash had torn off the cockpit door, exposing them. Marshall moved away from the open door until his back rammed the shattered flight controls.

From his tight vantage point, Marshall watched one of the men use his foot-long serrated knife to pry open a crate. The man howled with delight at the sight of the packaged rations inside. The three men ripped open packets with their teeth and devoured the provisions as though eating their first meal in days. Marshall hoped that once satisfied, they would move on.

Nick threw him a questioning glance. Marshall put a finger to his lips and shook his head. Nick nodded that he understood.

One of the intruders appeared in the cockpit doorway, his features hidden beneath a layer of dirt. Marshall's breath caught in his throat. The intruder's dark eyes glared at him while he ate a brown food bar out of a package. Marshall didn't move or say anything. The man watched him while taking a long swallow from a water bottle from another pallet.

Finished, the intruder let out a sustained belch before calling for his comrades. More shouting. Marshall heard the snap of a rifle bolt.

"How bad is it, doc?" Nick asked.

"Bad," Marshall said. "These men are armed."

A second man appeared in the doorway, pointing a rifle.

Marshall raised his hands.

The man glanced at Nick and then returned his gaze to Marshall with a grin. He used his rifle to motion the doctor out of the flight deck.

"Whatever you say." Marshall locked his fingers behind his head and stepped into the cargo area. Blood pounded in his ears. He had never looked down the barrel of a loaded gun before, and the experience shocked him to the core. He moved across the hold away from Weissmann, careful not to provoke either man. He saw no other firearms among the intruders.

The man with the rifle motioned toward the cockpit. "I want him too."

He spoke Arabic, yet Marshall understood him. That meant they would understand him as well.

Marshall lifted a hand and pointed. "The pilot's critically injured. His leg is shattered."

The rifleman grinned. "I will make him dance for us."

"He can't be moved—"

Another man unsheathed his wicked-looking knife and thrust its point at the doctor's throat, driving him backward.

Marshall put up a hand. "Take whatever you want."

An amplified shriek blasted through the hold, startling everyone into silence. Marshall whirled toward the source. The man with the rifle had found a bullhorn among the supplies. Laughing, he put the horn back to his lips and let loose another ear-numbing howl. His comrade with the knife screamed with delight and insisted on trying the bullhorn himself.

Their elder, a man with dark angular features and a full beard, raised a hand to silence the two. The elder approached until his nose almost touched Marshall's. His dark, narrow eyes stared at the doctor's unconventional cap, and then they darted down to his face. He removed Marshall's respirator with a hard, swift pull that broke the strap around the back of his head. He tossed it aside.

"I am called Jamal, the cleric," he said, "and these are my sons. Everything on this land is my property. You are trespassing."

"I'm a doctor," Marshall said. "I brought medical supplies."

"Your medicine will not help us," Jamal said, his tone bitter. "Allah has taken my people but spared my sons. Three days ago, they were young men. Each day they grow older until I no longer recognize them. My bones grow more brittle each day. We are dying."

Jamal and his sons were aging rapidly, just like Wissemann, transforming the boys into scared, bitter men. Nevertheless, Marshall knew they hadn't killed anyone—at least not yet.

Jamal's son waved his knife. "Let me kill him."

The elder waved off his son's threat. "This curse has brought madness that is turning my sons into voracious wolves," Jamal said. "They believe blood will cleanse the curse and return their youth. They are impatient for redemption. If I try to dissuade them, they will kill me as well."

"Your sons may look like men," Marshall said, "but they're frightened boys. If they take a life, they'll die too. Meanwhile, your hatred is killing you and your sons. I can explain—"

A cry erupted from the other side of the pallet. Marshall heard Weissmann let out a gargled gasp, and one of the men began laughing. Marshall disregarded the danger and rushed to the other side of the hold, where he found the professor choking and coughing up blood. Weissmann stared at Marshall in terror while making a feeble attempt to staunch a crimson river gushing from a deep slash across his throat. The bloody glass sliver he intended as a weapon lay in his lap. The man with the rifle stood over him, laughing, watching the blood flow from Weissmann's open wound.

Weissmann's eyes glazed, and his head bowed. He was gone.

The man with the knife prodded Marshall and forced him to his knees in front of Jamal. Paralyzed with fear, Marshall thought he was going to blackout. How could this happen? Are we that expendable to Aman?

He watched the man with the rifle charge into the flight deck and point his firearm at the center of Nick's chest. Nick tried to lift himself onto his elbows. But he had no chance.

Marshall couldn't watch Nick's execution. He bowed his head, a storm of regrets shooting through him, numbing him. *Goodbye, my friend. I'm sorry it came to this. You deserved better after what you gave.*

He thought about Samantha. His jaw clenched. *I'll never see her again.* "Aman, where the hell are you?"

The report of a gunshot in the cockpit made Marshall jump. He lost his balance and tumbled onto his back at Jamal's feet.

"Damn your sorry soul," Marshall spat.

Jamal gave his son a shallow nod.

The knife-wielding son pounced on Marshall and straddled his chest, pinning his arms. Marshall struggled beneath him and felt the cap fall from his head. He was unable to draw a breath as though his lungs had collapsed. The assailant put the tip of the serrated blade against the doctor's throat. The plane's hold spun out of control before Marshall's eyes. The assailant's hand trembled while he mumbled something that might have been a prayer.

With one swift movement, he thrust the blade downward with all his strength.

RETRIBUTION

"STOP THIS VEHICLE," Aman shouted up to Kirby.

Kirby eased off the gas. "How close are we?"

"We have arrived. The facility is beneath us."

Samantha leaned against the side window and watched the Humvee roll to a stop in front of a steep hillside, its features erased by the fierce weather. She tightened the straps on her respirator while Aman put on a pair of desert goggles.

"How are you going to breathe without a mask?" she asked.

"I will hold my breath," he said with a grin.

"Seriously—"

Aman opened the rear hatch and stepped out into the sandstorm. If the weather affected him, Samantha saw no sign of it. The wind howled into the passenger compartment, blasting her with needle-like grains of sand. *Screw this!*

"I'm going with you." Samantha put on her airtight goggles and followed Aman outside. She could make out little beyond the front of the vehicle but heard what sounded like distant thunder. This time she realized the deep sound emanated from beneath her feet, sending tremors through her legs and up through her head. *What is that?*

Kirby opened his door and stood on the truck's runner, his face hidden beneath his goggles and respirator.

"Uncouple the backhoe, Mr. Dawson," Aman shouted over the vicious wind.

Kirby nodded and climbed down between the vehicles.

Samantha turned toward Aman and gasped in surprise. The silhouettes of three men on horseback appeared several hundred feet beyond him. "Aman—"

Aman threw up a hand in warning. "Do not engage these men in any way. Mr. Dawson, uncouple that machine." He said to Samantha, "Stay here."

Aman, his head down against the gale, trudged through a howling curtain of sand to meet the horsemen. The lead rider urged his horse forward until he towered over Aman. He, too, wore goggles, and his face was wrapped in strips of shredded fabric like a leper. Even his horse's muzzle was covered.

Aman placed a fist over his heart and bowed slightly. The rider watched Aman through dark convex goggles that reminded Samantha of bulging insect eyes. The rider looked at her and then Kirby.

The horseman withdrew a large-caliber revolver from beneath his desert robe and pointed it at Aman. Aman didn't move.

Samantha raced toward them. *"No!"*

The rider said, *"Allahu Akbar,"* before discharging two quick rounds at the center of Aman's chest.

Aman didn't waver. The horse reared and threw the rider backward onto the sand. Samantha stopped. Twin gunshot wounds had torn apart the horseman's chest. The horse bolted past her and disappeared behind a cloud of dust. *What the—?*

The two remaining horsemen watched the wind and sand quickly bury their comrade. The sight was so unbelievable that Samantha expected the fallen rider to rise and rejoin them. But that didn't happen.

Aman called to her, "Stay with the vehicles."

One of the riders bolted forward with a yelp. The other followed at a gallop. The first rider unsheathed a saber and charged Samantha. She turned and struggled to run against the storm, terrified for her life. She could hear the horse's fast tread approaching.

The horseman quickly overtook her. Samantha glanced up as the rider swung his sword down across her neck with a great whoosh. She dropped onto the sand, a hand on her throat. The rider's headless body spilled sideways off the horse while his head rolled toward her like a beach ball. Samantha scrambled back in horror.

The third rider circled the vehicles. Kirby grabbed a crowbar from the rear of the Humvee and stepped away from the vehicle.

Aman raced toward Kirby, waving his arms. "Do not assail him!"

The bandit slid off his horse and hit the ground in a run. He pulled a dagger with a short, curved blade from beneath his robe as he charged. Kirby drew back the crowbar like a major-league batter preparing for a home-run swing.

"No, Mr. Dawson!" Aman shouted through cupped hands. "Do not lay a hand on him." His words were lost in the storm.

Samantha understood Aman's warning and sprang to her feet. "Kirby! *Drop it!*"

Kirby took two practice swings with the crowbar that did nothing to dissuade his attacker. Of course he would try to protect himself, she thought. Instinct.

She bolted toward him. *"Kirby! Please!"*

She heard Kirby yell, *"Shee-it!"* He threw down the bar and raised his fists like a boxer, his eyes fixed on the charging knife-wielder.

The bandit launched himself at his target. Kirby pivoted his body and delivered a straight punch into his attacker's face. Samantha winced. *I warned you.*

Kirby's goggles flew off, and he tumbled backward onto the sand as though a board had smacked his face. He lay on his back, stunned. The assailant, laughing, dove on top of him, his knife hurtling toward Kirby's face. Kirby was too dazed to defend himself.

The attacker let out a howl, and both men grew still.

Samantha ran to them. "Kirby?"

Kirby slid from beneath his would-be assailant and fumbled to put on his goggles while rising to his feet.

"Are you all right?" she asked.

Kirby put a hand to his jaw and worked it from side to side. "A pussy punch." He snatched up his crowbar and rolled his attacker onto his back with his boot. The man's face was a bag of bloody bones and rags.

Kirby let the crowbar dangle at his side. "Now I've seen everything."

Aman caught up with them.

Samantha turned away from the fallen horseman. "What happened to these men?"

"The Field no longer permits violence of any kind among men and has created a mirror," Aman said. "A blow delivered will be felt only by the attacker."

"You're *shittin'* me," Kirby said.

"Why didn't you warn us?" Samantha shouted. "I saw my whole life flash before me."

"In my haste," Aman said, "I failed to foresee these men coming."

Samantha figured that was as close to an apology as she would get.

"You want me to bury them?" Kirby asked.

"No, Mr. Dawson," Aman said. "The desert will reclaim them. You must begin your work in haste."

. . .

Jamal's son tumbled off Marshall and landed with a grunt on the floor at his father's feet. Marshall blinked in disbelief. He felt his neck for a wound. Not a scratch.

The assassin wasn't so fortunate. He lay on his back, making a lame sucking noise, while his hands clawed at his throat, unable to contain the copious spurts of blood from his jugular. His eyes, wide with surprise, stared up at his father standing over him. The boy sobbed, expelling a great gush of blood from his mouth. Marshall heard a final guttural gasp as the last breath left his lungs.

The man with the rifle staggered from the cockpit, a bloody hand covering a severe chest wound. "*Father—*"

His terrified eyes rolled up into his head, and he collapsed in front of the cockpit doorway.

Marshall pushed himself to his knees and looked up into the business end of a large-caliber revolver. Jamal drew back the hammer with a shaking thumb. Marshall could read the rage that blamed him for his sons' death.

"Don't do it," Marshall said, "for your own sake."

Sneering, Jamal pressed the barrel to Marshall's forehead and fired. Marshall flinched and rolled backward. But he felt nothing, not even a burst of air from the blast.

Jamal collapsed on the floor, the revolver still clenched in his fist. A long sigh of defeat poured from his lips. And then silence.

Marshall crawled to his would-be killer. The bullet entered Jamal's forehead and blew off the top of his skull, spraying the bulk of his brain mass across the cargo floor. Jamal's fear of his sons' violent aggression proved unwarranted—his own hatred killed him.

Marshall stood, his head spinning. He retrieved his cap and pulled it over his head while making his way forward. The dizziness passed. He glanced at Weissmann's corpse with the bloody glass shard still in his lap. He understood now. When Jamal's son attacked him, Weissmann plunged the glass shard into the assailant's neck. But Weissmann only succeeded in cutting his own throat.

Marshall entered the flight deck and knelt beside Nick.

His patient forced a smile. "That's twice today I cheated last rites. Next time I may not be so lucky."

"The Fold must need us," Marshall said. "It's finding ingenious ways to keep us alive."

EXHUMATION

SAMANTHA STAYED INSIDE the Humvee by Aman's side and watched Kirby carve a channel into the hillside with his backhoe. She saw nothing unusual about this mound in an otherwise barren landscape. Aman had instructed Kirby to start digging here—and that's just what he was doing.

Aman sat down between several large cases, his eyes fixed, waiting.

"What are you thinking?" she asked.

"I have very little time." He seemed composed, but his impatience with their progress conveyed something ominous. And that terrified her.

Samantha returned to the window. The farther Kirby clawed through the hillside with the backhoe, the slower he seemed to go. *Something terrible is going to happen to us out here.* She touched her ceramic cap and wondered how much longer this thing would keep blocking the lethal signals. *Please hurry, Kirby.*

Aman shifted restlessly. "We must get inside."

Samantha saw Kirby give a thumbs-up signal. "Aman—I think he found something."

Kirby cleared out more sediment until the bucket's teeth exposed what looked like a cement wall.

"He definitely found something," she said.

Aman put on his goggles. "He has reached our access point. Do not leave this vehicle until I call you."

Aman slipped out of the cargo compartment and closed the rear hatch behind him. Samantha watched him trudge a short distance through blowing sheets of sand and climb up into the backhoe's driver cage. He gestured for Kirby to proceed.

Samantha heard the hard screech of metal against cement when Kirby brought the bucket's teeth down against what appeared to be cinderblocks. He urged the backhoe forward. The vehicle's treads slipped over the sand, but he kept pushing until gaps appeared between the blocks. Aman's gestures became more animated. Kirby pressed forward and knocked in the cement blocks, exposing a dark cavity beyond. Samantha put a hand on the window. *What have you found, guys?*

Kirby continued digging until he had carved a trench wide enough for the Humvee. She saw Aman squeeze Kirby's shoulder and direct him to withdraw the backhoe. *Now what?*

Aman remained outside while Kirby limped back to the Humvee and slipped into the driver's seat.

"What the heck did you find?" she asked him.

"A wall," he called back to her, "and it's creepy inside."

"This whole desert is creepy."

Kirby backed the Humvee into the channel while Aman directed him with hand signals until the vehicle's rear hatch stood several feet from the wall. He waved him to a stop.

"Houston, we've landed," Kirby said.

Samantha didn't share his enthusiasm. Sea of Tranquility, my ass. *This is a friggin' war zone.*

Samantha returned to the back window and tried to see inside the wall's gaping hole. She felt a foreboding she couldn't shake as if an ancient curse were lurking in the darkness inside with certain doom. She thought about Marshall and wished like hell he was here with her. *What's he thinking right now,* she wondered?

She jumped when the Humvee's rear hatch opened. Aman retrieved a handheld spotlight.

"You may exit now," he said.

Samantha put on her goggles and stepped outside. The violent winds had grown worse and threatened to bury them. *No wonder he's in a hurry,* she thought. She couldn't see much beyond the trench. The desert looked oddly surreal, its shape and colors muted. She felt detached as if someone else was standing here in this terrible storm. Is this how soldiers felt going into battle, she wondered?

At least the narrow channel offered them some shelter. But it wasn't enough. They couldn't stay out here much longer.

Samantha joined Aman at the wall's opening. She saw the top of a broken metal stairwell, its few remaining steps hovering over the blackness below. "What is this place?" She barely heard her voice over the roar of the wind.

Aman didn't answer. He directed his lamp's powerful beam onto the walls inside and then down into a large room, revealing the remains of smashed machinery.

"What's down there?" Samantha said.

"The collider's heat exchangers. Or what remains of them." Aman handed her his light. "This is an emergency access. The main entrance is one mile east of here."

Kirby joined her for a look inside. "Isn't this lovely."

Aman retrieved a rolled chain ladder from the cargo compartment and attached one end to the back of the vehicle. He tossed the bundle into the opening. Samantha directed her light into the darkness and watched the ladder unfurl about thirty feet, finishing inches above the concrete floor.

Aman passed Kirby a steel winch cable with a clasp. "Handle these three containers with great care." He lifted the first out of the Humvee and passed it to Kirby. "I cannot continue if we lose the contents of even one of these."

Kirby's head bobbed, and he secured the winch cable's clasp to the case.

"Follow me," Aman said to Samantha.

Aman stepped onto the ladder and disappeared over the edge of the opening. Samantha directed her light down the wall and watched him climb to the bottom—a bit too fast, she thought. His words kept haunting her. *I am out of time.*

Kirby used the vehicle's electric winch to lower the first case. When it reached the bottom, Aman quickly unclasped it.

He called up to Samantha, "Come down here out of the weather."

Despite concerns for her safety, Samantha had no choice

but to trust him—supported by a healthy dose of self-preservation. She climbed onto the ladder, which seemed solid enough. She glanced down. Aman placed a foot on the last rung to steady the ladder while she climbed down, but much slower.

When she reached the bottom, Aman led her among the twisted wreckage just beyond his work area. Samantha welcomed the respite from the storm. At least it's quieter down here, she thought, and cooler.

"What do you want me to do?" she asked.

"Remove your respirator." Aman returned and unhooked the second case Kirby had lowered.

Samantha removed her face mask and filled her lungs with cool air, then touched her cap to make sure it was still seated securely.

She directed her light along the walls and over the high ceiling. What remained of these exchangers had become a high-tech junkyard. Heaps of twisted conduits conjured up frightening visages in her mind of faces staring down at her. A shiver ran through her as the enormity of their journey assailed her like a beast, even though she hadn't a clue what they would do in here.

Samantha felt another wave of deep rumbles beneath her feet. The hair on the back of her neck bristled, and her head thumped. She detected a pattern of tremors against her soles—a machine-like pounding. Was the collider still working?

The pounding stopped.

Aman assembled a small but powerful flood lamp with three halogen lights mounted on a stand. He switched on the array, which turned the area into daylight. He began inspecting the contents of the first two cases Kirby had lowered.

"Please hurry, Mr. Dawson," he called up to him.

The storm had grown worse, and Samantha saw only Kirby's silhouette working behind ferocious swirls of dust and sand pouring through the opening.

Kirby began lowering the third case. "The last one—" Suddenly, the case broke loose from the winch cable and struck the lamp assembly with a great crash.

"Oh shit!" Kirby shouted.

Samantha put a hand to her mouth.

Pieces of the lampstand scattered everywhere while the case tumbled across the floor and slammed against a pillar. Aman ran after it. Miraculously, one of the halogens laying on the floor remained lit, offering some light. Samantha noted several dents, but the case appeared intact.

Kirby turned off the winch and scrambled down the ladder. "Sorry, boss." He reached the bottom and collapsed into a sitting position, a hand on his injured knee. He removed his respirator and wiped the sweat from his face. "Damn storm almost killed me."

Aman ignored him and pried open the damaged case. Samantha saw a long, thin tool with a point at one end embedded in custom-fitted gray foam.

"Looks like a pogo stick," Samantha said.

"This is an electric pneumatic demolition hammer." Aman removed the tool from its case and inspected it. "We desperately need it."

"Is it okay?" she asked.

Aman nodded, and she could see his relief. "We are fortunate it did not sustain damage."

Kirby ran his fingers through layers of sweat-soaked hair. "I've worked jackhammers before but never seen one this compact."

"A prototype," Aman said.

Kirby took the tool from him for inspection. "Aerospace aluminum casing. Substantial, yet lightweight. Sweet." He lifted the battery backpack. "How many watts?"

"Twelve hundred," Aman said. "Sufficient for our needs."

Kirby nodded his approval.

"What about a radio?" Samantha asked. "We need to contact David."

"That is not possible," Aman said. "No communication device will work in this region."

"What about handguns?" Kirby asked. "We need something to defend ourselves if we have to."

"That will not be necessary."

Aman withdrew three white overcoats from a case and shoved one at Samantha and another at Kirby. He also gave them each a pair of bright-orange waterproof boots with thick tread soles.

Kirby held up the coat. "Are we hiking across the Arctic?"

Aman slipped on his coat. "The air below is dangerously cold."

Samantha put on the overcoat with a hood. Her size.

Aman retrieved another set of face masks with dual cartridge breathing ports the size of small cans. The shields were large enough to cover their entire face.

"You must wear these when we go below," Aman said. "They will filter out the ion particles that would otherwise destroy your lungs. I will instruct you when to put them on."

Kirby held up his new mask. "What other hazards haven't you told us about?"

"I do not have time to explain everything," Aman said, his voice strained. "You must do as I tell you."

Aman retrieved a small, ancient-looking wooden box from the second container. He shoved it into a deep pocket of his thermal coat.

"What's that?" Samantha asked.

"A key," he said. Before she could ask another question, Aman said to her, "I must return this to you."

He removed Samantha's quartz wand amulet from around his neck and presented it to her. "Do not take this off."

She welcomed the return of her wand's protective energy. She loved the quartz's unique green-tinted facets. But, as she turned its cluster points toward the light, the facets gave off a blue hue. *Now that's interesting.* She slipped its leather lace over her head and felt remarkably calmer.

"I will tell you why you are here," Aman said to her.

Samantha watched him with intense, curious eyes.

"You are here to save my life," he said, "if such a thing is possible."

TUNNEL

"HOW AM I supposed to save your life?" Samantha said. "I don't understand."

"I do not know," Aman said. "You will understand if and when the time comes."

Samantha shook her head in frustration. "Why are you doing this? Who picked you for this journey?"

"I made a vow to protect all."

Samantha waited for elaboration, but Aman returned to the cases without offering more.

He retrieved three LED flashlights with neck straps and gave one to each of them. Then he said to Kirby, "Are you ready, Mr. Dawson?"

Kirby lifted the drill's battery pack onto his shoulder and tightened the strap around his thermal coat. "Ready or not, I suppose."

"One important point both of you must heed," Aman said. "Always stay behind me."

Samantha forced a nod and felt the blood drain from her face. This is the moment, she thought—the point of no return. She wished she was anywhere but here. Samantha stifled a wave of anger over her trepidation. Giving up now meant certain death—not just for her, but for all. *I'll do whatever I can to help Aman—whatever he asks of me.*

Aman led the way around the wrecked machines and entered a narrow opening created by a fissure in the cinderblock wall. The tunnel beyond, wide enough for them to pass single file, sloped downward as far as their light beams could reach.

She recalled an instruction from a self-defense class years ago: heed your surroundings. Don't show fear. *Fight. Survive!*

Aman walked briskly down the tunnel ahead of them. Samantha hurried to keep up. Kirby trailed with a limp, the high-tech drill tucked under his arm.

Samantha heard that strange pounding again. The sound was louder in here, deep and primordial, booming from the darkness below. It reminded her of a giant heartbeat.

"That *friggin'* pounding," she said, her voice echoing off the narrow stone walls. "Does it have anything to do with the breach?"

"Yes. Each beat is a burst of dark radiation that corrupts our world."

"Scary," Kirby called after them.

The pounding ceased.

"How will you fix something like that?" she asked.

"That is complicated," Aman said. "The work requires manipulating energy of a different physics not known to our dimension."

"I see."

The tunnel narrowed, and the air grew cold and stale. Samantha's flashlight revealed stone walls carved out of the bedrock.

"What's up with this tunnel?" she asked.

"Yeah, where are we, Boss?" Kirby said.

"The engineers created this passage to test the integrity of the bedrock," Aman explained. "Once the stratum proved adequate, they built the main tunnels for the high-energy particle accelerators below."

Samantha found herself nearly running to keep up with Aman. The sound of Kirby's tread faded behind her.

The floor's angle steepened. She slowed her pace.

"*No farther!*" Aman shouted, raising a hand.

Samantha stopped on a daunting sixty-degree ramp. Her light beam revealed only blackness beyond Aman. Kirby, his breaths expelling in short puffs, stopped a few yards back.

"Do not move." Aman inched forward, scanning the tunnel ahead with his light. His beam lingered on a precipice where the stone floor ended abruptly, giving way to a treacherous drop-off. "This aperture is two hundred forty-two feet deep," he said.

"*Jeezis.*" Kirby took an anxious step back up the tunnel. "I thought you said this place was solid. It's a booby trap?"

Samantha inched her way up the ramp. "So, we're going back?"

Aman directed his light onto the wall behind them, revealing a waist-high opening. He beckoned them to follow. "There are steps through here."

Aman crawled under the opening and disappeared. Samantha followed. Kirby squeezed through with his battery backpack.

They emerged into a storage area filled with broken planks from discarded wooden crates. Aman led the way down a flight of narrow metal steps that barely allowed enough room to descend. No place for someone afraid of tight spaces, Samantha thought. She let the light dangle around her neck so she could press her hands against the stone walls for support. She moved slowly, cautiously, terrified of losing her footing and tumbling headlong to the bottom. Suppose Kirby stumbled behind her? One misstep could injure them all.

The stairwell felt colder the farther they descended, and she could feel a steady stream of frigid air from below. Samantha noticed her palm prints on the stone. *Frost.*

"Aman?"

He didn't answer and continued negotiating the steps well below her. He showed no indication of wanting to abandon this route.

They exited through an open metal security door that led to a shattered hallway, its tile flooring crushed into pebbles. They passed through a broken security door to a large circular room with heaps of computing workstations, screens, and overturned desks. Samantha ran her powerful beam across the area and saw a human arm reaching from beneath a pile of rubble.

She turned away. "Do we need to go through here?"

"This is one of the collider's control centers," Aman said. "It is the only way."

She swept her beam around, making quick swaths in the blackness. Her light bounced across one pile of debris after another—stacks of broken desks, papers, computer screens, and cabinets.

Kirby whistled his amazement.

The machine-like pounding resumed, much louder down here and accelerating. Dust and debris rained on them in sync with its rhythmic strokes. The pounding stopped.

Aman hastened his pace between the crushed cinderblocks and twisted beams. The damage was extensive.

Samantha hustled to keep up. "So, what destroyed this place?"

"A shock wave," he said. "No one survived the initial blast from the breach. The shock wave killed everyone in an instant. We are fortunate the way is still passable."

"Charming." Samantha felt dreadfully cold. She zipped up her coat and pulled its insulated hood over her head, then slipped her hands into the coat's pockets for warmth and found gloves. She hurried to put them on.

Samantha resumed her inspection of the area. Her light settled on a woman's corpse in a white frock sitting upright at a desk, her fingers touching the surface where the keyboard once sat. They passed more desks, some of which had bodies frozen upright in their chairs as though Medusa had come through here and turned them to stone.

"I need a second," Kirby called after them, a hand on his knee. He stopped to ease his weight against an upright metal desk.

"You must not fall behind, Mr. Dawson," Aman called back.

"You're *killing* me." Kirby pushed himself off the desk and struggled to keep up.

Aman entered a room with rows of overturned floor-to-ceiling racks of servers. The server farm lay in ruin, allowing just enough space between the toppled equipment to pass.

"This way, Mr. Dawson." Aman reached the far wall and put a hand on its surface. "Use your tool to break through this wall."

"Now you're talkin', Boss." Kirby put on his gloves and pulled up his hood. When he pulled the trigger, the jackhammer's battery-powered motor roared to life, its shrill whine amplified in the small space. Samantha winced and chanced a tentative glance behind her—no audience of dead men rising from their desks. *Get hold of yourself.*

Kirby jammed the chisel's sharp bit into the wall. The plaster yielded readily, as did the planks and mortar beneath. He gave Aman a grin of approval. Samantha felt a great gust of frigid air pour through the opening he was making.

"Wider," Aman shouted over the tool's whine. The chisel's hammering created a steady rain of plaster and dust. When Kirby had demolished a third of the wall, Aman motioned him to stop. He withdrew the new face shield from his coat pocket. "Put these on."

Samantha fumbled to slip the mask over her face. Kirby did the same.

Aman worked his hands into his gloves. "Do not allow your skin to touch any surface, or the tissue will die."

Samantha jammed her gloved hands into her coat pockets to keep them safe. "What's in there?"

"Ice." Aman stooped and disappeared through the wall. Samantha shrugged and followed. *Stay alert. Heed your surroundings.*

The three entered a large curved tunnel made of ice. The frigid temperature struck Samantha like a physical blow. Is this what the inside of a hollowed iceberg looks and feels like, she wondered?

Samantha noted some natural light—or rather twilight—coming through the ice. She snapped off her flashlight to observe the glowing effect. The illumination appeared to refract through the ice from a source deep within the tunnel.

"We are in a utility corridor above the collider assembly," Aman said.

"Why so cold in here?" Samantha asked.

"The gateway must protect itself from the massive heat it is generating," Aman said.

The pounding resumed. The sound was much louder in here, its resounding thud shaking the walls. Samantha couldn't stop trembling. They were close.

A section of ice as large as a truck fell in front of them with a great crash. Samantha recoiled from the shattered pile that could have crushed them all. She heard ice cracking all around them.

"This tunnel could collapse on us at any moment," she said. "Is turning back an option?"

"Come." Aman resumed his trek down the tunnel. The ice's split and uneven surface gave their thick boots some traction.

They came upon a cluster of human-sized pillars scattered across the tunnel like a field of tombstones. Aman weaved his way around them, ignoring them as he continued. Samantha directed her light beam at one of the pillars. Statues? Here? A gloved hand leaped to her face shield in surprise. *"No way—!"*

The pillars were men dressed in long, dark robes, frozen upright with agonized expressions on their porcelain-like faces. She just stared, unable to move.

Kirby caught up and added his light to hers. *"Mother Mary—!"*

"Are we're going to end up like them?" she said.

Kirby called down to Aman. "What the hell happened to these guys? Who are they?"

"Never mind them," Aman called back. "We must proceed in haste."

Samantha hurried after him. "Aman, wait—!"

She slid to a stop. A rugged mountain of ice from a collapsed wall blocked the tunnel. She saw no way around it.

"We must make our way over it," Aman called back to her.

He stepped up onto a block of ice and began picking his way up and over the pile like a veteran rock climber. Samantha climbed after him, following his path. At least the jumbo ice cubes under her feet felt solid enough, she thought. Kirby, saddled with his jackhammer and battery backpack, began his climb behind her.

Samantha crawled over the top just as Aman reached the bottom below her. As she started climbing down, the ice beneath her feet shifted, and her boots slipped from under her. Samantha fell hard and tumbled down the uneven pile. She heard her coat tear. Panic seized her—all she could think about was her white and atrophied skin. She hit the floor and slid to a stop. *Damnit!* She sat up quickly to inspect her coat for damage. She found a rip on the sleeve but no exposed skin. The material beneath held.

"This place is trying to kill me."

Aman extended a hand to her. "You must focus on the present moment and be aware of what is occurring around you."

Samantha grabbed his hand and climbed to her feet. She adjusted and secured her face shield while Kirby reached the bottom of the pile and joined them.

The tunnel beyond grew brighter, and they followed Aman to a wall made of luminescent blue ice. A human-shaped silhouette wielding a spear-like object was visible beneath the ice. *Surreal.* Samantha felt lightheaded while staring at it.

Aman placed a gloved hand on the ice surface. "Mr. Dawson, start excavating here until you reach the inner wall. Please hurry."

Kirby's wide eyes looked spooked beneath his face shield. *He doesn't like it here any more than I do.*

"Will do, Boss."

Kirby started the jackhammer and jammed its tip into the ice. Wafer-sized chips flew away under the high-speed hammering.

Samantha turned and realized that Aman had left them. She spotted him approaching the end of the tunnel.

"Don't you dare leave us!" Samantha raced after him.

Aman stood before a sheer wall of glowing ice—a dead end. He turned toward her. When he saw her racing toward him, he raised both hands as a warning. "Do not take a step closer."

Samantha's boots slid to a stop. The heavy pounding resumed beneath them, earth-shattering in its force. She could scarcely stand. Sweat continued to roll down her face—the air temperature was rising. Condensation building inside her face shield made it difficult to see.

The pounding stopped.

The tunnel's strange glow brightened. Samantha switched off her flashlight and saw the ice floor around them gleaming a fluorescent blue. She felt its heat. *What the—?*

"Step away," Aman shouted. "Stay with Mr. Dawson."

Samantha scrambled backward. "We need to get out of here."

Aman removed his face shield and gloves and tossed them aside. He retrieved the wooden box from his overcoat's pocket before taking off the garment and dropping it beside him. He pressed the box against his chest with both hands like a sacred book.

Samantha could see only his shape through the fog buildup inside her face shield. She reached for her mask but quickly reconsidered. What's safe for Aman could prove fatal to her.

Samantha heard more ice cracking. She looked up quickly, expecting to see an avalanche crashing down on them. Instead, she felt movement under her feet. Large concentric fractures appeared beneath her, a circular web that started under Aman and radiated past her. She scrambled up the tunnel until clear of it.

"Make a run for it, Aman!" she shouted.

Aman closed his eyes and lowered his head. The ice beneath his feet collapsed, dumping him into a circular pool of milky water amid bobbing chunks of ice.

"*Aman!*" Samantha crawled to the edge of the pool and thrust a hand toward him.

"Take my hand!"

His head disappeared beneath the swirling water.

VOID

"AMAN!" SAMANTHA SHOUTED.

Samantha pulled off a glove and sunk her arm into the water's cold, powerful suction. Aman was gone.

Samantha sat back on the ice and listened for any sign of him while stretching her numb hand. All she could hear was the whine of Kirby's jackhammer. Rain from melting ice began falling.

Am I supposed to save Aman's life—now? She stared into the frigid pool. *Hell no! You're going to kill yourself, girl.* She needed to find him some other way.

"Kirby!" She scrambled to her feet and made her way up the tunnel.

• • •

Turbulence, more violent than he expected, propelled Aman along a cold underground water shaft. The powerful suction tore the shirt off his back. He wrapped his arms around the box like a steel clamp.

He dropped his heart rate to a nearly undetectable rate to conserve the oxygen in his bloodstream. But the trip didn't take long. Aman's body shot through a dry aperture that delivered him into—*nothingness.*

Aman found himself enveloped in an unknowable and undefinable void—a space endlessly empty and black. He saw and heard nothing, an experience he likened to existence before his birth, separated from life or any reality. He felt nothing beneath his feet. Most would find the utter cosmic isolation deeply disturbing. But he still connected with physical reality through the presence of the box he carried.

Aman sensed movement. Yet, he was not moving. He felt another dimension of space, as black as the first, merging. Then another. High-density waves were changing and shifting through dimensions as though attempting to become something else, pulling him in every direction at once. This powerful convergence brought a disorientation he feared would debilitate him.

The relentless pounding resumed, unbelievably loud, producing powerful shock waves of cataclysmic energy.

Aman placed his right hand on the wooden box. The strange disorientation and the awful pounding made his contorted fingers jerk and spasm. *This is a time for mastery, not chaos.*

The box's twin metal straps broke under his touch, and he eased open the lid with shaking fingers. Despite the complete absence of light, he could see the remains of an ancient cushion inside that had dried and withered centuries ago. Amid the disintegrated fibers sat a unique dagger—a double-edged blood-red eight-inch-long gemstone that had once been a diamond. The flawless gem was not of this world. An interstellar asteroid carried it to Earth more than 400-million years ago. An elder from a long-forgotten civilization manipulated the gem's crystalline molecular structure to merge the blade with Earth's vital energies. The dagger would serve as a catalyst, amplifying his abilities countless fold.

Aman lifted the crimson dagger from the box and turned it slowly for inspection. The prehistoric gemstone had been cut and polished to reveal its extraordinary perfection and absolute clarity. Long facets along its sides reflected light from an unseen source in extraordinary ways. *A masterpiece.* He allowed his lips a faint smile of admiration.

His smile vanished when his hand fumbled to hold onto the dagger, nearly dropping it into the black abyss. The jewel was indeed a unique key. Losing it now would bring a rapid end to everything.

Aman rebuffed thoughts of failure—this was not a time for weakness. He raised the crystalline blade into the void's shifting energy matrix above his head. The energy waves slowed and stabilized. With deliberate slowness, he rotated the gem counterclockwise, creating unusual patterns of light off its facets.

The great pounding ceased, temporarily staunching the deadly radiation flooding Earth's realm. Aman bowed his head, his slim frame trembling. *Thank you.*

A single point of light appeared far below him—a lone star in the infinite blackness, pulsing like a beacon. The orb, indescribably bright, accelerated toward him. Yet, it did not dazzle him.

The orb stopped just below his feet. Aman continued rotating the gem until the light faded, providing a window of sorts to a physical room below.

Aman scrutinized the remains of the accelerator's particle detector. His eyes took in every detail of the vast chamber that housed the accelerator's solenoid magnetic core. He saw something else down there—an object unimaginably powerful and terrifying floating above the shattered equipment.

A gateway.

He had found the vortex, an inadvertent alien conduit to this world that upset Earth's balance and would destroy all life on this living planet.

The ethereal structure was alive and fluid. Aman stared into a cosmic tunnel of shifting lights and bands of colors. Thousands of stars were in constant motion, moving in both directions around a translucent doughnut-shaped rim that bent and distorted space behind it like a concave lens. The stars flowed around the perimeter and into the whirlpool-like tunnel, where they merged with the wall's multihued rings of radiation and vanished into a black abyss beyond.

The void faded, and Aman settled on a sheet of metal next to the gateway. From this lower vantage, he could see the donut-shaped rim floating above him but nothing below it.

Visible waves of energy gyrated above the gateway while its otherworldly glow painted the giant chamber bluish-white. He glanced upward and saw no trace of the black nothingness from which he had descended. But he knew it would return soon to reclaim the chamber. *Act quickly.*

The water tunnel's turbulence had torn every shred of clothing from his body. He didn't care about that. His mind was racing, taking in everything at once. The chamber's destruction appalled him. A massive explosion tore apart the collider and blew a five-story hole through the concrete ceiling. The specter of a human-made breach seemed impossible, as unlikely as humankind relearning physical field regeneration in a single lifetime. But the unthinkable had occurred. Humanity's recklessness far exceeded its shallow comprehension. What a sorry state. A global tragedy. *Unthinkable.*

A steady rain fell from the thick layers of melting ice covering every surface. The metal beneath his feet grew unbearably hot, and he labored for each breath. *I cannot survive long down here.*

But he had much to do—and little time. Creating twin work platforms to construct an apparatus to close the gateway would be difficult but not impossible. At least he halted the brutal bursts of energy—for the moment—which would provide the world with modest relief, albeit a temporary hiatus from the disaster it now faced.

Aman thrust the crystal dagger into the gateway's thick, blue corona—its atmosphere—and felt a force, sharp and angry, ripple through him like a dangerous electrical current. He winced, dismayed by what he felt. The corona was hot and expanding—very little malleability. *Work quickly!*

He manipulated the energy waves until a translucent three-dimensional globe appeared above the gateway's tunnel like a floating hologram. The globe's symmetric points intersected to create a 248-sided geometric sphere on which all laws of the universe were elegantly revealed to him—a blueprint of all physical matter from the Source. And his to command.

The luminous sphere began rotating. Aman wiped the rain

from his eyes and held his gaze in wonder. New energy coursed through him, remapping his mind, bestowing him with sacred knowledge of creation. His body tensed.

He shut his eyes tight and allowed his mind to become one with the gateway's cosmic field.

. . .

The C-130's flight deck grew quiet. Marshall stood and listened. He could no longer hear wind-swept sand battering the airframe. In fact, there was no sound at all.

"Nick?"

He checked his patient. Nick slept thanks to another injection of morphine. His vitals were stable. *Let him rest.* Marshall's thoughts returned to Samantha. Was she safe?

He moved through the cargo area and onto the aircraft's twisted rear ramp. The violent sandstorm with its swirling dark funnel clouds had stopped, leaving a thick haze. He felt no trace of wind to carry it away. *Aman's doing? Is it truly over?*

Marshall walked down the ramp and onto the sand. He stopped to listen. A peaceful silence had overtaken the desert.

Marshall looked skyward, a hand shielding his eyes. He saw blue sky through the broken folds of dust clouds. A hot day in the desert, he concluded. A very hot day indeed.

"Please keep Samantha safe," he prayed.

. . .

Harlan Municipal Airport, Iowa

Mel Arterberry slogged through the filthy water around his knees and pushed open one of the hangar's tall doors. More mud flowed inside. He gazed across the remains of his beloved airfield. The devastating storm had stopped. But not before floodwaters had buried the twin runways and claimed his administration office and every one of the field's single-engine aircraft. Only this flooded hanger remained standing.

Mel removed a stained rag from his overalls and wiped his

dripping forehead. *Now, if only this goddamned heat would break.*
The layers of clouds gave way to patches of sunlight.

Mel's eyes brimmed with tears. "*Sonvbitch,* Aman. It's you, isn't it?"

. . .

Leighton Command Center
Wuerzburg, Germany

The underground emergency lights flickered back on, startling Chancellor Anne Osthoff from her prayers. She sat up on the edge of her bed in surprise and listened to the low drone of reprocessed air once again flowing through the bunker's ventilators.

She inhaled deeply to reverse the effect of slow suffocation. Nothing in the world tasted so sweet. She thought this would be her deathbed. Dare she hope otherwise?

Osthoff touched the Bible on the bed beside her and made the sign of the cross. "God bless you, Aman."

. . .

Leighton Airfield
Wuerzburg, Germany

"Mr. Cohen? Mr. Cohen?"

Jacob Cohen's eyes fluttered open. He looked up into the face of the young curly-haired American soldier who had saved his life. The deep gash down the youth's temple he sustained when the hanger's roof collapsed had coagulated into an ugly brown scab. He hadn't bothered to bandage it. Jacob didn't blame him. Why treat a cut when you're about to die?

"Mr. Cohen? Can you stand? I want you to see this."

The young man lifted Jacob's slim frame into a sitting position on the crawlspace's concrete floor, where he laid since a freak tornado leveled the hanger above them. Jacob's bandaged head throbbed, and he rose to his feet unsteadily with the young man's assistance.

Jacob refused to complain. He felt very fortunate to be alive while so many others weren't so lucky.

"You look much better," the soldier said. He belted laughter. "Since when is there black in your beard?"

Jacob touched his facial hair, puzzled. *What does he mean?*

The soldier wrapped Jacob's arm over his shoulder and half-led, half-carried him past the others who had huddled here with them during the worst of it. Some lay still, covered with sheets.

The youth helped Jacob up a short flight of steps to a concrete slab that had once been the hangar's floor. The heat above struck him like an open blast furnace. Still, he was glad to be on his feet again. Jacob spotted a twisted door frame leaning at an odd angle, the only fixture he recognized. The rest of the structure sat heaped in large piles of debris.

"You see that, Mr. Cohen?" The young man extended his hand toward the horizon. "The storm's passed."

Jacob's gaze scanned the flooded fields. The sun, huge and red, sank toward the horizon. Such deadly heat, he thought. He refused to share the soldier's child-like delight. *This isn't right. Is my friend in trouble?*

"The man you came here to find?" the youth said. "The man who left last night in a cargo plane? I don't recall his name."

"Aman," Jacob said, staring at the blazing horizon. "His name is Aman."

· · ·

Once again, Aman pushed the gemstone dagger into the corona and felt his hand spasm painfully from the strong current streaming up his arm. Yet, he did not waver. He visualized giant twin work platforms in incredible detail and then moved that mental image from a higher dimension to this dense three-dimensional realm.

A potent crack of thunder ripped through the chamber, and sparklets appeared high above like the birth of a mini star cluster. The starbursts solidified into a colossal work tower with its base anchored deep beneath the collider's floor. He was manifesting matter from subatomic particles, just as the Universe had done since the beginning of time.

Faster!

Another flurry of sparks appeared on the opposite side of the gateway and formed a second tower, a mirror image of the first. Aman continued manipulating energy until two extraordinary construction towers stood like sentries on opposite sides of the gateway, waiting to begin their work. These twin work platforms, each with a pair of long flexible robotic arm systems, would help construct a powerful device to close the breach. Finally, he created a holographic control platform a safe distance from the gateway to monitor the construction.

But he wasn't finished.

Aman once again pressed the gemstone into the corona. He winced from another surge of energy that threatened to cripple his arm. Sweat mixed with rain flooded his eyes. *Hold still!* A thick, oscillating sound shook the chamber like an earthquake, its harsh noise more felt than heard. A large ring of white light, pure and radiant, appeared around the gateway.

The ring's edge expanded and bent inward, ripping open space-time to reveal a dimension far different from his physical world. The opening—a door—stretched until it touched the chamber's floor. He struggled to hold his hand steady. Dropping the gem would seal the orifice he so desperately needed to keep open.

Aman saw movement within. A single radiant orb broke into three figures made of light moving through a strange white mist. Their extremities, surrounded by sparkles and lacking any skeletal structure, stretched and undulated in mischievous motions. As they approached, the malleable shapes coalesced into three human figures—a man and two women dressed in festive color clothing. He forgot his distress and allowed a euphoric smile to replace his drawn features.

The three figures stepped onto the shattered platform and marched toward him with pride and purpose. Each returned a splendid smile of greeting.

Aman lowered his arm with a heavy sigh and let the gemstone dangle at his side. The interdimensional ring vanished behind the three, its deep oscillating sound silenced. A bitter thought eclipsed his elation. Their frequencies would soon rise again until they would be drawn back into the realm they called home. And he would be alone again.

Aman could hardly speak. "Eos and Dorea," he said to his children. "Welcome."

"Always a pleasure to see you in the flesh, father," said the young man, Eos, slicking back his shoulder-length hair with rainwater. His curious eyes scanned the twin work towers. His expression beamed with a generous smile. "These will do nicely, father. In fact, they are perfect."

His sister Dorea presented Aman with a robe she had brought with her. Aman accepted the garment and slipped it on, and the three embraced with unspoken joy. He wished to hold his children forever.

Aman broke away with reluctance and turned to the woman with white flowing hair and dressed in a red robe, watching him with a smile. "My Sheema." He bowed his head to hide tears. Her intense green eyes never wavered from him.

"The melting ice will complicate our work," Eos said, interrupting their reunion.

Aman nodded. *He wishes to remind me why we are here.* "You must excuse my world's precarious state."

"How will you keep the realms apart?" Eos inquired.

"With this." Aman held up the blood-red gemstone. "I will tap the corona's energy field to link to the gateway."

Eos scowled. "A dangerous method. What are our other options?"

"None, given our time constraints," Aman said.

His daughter, Dorea, her eyes fixed on the floating gateway, grew impatient, her expression taut. "It's expanding, and the heat will cause our physical bodies great pain," she said. "You should have summoned us much sooner. This frightens me. Forgive our haste, father, but we must begin."

Eos placed a hand on his sister's shoulder. "I agree."

Aman nodded. "Of course. Proceed."

Eos and Dorea raced in opposite directions, each to their respective work tower. They stepped onto circular plates that lifted them rapidly inside the machines' scaffolding to their control stations high atop of their tower. Within seconds, the twin platforms came to life. Each machine's twin agile robotic arms began probing the chamber's scrap heaps at a dizzying rate and accuracy, collecting rare alloys needed to build their device.

Aman gazed into Sheema's eyes. "I miss you so."

She smiled and extended her hand to him. "The waiting is difficult. I want so much to be together—a family again."

His fingers touched hers for the first time in a very long while. His eyes again filled with tears of deep longing. *Yes, I want that too—very much so.*

A gentle current flowed between them. Forces from two profoundly different worlds that could not merge.

ARUK

SAMANTHA FOUND KIRBY working inside a sizeable hole he had carved into the tunnel's ice wall with his industrial chisel. "Kirby," she shouted. "Aman's gone."

Kirby didn't hear her over the whine of his jackhammer. He worked undistracted, the ice falling away in large, wet chunks thanks to the rapid rise in the tunnel's temperature, which Samantha figured had climbed over one-hundred degrees. Water fell from the ceiling like a steady rain. The ice kept the air cool and breathable.

Kirby uncovered a corpse holding a shaft with a spear-like tip, blocking his way. He wrenched the shaft free and tossed it into the tunnel, landing in the slush at Samantha's feet. Water flowed over her boots as though she were standing in a shallow stream.

The jackhammer's electric motor grew sluggish. Samantha reached into the hole and yanked Kirby's leg. "Turn that thing off!" she shouted.

Kirby stopped, shrugged the battery pack from his shoulders, and took off his thermal coat. "Damn battery's almost dead. Aman didn't bring a spare."

"Forget the battery," she said. "Aman's gone."

Kirby looked at her, puzzled. "Gone? Where?"

"I don't know where." She pointed down the tunnel. "He took off his mask and coat and disappeared through the ice."

"He dumped his mask?"

"Yes. And his coat."

Kirby yanked off his face shield. "Damn thing's smothering

me. I can't see through it."

"Are you *crazy*? The air could still be dangerous."

"Screw it. The air's fine." Kirby tossed the mask aside and used his sleeve to clear the sweat from his face and eyes. "My lungs feel great."

A stiff hand came down on Samantha's right shoulder.

She spun around. "Aman—"

Samantha recoiled in shock. One of the tunnel's frozen men stood before her—a walking corpse, his face shockingly white. He wore a helmet-like leather cap and a dark, tattered robe that hung off him like seaweed.

A hiss poured from his lips that sounded like, "Free ... him..."

Samantha stumbled backward, slipped, and fell into the water. The man struggled forward, his bone-white fingers reaching for her. The sight of the ghastly figure terrified her.

"*Kirby!*" she screamed.

"What the—" Kirby scrambled out of the hole and stepped between them with raised fists, like a boxer.

"*Release him,*" the frozen man gasped. His dull eyes rolled up inside his head, and he collapsed onto the tunnel's floor with a splash. His lips were still moving while his face sunk beneath the rising water.

Samantha scrambled to her feet and adjusted her face shield. "Pull him out of the water."

"Are you nuts?" Steam puttered from his lips in short bursts.

She didn't blame him for being freaked out. *I'm freaked too.* "I don't think he means to hurt us. We need to find out what he wants."

Kirby yanked the man's body from the water and dragged him to a high spot next to the ice wall. His body contorted and twisted as though in a seizure.

"Forget it," Samantha said. "He's not conscious."

"This is crazy. Let's get out of here."

"No." She glanced at the hole Kirby had carved out of the ice. *Why here?* "Aman told you to dig to the inner wall."

Kirby ran a hand through his sopping hair. "That was before

this guy showed up." He glanced up the tunnel with a wary expression. "What if his buddies wake up?" He shook his head. "No friggin way I'm staying here without Aman. I say we go topside and wait."

Samantha felt a surge of desperation. "No!"

"You're insane."

She snatched up the spear-like tool from the tunnel's flooded floor and ducked into the ice hole Kirby had created. She rammed the rod's chisel tip into the ice. *What did he want us to find here?* She pounded the rod, again and again, venting her frustration. She heard the tip strike metal. A final layer of ice fell away in a single sheet, exposing a large black box with ornate metal plating.

Samantha stared. Strange, hieroglyphic-like symbols were carved into the oblong box. "Look at this." She jabbed at the remaining ice to clean its surface.

Kirby squeezed next to her. "What the hell is that?"

"Aman wanted us to find it," she said. "Can you open it?"

Kirby touched a small hole on the side. "Looks like it needs a key."

"There." Samantha thrust a finger at the worker Kirby had uncovered beneath the ice. He held a small metal object with wavy ridges that could pass for a key. "Maybe he was going to use that to open the box."

Kirby grabbed the pole from her and dug its tip into the ice until he exposed the object in the corpse's hand. He wrestled it from the claw-like fingers, breaking off several digits in the process. "Mother F—"

Samantha flinched.

Kirby fumbled to insert the key into the box's hole. It fit perfectly. The side of the metal box came off in his hand. Samantha felt a draft of cold, fetid air blow past her.

Kirby directed his light inside the box. "Christ, it's a goddamn coffin!"

• • •

Sheema followed Aman to the edge of the gateway's corona, a blue translucent wall of lethal radiation that terrified her. Aman stood there, considering the gemstone in his hand, mentally questioning whether it would give him the strength to complete his task. It didn't matter—he had no other options.

Sheema's expression betrayed her deep concern. "Please reconsider. Your method requires great strength and endurance. It could kill you."

For an instant, Aman's eyes fluttered with uncertainty. Then, "I have no choice."

Before she could respond, Aman turned away from her and thrust the gemstone into the corona's energy field. Sheema watched in dismay as his body grew rigid and began trembling. She reached out to touch him but thought better of it and backed away.

Aman gritted his teeth as a powerful energy stream surged up his arm. *I have no choice.*

• • •

"*A coffin?*" Samantha shouted.

"Yeah. With a body."

Samantha squeezed beside him and directed her light inside. Her throat tightened. Those weren't ancient skeletal remains. She saw a frail man covered with ice chunks, wearing a dark robe similar to the others in the tunnel, his hands folded over his chest.

Kirby turned away. "I'm outta here."

"He *moved!*" Samantha shouted, pointing.

Kirby whirled.

A hand dropped from the body's chest and slid away until his fingers touched the box's other side.

Kirby slid backward. "*Whoa!*"

Samantha directed her light into the man's pallid face. His lips were moving.

"That's no corpse." She reached inside the box, grabbed the garment around the man's shoulder, and pulled. The fabric came apart in threads. "Help me, Kirby."

"*Jesus.*" Kirby, scowling, slipped both hands under the man's arms.

Samantha backed out of the hole to allow Kirby room to pull the body from the box with one swift yank. He appeared to weigh very little. Kirby grabbed the man around his chest and dragged him out into the tunnel.

Water poured down on them like heavy rain from the rapidly melting ice. Samantha stood knee-deep in the swift-flowing current. Despite the rising heat, the water still was exceedingly cold.

Kirby set the anemic-looking man on his back on a mound of fallen ice. Samantha moved to his side. He was older, perhaps in his seventies, short and thin, with gray shoulder-length hair. His angular features reminded her of Aman.

She felt his bony wrist for a pulse. His head jerked suddenly, and his eyes opened wide. Samantha stumbled back in surprise, nearly losing her footing again. He blinked incessantly against the rain, his breathing short and rapid. He couldn't seem to focus his eyes.

Samantha stepped closer. *This is too strange—but what isn't?*

The man pushed air through his lips in small puffs. "Hel ... hel ... help ... help ... meeeeee...."

Samantha leaned over him. "Who are you?"

The man grabbed the front of her coat into his wrinkled fist. "Help ... me ... rise..."

"He wants to sit up," Samantha said.

Kirby pulled him into a sitting position.

The man let out a hacking cough that wracked his small frame. His breaths came in fits and huffs. He trembled terribly from hyperthermia, and Samantha feared he would collapse in a seizure like the other man. Instead, his trembling decreased, and he gasped, "Thank you."

She detected an accent, not unlike Aman's speech. The man's breathing improved, and a trace of color crept onto his features.

"What is your name, my son?" he asked Kirby.

"Kirby Dawson."

"Yes, yes, yes," the man said, his speech rushed. "I have heard about you." His trembling subsided. He stared at Kirby's face as though reading him. "You are skilled with tools. You are a man who gets things done."

"Yes, sir."

The man frowned when he shifted his gaze to Samantha. "You may uncover your face now and remove your cap. We are safe for the moment."

Kirby seemed okay without his. So did this old man. Fine. She pulled off her mask with a grateful sigh and drew in a deep breath.

The man continued staring, his eyes narrow, studying her. "The cap, too."

Samantha removed the ceramic cap and brushed the wet hair from her face. She felt no ill effects from the lethal signal. "My name's—"

"Samantha Coyote," he said. "I've heard much about you. I'm happy to meet you finally."

Samantha watched him suspiciously. "Who are you?"

He shifted around the ice heap and sank his sandaled feet into the frigid water. "My name is Aruk. It was my task to close the breach. But the unimaginable destruction here came quickly. The explosion destroyed everything—including most of my men."

"You're a sentinel," Samantha said.

Aruk nodded. "The gateway froze this complex in an instant to prevent catastrophic incineration. The deep freeze trapped me inside that box."

"When you didn't fix the breach," she said, "Aman came in your place."

"Yes," he said, "yes, yes. You see, Aman is my brother."

Samantha looked at him, stunned.

"I'll be damned," Kirby said.

"His journey here in my stead took much too long." Aruk ran his brittle fingers through his long gray hair, raking it back. "He has come too late."

ASSEMBLY

"I DON'T LIKE what I see," Sheema said to her husband. She stood on a small platform with holographic displays Aman had created for her to oversee the construction of the device to close the breach.

Aman did not need a warning. Creating the twin work towers and bringing his family into this world had caused gross instability in the gateway's plasma core. But he had no choice. However, his family faced annihilation if they didn't complete their work swiftly. *Our task here is growing increasingly futile,* he thought. *And my Sheema is aware of the grave danger.*

A blue glow enveloped the crystal blade Aman held firmly inside the corona. The heat buildup had become extreme.

"Aman?" Sheema called.

He kept his back to her to hide his distress. He didn't want her to see him this way, and he feared any distraction. Breaking his connection with the energy field, even for an instant, would be cataclysmic. The twin towers would revert to their primordial energy state in a violent implosion. His children, in their temporary state of flesh and blood, would disintegrate in that maelstrom. He would not allow that to happen—even at the cost of his life.

· · ·

A torrent of water roared down the tunnel like a flooded storm drain. Samantha struggled to maintain her footing under the swirling water that flowed around her waist.

The end of the tunnel had become a hard waterfall that crashed and churned around the same treacherous whirlpool where Aman disappeared. One slip, and they all would be swept into it.

"We can't stay here," Samantha shouted over the roar of water.

"Agreed," Aruk said. He extended his hands to Kirby. "You must help me."

Kirby swung Aruk's right arm over his shoulder before the current could sweep away his thin frame. Samantha grabbed his other arm for support.

"I will go alone to find my brother," Aruk said.

"The hell you will," Samantha shouted over the crashing water. "You're taking me with you."

"That may not be possible—"

"How do we get to him?" Samantha insisted.

Aruk gestured up the tunnel. "Steps. But ice sealed the passage."

Samantha saw huge ice sheets falling away, exposing the tunnel's curved concrete walls. "Show me."

The three fought the swift current back up the tunnel.

"Just up there," Aruk wheezed.

Samantha scanned the tunnel wall with her light beam. "There's nothing here."

"A bit farther on," Aruk said. "There, there."

They came to an opening in the wall. Kirby climbed onto a ledge and helped the others out of the water. Aruk put a shaking hand on the wall to steady himself while taking several deep breaths. Samantha feared he might be too exhausted to continue.

She peered inside the service doorway and directed her light down a long flight of metal steps. No ice, only water cascading down the staircase like a stepped fountain.

"It's pretty steep," she said to Kirby. "Can your knee handle it?"

"The knee's not bothering me," Kirby huffed, "much."

Samantha glanced back at the tunnel's rising water. Their

options were shrinking by the second. "I don't think we have a choice."

"We must proceed in haste," Aruk said.

Kirby let the light dangle around his neck and pressed his gloved hands against the cinderblock walls. "I'll go first."

Samantha followed Kirby down the staircase with Aruk close behind her. She couldn't see the metal steps beneath the cascading water, but they felt firm and even under her boots. The walls felt hot through her gloved palms.

The heated air thickened as they proceeded, making breathing a chore. Kirby moved quickly—too quickly, Samantha thought. She slowed as a precaution only to feel Aruk's urgent hand on her shoulder, pressing her forward.

"Don't get so close, Aruk," she said. "I'm not comfortable on these steps."

"Imagined fears will not serve us," Aruk said. "We must proceed quickly."

• • •

"Aman," Sheema said, her voice unsteady, "This is not going to work. We should stop and leave here now."

"*No!*" Aman, his face a mix of determination and agony, refused to look at his hand, which had become a charred claw. The intense pain worked its way up his outstretched arm like a slow-burning fuse. "We will not have another chance."

He raised his eyes to the gateway, its perimeter alive with angry pulses of intense white light. Aman struggled to maintain his control of its brutal energy while the same disorientation he experienced inside the void returned. *You must not lose this fight.*

His gaze shifted to the twin towers, where his children worked swiftly to create a powerful device to insert into the celestial vortex. The construction continued at a furious pace, the towers' robotic arms salvaging scrap metal and pieces from the collider's shattered machinery in a blur. A heavy shower of sparks rained down from the bonding process like a burning waterfall.

The construction task was enormous, the towering machines performing the labors of countless workers, far exceeding current industrial capabilities. He did not doubt Eos and Dorea's abilities and exceptional skills. But they needed time, the one thing he could not give them.

His expression tensed when he spotted dark, shifting sheets of radiation unfurling like gathering storm clouds above the towers. The void intended to keep them inside its dark prison, an existence of hellish isolation and inescapable madness. His children would be absorbed first.

"Focus," Sheema shouted to him, her voice terse.

Aman lowered his eyes. Weary with frustration and regret, his shoulders sagged, and he felt very old again. He longed for order and control. *Our children are at great risk because I brought them here. And my Sheema is terrified. I must not fail them—I must not fail humanity. This is why I was born.*

"I want more time," Aman shouted. "With you. With my family."

"Nothing must happen to you," Sheema shouted back to him. "Nothing must happen to our children. *Nothing.*"

Aman felt her fear. *No!—I need your courage to give me strength.*

Sheema touched the controls and called up to her children. "Eos. Dorea. The core is critical. How much longer?"

High above them, Eos' fingers danced across the control surface like a virtuoso. He heard the alarm in his mother's voice and scowled at the distraction. His jaw tightened. The device wasn't ready.

"We are not progressing as fast as planned," he said to his mother, curter than he intended.

"Finish immediately," Sheema implored. "No exceptions."

Eos understood. He opened a channel to his sister. "Status?"

"I am applying additional hardening to the casing," she said. "Just moments more."

"Are you expecting trouble?"

"I always expect trouble in this realm," she said. "Is the interior ready?"

"Negative," Eos said. "Charging the power supply is stubbornly difficult. The quantum nucleation system needs more mass."

"There is no time," she said. "Use your imagination and improvise."

Eos frowned and shook his head. *I sincerely hope we're not wasting our time here.*

ORIGINS

SAMANTHA'S LEG MUSCLES ached from the rapid descent. She let out a welcomed sigh when the stairwell gave way to a curved service tunnel. Large chunks of ice lay scattered everywhere. "How much farther?"

"Just ahead," Aruk said, still on her heels. His pace impressed her, considering his poor physical state only a short time ago.

The three proceeded swiftly, splashing through puddles of melted ice until the tunnel opened into a giant, dark room. Except this was no room. Samantha had stepped into profound darkness that seemed to stretch to infinity in every direction. She couldn't see her body, nor could she see a way back. She had the sense of being suspended, of floating but not moving. What had they done?

"Kirby?" the odd sound of her voice dissipated without a trace of acoustics. Samantha heard nothing from the others. In fact, she could hear no sound at all, which terrified her. She existed in an abyss of empty, joyless, nothingness.

A strange force accosted her, producing mounting vertigo. She felt energy streams shimmered through her like Jell-O, spinning her brain one way and then the other. The sensation was about to make her violently ill.

"Kirby?" Her voice traveled nowhere. She was lost and alone in this non-place.

A sudden panic seized her. *I'm dead, aren't I?*

Yes, of course, and this would be her existence for all eternity—alone, without a body, her consciousness absorbed in absolute, endless darkness in total silence. Forever.

"HELP! PLEASE HELP ME!"

Samantha felt a cold, hard surface against her back. Her eyes fluttered open with a start, and she looked up at Aruk standing over her. She tried to sit up quickly, but she fell back onto an ice-covered floor with a dull pounding inside her head.

Kirby sat up with a groan beside her. "Another second, and my skull would've exploded."

"We are very fortunate," Aruk said.

"What—what just happened?" Samantha said.

"Our consciousness entered a multidimensional space that separates all there is from infinity," Aruk said.

Samantha pushed herself into a sitting position. "Say again?"

"The empty region is a product of the breach," Aruk said.

Kirby struggled to his feet. "How did we get out of that hell hole?"

"Aman hid it temporarily," Aruk said. "He must be unable to keep the gateway stable, which threatens what he must finish here. If Aman fails, the void will swallow us and condemn us all to a madness worse than death. Earth would lay barren within days."

Samantha put out a hand to Kirby. "Help me up."

Kirby pulled Samantha to her feet. They stood on a deep concrete shelf covered with a thick layer of ice that overlooked a vast room with towering walls and a high ceiling. The rising heat was rapidly melting the ice down here, too. Samantha shed her coat while Kirby pulled off his gloves.

A waterfall of melted ice flowed over the side of the shelf. Samantha moved carefully to the edge and saw a large pond at least ten stories below. She shifted her gaze to take in the rest of the chamber.

"Oh, my God!"

Kirby stepped beside her and stared in awe. "What in hell am I looking at?"

They gazed across a vast area that housed the collider's magnetic core, one of the most formidable machines humanity had ever created. The damage to the equipment below was massive—a forest of twisted steel, broken conduits, and shattered machinery, the purpose of which she couldn't fathom. Floating above the destruction was a most wondrous swirling mass made of countless points of light—the same galactic tunnel she saw just before they landed. The stars flowed into a wide, multi-colored tunnel like a celestial drain.

She knew the object was not of this world. Globules of white lightning pulsating from deep within the tunnel touched her in a profound, physical way.

"Beautiful!" Samantha uttered, spellbound.

Something like this couldn't exist, she thought. Only Divine intelligence could create such a thing. *I'm looking through the very gates of heaven.*

Equally astounding were two remarkable crane-like construction towers on opposite sides of the extraordinary object. The twin towers' thin robot-like arms were picking through the collider's wreckage, plucking out and reshaping materials at an astonishing pace. They were constructing what looked like a high-tech missile. Where in the Lord's almighty kingdom did this technology come from, she wondered?

"You are blessed to witness what few will ever see," Aruk said.

Samantha tore her eyes away to face him. Aruk was watching her with a trace of a smile, perhaps amused by her naive awe.

"You are in the presence of an extraordinary portal not unlike the one that long ago breathed life in all its abundance across the earth," Aruk said. "The energy flowing through the original portal eons ago shaped a beautiful world full of life and balance. But humanity should never have opened another gateway, not now, not like this. The discordant energy forcing its way into our world comes from a dark, parallel plane—not from the Source. As you have witnessed, the uncontrolled release is creating chaos and death on a global scale. This could very well result in our extinction."

Samantha felt lightheaded. His words made about as much

sense as talking to a man they just dug out of an ice coffin.

"Why, Aruk?" she asked.

"A highly evolved civilization created a cosmic tunnel to this world in a desperate attempt to preserve their species," he said. "They exhausted the energy of their star system and tapped their region's dark antigravity ether to build a bridge to this galaxy. They inventoried millions of star systems, seeking out those few planets that could sustain them before their dying world disappeared into the cold, dark vastness. They selected this planet for their new home."

"Wait just a second," Kirby said, his face beet-red. "You mean this is all about helping aliens repair a tunnel to our world?"

"I wouldn't describe it that way," Aruk said.

Samantha shook her head, confused. "Why Earth?"

"Because the planet's carbon-based biochemistry is compatible with their own," he said. "They planted their seeds here and allowed the energy flowing from their home system to transform a barren planet into a bountiful garden. They even improved the ecosystem by introducing viable creatures from other worlds. The survival of their species depended on the fruition of those seeds."

"So now they want our planet for themselves?" Kirby said. "All those deaths, all the destruction in one week—it's an invasion, isn't it?"

"No," Aruk scoffed. "They are already here, and they have been for eons."

Samantha could scarcely breathe. "If they're here, why are they hiding?"

"Their species is not hiding." Aruk looked at Samantha, eyebrows raised, and then at Kirby as though the answer should have been obvious. "They are you and me."

Samantha cocked her head. "*What?*"

"They are us, and we are them," Aruk said. "Humanity is the product of their seeds. The elders gave their descendants everything they needed to make this planet their prosperous new home, and the honor and respect for its safekeeping was ours. The elders watch over this planet from their higher realm."

"You're creeping me out," Samantha said.

"You should not fear the Masters," Aruk said, "but welcome them as our ancestors, our brothers, our guardians. They are Earth's only hope."

"Then why aren't they fixing this shitstorm?" Kirby said. "Why aren't they here with us now?"

"The original ones have evolved into highly intelligent light beings. They cannot exist in our dense, heavy dimension, even for a short time. So they sent Aman."

"They're not doing jack shit, for *chrissake*," Samantha shouted.

"Not so. The Masters need to expand the human genome so our bodies can survive Earth's vibrational frequency shift. Those who cannot adapt will not be part of the New Earth. They must complete a vast amount of work on our bodies in a very short time. But this will mean nothing if Aman fails here."

Samantha looked at Kirby, unsure what to make of Aruk's strange explanation. He didn't appear convinced either. *Ancestors from another dimension?* A week ago, she never would have listened. Today, she didn't know what to believe and wanted to know more.

She appealed to Aruk. "Tell me something."

"If I can."

"Why did Aman bring me here?"

OBLIVION

ARUK LOOKED DEEP into Samantha's eyes. "Only Aman can answer that question."

Samantha stared at him. *He doesn't know.*

A violent tremor rocked the shelf. Samantha fell onto her back and slid to a stop at the edge of the shelf. The shaking subsided.

"What the hell was that?" Kirby said, crawling to the back wall on his hands and knees.

"Plasma is venting from the gateway's core," Aruk said. "That is concerning."

Samantha stood and looked over the edge into the chamber below. The height spooked her, like looking over the side of a skyscraper. "Where is he?"

Aruk stepped beside her and pointed. "There."

Samantha spotted Aman standing beneath the strange tunnel, his arm seemingly connected to its blue halo. Not far from him, a woman with long white hair and a red robe stood on a translucent circular platform surrounded by floating displays—a control station of sorts.

Seeing her again took Samantha's breath away. "Sheema's with him. And she's *alive.*"

Kirby moved to the edge. "What the hell are they doing?"

"Aman is manipulating the gateway's energy strings to manifest what he needs to close the breach," Aruk said. "He gave his wife and two children flesh and blood to return to our three-dimensional realm to help him. But only temporarily. They have very little time to create a tool to reverse the quantum gravitational singularity keeping the vortex open. They are rushing to build an apparatus that can generate an electromagnetic field powerful enough to cancel the breach's gravity anomaly and allow the vortex to collapse."

"Have you thought about becoming a college science professor?" Kirby said. Aruk ignored the question.

Samantha's eyes remained fixed below, watching them work. "Unbelievable."

"His children are highly skilled," Aruk said with a note of pride. "A gift that flows through our bloodline—"

A horrific blast rocked the chamber. The shock wave lifted Aruk off his feet and dumped his small frame against the back wall. Samantha dropped to her knees and spread her hands across the bucking ice surface for support. The tall work towers on either side of the gateway wobbled dangerously.

The shock wave subsided.

"Now what?" Kirby said, lying spread eagle on the ice.

Samantha crawled back to Aruk. He lay on his back, his breathing rapid. The air was growing thin, and she couldn't get enough of it.

Aruk put a hand on his forehead. "No. No. No."

"Aruk? What's wrong?"

He struggled to rise. Samantha helped pull him into a sitting position.

"Did that tunnel thing do this?" she said.

"Aman is averting a full breach—but there is a limit to what he can do," he said. "He has separated the two dimensions and must keep them apart. He must not lose his connection with the Field, not even for an instant."

"And if he does?"

"Total oblivion."

"That's just great," Kirby said. "So, we're screwed."

Aruk crawled to the edge, his eyes scanning the chamber below. Samantha followed, inching forward on her hands and knees, wary of another blast. Large sections of ice were falling away from the walls and ceiling at an ever-increasing rate. She didn't see a way down. "How do we reach him?"

Aruk sat back. "We don't."

"NO! We need to help him."

"The task of closing the breach is his alone," Aruka said.

Samantha rose to her knees and glowered over him. "How do I get down there?"

Aruk kept shaking his head. "My child, your presence would be a mistake—a gross distraction."

Another boom, less severe, shook the ledge. The sound reverberated like thunder.

Sweat streamed down Kirby's crimson features. "*Goddamnit,* I didn't come all this way to buy it in some interstellar explosion." He thrust a finger at Aruk. "How do we get down there to help the man?"

"I will go," Aruk said. "Alone."

He draped his thin legs over the side and looked down into the rising pool of water ten stories below. Samantha heard more ice cracking beneath him.

"Aruk? What are you doing?" she said.

He pushed himself off the ledge.

Kirby slid to the edge. "*Sonovabitch.*"

Samantha flattened onto her stomach and peered over the side just as Aruk struck the water. She refused to release her breath until his head broke the surface, and he began splashing his way across the pool.

"The man's got big brass ones," Kirby said, "I'll give him that."

"It's too high for us," Samantha said.

"I'll get the truck's cable ladder," Kirby said.

"Too short." Samantha moved to the back of the shelf, her mind spinning.

Kirby eased against the wall next to her. He looked exhausted and beaten, and she feared he might pass out from the chamber's low oxygen and rising heat.

"We're so screwed," he said.

Samantha grabbed the quartz amulet around her neck. *What am I supposed to do?*

. . .

Aman's flesh sizzled. Sheema watched him drop to his knees beside the gateway's expanding corona, his breath coming as sobbing gasps. She could not bear to see him suffer this way. Despite his anguish, she knew her husband would never give up—not with their children at risk.

Sheema stepped off her control platform and raised a hand to him. She stopped. Her bone-white fingers had lost the color of life. Her physical form was deteriorating. She and her children were returning to their realm. *We will not finish here.*

Sheema began sobbing. "My Aman."

. . .

Aruk staggered out of the water and limped toward the gateway while the rain intensified from the rapidly melting ice. Sparks pouring from the construction towers high above provided precipitation of its own in the form of a shower of embers. But that wasn't his concern. The chamber was filling with acrid, toxic smoke, making breathing dangerous.

He found Aman kneeling beside the corona, his face twisted in agony. Yet, he would not release his grip on the crystal blade inside the corona. The odor of burning flesh stunned Aruk. His brother's forearm was thin and blackened, the remains of bone visible. High above, he saw the void's dark plumes oscillating around each other, eager to retake the chamber. Aman's bond with the field was about to break.

We are doomed.

Aruk extended a hand but stopped short of touching him. *What am I thinking?* Merging their energy could create disastrous instability and hasten their end. "I am afraid, brother."

Aman raised his head while sweat poured over his beaten features. *His suffering must be inconceivable.* Yet, Aruk could do nothing to ease his brother's anguish.

"He's dying," Sheema called to him.

Aruk put up a hand for her to stay back.

"I have failed," Aman gasped. "Open the portal and take my family back to safety before I kill them. Take Samantha and Mr. Dawson as well. There is no future in this world. *Hurry!*"

Aruk knelt before him. "Listen to me. You have done re-markable work here. Creating these machines and bringing your family back to operate them was genius. You must allow your children to complete their task."

Aman shut his eyes tight. *"Do as I ask."*

"I will do no such thing!" Aruk shouted. "We will all stay until you finish what you came here to do. That is the only way we will be together again as a family in a much better world you helped create. That is our dream—your destiny."

Aman's eyes flared open, and Aruk saw his deep anger. *"Do it now."*

Another burst of plasma roared across the chamber. The discharge slammed Aruk onto the floor while Sheema crouched beside her station. The holographic control screens above her sputtered.

Aruk shook his head. *Our time is over, brother.*

COCOON

THE CHAMBER REVERBERATED with a relentless roar of thunder. Angry bursts of lightning emanating from the tunnel reminded Samantha of the discharge from a novelty plasma ball. She felt the heat rising and beckoned Kirby with an urgent wave. "Something's changing, and not for the better."

Kirby moved to the edge beside her to see the gateway. "We're into some deep shit."

Another burst rocked the shelf.

Kirby grabbed Samantha's arm in a tight grip of panic and looked back at the passageway that led them down here. "Let's get out of here before we deep-fry."

Samantha didn't hear him—she was thinking about Marshall. If they were going to die, she wanted to be with him. But what if he was already dead? What if everyone she ever knew was dead? If so, what's the point of it all?

Her thoughts shifted to Aman. *He brought me here to help him, and I've done nothing.* "I need to find a way down there."

• • •

Aruk struggled to draw in a breath. The field's ionized discharges depleted most of the chamber's oxygen.

He put out a hand to his brother. "No, this cannot be."

"Do not distract him," Sheema said, approaching. Her pale, translucent skin indicated that she and her children were leaving this dying world and returning to their higher-dimensional realm—and safety. *Yes, at least Aman's family would be safe.*

"My dear Sheema."

"I cannot watch him die," she sobbed. "I cannot."

Aruk exhaled what little breath he held. He felt powerless to help his brother. "Sheema, he wants you and your children safe."

More lightning discharging from the corona pounded the walls, dislodging great ice blocks that crashed down around them.

"It's hopeless," Sheema said. She wiped her eyes and opened the channel to her children. "Eos. Dorea. Disembark immediately."

• • •

Dorea could no longer ignore her hands' strange luminance, making it impossible to operate the controls. The flesh and blood her father gave her were dissolving. She fought a growing panic. The construction was sloppy, and she questioned whether the device would work in its crude state. Regardless, they were out of time. She glanced across at Eos' workstation. Flailing streams of light flowed like tentacles around his tower. The twin structures were disintegrating, too.

"Disembark," she called to Eos.

No response.

"Eos?"

"One moment, please," he shouted.

"No—"

A thunderous blast sent another quake through the chamber. Dorea's tower shook and swayed while searing white light whirled around her, blinding her, burning her. She cursed the fragile human physique, vulnerable to so much physical pain. She felt lightheaded and began to black out. *If I stay up here in this body, the pain will be unimaginable.*

• • •

Another severe concussion struck the face of the wall below Samantha and Kirby. The ice-covered shelf buckled under the impact. Samantha landed with a grunt, her ears ringing from the blast.

Cracks appeared on the surface beneath Samantha. Her hands brushed the ground for something, anything, to grasp. But she felt only ice and water.

The cracks widened. Her eyes locked with Kirby's, and she could see his terror.

The front of the ledge collapsed. Samantha slipped into an ice fracture, her arms flailing for a handhold as she slid toward the edge.

Kirby grabbed her as she slid past him and jerked her to a stop. He held her full weight while water and debris flowed around her.

"Find something solid and grab it," Kirby instructed her.

His voice sounded muffled in her ears from the blast. Samantha saw a protruding chunk of cement by her feet. Her arm slipped from his grip. She scrambled onto the small stone haven and clung desperately to it.

"Kirby," she gasped, "you saved my—"

The ice slab beneath Kirby shifted, dumping him into the channel of ice and rubble. He slid past her with a yell.

She reached for him. Too late. "Kirby!"

He grabbed an ice outcrop at the edge to stop his fall over the side. A steady stream of ice chunks and gravel hurtled past him, hammering his face like mallet blows. This is it, Samantha thought. *This is how God will send for us.*

She watched helplessly as Kirby clung to the ice cantilever for his life. His fingers were brushed raw, and he spat out a mouthful of blood. His feet scraped the melting ice wall below him, searching for support. There wasn't any.

More ice fell away beneath him and splashed into the pool ten stories below. She could see his panic.

It's not fair, she thought. *It's not fucking fair.*

· · ·

Aruk appealed to Aman. "Brother, you must keep the core stable. Only moments more."

Aman didn't answer. Could he hear him? Aruk watched a translucent cocoon-like bubble envelope Aman, something he had never observed before. What was this? His brother had become a parasite to the gateway, exploiting its power, and the portal was purging him. Still, Aman refused to abandon his hold on the gem.

Aruk peered closely at the bubble. Would it help or hurt Aman? He didn't know. "You are keeping us alive, brother."

Aman's muffled words came slowly inside the viscous bubble. "Are ... they ... finished?"

Aruk glanced up at the extraordinary projectile floating high above. Its odd geometric markings and seals appeared coarse, unfinished. Would it descend properly? Would it descend at all? And would its extreme electromagnetic radiation deliver enough energy to close the breach? He had no way of knowing.

"I — I am not certain."

Aman's eyes took on a distant look of resignation before closing. His head dropped. A deep rumble shook the chamber. The lofty work towers began to crumble in a livid flurry of stars, returning to a primordial quantum state.

Aruk saw no further movement from Aman's shrinking body. "My dear brother. I am sorry."

• • •

Eos activated the projectile's quantum thermionic system that would generate the extreme electromagnetic discharge they needed. "That's it—I hope."

The control surface disappeared under Eos' hands in an angry spasm of light. The tower's framework began collapsing around him. Finished or not, he needed to leave.

"Dorea?" he called to his sister. He heard no response and trusted she had already descended.

Eos stepped onto the circular plate that would take him

down to the chamber's floor. He grabbed a strut for support, but the metal vanished under his hand in an undulating wave of light and heat.

The plate under his feet began descending. He stood very still and prayed it stayed solid until he reached the ground.

· · ·

Kirby couldn't pull himself up onto the shattered ledge. Samantha held onto the outcrop of concrete for her life. She shifted her foot. More debris flowed over the edge. The next tremor would shake loose more ice and kill them both. *Dear God ... dear God...*

"Don't you move!" Kirby shouted.

Samantha's mind raced. Leaving this rock refuge would be suicide, a one-way free fall over the side for both of them. She couldn't see any way to save him. She couldn't save herself.

"How can I help you?" she shouted.

"Stay put."

She saw more cracks appear across the ice sheet. Kirby glanced down at the pool below. When he looked back at her, he was grinning without a trace of fear in his eyes. "I can do this."

"*No, Kirby, we're not like them—*"

He released his grip and fell.

BLOODLINE

KIRBY ROSE TO the surface in a daze and dragged himself through the pool's shallows. He knew he had broken lots of bones in the fall, and he couldn't feel his legs. At least he hadn't broken his neck or blacked out from a concussion and drowned, he thought. That was something.

A woman appeared above him—Sheema, dressed in the purest white. Her features were unearthly pale and marred by deep creases of concern.

Kirby tried to speak to her but only managed to cough up water. Finally, he groaned, "I can't walk. My legs..." His broken arm buckled beneath him, plunging his head back under the water.

Aruk splashed through the surf beside him. He wrapped his arms around Kirby's chest and dragged him out of the pool with more strength than a man of his slim frame could generally muster.

"Damn," Kirby moaned, "I screwed myself bad."

"What you did was stupid," Aruk said, pulling him onto a dry surface.

"Didn't have a choice."

Samantha shouted down to him, "Kirby, are you all right?" She still clung precariously to the loose cement section high above them.

Kirby lifted an arm and offered her a feeble wave that caused him considerable pain, his wrist bent at a frightening angle. He looked to Sheema. "Help her ... please..."

Sheema whirled and shouted at Aruk, "Get her down from

there."

"Yes," Aruk said. "Yes, of course."

Aruk scurried up the platform and drove his hand into the corona's energy field. His palm glowed a deep red, and he winced at the strength of the current. He kept his narrowed eyes fixed on Samantha while his mind visualized a way to get her down.

Aruk jerked his hand from the blistering corona with a howl.

A long, spiral staircase, three feet wide with pencil-thin handrails, materialized in front of Samantha. She stared in awe. *Now he thinks of steps.* She saw Aruk's tiny figure below waving his arms, beckoning her down.

Samantha released her grip on the cement chunks and lept onto the metal staircase anchored solidly below. She negotiated the first few steps carefully, keeping both hands on the rails for support. Reassured, she began clattering quickly around and around the spiral staircase toward the main floor.

A large ring of white light appeared around the gateway like Saturn's ring. Samantha slowed to watch it. The ring became so bright that it pained her to look at it. A halo mist flowed from the ring and twirled around Sheema, turning her body a ghastly white. Somehow the light was taking her from this place.

Samantha reached the bottom of the staircase and raced toward the others. She found a young woman kneeling before a basketball-size sphere sitting inside the corona. A young man with sharp, noble features stood behind her. Aman's children!

Their ghostly white appearance frightened Samantha. What remained of their flesh was falling away like powder. The strange light from the ring was taking the three of them back to wherever they came from but leaving their bodies here.

The young woman sobbed, *"Father."*

Aman? Samantha pushed Aruk aside to get a closer look. The woman reached into the corona, but her hand passed through the pod as pure energy.

Dorea's head flew back, and out poured a cry of despair.

Sheema placed a ghostly hand on her daughter's shoulder.

Samantha knelt beside Dorea and stared, astonished, at Aman—or what had become of him. She saw a withered caricature of a man the size of a doll inside the transparent shell wrapped around a long red crystal.

Samantha reached into the corona. A vicious spark knocked her back. *Jesus!*

"How do we get him out of there?" she said, flexing her throbbing hand.

"We cannot," Dorea said bitterly. "We lost him."

Anger shot through Samantha. *No!—This isn't happening.* "He brought me here to save him." She lowered her eyes to the pod and whispered, "I failed you miserably."

Sheema gestured toward the water. "Your friend needs your attention."

Samantha saw Kirby on his back by the pool. *"Kirby."*

She dashed down the platform and knelt beside him. The floor scorched through her jeans, like kneeling in a heated frying pan. How could he lay here?

Kirby looked awful. His eyes were closed, his breathing rapid. His injuries were far worse than she realized. He was dying.

Aman's son knelt on the other side of Kirby and said to his mother, "There's no way he can walk out of here. And if he stays, he'll die."

Sheema knelt beside Samantha. "I am very sorry about your friend."

"Can you fix him?" Samantha said.

"His injuries will need time to regenerate," Sheema said, "something he does not have."

Samantha leaned over him and shouted, *"Kirby."*

Kirby's eyes fluttered open with a start. "Sam…" He forced a grin. "I've always had a crush on you."

Samantha let out a huff of laughter and wiped her tearing eyes.

"We can't leave him," Dorea said.

"Of course not." Sheema said to Kirby, "You cannot stay here. If your friends try to take you out, none of you will survive."

"Leave me," Kirby said.

"Come with us," Sheema said.

"With you? Where?"

"Our home," she said, "for now."

"Do I have a choice?" Kirby raised a twisted hand. "Someone help me up."

Eos pushed him back onto the surface. "You cannot take that broken body with you."

"What the hell are you talking about?"

"Our dimension doesn't require flesh and blood," Eos said. "I'm certain you will find the experience agreeable."

"You're scaring the crap out of me." Kirby grabbed Samantha's hand. "Come with me."

"She cannot," Sheema said. "She would need to shed her physical form."

Samantha squeezed his hand gently. "I'm staying here with my body, thank you. At least for a while longer."

"Goodbye, Sam," Kirby said. "When you think of me, I hope the memories make you smile."

She took his hand in both of hers. She didn't want him to see her grief, but her eyes welled with more tears. "Kirby—"

His startled expression froze as the soft halo curled around him. Kirby's chest grew still, and his skin turned dreadfully white. She released his hand.

Samantha watched, stunned, as his body deflated inside his clothes. At the same time, a steam-like mist flowed from his body. They were taking his essence with them. Samantha saw Kirby's face stamped onto that stream. His lips were moving as though speaking to her, but she heard nothing. Dorea took his hand as he merged with Aman's family, and together they flowed inside the portal's peculiar ring of light. Only Sheema's features remained recognizable.

"You should know that you are a descendant of the sentinels," she said to Samantha. "We are your family."

"Family?" she said, puzzled. "My parents died when I was nine."

"I am your original mother. Aman is your original father—many, many generations ago."

Samantha stared, dumbstruck. *Family?* She felt deeply moved.

Sheema's features continued to meld into the light. Very little of her remained. "You were his connection in this world, the last of our lineage." Her essence was fading. "You must not leave him here—"

The ring vanished, taking Sheema, her children, and Kirby with it. The chamber darkened. They were gone.

Aruk laid a hand on Samantha's shoulder. "Aman has done remarkable work." He looked up at the gateway and added in a low voice, "If only the device descends. It must descend."

That's just great, she thought. After all this, nothing is certain. "Where did they go?"

Aruk took her arm and began leading her toward the staircase, his grip firm as he hurried her along. "Aman's family lived full lives many millennia ago. They now dwell in a higher realm that preserves their essence as they were until they can walk the earth again. There are many others like them, waiting."

Samantha pulled Aruk to a stop. "Why didn't they take Aman with them?"

"My brother's essence has evolved to a level that surpasses his family's realm," he said. "He will dwell in a higher plane and become one with the Source. Unfortunately, this realm will separate him from his family for eons until they evolve to his level."

Samantha pulled Aruk to a stop. "*No!* Sheema wants me to get him out of here."

Aruk scowled. "You cannot save him. No one can. Aman is gone. If you try, you will kill yourself."

She whirled toward Aman's basketball-size cocoon. Soon there would be nothing left.

"I'll take my chances." She sprinted toward the corona.

"Child," Aruk shouted after her. "Sheema is wrong!"

Samantha ignored him. Without hesitating, she stepped into the gateway's corona. A powerful charge ripped through her, paralyzing her.

CORONA

SAMANTHA SOARED OVER a sprawling landscape while a curious mosaic of images and sounds enveloped her. She tried to cry out but had no voice. Minutes, maybe hours passed before she slowed to a hover over a picturesque community with tall spires and stucco dwellings painted pastel colors.

She settled onto a cobblestoned street where children sang and ran past her with their dolls. An overwhelming feeling of love and peace filled her heart. This was a dream, wasn't it? She felt a warm, dry breeze tousle her hair, and the street felt solid beneath her feet. This was no dream.

A young woman passed her with two small children, a boy and a girl, clinging to each of her hands. The woman had tied her long black hair into a loose tail that reached to her waist, and she wore a bright red dress that touched her ankles.

The young woman's elegant features looked teasingly familiar. Sheema? The young boy turned his head and smiled back at her before his mother took the two inside a two-story dwelling.

"You look lost," said a voice above her.

A striking young man in a green tunic watched her from a second-story window.

Samantha's eyes widened. "Aman?—how—?"

He gave her a smile of greeting.

Her surprise turned to confusion. Had she somehow crossed a vast chasm of time and space to a moment in Aman's life long ago when he walked the earth with his wife and children? *Or did I really die this time?*

Aman leaned out the window, his warm expression turned

somber. "Don't leave me in there. Or I will not see my family for a very long time. Please—"

"My child? Can you hear me? *My child?*"

Samantha opened her eyes and saw Aruk kneeling over her. She couldn't move. The last of the ice was gone, taking the rain with it. High above, she saw the void's odd black angles expanding. She shuddered at the sight of it.

Her paralysis faded, and she pushed herself into a sitting position, which made her lightheaded and dizzy. She was sitting next to Aruk, twenty feet from the corona. Her head throbbed, and every joint protested in pain. A weird current flowed down her arms and ended at her tingling fingertips.

Aruk's taut expression softened with relief. "I thought the corona had killed you."

"You pulled me out?"

"Yes. But that is not our concern now. The void will claim everything Aman has done if the device isn't lowered before it overtakes this space."

Samantha wiped the sweat-soaked hair from her face. "I saw Aman."

"Aman is gone."

"But—"

"We will talk later," Aruk said, standing. He indicated the spiral staircase created for her. "Mount those steps and return to the tunnel from which we came. Leave this place. Your life depends on it."

"I spoke with him."

"Do as I say. *In haste.*"

Aruk turned and ran to the gateway, using the inside of an elbow to shield his face from the intense heat. He stayed well away from Aman's remains as though afraid to look at it.

Aruk thrust his right hand into the corona, his fingers angled upward. His palm glowed red like before, and Samantha saw flashes of light sputtering off his fingertips. He struggled to stay upright.

"Aruk?" she said.

A powerful hiss filled the chamber, startling her. High above the gateway, the projectile came to life with an ear-shattering screech and began rotating.

Aruk peeked over his elbow and watched it closely. The projectile's rotation increased as it began descending. "Yes, YES."

Samantha heard Aman's weak voice. *"Do not leave me."*

"Aman?" She whirled and saw only the barest outline of Aman's remains inside that shell. *That bomb will destroy what's left of him.*

Samantha tried to clear her mind. Aman had given her a single task—save him. Somehow she needed to take the pod with her.

She rose and staggered to the edge of the blue corona, a lethal field that protected the gateway like a moat of fire. Perhaps she was too late to help him. What if there's nothing left to save? *He needs me.* She drew in a long breath and held it.

Samantha heard Aruk shouting at her. "Dear child—*no!*" He jerked his hand from the corona. A puff of smoke spiraled from his fingertips.

She stepped inside the corona.

A giant unseen hand began crushing her while the extreme heat scorched every inch of her body. She heard crackling all around her like an electrical discharge. But this time, she remained conscious.

Samatha glanced up at the descending missile, its geometric markings reflecting light in bewildering patterns. *Let's do this.*

Samantha's mind raced. She fought back a growing panic and collapsed onto her knees in front of Aman's shell. A tiny pair of eyes inside opened and locked with hers. *There's still life! And you can see me.*

Her vision dimmed, and she began to sway. Samantha made a desperate effort to fill her lungs, but there was no air inside the corona. She struggled to stay upright. *You'll die if you black out!* "I ... can ... do this..."

A glass-like sphere enveloped her. The heat dissipated until it became tolerable, and she could draw in shallow breaths. *It's shielding me—just like that cacoon is shielding Aman!* She glanced at her quartz wand amulet, glowing a bright blue.

Samantha spotted Aman's smock under the pod. She yanked it free and spread out the fabric before her, then drove her fist into Aman's shell, splitting it. Scorching crimson fluid flowed over her hand and between her fingers, burning her in the process.

Samantha reached into the pod and lifted the blistered clump of tissue that had once been Aman. She pulled until the mass detached from its shell and placed it in the center of the smock. A blood-red crystalline knife remained embedded in the tissue.

She spotted Aman's old wooden box—his key. The wood had blackened from the heat, its metal straps melted. She grabbed the box and set it next to Aman's remains and wrapped them both in the smock.

"Let's get out of here, Aman."

Samantha tucked the bundle under her arm and bolted from the corona, leaving a trail of smoke from her hair and clothing.

Aruk waved his arms from the top of the circular staircase. "Hurry, child!"

Samantha glanced back and saw the projectile spinning like a drill bit right above the gateway's tunnel. She charged up the staircase with her bundle, her free hand on the rail.

The corona grew more violent, reacting angrily to the projectile's arrival. Intense bursts of energy shot in random directions like death rays, some of them vaporizing the water below her in fierce sprays.

Samantha reached the top of the staircase, and Aruk pulled her onto the concrete shelf.

"Aruk," she managed, cradling her bundle, "I think he's—"

"Come!"

Aruk yanked her into the service tunnel and began climbing the staircase leading to the next level. He released her hand and stormed up the steps, taking them two and three at a time. Samantha raced after him. She chanced a look back and saw a radiant white fluid flooding the lower steps.

"Eyes forward," Aruk warned, as though he could see behind him.

Samantha focused on the steps ahead, her leg muscles protesting the rapid climb. They reached the top and climbed down into the accelerator's service tunnel. Every trace of ice and water had vanished, revealing cement walls lined with utility pipes.

She followed Aruk far up the tunnel until he could go no farther and collapsed into a sitting position on the grated metal floor, his chest heaving.

Samantha settled beside him with a groan. The ends of her hair had withered from the heat. Her arms were blistered, and the rubber soles of her orange boots had melted. She wondered why her injuries were not more severe. *I should've been incinerated.*

She grasped the wand amulet hanging around her neck. Only a stump of quartz remained. "I'll be damned."

Aruk looked exhausted, and she figured he hadn't yet reached the physical peak Aman had achieved over the week. "Are you okay?"

Aruk couldn't catch his breath and began hyperventilating. "Give me one moment. Just one moment, please."

. . .

The projectile entered the gateway's tunnel, producing a blaring moan-like noise that sounded almost human. Superheated plasma from deep within the tunnel assaulted the device, attempting to vaporize it. Its surface glowed white from the intense heat.

The projectile's rotation accelerated to a blur. Although Aman's children created a shell that could survive temperatures equal to the sun's surface, the device's reinforced exterior began breaking down. A thermal expansion threatened to destroy it.

But the projectile refused to concede. The device's power

system activated and blasted extremely high electromagnetic pulses deep inside the tunnel, creating gross instability. The gateway's plasma flow ionized and dissipated. What remained of the blue corona disbursed in a powerful detonation that incinerated the remains of the chamber in an instant.

Within that maelstrom, the gateway grew to twice its size before shrinking to a brilliant floating orb, pulsating as though considering its options. There were none. The translucent sphere darkened until every trace of it vanished into the inter-dimensional ether, taking the projectile with it. The roar faded.

The chamber grew still and dark—and very quiet.

• • •

The tunnel brightened, and Samantha felt the surface beneath her shaking. An intense light appeared around a bend in the curving tunnel, heading toward them. The sudden wave of heat felt like an open furnace.

Aruk rose to his feet. "Go!"

He scrambled up the tunnel. Samantha grabbed her bundle and ran after him. Aruk slipped into the computer room through the opening Kirby had created with his jackhammer. Samantha followed. She looked back and saw a fireball roaring toward them.

Aruk yanked her away, and they raced between rows of toppled server racks. They hadn't gone far when Aruk hurled himself onto Samantha and slammed her to the floor behind a metal desk. She pressed the bundle against her chest and pushed her face into it. An instant later, an explosion destroyed the wall behind them, tearing through the room like a rocket, hurling debris in a great upheaval.

As the blast subsided, glowing embers rained down like the fallout of a volcano, burying everything in ash.

REGENERATION

DUSK SETTLED OVER the quiet desert. Marshall dug into one of the cargo lockers and found a battery-operated lantern. He carried it into the shattered cockpit and knelt beside Nick, raising the lamp over his patient.

Nick sat up and shifted his leg, testing his mobility. Hours had passed since his last morphine injection, yet he didn't appear to be in pain now.

Marshall placed a hand on Nick's chest to keep him down. "Lie still."

"Doc," Nick said. "I need to stretch."

"I need you to lie still."

Nick frowned. "Damn, my forehead itches like a sonofabitch." He slipped a thumb under the gauze to scratch the wound. The wrap fell away.

Marshall moved the lamp close to examine Nick's head wound—or lack of one. Instead of a deep, bleeding gash, he found scarcely a crease. Not even a scab. Nick's complexion even held decent color.

"Well, I'll be damned." Marshall set down the lantern with a thump and sat back on the floor. "The tissue's healed."

"Huh?" Nick felt his forehead and broke into a broad smile. "Awesome!"

"Let me take a look at your leg—"

Marshall heard distant voices. He rose to listen. Was Samantha returning? His heart soared with the possibility. But there were too many.

"Is Aman back?" Nick asked.

"No. I hear a lot of people."

Nick's eyes widened. "Doc, what if they're bandits?"

Marshall stood very still, listening to the voices outside. He needed to check it out. "Stay put."

Marshall moved through the cargo bay and stood at the top of the aircraft's rear ramp. The last rays of sunlight had retreated, casting colors across the horizon, a beautiful sky the likes of which he had never seen before. But there still was enough twilight to reveal the wreckage to anyone passing by, particularly desperate bandits. The voices grew louder, closer, and he heard children shouting.

Marshall walked down the ramp and out across the sand under a cloudless, azure sky. He loved the way the evening felt. The air was crisp and clear, a remarkable contrast from the day's violent storms and heat. Countless stars were visible.

His pace slowed. About a half-mile away, a long caravan of people carrying torches streamed across the sand as though on a pilgrimage—men, women, and children dressed for the desert. A few rode on camels and mules while the majority walked. These weren't bandits. They were families heading in the same direction Aman and the others had gone. He felt oddly drawn to follow them.

"Great night for a walk," Nick said.

Marshall turned and saw Nick standing at the top of the cargo ramp, a hand on the airframe for support.

"You shouldn't be standing," Marshall said.

"I shouldn't be alive." Nick jammed his Beatles cap onto his head and hobbled down the ramp. He looked alert and didn't seem in any pain, ready for a night at a rock concert.

"Slow and easy, Nick," Marshall said. "I still want a look at your leg."

Nick spotted the corpses Marshall had placed in a neat row beside the airframe. He looked away and limped out across the sand, taking in the desert twilight. He wouldn't stop grinning and filled his lungs with the night's air, relishing the experience. His steps were unsteady, but he appeared to gain strength and confidence as he walked. Getting up on his feet seemed to revitalize him.

Nick watched the long procession a half-mile away. "Bedouin refugees?"

Marshall hadn't a clue who they were. "They're not interested in us. Maybe they've come to see Aman."

"Let's find out."

Marshall wasn't comfortable with Nick's sudden physical activity. But he understood his need to go—he felt the same allure to join these people. "You should take it easy for one night."

"I thought you wanted to find Samantha," Nick said over his shoulder with a grin.

Nick resumed his trek toward the caravan. Marshall hurried after him, and together they began crossing the rippled desert carpet.

• • •

Samantha lifted her head from the ash and sat up, dazed, her ears ringing. Small fires throughout the room provided light. She wiped soot from her face and hair and surveyed what remained of the wrecked hi-tech room that looked like a battlefield. The toppled metal desks and computer racks had saved her life.

She spotted a shoulder jutting from the ash next to her. "Aruk?"

Samantha rose awkwardly and set her bundle on top of a desk that had somehow remained upright. She reached under Aruk's arms and pulled him into a sitting position. He blinked incessantly to clear his eyes while exchanging a wary glance with her.

"We are very fortunate," he said, climbing to his feet.

"The gateway. Is it—?"

"Gone," Aruk said. "The breach is closed."

Samantha let out a long, sustained sigh of relief. "I still can't believe what I saw down there. Aman created a miracle."

"Humanity owes Aman a great debt for what he gave his life

for."

Samantha reached for the bundle. "Let's get out of here."

Aruk placed a hand on the bundle to stop her. "Yes, but first, show me."

Samantha hesitated, afraid to unwrap what she carried from below. "There isn't much left."

"Allow me to see," Aruk said.

Samantha stepped back and watched Aruk pull aside the fabric, releasing a stench of burnt flesh.

Samantha let out a gasp, horrified by what she saw. A dark mass of tissue lay quivering next to the crystal blade. She moved closer and forced herself to look at it. The gateway's energy shrunk Aman's physical body to a bloated, fetus-like mass small enough to carry under her arm. She looked closely at its face and recognized a few human features, or at least what remained of them, but this thing wasn't a man. Samantha wasn't sure what it was. Certainly not Aman. Its round, bulging eyes locked with hers while the undeveloped extremities stirred clumsily as though struggling to reach for her.

"What have I done?" she said. "You were right, Aruk. I should never have taken him. He can't live like this."

Aruk drew closer and stared in astonishment. "Child, I was wrong to dissuade you. Aman should have passed on. Yet you brought him here—alive. You truly are a special part of his bloodline."

Aruk leaned over the form and said, "Brother, I am so sorry I gave up on you. I am an impatient man." He looked at Samantha, his eyes hopeful. "Yes, yes, perhaps you can help him."

"What can I do?"

"Cleanse him."

"What? Give him a bath?"

"Place your left hand around the back of his head and your right palm against his forehead," he said.

"You do it."

"It must be you, as Sheema said," Aruk said.

"But—"

"You are vibrating at a higher frequency with new energy, allowing you to touch others in a way not possible before."

"New energy?" she said.

"An energy that rejuvenates, heals, cleanses, energizes, and purifies."

Samantha didn't understand any of this, but she was willing to try something, anything, to help Aman. She slipped her left hand behind Aman's head and placed the palm of her right hand over his forehead. His flesh felt moist and spongy. Her fingers trembled.

"I don't know what to do—"

"You are too busy thinking. Allow your mind to be still and, when you are ready, you will understand."

Samantha struggled to push every thought from her raucous mind and focused on the pitiful form under her hands. At first, she saw and felt nothing. Then her mind gave way to intense awareness. A current flowed down her arms and bathed her fingertips with unusual energy. She wasn't frightened. This was a good feeling that enthralled her.

She glanced at Aruk, her expression a blend of confusion and amazement. "I feel something."

Aruk nodded.

Her hands took on a metallic-like luster that reflected the room's scattered fires. She felt an extraordinary vibration throughout her whole being and allowed this energy to flow into Aman, cleansing him. But more than her hands had changed. Her senses awakened to a new dimension of consciousness. Everything around her glistened with deep meaning. She absorbed every detail—the amazing structure of her hands, the intensity of every color, Aruk's majestic pose standing beside her, the gem's incredible masterwork, the beautiful wood grains of the seared box—everything. The beauty she perceived grew beyond anything she had experienced before. And everything she saw was alive and wonderful.

"Welcome to the New Earth," Aruk said.

"Am I helping him?"

"You have stirred his cellular memories. His genetic sequence is returning to crucial equilibrium and regenerating his cells' protein molecules."

"I'm doing *what?*"

"The amino acids will follow alternate pathways to his former three-dimensional physical structure."

The tiny body tensed and began to thrash and twist as though in agony. She heard a faint cry.

Samantha jerked her hands away. "I'm killing him."

For an instant, the mass transmuted into a pure ball of light before melding back into flesh and blood, its tiny chest rising and falling in quick breaths.

REUNION

MARSHALL WORKED HIS way through a growing crowd of men, women, and children gathering at the base of a dune. They numbered in the hundreds, with more filing into the makeshift encampment under the abundant and brilliant stars. Where were these people coming from, he wondered?

The place felt alive and inviting with exciting energy. Marshall observed youngsters singing songs while the elders told stories and others talked fervently while readying tents and bedrolls by the light of their torches. He searched the faces and listened for Samantha's voice. But he saw and heard only strangers.

No one seemed to mind Marshall or Nick as they mingled. All newcomers summoned from the desert appeared to be welcome to this outdoor community. Marshall recalled the crowd in Germany that came to watch Aman depart from the airfield. Were these people following a similar call? And if Aman was here, what about Sam?

"Throw in some dope," Nick said, "and we'd have another Woodstock."

Marshall's keen eyes scanned the crowd. These people looked content and happy. But he felt neither. He wouldn't know contentment until he found Samantha.

"Bingo." Nick pointed toward the dune. "Our backhoe."

Marshall made his way to the buried machine. Only the roof cage and shovel arm remained exposed. Mothers were letting their children play on the backhoe's roof and take turns sitting in its sand-filled shovel.

Marshall's pulse quickened. Aman had been here—and done what? *Where are they?*

Too many people were arriving and getting in the way of his search. Marshall pushed past several families to get to the backhoe. He picked up a little girl from the shovel's dangerous teeth and set her on the ground before she injured herself.

"Use common sense, people," he shouted. "This isn't a playground."

Those closest to him fell silent and stared. A woman dressed in a beautiful red and black swirl gave him a disarming smile and spoke to him in Arabic. "The children are happy here. Please allow them to play."

Marshall's expression softened, and he regretted his outburst. These benevolent people had shown him only kindness. And he returned that kindness with beratement.

Marshall bowed apologetically to the woman. "I don't want to see anyone get hurt." He spotted a tiny dark-haired girl with big eyes standing in front of him, holding an exotic red flower the likes of which he had never seen before. He couldn't imagine where she found it out here.

He rejoined Nick.

"So we found the backhoe," Nick said, "but I don't see anything dug up."

The deep drifts of sand and the lack of daylight made it impossible to determine what Aman had unearthed. Marshall's heart sank. He saw no other evidence of Aman's presence here.

"The Humvee's gone," Marshall said. "They could be miles from here."

"Or maybe not." Nick pointed toward another spot farther along the base of the hill.

The torch flames caught the reflection of what looked like a windshield jutting from the hillside. Marshall ran to it and began brushing sand from the Humvee's grill and headlights.

"They're buried inside," he shouted to Nick.

Marshall appealed to a group of men to find shovels, hoes, anything to dig out the vehicle. While the men grabbed their tools, Nick used his hands like garden spades to claw his way into the Humvee's driver compartment. The vehicle was empty. He climbed behind the wheel but couldn't start the engine. *The easy way won't work.*

"No one's inside," Nick called out to Marshall. "We're going to need lots of muscle to pull out this bad boy."

"Leave it in neutral," Marshall said. He appealed to an older man wearing a simple gray tunic to find several strong volunteers. The man nodded and conferred with his companions. A buzz of activity followed.

A young man brought yards of heavy rope, flattened onto his back, and tied it to the Humvee's undercarriage. The youngest and strongest used their collective strength to pull the truck out of the trench. Sand cascaded off the vehicle until the Humvee sat in front of the crowd gathered to watch.

Marshall discovered the rear cargo door open and a broken cable dangling off a winch. The truck's cargo area was empty.

"Aman took everything with him," he said to Nick.

"But where to?"

Three men with shovels kept digging into the area where the Humvee sat until they all heard their metal tools scraping stone. Marshall rushed to join them and used his hands to push sand away until they exposed a cinderblock wall with a hole large enough to climb through.

"Hello?" a man's voice reverberated from the hollow darkness inside the wall. "Hello?"

Marshall called for a light, and the workers passed several torches forward.

A face appeared in the opening, prompting gasps and whispers. One of the men pulled a slight wizened man off a cable ladder that had been lowered inside.

The stranger was short and frail-looking, with stringy gray hair to his shoulders, and dressed in a plain dark robe.

"That's not Aman," Nick said.

"Maybe he knows where they are." Marshall headed toward him.

The man spotted Marshall approaching and met him with extended hands. "Dr. David Marshall. I have looked forward to this moment."

Marshall grasped the man's bony hands and studied his features, so much like Aman's.

"Who are you?" Marshall asked.

The slight man broke into a genuine smile of fellowship. "My name is Aruk. I'm Aman's brother."

Marshall looked at him in surprise. "*Brother?*"

Aruk turned to Nick and grasped both the pilot's hands. "Captain Nick Judge."

Nick said nothing. He seemed uneasy, perhaps even afraid of the odd man.

"Where are the others?" Marshall asked. "Samantha? Kirby?"

Aruk released Nick's hands, and his bright expression dimmed. "Your friend Kirby is no longer part of this world."

"You mean he's dead?" Marshall said, astonished.

"No frigging way," Nick said.

Marshall placed a hand over his forehead in disbelief. "My God—what happened down there? Where's Samantha?"

"Your friend Kirby will return one day as flesh and blood when the earth's conversion is complete." Aruk's eyes took on a far-away gaze as though he could already see the event. "What a wonderful day that shall be."

Marshall scowled and squatted next to the wall's opening. "I need a light."

A woman handed him a torch. Marshall thrust the flame into the opening that lit up a large area of broken machinery. Someone was climbing up the ladder. She looked up at him.

"*Sam!*"

Samantha offered him a broad smile. "David." She hurried up the remaining rungs. "*David!*"

Marshall passed his torch to Nick and helped Samantha up off the ladder. Her skin was red like a bad sunburn, the ends of her hair singed. She reeked of smoke. Still, she looked gorgeous, even younger and fairer than when he last saw her.

Samantha sprang into his arms and gave him a colossal hug. Marshall held her tight, afraid he'd lose her again if he let go. Her body resonated with wonderful energy. "Thank God you're okay."

"It's done. It's over," she said. "We're safe now, and you're a part of it."

"That Aruk fella told me about Kirby," Marshall said. "I'm so sorry—"

"He's not lost," Samantha said, beaming. "His transition from this world was an incredible miracle. We'll see him again."

He peered deep into her eyes. "I was afraid I'd never see you again."

Samantha let out a huff of laughter. "You worry too much, Doctor." She looked up into the sky. "I never thought I'd see stars again, let alone so many and so bright. They're speaking to us. They're happy for us."

Nick touched her shoulder.

Samantha turned, and her eyes widened. "Nick! I can't believe you're on your feet already." She released Marshall and hugged Nick, almost knocking the torch from his grip.

"Where's Aman?" Marshall asked.

Samantha released Nick. "David, you're not going to believe—"

"He is here," Aruk said. "She saved him."

The crowd of spectators grew quiet when a hand appeared over the edge of the opening. Aruk knelt and lifted a small figure off the ladder.

Marshall grabbed the torch from Nick. The additional light revealed a boy, perhaps five years old, wearing a plain, one-piece brown smock torn just above his knees to fit him. He held an old wooden box blackened by fire. The boy's black hair touched his shoulders, and his dark complexion looked painted on. The child's penetrating eyes shifted from Marshall to Aruk.

Samantha stepped behind the boy and placed her hands on his shoulders.

"This is Aman," she said.

Nick and the boy exchanged bewildered looks. "Chief?"

"You can't be serious." Marshall dropped to his knees in front of the boy. He searched his face but found no familiar features. The boy returned a curious look of his own without saying a word.

"If you're Aman," Marshall said, "you need to get a handle on this aging thing before you become an embryo."

"He already has," Samantha said. "Now he's coming back to us."

The little girl stepped forward and held out her exotic red desert flower. The boy took the bloom from her tiny fingers and smiled at its beauty.

"Incredible," Marshall said.

"In time," Aruk said, "the boy will become the man he was."

AWAKENING

THE CROWD GREW restless and began asking for information. Samantha scanned the multitude, hundreds of men, women, and children, stretching out into the desert under a canopy of torches. This spot represented the end of their pilgrimage, and she knew everyone wanted to know why they had been summoned here.

"We should tell them something," she said.

"Most won't hear us," Marshall said. "Let's brief a few who can spread the word."

Aruk pointed to a cluster of people by the mouth of the trench. "Perhaps he can help you."

Samantha spotted a boy wielding a bullhorn. Behind him, two older boys carried pallets of bottled water from the plane's cargo hold. Her face lit with a knowing smile. Aman had thought of everything.

She squatted before the boy and placed a hand on the bullhorn. "May I borrow this for a moment? Afterward, I promise it's all yours."

The youth, beaming, presented the bullhorn to her with both hands.

Samantha touched the boy's chin. "Thank you."

She rose and considered the bullhorn. I'm out of my league here, she thought. *I hate public speaking.* She offered the bullhorn to Aruk. "You tell them what happened."

"It is not my place," Aruk said. "Aman chose you."

"But—"

"Go for it, Sam," Marshall said, grinning. "Tell them what

you're feeling right now."

Samantha relented with a shrug. This won't be pretty. She mounted the hillside beside the trench and faced them. The crowd rumbled with expectation. *What the hell do I tell them?* She switched on the bullhorn and put it to her lips. "Can everyone hear me?"

Samantha's voice boomed across the desert. Her audience quieted. Heads throughout the crowd bobbed in response to her question. Marshall, impressed by the volume, gave her thumbs-up approval to continue.

"The worst of our kind that made this world a cruel and violent place are gone," she began. "Others with negative unresolved energy will follow. We are the survivors—the awakened. We will leave behind humanity's wars and darkness and become a loving and compassionate people in a beautiful new world free of misery. As our collective vibration continues to rise and takes us into a new dimension, unconditional love will complete the awareness that unites all of us—a single loving consciousness. Our expanded awareness of this divine connection of our souls will be our new reality. We are all one love."

The words poured from Samantha from a place within she didn't know existed. Her mind was sharp and focused. She looked over at young Aman. He watched her curiously as though trying to understand what was happening. For an instant, she thought she spotted Sheema standing behind him, as pale and wispy as a ghost. But as she stared, she saw only the child watching her.

Samantha once again directed the bullhorn at the crowd. "All of us owe a great debt to a man we met just days ago. A man who calls himself Aman."

His name sparked whispers and movement throughout the gathering.

"He is a highly evolved soul and a master of the Divine Knowledge our species forgot long ago," she said. "We don't know much about him or how he came to us. But without him, the world was doomed. Because of what Aman achieved here today, we now begin a wonderful new life full of wonder and possibilities, free of sickness and disease. A place of love, beauty, and peace. A voice called you to this sacred place—the same voice that awakened our single consciousness to the truth. Aman is the father of our future, and we have much to learn from him."

Samantha lowered the bullhorn and let her words reverberate across the desert. The crowd remained still and attentive to her every word. The experience stunned her. Never before did her words command such power over people. Although she wished to tell them more, she didn't feel this was the right moment for long speeches. In a few hours, the first rays of daylight would brighten the horizon. They had all the time in the world.

Aruk brought his palms together with a sharp *whack* that broke the silence. He repeated the gesture. Others followed likewise until everyone was clapping. Nick put two fingers in his mouth and let loose the loudest, shrillest, drawn-out whistle Samantha had ever heard, leaving her ears ringing. A little boy climbed the hillside, grabbed his bullhorn, and ran off.

People began cheering and singing. Others danced. The jubilation grew until the roar became overpowering. The outpouring of gratitude flowed through her like an unyielding river, a fantastic feeling that amazed her. They were thanking her—thanking Aman—with a single voice.

She looked at Marshall, who was smiling and applauding her. The light from the torches caught his eyes and made them sparkle.

An elder in a bright red tunic and matching headdress climbed the hillside and grasped her hands. His touch sent a wave through her that made her shiver. Samantha saw the man's life unfold in an instant in her mind. He was a good man, a good leader, who would make a significant difference in their new lives. She looked into his compassionate eyes while he spoke to her in Arabic. He was the leader of the neighboring region, and his people had come from many villages. He wanted Samantha and her friends to become part of his family. With a broad wave of his hand, he promised that his people would open their homes and treat them to the grandest celebration of their lives.

Tears flowed down Samantha's cheeks. Yes, there was much to celebrate.

The vigorous applause continued without end. Samantha followed the elder chief down the hillside to rejoin the others. Young Aman scurried to Samantha. He grabbed her hand and beckoned her down to his level with anxious tugs. She knelt beside him. He whispered into her ear, "Don't ... leave ... me."

Samantha looked into his large brown eyes, and another swell of emotion caused a lump in her throat. Here stood the man who changed the world, yet he clung to her hand as a frightened boy. "Of course you will come with us. We are family."

The crowd parted and formed a long row that led out into the desert. Samantha rose and took Aman's hand. Marshall stood next to her, his eager eyes glowing, and placed a hand on her cheek. She closed her eyes and leaned into his palm, wishing to feel his touch forever. The world seemed to dissolve into a lovely distant place. Time ceased, and she felt highly sensitized to each delicate nuance of his touch. When she opened her eyes, she saw his eyes glistening with tears.

Samantha took Marshall's hand into hers and gently squeezed the boy's hand with the other. They escorted young Aman past the villagers while Aruk and Nick followed with torches. The boy stared timidly at the onlookers who watched and applauded him with an equal blend of curious eyes and welcoming smiles.

As they walked into the desert together, Samantha felt whole and alive. Everything she saw, every face, every grain of sand, held deep and perfect meaning and connection. The universe was speaking volumes to her in a beautiful voice. She felt utter contentment and great compassion. They had done so much in six days. There was so much more to do.

And today, on the seventh day of Aman's awakening, they would begin a new life together in an extraordinary world far different from the one they had known before.

"When we dream alone, it is only a dream, but when many dream together, it is the beginning of a new reality."

Friedensreich Hundertwasser

"We have found a strange footprint
on the shores of the unknown.
We have devised profound theories,
one after another, to account for its origin.
At last we have succeeded in reconstructing
the creature that made the footprint.
And lo! It is our own."

Sir Arthur Stanley Eddington

ACKNOWLEDGMENTS

I am hopelessly indebted to my special friends and colleagues who gave generously of their time to offer me feedback and encouragement: Frank Baker, Chris Beakey, Greg Beaubien, Darlene Bissonnette, William Burns Jr., Patti Green, Stephanie Johnson, Mary Orjansen, Patricia Pedersen, Marlyn Savage, Annie Smith, and Patricia Wiebe. And to a fantastic group of fellow writers with keen eyes and terrific ideas: Leann, Kay, Amy, Laura, Charlie, Millie, and Dean.

Thank you all.

When Andrew Finsbury realizes he's dead, he journeys to the darkest valleys of hell to confront his murderer and save the woman he loves.

THE RESURRECTION OF ANDREW FINSBURY

A paranormal thriller by Joseph Massucci

Turn the page for a sneak preview.

My Dear Eben,

However bizarre this story may seem, I assure you every word is the truth. My faculties are still acutely sane, and the details of my extraordinary adventure are etched indelibly upon my mind. Only now in the winter of my life do I feel compelled to share my story with you. Your mother and I agreed that you are ready. You see, I fear the Almighty will soon see fit to take my soul into his own for the final time and forever silence the account of one mortal's journey through the Otherworld of the Dead.

—Your Father

CAPTAIN MYLES EDWARDS
ACCOUNT OF THE LOSS
OF THE *H.M.S. TIMONIUM*

THE BEAST HAD RETURNED. Captain Myles Edwards, master of the frigate *Timonium,* could no longer see the creature, for the encroaching night hid it from him like a black veil. Despite the darkness, he could sense its presence, its cold, malevolent spirit, watching him from behind the mounting waves off his ship's starboard beam like a snake waiting to strike. He knew nothing of its origin, but he did not doubt the creature possessed the power and the purpose of crushing his ship and dragging its twisted planks along with his passengers and crew to the bottom of the North Atlantic.

The night droned with rolls of approaching thunder. Captain Edwards pulled his oilskin jacket around his neck but found no warmth on this black night. The pallor of his hands matched the color of the ship's bone-white canvas. Although he had just passed his forty-fourth birthday, those who saw him on this hellish night would declare him at least half again that old.

Edwards watched the mast's brass oil lamp swing and turn as though shaking its glowing head in warning. The weather stalks me as well, he thought. Very soon his ship would be in the midst of a North Atlantic storm. Intent on the lantern's pendulum lurching, he tried to calm his pounding heart and staunch the twisting in his bowels. *For chrissake, do something!*

A hand fell upon his shoulder and spun him around with a

start. A black seaman, his first officer, stood uneasily before him. Something terrified him beyond reason. "Myles ... it's come back. I seen it."

Edwards looked deeply into the Negro's sea-weathered face. What he saw—those terror-filled eyes, sunken cheeks, twisted mats of gray hair flecked with dew-like sleet—made him shudder. "C.J., tell the others that this foul weather will delay our arrival in Baltimore."

"Myles," the old mate whispered, moving closer, his glistening eyes reflecting the lantern's glow, "I seen it clear tonight. That thing ... *it ain't of this world*. What harm does it mean us?"

The captain closed his eyes to shut out the image of the frightened seaman and shook the lingering dread from his mind. "I cannot tell you the future, C.J."

The old mate stammered, "Myles ... Myles..."

"Come below with me," Edwards said, anxious for something, anything, to distract them. "I want to record the new sighting in the log," and added under his breath, "and pray it won't be my last."

Edwards opened the hatchway and descended the ladder into his cabin. His first mate followed. The captain waved the sailor into the cabin's only chair and sat down heavily on his cramped box bunk.

C.J. sat down at the desk and brushed several charts and maps to one side to clear the blotter. He slid open the drawer and withdrew the bound log, treating it with peculiar reverence as though it were a holy book. His stringy, rope-worn fingers riffled through the pages until he found the last entry. He uncorked the ink, dipped a quill pen and dripped a trail of black dots across the page. Ready, he looked at the captain, awaiting his dictation.

Edwards rubbed a hand over a week-old beard, gathering his thoughts. "Supplementary log entry," he began, feigning calm control, "this ... this..." He snapped his fingers. "What day is this?"

"It's Sunday, the sixteenth of March."

"This sixteenth day of March," he continued, "in the year of our Lord eighteen hundred and ninety-four. Sighting confirmed at approximately 1830 hours. The bastard appeared again off our starboard beam as black as evil, lurking, matching our speed and course, watching us—waiting for..." he paused and shook his head "... only the devil knows for what. The weather is deteriorating, and I can see nothing now that night has fallen. All decks secured, and passengers confined below."

Edwards closed his bloodshot eyes and rubbed them hard with his thumbs, nearly mashing them into the back of his skull. "Make one more note, C.J."

The mate dunked his pen and held it over the page, spotting the last entry with black droplets.

"I will ready the lifeboats as a precaution." He added in a whisper, "God be with my passengers."

C.J. stiffened, his face a mask of unchecked fear, an expression that sent tremors of dread through the captain. "What is it, man?" Edwards hissed.

C.J.'s terrified gaze shifted to the captain. "I smell smoke." He threw a trembling finger at the cabin door. *"There!"*

Edwards sprang from the bunk and saw a tail of smoke slithering under the door like a serpent. He drew a deep breath and winced at the acrid smell.

"What the hell—" Edwards threw open the door, admitting a thick cloud of smoke. His eyes burned terribly, and he began choking. The passageway outside was impassable.

"Move," the captain shouted between fits of coughing. *"Move!"* He could no longer open his streaming eyes. "Get to the lifeboats."

C.J.'s vague outline groped for the ladder. Before he could secure a foothold, a violent crash jarred the ship, hurling both men to the floor. The corridor resounded with screaming passengers. Edwards felt his way to the old sailor and pulled him into a sitting position.

C.J.'s breathing came in short huffs. "We can't launch boats in this weather. We're dead men—"

"Listen to me, C.J.," Edwards implored. "I want you to get my passengers off this ship."

The mate's eyes widened. "But the storm, Myles. We'll be washed under."

"Have you another suggestion?"

C.J. stared at the captain and then finally shook his head, conceding the obvious that they had no other course.

"Then see to it—and *quickly.*" Edwards knew the old mate would perform his duty as long as breath remained in him.

Before C.J. could carry out his captain's order, another crash sent a violent quake through the ship, then another. More shouting and screaming resounded from the corridor. The planks shook and splintered as blast after blast pounded the frigate.

The first mate's eyes darted wildly about. "What's happening, Myles? *What in God's name is happening?*"

"C.J.—"

The cabin exploded in an upheaval of wood and shrapnel.

Edward's eyes fluttered open. A frigid blast of air mercifully purged the compartment of the foul smoke and roused him back to his senses. He could hear sobbing far off and, worse, the sound of the sea roaring into the ship's hold. He knew the *Timonium* would soon make her final journey to the bottom of the Atlantic.

He lay on his back staring up at an inferno of burning rafters. Beyond the fire, he could discern the ship's shredded sails flapping in the raging wind against a black sky. *I am peering through a hole into hell.*

Then came the pain.

Edwards shifted his body amidst the debris and cried out from the agony of shattered ribs. He could feel nothing below his waist. He glanced down and saw his lower torso twisted at an angle severe enough to sever his spine. He grabbed a beam and struggled to pull himself into a sitting position. Wiping his eyes, he scanned what remained of his quarters and spotted a fist jutting from the broken timbers.

"God, no..."

The hand remained clenched.

Fighting back the bile boiling in his throat, Edwards dragged his shattered legs over the debris and pushed away the beams to reveal the crushed remains of the man who had served faithfully at his side for more than two decades. Emotion swelled in his throat.

"I'm sorry, C.J."

Edwards spotted the ragged edges of the ship's log half-buried beneath his body. He wrenched the book free and held close to his chest the only record of this night's horror. Somehow this must reach British naval authorities. But how?

"Who is in there?" called a voice with a heavy French accent.

Edwards cocked his head towards the source and listened—someone was moving through the rubble.

"In here," the Captain shouted. "*Quickly. I need help.*"

A shadow stumbled over the debris, and a face appeared over him, the face of a slight French merchantman whose hundred casks of wine were stored in the ship's hold. He couldn't recall his name. *DuMont?*

The Frenchman's eyes were fixed on the logbook pressed against the Captain's chest. His nose wrinkled in repugnance when those eyes shifted to the remains of the first officer. "A dead colored."

Edwards reached for him. "For the love of God, help me out of here, DuMont. I've been crippled."

The Frenchman sat upon a fallen beam. "Ducreux," he corrected me. "My name is Ducreux."

Edwards thrust the logbook at the Frenchman. "Take this. You must give it to Admiral Joshua Finsbury in Potters Bay."

Ducreux made no move to assist me.

By the light of the burning timber, the Captain saw a twisted look of lunacy on the Frenchman's face. He appeared oblivious to the ship's sinking and showed no regret for the fading sounds of dying women and children topside. Was he injured? No, he saw something more sinister in his dark features. Madness? His tone became desperate. "Save yourself.

Get to a lifeboat. You must take this to Admiral Finsbury. *Please.*"

The little man's lips broadened into a grin. Edwards' gaze shifted, and his eyes widened. The Frenchman's right hand rested in the flames of a burning section of beam. Yet there was no trace of pain in Ducreux's eyes or any sign of corruption of his flesh.

The sight left him stunned.

The Frenchman removed his hand from the fire and took the book from the Captain's trembling fingers. He leafed through the pages, pausing to read the last few entries, his manner casual as though browsing the morning news over tea. Water foamed through the door of the compartment while he read and washed over the debris—icy claws that had come to drag the *Timonium* to her grave.

The little man shut the book with a snap and offered his broadest smile. "Thank you. I can assure you that this will be read carefully—although not by the man you had hoped." He waved the book at him. "It will bring a satisfied smile to his face."

Ducreux rose, bowed awkwardly, then ducked under the beams and vanished into the fire's haze like a ghost.

Anger broke the Captain's incredulity. "Joshua, you son of a bitch." He rammed his fist hard against a fallen beam. "Where are you?"

No one could hear him. The ship listed heavily to starboard, dumping debris, fixtures, and furniture onto the walls of the cabin. As the fast-rising black water swirled around him, Edwards vowed to survive this night. He would return to Potters Bay and tell the admiral how his ship was destroyed.

Fending off the debilitating cold, Edwards groped among the flotsam until his hands found a shattered beam. He embraced it in a desperate bear hug. He found a frayed rope and tied his broken torso to the beam until he and the improvised raft were inseparable.

An explosion in the ship's hold tore the doomed vessel in two. The compartment turned over and the planks burst inward, admitting a raging sea. He managed a final, shallow breath before the thick, icy water enveloped him. Tied to the beam, he rode submerged into the cold blackness, fighting the insistent hand dragging his wrecked ship to the distant seabed. The water transformed his arms into useless boards. Further struggle became futile. His mind grew numb, and he lost all bearings. He prayed that the beam on which he rode would break the surface in the next seconds before his lungs collapsed. But fate decreed that Captain Myles Edwards would die with his vessel tonight. Only one meter from the surface, reflex forced him to inhale deeply. Black saltwater imploded into his lungs.

Teetering on the rim between life and the unknown, Edwards came to the stark realization that his ship had been lured into a death trap—for its cargo. He felt the spirit of each doomed passenger and crewmember rush through him like a sacred wind. Dead—all of them murdered because of a cargo only he knew had been stowed aboard.

Their spirits cursed him bitterly, holding the ship's captain alone responsible for this massacre. Edwards water-swelled throat emitted a bitter cry of despair.

MY GRAVE

BLACKNESS. I COULD NOT MOVE. Where am I? Only silence, absolute and frightening. I flexed my fingers and felt damp, pliable earth. A swell of terror overtook me when I realized my predicament. *I was buried alive.*

Summoning all my strength, I hoisted myself up through the earth and thrust my head above ground with a deep breath like a swimmer surfacing after a dangerously long plunge.

I stared soberly at my surroundings. This was a neglected graveyard with hundreds of crooked headstones that reminded me of a field of hunched and crumbling men. The dark, overcast sky turned the landscape into an eerie twilight.

What was this place? And how did I get here? I had no memories of this, only swirls of puzzling images.

I pulled my feet out of the earth and sat down beside the hole from which I had just crawled. There were no freshly dug plots in this old cemetery, only long-forgotten headstones of souls laid to rest long ago.

Was I dreaming? Impossible. Never before had I experienced a dream of such clarity, far more real than waking life. I felt no discomfort, hunger, or thirst. Instead, a strange serenity settled over me. I could not deny that a profound change had befallen me. But in what way? And why?

I grabbed the towering stone crucifix and climbed to my feet. My stomach knotted when I read the inscription on the cracked and faded marker:

Here lieth the Body of Andrew M. Finsbury,
faithful Christian and proud Captain.
Born on the second day of August in the year
of our Lord Eighteen Hundred and Sixty One,
departed on the twenty-third day of April
Eighteen Hundred and Ninety Four, age 32 Years

Reading the chiseled words describing my life unsettled me. Was I to die in four weeks hence? I turned away with a shiver. I desperately needed to know the name of this place and how I had come to be here.

I heard a muffled groan, and then the earth next to me began to crack and rise from a pressure beneath. As I watched, breathless, a hand reached through the soil and began pulling himself from the clinging earth as I did moments before. This was no corpse. I watched a tall, lean man dressed in a muddy sea captain's uniform pull himself free of the ground and rise to his full height before me. At first I didn't recognize him. His eyes, bright brown, radiated warmth and kindness. His solid angular features hosted a trimmed beard and a full head of curly hair topped a blithe expression.

"Myles," I gasped. "By all of God's glory…"

My old friend Captain Myles Edwards, master of the merchant frigate *Timonium*, offered me a broad grin of greeting. He appeared more handsome than I had ever seen him without the hard lines that in later years etched cynicism and weariness onto his noble features. Despite his youthful appearance, his eyes revealed an intensity that humbled me.

Myles scratched a dirt-smudged nose and said to me, "I traveled a long way to meet you here, mate." His voice, deep and resonant, lacked the hard rasp of age.

"Where did you come from?"

He waved his hand at the disturbed soil over the grave next to mine. "From the same place as you." He gave my shoulder a friendly slap that startled me. "What'd you expect? That I'd leave you to wander this land alone? I've been racing to catch you. We have much to do in a very short time."

I could scarcely find the words to respond. "What is this place? Why are we here?"

"You're joking, are you not?" His grin faded, and he looked at me quizzically. "You don't know yet, do ya, mate?"

"Myles, I don't remember anything. I don't know where I am or how I came here."

"Would it spook you to tell ya we're dead, mate?"

I let out a huff of incredulous laughter. "*Dead!?* Impossible. I am alive and real as you are."

Myles offered me a sympathetic look. He beckoned me to sit, and then he sat down beside me, his back propped against the giant stone crucifix, his legs stretched out before him. His eyes fixed on some far-off point as he peered into his past.

"The beast came in the night and devoured my ship, my crew, and my passengers," he said. "I died in the North Atlantic, the sixteenth day of March."

Before Myles could tell me more, his voice trailed off, and the air grew quiet. I looked up. He was gone. I felt a profound sense of loss and foreboding.

I was on my feet in an instant, charging down a hillside to find him. I had no destination in mind, only a need to run. Unlike the dreary graveyard at the top of the hill, this beautiful valley hosted rolling meadows and thick groves of trees, all bathed in the warmest sunlight. As I ran, more wonders overtook me. I discovered that my body did not experience the usual fatigue after such exertion. I could run forever.

The field gave way to a lovely garden at the edge of a tall forest that seemed to beckon me. The blend of sight and smell was indescribably delightful. What was this place? If it were possible, I would remain here forever.

A strange sight brought me to an abrupt halt. I found my friend sitting in an ornate wooden chair in the center of the garden with a young boy, hardly more than an infant, seated in his lap. Like Myles, the child possessed an aura of wisdom far beyond his first years. From their expressions, I knew we were in some sort of danger.

"It's not your time yet, mate," Myles said to me. "Be patient,